ONCE UPON A ZOMBIE

BOOK TWO: THE LORD OF THE CURTAIN

BILLY PHILLIPS
&
JENNY NISSENSON

ONCE UPON A ZOMBIE

BOOK TWO: THE LORD OF THE CURTAIN

BILLY PHILLIPS
&
JENNY NISSENSON

THE TOON STUDIO PRESS

Beverly Hills

This book is a work of fiction. The names, characters and events in this book are the products of the author's imagination or are used fictitiously. Any similarity to real persons living or dead is coincidental and not intended by the author.

ONCE UPON A ZOMBIE: BOOK TWO: THE LORD OF THE CURTAIN

Published by Gatekeeper Press
2167 Stringtown Rd, Suite 109
Columbus, OH 43123-2989
www.GatekeeperPress.com

ISBN: 9781935668398
ISBN: 9781642370232
eISBN: 9781642370225

Printed in the United States of America

For Marianne

THE COLORS OF
THE SPECTRUM

RED	GREEN	VIOLET
Fear	Will to Resist	Courage
Anxiousness		Calm
Jealousy		Contentment
Entitlement		Appreciation
Panic		Serenity
Sadness		Happiness
Doubt		Certainty
Worry		Confidence
Cynicism		Conviction
Pessimism		Optimism
Apathy		Passion

When one resists the reactions arising out of the
Red Spectrum, through their willpower, this
free-willed act unleashes the attributes shining from
the violet end of the spectrum. Resistance is the key.

—*The Colours of Our Character*
Dr. J. L. Kyle

OUR STORY SO FAR

THEY SAY HARDSHIPS COME IN *THREES*, BUT CAITLIN FLETCHER was inclined to believe that *they* miscalculated by a digit or two. Thirty-three or 303 seemed more like it. Because that's how it had felt since that very first hardship hit.

That first one had occurred on the day that Caitlin had turned ten years old—Halloween—and her mom, Evelyn Fletcher, had gone missing.

I won't even calculate the number of anxiety attacks I had.

Three years later, evidence surfaced suggesting she had died, leading police to end their missing-persons investigation. Evelyn Fletcher was declared deceased. Thirteen-year-old Caitlin was inconsolable—so much so, she had blocked out the devastating truth of her mom's passing, repressing the memory into one of those proverbial hidden recesses of the mind.

Then came hardship one hundred thirty-whatever.

It was one year later. Fate had intervened. On Caitlin's fourteenth birthday, and the night of Halloween, Caitlin was forced to come to terms with what had really happened to her mom.

She underwent an extraordinary, surreal experience—one that would never be believed by any rational, lucid human being.

I'm still having trouble believing it happened!

Caitlin had tumbled down a rather unusual rabbit hole. Unusual because the rabbit hole in question was, in fact, a *wormhole* beneath the grave of author Lewis Carroll, who was the first to dream up the idea of an interdimensional rabbit hole. When Caitlin had emerged, she'd landed in the authentic Wonderland. The land of wonder and the entire *fairy-tale* universe were verging on an apocalypse of undeadly proportions. All the revered literary characters of history were slowly but surely degenerating into ghastly, blood-eyed zombies.

Except for those with royal blood.

Zombie princesses Snow White, Cinderella, Sleeping Beauty, and Rapunzel, though cold, pale, and distinctly undead, had retained the inner strength of will to resist the ferocious impulses that compel the walking dead to feast on flesh, blood, brains, and other vital organs.

At the behest of another royal—the wise and enlightened blue caterpillar of Wonderland fame, Lord Amethyst Bartholomew—Jack Spriggins, the famous giant slayer, climbed a great beanstalk and popped out of the wormhole that was Lewis Carroll's grave to seek out Caitlin so that she could help prevent the total collapse of all the kingdoms.

Jack, going incognito in the world of humans as a high school hottie, befriended Caitlin as part of his plan to coax her into visiting the fairy-tale universe on Halloween night—the cosmic window when the graves of the most famous fairy-tale authors transformed into interdimensional portals.

The situation became altogether strange when Caitlin discovered that the Queen of Hearts was the culprit and villain who had cursed these kingdoms with this vile affliction. The *altogether strange* had become deeply personal when Caitlin further discovered that her mother was still alive—she was the fairy-tale world's Queen of Hearts, under a hypnotic spell placed on her by the wicked Enchanter.

My poor mom!

Caitlin had courageously fought through a tidal wave of debilitating fears by resisting the rash reactions radiating from the Red Spectrum. These valiant acts of free will had allowed her to liberate her mom from her emotional and psychic prison. In the process, she'd prevented the devastation of all these storied worlds.

And then Caitlin's heart was shattered. Her mom, though free from the curse of the Enchanter, was, in fact, dead in Caitlin's normal world—but somehow very much alive in this other reality.

Which meant her mom couldn't come home with her.

Caitlin had finally found peace by coming to terms with the tragedy that had devastated a heartbroken ten-year-old girl. When she'd finally returned home after preventing the collapse of the kingdoms, Caitlin had said goodbye to her mom at Mount Cemetery, in Guildford—the same cemetery where Lewis Carroll was interred. Her mom's temporal body rested in peace by the grave of Caitlin's granddad Robert "Bobby" Blackshaw.

Caitlin had also come to terms with the fact that her new, dear friend Jack was, in fact, Jack Spriggins—which meant she had been harboring deep affections for a fictional being.

Bizarre, to say the least.

But the kiss they'd shared while standing under a crescent moon outside Mount Cemetery in Guildford was anything but fictional.

After Caitlin's breakthrough at Mount Cemetery, Jack had to return to his own world. However, he'd promised to return on a regular basis to keep their new friendship—*and perhaps a new romance?*—alive.

CHAPTER ONE

THE AFOREMENTIONED EVENTS TOOK PLACE EXACTLY TEN YEARS ago to this very day. *This very day!*

Halloween.

And Caitlin Fletcher's twenty-fourth birthday, which also happened to be her wedding day.

The lovely young bride looked and felt angelic in her flowing, white silk gown with lace overlay and a tulle veil embellished with pearls that covered her face with distinct elegance and grace.

She fidgeted with her bouquet of flowers as she waited nervously at the head of a candlelit aisle. Ivory rose petals adorned the matrimonial walkway that led to a white canopy upheld by birch poles trimmed with hanging grapevines and cascading florals. Truly enchanting.

And so was the band, whose lead singer was crooning

"Then You Can Tell Me Goodbye." Caitlin had chosen the song in memory of her mother; it was the same song that her mom and dad, Harold and Evelyn Fletcher, had selected for their wedding dance after exchanging their own marriage vows.

Tonight, Caitlin was certain her life was about to change. October 31, which had always been a deeply traumatic date for her, was about to be transformed into a day of joy, life, hope, and celebration.

She felt beautiful, ridiculously happy, and deeply in love.

Caitlin's sister, Natalie, strode over, lifted her sister's veil, and kissed her cheeks.

"You look absolutely beautiful, sweet sibling!" Natalie said. "The perfect October bride." She gave Caitlin a head butt. They shared a laugh.

Caitlin was delighted at how beautiful Natalie looked. Her brainiac, child-prodigy kid sister had grown into a lovely and gracious young woman. Caitlin shook her head.

How quickly the last ten years have flown by!

She gazed into her sister's eyes as a flood of memories stirred a gentle pang in her chest.

Natalie was already a few years into a promising career as a highly regarded quantum biologist. The former little twerp was now the leading light in her field, responsible for some of the major advances in quantum biology.

Whatever the heck that is!

Caitlin was proud of her. Yet she secretly hoped Natalie would find a boyfriend already instead of staying married to her work. Guys were always lined up for blocks trying to score a date with the adorable hottie with the petite bod and the big brain.

"Can't wait to be an aunty," Natalie said. Caitlin hugged her again.

Harold Fletcher interrupted his daughters as he slid in next to Caitlin. He gently placed his daughter's arm around his, patting it lovingly.

"Ready, Caity-Pie?" her dad asked.

She smiled. She had long dreamed of the day when her dad would walk her down the aisle.

"Good to go, Papa Bear."

She sniffled. Caitlin so missed her mom at that moment.

Her dad smiled. He gazed down the aisle toward the wedding canopy where Caitlin's husband-to-be stood tall and graceful in his elegant black tux with the grosgrain-textured lapels.

Caitlin laughed inwardly. Who could ever have imagined such a scene when she met up with Barton Sullivan in college three years ago? They had remained friends during their high school years, bonded by their mutual friendship with Jack.

Jack.

Caitlin swallowed.

It had been ten long years since Caitlin had seen or heard from Jack. She lifted her veil and dabbed the wetness from her eyes with her pinkie.

Not now, Caity-Cry—your mascara will run!

Both she and Barton deeply missed Jack during their high school years at the Kingshire American School in London.

Caitlin had never told Barton that Jack was actually *storybook* Jack Spriggins, the boy who climbed a beanstalk and faced off against the famous fee-fi-fo-fum-yelling giant.

When Caitlin and Barton had met again in college, she'd found that the cocky high school rugby star had turned into a sweet and incredible guy. He was kind, graciously thoughtful, and never affected by his family's wealth. Caitlin was certain that the punch on the nose from Jack on that first day of high school ten years ago, along with Barton and Jack's deep-yet-brief friendship, had made a lasting impression on Barton Sullivan.

Caitlin and Barton's platonic relationship had blossomed into romance by her final year of college.

Caitlin gazed at him through her veil as he stood under the canopy, lit by warm candlelight.

How impressively handsome!

Barton's parents began their stroll down the aisle, and just like that, the wedding ceremony was under way. Natalie winked at her big sister, then followed.

Caitlin became teary-eyed again as her dad softly tugged her arm.

Together, father and daughter began their procession toward Caitlin's husband-to-be.

Butterflies flitted about in Caitlin's tummy. She squeezed her dad's hand. Rows of guests along the aisle nodded and smiled lovingly. The music stirred Caitlin's emotions. Halfway down the aisle, Barton moved to claim his bride.

Totally handsome dude!

She couldn't contain her feelings. She broke out in clipped sobs when her dad kissed her on the forehead, began to cry himself, and handed her off to Barton.

The walk with Barton to the canopy and the marriage ceremony seemed a complete blur. Before she knew it, Caitlin and Barton had exchanged their vows and kissed. They were now husband and wife.

Thunderous applause rang out. Band music filled the air.

Family and friends circled the newlyweds. A barrage of congratulatory hugs and kisses ensued. Caitlin leaned in to hug Barton's cousin Amanda, and as she leaned over Amanda's shoulder, her eyes caught a glimpse of something that made her freeze: a familiar figure moving deftly through the crowd.

Jack?

He had crossed the room like a fleeting shadow, his face the same as Jack's, but older.

Caitlin craned her neck above the people swarming around her. She rose on the balls of her feet to scan the crowded room.

Did I imagine it? Was it a look-alike, perhaps a relative of Barton's?

Her eyes darted around furiously.

Then she lost her breath.

Cinderella?

The girl, a dead ringer for Cindy, was beautiful, fashion-ably attired, and without a trace of paleness or death upon her.

Is she wearing makeup to hide the affliction? Is she cured? Is it even Cindy?

Caitlin broke away, pushed past a throng of guests, and fought her way over to the girl who seemed to be the spitting image of Cinderella.

Caitlin stopped before getting too close. The girl smiled tentatively.

Caitlin cupped her mouth over her hand.

The words fell out. "Is it you?"

The girl held Caitlin's gaze but didn't reply. Instead, she approached Caitlin and warmly wrapped her arms around her.

My God, it is her!

She whispered in Caitlin's ear, "Jack is here, too. We're *all* here."

Caitlin let her go. She turned. Rapunzel was now right there behind her; her long golden locks pinned and wrapped, obviously to avoid drawing attention.

And there was Snow White . . . and Sleeping Beauty, both smiling lovingly and dressed exquisitely, not a single trace of their former affliction on their faces.

Emotions let loose and Caitlin corralled her royal friends into a group hug. Tears and kisses erupted as the girls gabbed a mile a minute, laughing like giddy schoolchildren, catching up on ten years in ten seconds.

And then, Caitlin looked over at Rapunzel.

He was standing right behind her.

Jack.

Caitlin's royal friends retreated, leaving her and Jack alone and staring at each other.

Jack nodded. That boy Spriggins was still adorable and as fresh as the countryside air, just as he had been when she last saw him a decade ago. Except he was now twenty-four, and old enough for marriage.

A delicate smile formed on his face as he moved closer. Caitlin threw her arms around him. Jack embraced her warmly. She smelled his musky cologne, his hair, and his magic.

Caitlin's brow abruptly sharpened into an unhappy arch. She broke away from Jack's embrace. Years of hurt and pent-up anger ignited a fiery glare. Her tone was thick with ire.

"How could you not have contacted me all these years? I looked for you, Jack. I waited for you!"

Silent grief lit his eyes. "I was here the whole time."

The words chilled her. She pressed a fist against her mouth, shaking her head in disbelief.

What's he talking about?

"You never saw me," Jack said. "I called for you, over and over. But you never heard. Never saw." He took hold of her hands. She was trembling. "I never left you."

Jack raised his eyes, gazing past Caitlin . . .

She turned to see what had caught Jack's attention. Barton was coming to retrieve his new bride. Her husband's eyes widened, and his mouth dropped.

"Jack!" Barton called out.

Jack let her go.

He and Barton exchanged handshakes. Then they froze, gawking in disbelief at their formally locked hands. They broke out in laughter and immediately hugged each other like long-lost brothers.

"What the hell happened to you, mate?" Barton asked. "All these years!"

Jack smiled broadly. He stole a fleeting glance back at Caitlin. She saw it in his eyes. He was uncomfortable.

Her heart fluttered. A palpable awkwardness had descended on the moment, and Caitlin was suddenly feeling confused. And though Barton seemed genuinely happy to see Jack, she detected a shade of concern in his eyes as well.

A twinge of sadness crossed Barton's face as he turned to his new bride. "I'm sure you both have lots to catch up on. You should talk. I'll cover for you with the folks."

Caitlin's heart broke as her new husband walked away. Barton obviously knew that Caitlin had crushed on Jack back in high school. But she had only been fourteen years old back then.

Why should he be worried now, after all these years? Then again . . .

Caitlin never had told Barton about her experiences at the Mount Cemetery graveyard in Guildford. She knew he'd think she was a flipped-out psychotic if she did.

Jack took Caitlin's hand and led her out of the ballroom to a private hallway.

"I don't understand," Caitlin said, brushing away the tears.

"I never left," Jack said. "I swear. Look at me. Being in your world all this time, your sun aged me. I did it for you, Caitlin."

She shook her head in dismay. "How's that even possible? I see you now. I just saw Rapunzel. And Cindy. On my freaking wedding day, Jack! What am I supposed to do? What am I supposed to think? How could I have 'not seen' you for the last ten years of my life?"

A worried and hunted look crossed Jack's face.

"A curtain," Jack said. "The Lord of the Curtain. The Enchanter."

Her body went cold.

A sudden, strange thought knocked the breath out of her lungs.

I removed my contact lenses before getting my makeup done tonight.

Caitlin had never put her contacts back in. She'd been wearing contact lenses every day for the last ten years.

Had the Enchanter exchanged her lenses at some point ten years ago, after she'd returned home from Mount Cemetery in Guildford? Just like those cursed glasses he had put on her mom that reversed the truth in her mind? A shiver tremored down her spine.

Natalie burst through the ballroom doors and arrived in the hallway. She stormed toward her sister and placed her hands on Caitlin's shoulders.

She shook her vigorously and shouted, "What did you do, Caitlin? What did you do?"

Natalie had *never* screamed like that before.

Caitlin clutched at her chest as a river of tears ran down her cheeks.

Jack simply bowed his head, sad.

Rapunzel stood at the far end of the plush-carpeted hall-way. She unbound her enormous length of hair and corralled one long braid. She hurled the plait like a lasso toward a dumbfounded Caitlin.

Rapunzel jerked the braid . . .

CHAPTER TWO

CAITLIN JOLTED AWAKE. SLEEPING BEAUTY WAS STARING INTENTLY into her eyes and rocking her by the shoulders. Caitlin was snuggled under a floral-scented comforter, lying in a soft bed. Beauty rattled her again.

"What did you do, Caitlin? What did you do? Are you not getting this message?"

Caitlin shook her head back and forth, as if trying to shake off a dream. She blinked once. Twice. She squeezed her eyes shut for a third time and kept them shut for several long moments.

Then—

She opened her eyelids again.

A stern-faced Natalie was leaning over her.

Except this was *young* Natalie, her kid sister, just ten and a half years old. And Caitlin was lying in her own bed back on Royal Street, in Central London. She was fourteen and a half years old. And the morning light was slipping through the slats of the window blinds.

Whoa—what a totally freaky, bizarre nightmare that was!

"What did you do, Caitlin?" Natalie shouted.

"What do you mean?" Caitlin replied.

"You never set the alarm. We're late for school. You forgot again! You think you're hot stuff because your blog went viral? Get up off your butt, sleepy sibling, and let's get to school!"

Caitlin flew out of bed and jumped directly into the shower, where she sudsed her body with a creamy bar of soap and lathered her hair with green tea shampoo. She rinsed off in record time. She hopped out of the shower; dried herself off; wrapped an extra-long and ultra-thick, plush pink cotton towel around her body; did her makeup; threw off the towel; and got dressed. Through it all, Caitlin wondered why on earth Sleeping Beauty, Jack, and all the rest of her ghoul friends had showed up in such a surreal dream within a dream after all this time.

Eleven long months had passed since Caitlin last saw Jack Spriggins in the parking lot of Kingshire, on the night of Halloween. He had never called her—not even once. Not during the tedious, cold winter; not during the wet, blooming spring; not during the hazy, humid summer. Jack had never appeared at her window. Never even left a single garbanzo bean on her tenth-story ledge.

Nor did Caitlin ever hear from Cindy, Snow, Rapunzel, Beauty, or even Alice again—except during her bizarre dream.

And what a dream it was. Marrying Barton Sullivan? How outrageous was that? But Sleeping Beauty had wakened me from my dream, asking if I got a message from her.

What—like a text message?

Or a prophetic message?

Am I going to wind up marrying Barton Sullivan one day? Is Jack going to go missing for another ten years? Did that mysterious Deity of the Drapes, or rather, the Lord of the Curtain, somehow pull a wool curtain over my eyes? Has Jack had been trying to contact me all this time?

Caitlin glanced over at her contact-lens case on her nightstand.

Are they enchanted? Is that why I have not seen Jack since Halloween night eleven months ago?

"Let's go!" Natalie shouted as she slipped on her backpack.

She and Caitlin bolted downstairs to find their dad retrieving two plastic plates of scrambled eggs from the microwave.

"Morning, girls. Late, as usual."

"Your firstborn daughter never set the alarm," Natalie said, throwing the firstborn under the bus.

Some things never change.

"Miss Caitlin Rose Fletcher was blogging late into the night. She slept in *on purpose*. And now *I'm* late."

Caitlin glowered at Natalie. "Then get your own alarm, twerp. Stop relying on me."

Harold Fletcher set the plate of scrambled eggs on the counter. "I had to reheat your breakfast. It's been sitting here for twenty minutes."

Caitlin scooped up the plastic plate. Her lips sucked down the eggs like a Dyson vacuum.

"How ladylike," Natalie quipped. "You have a fear of cutlery now?"

"Let's get going, girls," her dad said. "I'm not writing another note explaining why you're late."

"Tell your daughter—Miss Mega-Popular Blogger—to stop blogging till all hours of the night," Natalie said.

Harold Fletcher rolled his eyes. "Caity-Cakes, did you take your meds?"

Caitlin froze. She wasn't going to lie to her dad again. She hated lying. She had never had to lie to him before.

"I haven't taken them in weeks. Months. They made me feel awful. And besides, there's nothing wrong with me."

Surprisingly—or more likely, not surprisingly—her dad didn't seem upset. Or miffed. In fact, he seemed to be as conflicted about the meds as Caitlin.

Is he kind of relieved I haven't been taking them?

"Let's talk about this later," he said.

She smiled warmly at him.

Dad is pretty freaking cool, as fathers go.

Caitlin dashed out the apartment door. She ran past the elevator and instead took the stairs ten flights down to the lobby. Some old lady from the fourteenth floor had gotten stuck in the elevator for an hour a few months back. Caitlin had avoided it ever since. It was true that her fears no longer ruled her life to the crippling degree that they once had, but she figured it was just plain stupidity to knowingly ride a faulty elevator when cramped, claustrophobic spaces were not your cup of tea.

* * *

The school day flew by lightning quick. Caitlin had to admit she felt totally awkward talking to Barton after the intensely realistic dream she'd had that morning. They were good friends now. Like in that dream. Along with Erwin Spencer. The trio had bonded over their shared friendship with Jack and their deep longing for him to return ever since he had "moved away" eleven months ago.

The three had been shocked when Jack had literally vanished, never to be heard from again. Supposedly his family had moved to Scotland—the very day after Caitlin and Jack had danced together at the Kingshire masquerade ball.

Caitlin knew Jack hadn't really moved to Scotland.

But Barton Sullivan and Erwin Spencer didn't. So they were befuddled when they couldn't find a forwarding address or a mobile number for him. Erwin, a bona-fide computer nerd and hacker, scoured the Internet and found nothing on Jack.

Meanwhile, that dream had made her wonder if she could ever like Barton Sullivan.

Am I supposed to like him? I mean, who wouldn't like him?

She *almost* admitted to herself that there had been more than a few moments over the past year when she had suggestive imaginings about him. Perhaps *suggestive* was too polite a word. But to fully admit this brought forth pangs of guilt, because of Jack—not because she was going on fifteen.

Jack. A fictional fairy-tale character. How insanely absurd am I?

Caitlin had also felt a twinge of jealousy when Piper and Barton had begun dating back in January.

Okay, a fierce and severe pang.

With Jack gone from Kingshire, Piper had wasted no time cornering the hottest dude left. In truth, she actually played it appropriately cool and balanced in the beginning, the right blend of hard-to-get aloofness mixed in with her seductive art of flirtation in just the right dosage. Barton had quickly showed serious interest and by their third date, Piper had prepared an official but private list of "Barton Dos and Don'ts" for him, which someone at Kingshire posted on Instagram in Piper's name, thereby making the private missive public.

THE BARTON SULLIVAN DOS AND DON'TS

Don't download any dating apps.
Delete all your existing dating apps.
Make a list of all the girls you dated previously.
Delete all the girls you dated previously from all your social media accounts.
Make a list why you prefer me to them.
Don't ever ignore any of my texts.
Don't flirt with girls anymore.
Don't friend any new girls on Facebook.
Don't make jokes about blonde girls—or any beautiful girls, for that matter.
Don't look twice at the same girl.
Don't joke with your friends about other girls.

Some kids are passive-aggressive. Piper turned out to be *hyperpossessive-aggressive*, on the verge of stalker. It was not that she was just trying to keep her new beau on a tight leash. No. Piper had dispensed with the whole idea of a leash. Instead, she kept the snap hook and collar firm and tight around Barton's neck—and superglued the leash handle to her palm.

It didn't take long for Barton to gently break it off with her. He made up a long list of fake reasons Piper gave *him* the boot, in her voice. He pretended it also had been leaked, and he posted it on social media. Fake news. But a gracious deed. Barton's chivalrous act helped Piper save face. The only person on planet Earth who knew the truth was Caitlin. And she was happy for that, because Piper just couldn't help herself.

Lots of girls behaved like that when they found themselves in similar circumstances. Obsessive thoughts and fears about a relationship could hold one prisoner. Girls and guys often confused obsessive infatuation, possessiveness, and jealousy for feelings of genuine affection and love.

Caitlin had similar issues involving her panic attacks in the past. Unhealthy thoughts and obsessions attacked her without warning. And they would never stop until there was a response. Like the time she had left her bottom dresser drawer open just a crack. It had gnawed at her brain throughout breakfast. She was determined not to respond by giving in and closing it. But halfway to school she just couldn't take it anymore. The relentless thought had finally compelled a response. She had turned around and traveled all the way back home just to close the drawer properly. She had been scared to death that the thought of an open drawer would stick in her brain all day, all week, or maybe even forever if she didn't respond!

Responses were quicksand. They made you fall deeper into the obsessions. Closing drawers and cupboards all the way had become a constant habit. Sometimes she had closed a drawer twenty times or more until it closed just right. Thankfully, she had learned to conquer a lot of her anxiety and OCD.

As she hurried home after school, Caitlin realized she had other issues to contend with now. She still had deep feelings for Jack—the boy who might not be real. But he *had* to be real. He *had* attended Kingshire. Barton remembered him. Barton admired him. Erwin totally appreciated Jack because he had saved Erwin from getting pummeled by bullies. All the kids dug Jack.

But was it in the realm of possibility that she might have hallucinated the entire episode of decaying kingdoms in another universe? Just as Dr. Kyle had said she did? Were the zombified characters from the world of children's books just a figment of a troubled mind, born of repressed pain relating to her mom's disappearance and eventual death?

Natalie remembered zilch about that night.

And now Jack was gone, never returning as promised. Not keeping promises and not showing up seemed uncharacteristic for Jack. His mysterious absence had left a decisive hole inside her. The hollowness that ached was painfully real.

Which means Jack has to be real.

And there was other evidence. Her signature butt-length, cinnamon-colored hair had been lopped off when she had woken up at the cemetery last Halloween night. A dream, no matter how realistic, cannot physically trim the locks off your head and give you a stylish and totally rocking Taylor Swift pixie haircut. Unless Caitlin was schizoid and she had cut off her own hair, then buried the scissors and her long bangs in her backyard and repressed the memory.

Perhaps I went off the meds too soon?

Then again, what about the extraordinary popularity she had experienced since that crucial night? And all the wonderful changes taking place in high schools around the world as a result of her blog?

All these thoughts danced in her head as she arrived home from school. She changed clothes, slipping on her favorite distressed jeans with the rips above the knee, a loose sweater, and black Converse sneakers.

Instead of taking the Tube as she normally did, Caitlin jumped on her bike and rode off along Royal Street toward Dr. J. L. Kyle's office.

Dr. J. L. Kyle—my freaking psychotherapist with the smug Brit accent and condescending attitude!

CONFIDENTIAL TRANSCRIPT OF
CAITLIN'S FIRST THERAPY SESSION

Dr. Kyle: As I understand it from your guidance counselor at Kingshire and from your father, you had quite an unusual experience on Halloween night a few months prior?

Caitlin: I did.

Dr. Kyle: Something about a fairy-tale universe overrun by the supposedly undead?

Caitlin: I suppose something like that.

Dr. Kyle: Cinderella, Snow White, Rapunzel, and other such characters from our childhood bedtime books were gradually decomposing into flesh-eating ghouls? Have I got it right thus far?

Caitlin Their decay wasn't gradual. It was pretty freaking fast. And it wasn't all of them.

Dr. Kyle: Oh? Well then, let's begin right there, shall we? Not *all* of the literary characters degenerated into the purported living dead?

Caitlin: What I mean is, those born of nobility, of royal blood—they didn't dine on flesh. Some of them just ate hot peppers.

Dr. Kyle: Peppers, you say?

Caitlin: Jalapeños.

Dr. Kyle: Why would a ghoul prefer a jalapeño pepper over human flesh?

Caitlin: The burn of the jalapeño curbed the burning hunger for flesh.

Dr. Kyle: Why would that be?

Caitlin: You'd have to ask a zombie chemist.

Dr. Kyle: And why were they even attempting to tame their appetites? I would assume a zombie to be a thoughtless, remorseless, and tenacious fiend.

Caitlin: Royal-blooded zombies were beautiful inside as well as on the outside. They still retained their beauty and, along with it, their self-control. They had decency.

Dr. Kyle: Resplendent zombies that preserved a modicum of decency?

Caitlin: The princesses, yes.

Dr. Kyle: That's some feat, young lady.

Caitlin: It certainly is. But the rest were blood-eyed ghouls, grotesque and dangerous, as one might expect. But why do I get the feeling you think I'm either making this up or just plain mad?

Dr. Kyle: Let's move on. Tell me about your mum.

Caitlin: She's dead.

Dr. Kyle: Yes, I am aware of that. Please tell me about her.

Caitlin: Her name is Evelyn. Married name Fletcher. Maiden name Blackshaw. How far back would you like me to go?

Dr. Kyle: I was referring to your relationship with her.

Caitlin: Oh. Well, she's interred at Mount Cemetery, in Guildford, so that makes it somewhat difficult to maintain a relationship with her. I was in denial about her death for many years. Deep-seated emotional wounds. Suppressed feelings. That sort of thing.

Dr. Kyle: Perhaps we should leave the analysis to me; just tell me about your mum.

Caitlin: About *Mum*? Okay. Well, I love my *mom*. It was hard as hell when she first disappeared. Sorry for curse word, *ahem* [throat clearing]. I had thought that maybe she had left my dad. But she hadn't. She was murdered. In a graveyard, of all places. I didn't want to believe that, so I clung to the false hope that she had just abandoned our family. I was forced to confront the truth as a result of my journey into that other world. But now I have come to accept her passing. And I do feel so much better. May I go now?

Dr. Kyle: Please carry on.

Caitlin: Hmmm. Well, I had a profound awakening when I reunited with my mom in Wonderland. My mother was the Queen of Hearts. At least she was under the delusion that she was.

Dr. Kyle: *She* was under the delusion?

Caitlin: [Pause] That's correct. She'd been put under a spell. By some evil dude with zero fashion sense, because he supposedly wore curtains for clothes. They called him the Enchanter. AKA the Lord of the Curtain—hence the curtain fashion wear. Please note that I have never met the Curtain Dude personally— that's just what I've been told. My mom is the one—under the spell of the Enchanter—who put the curse on the fairy-tale universe. She blocked out the Green Spectrum from the sun. The Green Spectrum is what gives the people of that world willpower to resist the Red Spectrum, which is full of fear, anger, anxiety, and panic. She blocked out the Green Spectrum by using her scepter to create a cloud filter in the sky. Except the scepter was really *my* toy wand. It was a sort of security blanket for me ever since I was a kid. This is what caused the zombie affliction . . . at least until I smashed the scepter to smithereens. The green was free to shine through again, but still not in full force because of some initial damage, so the folks in this other world were still somewhat zombified but no longer blood-eyed and dangerous. But you know what I think, Dr. Kyle?

Dr. Kyle: Please tell me.

Caitlin: I think the broken heart and mournful spirit of a ten-year-old child conjured up her dead mother as the wicked Queen of Hearts in her own mind. Get it—broken *heart* and Queen of *Hearts?* I'm not sure any of this ever really happened. Except for the part about me standing in front of my mom's grave on Halloween night last year and confronting the truth. It's rather difficult to deny your mother is dead when you're standing in front of her headstone. That's when I woke up, emotionally speaking. I think I dreamed the rest of the adventure as a way to help me cope with and overcome this deeply traumatic tragedy.

Dr. Kyle: Do you, now? Or perhaps you're telling me what you think I want to hear. Perhaps you're concerned that your tale sounds far too fantastical to be taken seriously. Perhaps you're worried you might find yourself bound in a straitjacket and placed under long-term observation in some old nineteenth-century asylum in some remote corner of the English countryside?

Caitlin: You read me like a book.

CHAPTER THREE

THE KINGSHIRE AMERICAN SCHOOL OF LONDON'S GUIDANCE counselor, Mrs. Buttersworth, had recommended Dr. J. L. Kyle to Caitlin. Her dad hadn't been entirely sold on the idea, but after thinking about it, he figured it might be a good opportunity for Caitlin to talk out a lot of issues involving her mom's death.

Officially, the *shrink* was supposed to help her deal with her outlandishly ludicrous claims about ghouls and degenerating fairy-tale kingdoms as well as how she claimed her mom, Evelyn Fletcher, had been kidnapped by some dark and devious being.

It did sound preposterous. Totally juvenile. But why *wouldn't* Mrs. Buttersworth think that Caitlin's story was merely her way of dealing with tragedy? Why not suggest that Caitlin write a book about it, as a therapeutic way to confront her inner demons?

So much had changed for Caitlin, and so much had changed in high schools around the world during the last eleven months. And all of the changes were a result of her experiences in that decomposing universe, which she had shared on her blog.

Had no one noticed all the changes?

That blog had gone viral after she had posted a few secrets that she gleaned from her experiences.

If that world wasn't real, why was the wisdom she was posting transforming the lives of so many hurting kids across the United Kingdom, the United States, and other countries?

At least, kids had been telling her over the last few months that the posts helped. She'd been inundated with emails and comments from bullies who gave up bullying, nerds who were making friends with jocks, and jocks who were making friends with stoners. And now the stoners were giving up the drugs because they were getting a natural high by forming new friendships with people they never dreamed or imagined ever being friends with. They were living the words of Lord Amethyst, mastering techniques for igniting the violet-blue end of the spectrum. These included resisting their fears and insecurities and no longer worrying about what other people thought. That temporary pain or embarrassment was like a bar of soap that washed away anxiety. She had written to kids about the power of performing random and totally uncomfortable positive actions instead of just making their lives all about themselves. These actions aroused light that vanquished the darkness of panic and anxiety. And it was eye-opening for Caitlin to learn that so many kids from all walks of life suffered, to one degree or another, from some aspect of anxiety, fear, pessimism, or obsessive-compulsive disorder.

Caitlin never wrote about the literal color spectrum. At least she hadn't yet. She'd only shared that with Dr. Kyle. But she shared basic concepts that she herself had experienced in a language others could understand without having to reveal its origin as being from some transdimensional fairy-tale realm.

All these conflicting thoughts gnawed at her brain as she rode her bike along the sun-splashed streets of Central London and a mild September wind tossed her hair around. Caitlin nevertheless kept pedaling toward Audley Street, near Hyde Park, for her weekly visit at the office of the prosecuting attorney—er, rather, her behavioral therapist.

She didn't care for the man. Didn't trust him. Didn't like his questions. Or his condescending manner and suspicious tone, which he seemingly tried his hardest to conceal but couldn't.

And then, in one single instant, Caitlin's worst suspicions about her shrink were confirmed. It happened in a flash, a single heartbeat, as she rode right by Foyles Bookshop.

Caitlin slammed on her brakes.

Her bike burned rubber as it skidded to a stop.

She backed it up until she was parallel with Foyles's window.

Caitlin glared at the display of new book releases, her

eyeballs narrowing. She clenched her fists. Then she locked her bike and stormed into the bookshop. She purchased the book that had seized her attention and returned to her bike, then rode off as her blood boiled like lava.

She soon arrived at the office of her psychotherapist, short of breath from the furious pedaling, heart racing in her still-rising anger. She locked her bike and entered the building.

"Good afternoon, Caitlin," Mrs. Caruthers, the wrinkled, ninety-year-old receptionist said. "Have a seat, and Doctor Kyle will be with you shortly." The reception area smelled of Mrs. Caruthers's old-lady floral perfume.

Caitlin took a chair and immediately opened the book she had just purchased. She turned the pages hard and fast, flicking the paper as she digested the content.

How could he do this?

"You can go in now," Mrs. Caruthers said, interrupting her thoughts. Caitlin shut the book, slid it back into her bag, and walked into Dr. Kyle's office.

He was yakking on the phone. He gestured for her to sit, making a face that suggested he'd be off momentarily. Caitlin sat there waiting, biting her lower lip, and trying to calm herself.

Dr. Kyle finally hung up the phone.

"Good afternoon, Caitlin. How are we doing today?"

"*We* are not doing well at all," Caitlin snapped. Her accusatory tone seemed to catch him off guard. He tilted his head.

"Is there something wrong?"

She wanted to tell him, wanted to scream. But she held

her breath for a moment, and then she let it out in a major huff.

"I'm fine."

He smiled. "Well, okay . . . that's good to hear." Dr. Kyle got up from behind his desk and sat on the leather chair next to the sofa where she was sitting. Dr. Kyle took out a notepad.

"How are things since we last met?" he asked.

He patted her on the leg, right by the tear in her jeans, his pinkie finger touching her bare leg.

That is, like, totally inappropriate and borderline illegal!

"Okay, I guess."

"Are you still experiencing the feeling of being watched?"

She was. She had told Dr. Kyle after her third visit that she often felt that a single eye was keeping watch over her. Or perhaps it was more like being spied on, or being monitored. She wasn't sure if it was a creepy kind of thing—like his pinkie grazing her flesh—or protective. But the one eyeball was ever present. At one point, Caitlin thought it might be Jack. Or Rapunzel. Or maybe even her mom. But then there were times when she was alone at night in her room, in the dark, and that feeling of being watched felt intrusive and frightening.

Anyway, Caitlin was too angry to start opening up to him.

"Nope," she replied. "No more peering eyeball."

Dr. Kyle jotted in his notepad and then said, "Do you have any new dreams to report?"

Yeah . . . I married Barton Sullivan last night, and my zombie BFFs crashed the wedding!

"Nope."

Not a chance I'm sharing that dream with creepoid Dr. Jekyll!

And then something registered as she shifted anxiously in her chair. The recollection caught her totally off guard.

A dream.

A second dream she had dreamed last night—*before* the wedding dream.

Wait.

It wasn't just an ordinary dream. It was a *recurring* dream. She had *also* dreamed it last week.

Whoa!

Like a budding flower bursting out of the soil in a time-lapse video, dream memories began to surface in her consciousness.

"Actually, I *did* have a dream last night," Caitlin said, feeling strangely compelled to talk about it, even though she absolutely did not want to.

"Tell me," Dr. Kyle said.

Absolutely not, Caitlin thought.

"There was a girl," she answered. "Older than me. Beautiful. Wearing all white. Lots of lace. She was waving at me. Calling for me. She stood by a forest . . . No! She stood by a black gate that *led* into a forest. Her stark-white body outlined against the polished black gate was extremely breathtaking."

Caitlin's initial thought was that the girl had to be a grown-up Alice. But it wasn't. It absolutely wasn't. Caitlin didn't recognize her . . . and yet, she seemed oddly familiar in a way Caitlin could not explain. It had made sense to her in the dream, but she could not articulate why now.

Dr. Kyle fiddled with the clip on his pen. "Is this the magical Zeno's Forest that you've been telling me about? Where the properties of time and space are nonexistent?"

She detected the tone of condescension in his voice. Nevertheless, the question was valid. Caitlin sensed that the forest could indeed transport her to a faraway place. Yet it didn't look or feel anything like Zeno's Forest.

"I don't think so. Not sure."

"Let's move on. Tell me about your daily routines. Are you still taking ten flights of stairs in order to avoid the lift in your building?"

Her eyes blinked rapidly. "As a matter of fact," her lie began, "I took the elevator down this morning."

He smiled slyly. "Did you, now? You know, Caitlin—your particular situation regarding irrational fears, social anxieties, and OCD are disturbingly rare in the annals of the psychiatric profession. I have yet to see or read about a case as extreme as yours. You're an anomaly, young lady. Therefore, I need you to be forthright if we're to make progress."

His eyes stole a quick glance at her bare leg again.

She shifted in her chair. She glanced at her Foyles bag. Her fingers drummed the armrest of the sofa. Then she directed her eyes back to Dr. Kyle.

"You don't believe me? You think I imagined riding the 'lift,' just like I imagined that boy Jack Spriggins . . ." Her tone sharpened. "And my mom, and all the dead people . . ." She cranked up the volume. "And that whole evening last October at Mount Cemetery?"

Dr. Kyle waved his pen. "Let's not raise our voice. Have you been taking your meds regularly?"

"Every day."

"Good. I want to prescribe a supplementary treatment. A new antidepressant."

"But I'm not depressed."

He wrote up a prescription as he spoke. "They've proven extremely effective in reducing intense anxiety and stress. And they will help you sleep better, hopefully curb those recurring nightmares."

"They weren't nightmares."

How does he know they're recurring?

"Besides, all these meds . . . they make me feel . . . different. Not myself. I don't like them. I don't think I need them anymore."

And that's when Dr. J. L. Kyle patted her on the knee again. That same pinkie touched the flesh of her thigh.

"I think you should let me prescribe the treatments best suited for your condition. This will help with your agitation as well."

Caitlin had already clenched her hands into fists. "You mean, I'm now under the control of the *Red Spectrum*, ruled by anger and fear and negative emotions that shine from the *red side* of our character?"

She whipped out the book she had bought at Foyles. Waved it in his face. Tossed it onto the coffee table in front of the sofa, where it landed with a thud. Dr. Kyle's face reddened.

"You stole my ideas!" Caitlin shouted. "You wrote about everything that I shared with you in confidence! And yet you've been telling me, and my dad, that I was making all of this up? And you've touched my leg twice today!"

Dr. J. L. Kyle's Adam's apple jiggled as he swallowed.

"I'm telling everyone," she declared. "Everyone! I'm telling my dad. Calling the newspapers. I'll call your publisher. I am going to post the truth on my blog." Her bitterness boiled over.

Just then, a black crow landed on the window ledge directly behind Dr. Kyle's desk.

It was as if someone had suddenly plunked an ice cube into her simmering soul.

Caitlin gasped.

Dr. Kyle sneered.

He slid his pen into his pocket and closed his notepad.

"Session's over," he said in a grim tone. "Time to leave."

Caitlin didn't need any coaxing. She snatched the book from the table and leaped up from the sofa. She stole a nervous glance at the black bird perched on the window ledge as she opened the door to leave the office.

It cawed.

Dr. Kyle grabbed her arm firmly before she opened the door. "I'd think twice, young lady, before doing something you'll surely regret."

Caitlin jerked her arm free. "You don't frighten me."

But he did.

He moved in close and put his hand under her chin, softly but firmly. She pulled her head away.

"I'm your therapist," he said. "I'm here to help you, if you'll let me." He inched closer. She smelled the pipe tobacco on his breath. "But if you carry on ranting about all these absurd allegations, I'll see to it that people categorically believe me—your psychotherapist—and certainly not you, the unwell patient with the rarest degree of an anxiety disorder ever recorded!"

Caitlin turned and opened the door. She suddenly felt a maddening compulsion to sneak a peek at one of the four corners of the ceiling.

He's right! I'm a freak. So don't look at it.

She did. But just one corner.

Okay—done.

Then she eyeballed a second corner.

No more!

Then a third—

Somehow she willed herself to stop her compulsive habit of making eye contact with all four corners of the ceiling. Instead, she glared at Dr. Kyle.

"You messed with the wrong person," she said, then fled the office.

She scrambled out of the building onto Audley Street, unlocked her bike, rode off, and pedaled at a breakneck pace.

Ghost-gray clouds began gathering over Central London.

CHAPTER FOUR

CAITLIN COULD ALMOST HEAR THAT CREEPY CROW CAWING BEHIND her as she rode swift and hard toward Hyde Park. She thought about the fact that she hadn't looked at the third and fourth corners of the ceiling of Dr. Kyle's office even though she desperately didn't want to. But what choice did she have?

She never *canceled* them out by looking at them.

Now these obsessive-compulsive thoughts would torment her to no end. And she was almost certain that she'd never again step foot inside that *Dr. Jekyll's* office. Which meant she'd never get another chance to cancel out the remaining ceiling corners. Which meant she'd never rid herself of these obsessive thoughts.

I thought I was over all this freaking OCD crap!

And what about the black crow on the window ledge? Beyond freaky. And Dr. Kyle's face? Wickedly unsavory.

The crow and the shrink seemed straight out of the

zombie universe. Caitlin's dread and discomfort over that turn of events made her forget all about the corners and ceiling in his office. She was also busy stealing quick glances behind her to see if that ghastly crow was following her.

She finally arrived at Hyde Park. She rode past the grand entrance and pulled up next to a bench, where she parked her bike. Her breathing began to slow and her shoulder and neck muscles relaxed as she settled in among the crowds milling about. She sat on the bench to gather her thoughts, comforted by the fact that she was one among thousands. The air was late-afternoon cool.

She pulled out a nutrition bar from her pocket. She squished it with a firm handgrip, then tore open the crumpled wrapper and poured crumbs into her palm. She tossed the crumbs onto the pavement to feed the pigeons skittering about.

"Excuse me, my young lady," a voice interrupted. "Feeding the pigeons is a crime. You can be fined or even face prosecution."

Her back stiffened. But then she relaxed as she realized the voice sounded vaguely familiar. Caitlin looked up but didn't immediately recognize the elderly man standing in front of her. He was short and plump with a tartan bow tie and a brown tweed vest. His light-gray beard grew to a sharp point, and he wore a herringbone ivy cap.

"Pay attention to the signs," he said.

"What signs?"

He smiled. "Precisely my point—you're oblivious to the

signs. Thus, you are breaking a law that bans the dispensing of pigeon feed."

The old man gestured with a finger toward the empty spot on the park bench beside her. "May I?"

Caitlin shrugged. "Sure."

Moving as if his bones were tired and sore, the old man gingerly sat down, letting out a weary huff and a laborious heave as he planted his bottom beside Caitlin.

He looked around suspiciously as his left eyebrow arched. When it seemed the coast was clear, he presented an open palm to Caitlin along with a mischievous smile.

She poured him a handful of crumbs, whereupon the old man sprinkled the feed onto the pavement for the pigeons bustling about; they eagerly gobbled up the morsels.

Caitlin drew her brows together playfully. "I suppose you don't pay attention to the signs either—or perhaps you're willfully choosing to commit a crime."

"Was that a question or a statement?"

How weird, Caitlin thought.

"Not many pigeons left in these parts," the old man continued. "Used to be about four thousand birds on an average day. Which made for one large lot of pigeon poop."

"You mean guano," Caitlin responded.

"Very good," the old man replied with an impressed nod. He pointed toward a menacing bird circling overhead. "Harris hawk," he said. "A bird of prey. The city brought them in to frighten off the pigeons in Trafalgar Square and now here. Pigeon pest control, you might say."

The hawk suddenly nose-dived, causing a flock of pigeons to scatter.

"That's cruel!" Caitlin said.

"Indeed." The old man agreed as he stroked his beard. "But while most pigeons fled as the hawk approached, a few remained. Apparently they were prepared to fight for their nourishment, despite their fear and the danger." His tone became foreboding as he went on.

"Unexpected turns of events, though painful and frightening, often serve to make us stronger. They impel us to become the person we are meant to be. Destiny holds both pain and blessings, my young lady. But make no mistake, *both* serve the same purpose: to help us evolve and contribute our very best to this world."

The old man presented an open palm again. Caitlin poured him more crumbs, which he tossed to the pigeons.

"Well, it's time for me to run," the old man said as he rose slowly. "Be well, my child. And be strong. And remember: we don't have a choice about the pain that comes to our lives, but we do have a choice about suffering." He removed his cap and bowed gracefully in a parting gesture.

No way!

Caitlin was certain she saw two insect antennae protruding from his head.

A majorly bizarre day, to say the least.

She pushed aside thoughts she was having about how the old man oddly resembled Amethyst, the green-tea-drinking caterpillar and butterfly. Instead, she pulled out Dr. Kyle's book and stared bitterly at the cover.

The Colours of Our Character
A New Technology for Eradicating Fears,
Phobias, and Anxiety
Dr. J. L. Kyle

She perused the book, heart palpitating the way it did whenever she was forced to confront a friend about an unpleasant issue. Dr. Kyle had pirated her deepest secrets. Plundered her painful experiences, then used them as his own insights into treating various anxiety disorders. He even used zombies as a metaphor for the onslaught of negative thoughts. Every page was a page from her life.

He used sunlight as a metaphor for the mind. The red and violet bands of color spectrum transmitted fear and courage, sadness and happiness, anxiety and serenity, respectively. The most important mind frequency the sun transmitted was the color green. He said we find our humanity when we activate our free will to resist the red-band emotions, which in turn lights up the feelings found in the violet end of the spectrum.

Duh. Who d'ya think told him all that?

And that snake was cynical to me about the whole idea of using colors to explain human nature. He didn't even understand it. Didn't get it.

She had tried explaining it, over and over.

He either purposely feigned ignorance, or the sketchy shrink really is totally ignorant.

That is, until the light bulb went out in his office during one session and the light bulb went on in Caitlin's head. When that light bulb had flashed and burned out, she suddenly found a way to explain it to him. The two of them had been sitting in near darkness. Totally creepy. Caitlin had quickly flicked on the flashlight on her phone. Then she explained it to him; a light bulb burns out when the filament breaks and the positive pole and the negative pole touch directly. There is a momentary flash, then total darkness. The light bulb shines only when the filament *resists.* Resistance creates light. And now Dr. Kyle had hijacked her philosophy and claimed as his own.

Contemptible thief! Plagiarist. Con man. Creep. Scoundr—

Something was wrong. Terribly wrong.

Suddenly, a menacing shadow was moving over Hyde Park. The rolling gloom seemed never-ending.

Caitlin's initial thought was that a giant blimp or a colossal low-hanging cloud must have been passing overhead. But she quickly realized that this was an unearthly presence. The humongous shadow moved over the parkland slowly and ominously. Before Caitlin could even look up, thousands of pigeons erupted in a flurry, fleeing the area in panic. Stranger still, the Harris hawk that was there to scare off the pigeons took flight as well, frightened off as if some malevolent force were descending upon the Earth.

Caitlin lifted her eyes. Her mouth hung open. The sky was paved in gleaming black tar.

But it wasn't black tar.

A vast and savage sea of black crows was winging overhead, packed so tightly together and in such vast numbers that they looked like the underbelly of some gargantuan alien ship—a ship with no sides and no end.

The black swarm blocked out sun and sky, its shadow rolling over the earth like the angel of death.

Thousands of frightened people came to a standstill, eyes wide at this implausible, intimidating spectacle in the sky.

And then the unthinkable happened.

Crowds scrambled frantically, fleeing Hyde Park as hordes of screaming crows began touching down.

They fell like black rain.

Caitlin's body went cold.

Tens of thousands of birds were landing by the second. Squawking like demons. Blanketing the full breadth of Hyde Park in a silken sea of feathered gloom. Devouring the grand entrance to the park and drowning Caitlin in black feathers.

A hundred thousand crows were suddenly on the ground, black beaks glistening, black bodies crammed so tight they swallowed every blade of grass and crack of concrete. They spread as far as Caitlin could see.

The stench of feathers, dead insects, and bird droppings invaded her nostrils.

And then, for some unexplainable reason, the wretched birds went silent. Not a caw. The silence was unnerving. The scene, surreal. Terrifying. Caitlin half expected to see that blonde lady—Tipper or Tippi-something-Hedren—from that old black-and-white movie her dad once showed her, *The Birds*, running through the scene.

The Enchanter is behind this.

She was positively certain, and her conviction filled her with nauseating dread.

The Lord of the Curtain.

Is it a warning? Is it connected in some way to that thieving plagiarist, Dr. J. L. Kyle? Aren't black crows an ominous sign of impending doom?

Caitlin bit her thumbnail. She needed to get home. Her eyes frantically searched her surroundings. The vast majority of people had already fled the scene. Her bike was buried beneath birds. She couldn't Uber her way out of there, because no vehicle could get close. And there was no escape route on foot because beady-eyed birds shrouded the earth. It looked like a scene out of the apocalypse.

She stretched out the collar around her neck.

Sirens suddenly screamed from afar.

A good sound!

Emergency responders were on the way.

The roar of helicopter rotors thrummed. She raised her eyes. News choppers hovered overhead. She glanced back to the streets. Fire trucks were pulling up curbside. She exhaled, sitting as still as stone, and watched as firemen drew their hoses from the fire trucks.

Cannons of water came gushing out of the nozzles. A

booming wave of squawks shook Hyde Park as the repulsive birds thrashed and flapped and took to the skies. Plumes of water swept the area. The crows smothering her bike abandoned it in a frenzy and returned to the sky. Pathways leading out of the ghastly scene began to open up.

Caitlin seized the moment.

She jumped up from the bench, hopped on her bike, and began to pedal. Fast. Faster. Maniacally.

She bolted from Hyde Park like a bat out of hell.

Should I glance back to see if crows are following me?

She didn't dare.

CHAPTER FIVE

CAITLIN TORE DOWN ROYAL STREET AND PULLED HER BIKE UP TO her apartment building. She couldn't wait to tell her dad what had just happened. She knew he was probably hearing about it on the news already.

During the last eleven months, Dr. Kyle had told Harold Fletcher that Caitlin's fanciful stories about her mom and her adventures down the grave of Lewis Carroll were just part of an overactive imagination fueled by an unwillingness to confront painful truths.

Nevertheless, her dad had always winked at her. Always given her a reassuring hug after such observations by that nasty shrink.

He believed in her. He might not have understood exactly what had happened to her, but he seemed certain that something out of the ordinary had occurred and that his daughter was not dreaming it all up.

Caitlin climbed ten flights of stairs. She zipped down the hallway, breathless and sore-legged from all the bike pedaling and stair climbing. She burst into her apartment.

"Dad, did you see the news?"

She took the stairs two at a time to the second floor of the split-level flat. She knocked on her dad's bedroom door. Silence. She nudged the door open just a crack, peeking in.

"Dad?"

Still no answer. She gently opened the door all the way and tiptoed into the room.

He wasn't in bed. Not at his desk. Bathroom lights were off. She looked by the side of the—

Her heart jumped!

Harold Fletcher lay face down on the floor.

Unconscious?

Heart in her mouth, she dashed over to her dad and grabbed his wrist.

God, no!

His skin was cold. No pulse. She whipped out her phone. Dialed 999. Summoned an ambulance. She didn't even hear herself speak. She turned back to her dad.

"Daddy, please wake up! Wake up!" She wiped the wet from her eyes.

"Sound the trumpets, I have returned home from school!" a spry voice called out from downstairs.

Natalie! No!

"Get into the kitchen—now!" Caitlin screamed, desperately trying not to sound hysterical but failing miserably.

She choked back her emotions. "And wait there—do *not* come upstairs!"

"When did you become sheriff of London Town?" Natalie shouted back in defiance.

Caitlin slid her hands underneath her dad's forehead and chest. She rolled him onto his back. With both hands, she pushed hard and quick on his chest. Again. And again. She placed her ear over his heart. No beat.

She pushed hard and fast on again. After five or six more thumps, she held his cold hand. Placed a finger on his wrist. No pulse.

A morbid sound made her skin crawl.

Cawing.

She turned to the bedroom window. A black-eyed bird was perched on the tenth-story ledge. Watching her. Its beak looked as though it were smiling.

The wail of an approaching siren seized her attention. She leaped up, ran out of the bedroom, and flew downstairs. Natalie was ambling out of the kitchen, her thumb sunk in a jar of peanut butter. She scooped out a thick, sticky globule and shoved it into her mouth.

"Wha up wid you?" she mumbled through a mouthful.

Caitlin beelined to the front door. Before opening it, she turned to her sister. "Get back in the kitchen! Now!"

Natalie was clearly taken aback by Caitlin's forceful manner and tone. Evidently this was not a moment to test her sister's patience, so Natalie slunk back into the kitchen.

Caitlin opened the apartment door and stepped out into

the hall. The elevator chimed. The door slid open. Paramedics rushed out.

"Upstairs!" Caitlin shouted. The responders ran into her apartment. "First bedroom on the left."

Caitlin walked gravely back into her apartment, head hung low. She leaned against the wall in the front foyer. Then she crumpled to the floor, knees tight against her chest. She buried her head in her arms. She absolutely refused to look up when the paramedics carried the stretcher down the stairs and out of the apartment.

She just sat there, head still bowed, eyes closed, drowning in a well of tearful grief.

Soft fingers suddenly caressed her hair. She smelled creamy peanut butter. Natalie had come out of the kitchen.

"What's wrong, Caity-Pie?"

Caitlin's throat throbbed as she stifled the urge to cry.

She raised her head, wiping away a warm roll of tears from her cheek with her sleeve.

Large sculptures of peanut butter that would make Michelangelo weep with envy were pasted on Natalie's nose, lips, and chin. Normally that would've cracked Caitlin up with laughter. But all cheer had abandoned her.

Slowly, carefully, and contemplatively, she made eye contact with each of the four corners of the ceiling in the front foyer of their flat. The OCD had beaten her down.

And despite her effort to regain her composure for her sister's sake, Caitlin's voice broke as she replied through a waterfall of salty tears, "Dad's gone."

CHAPTER SIX

SPY-GLASS HILL, TREASURE ISLAND

SCORES OF NIGHTINGALE BIRDS BOASTING A BRIGHT ARRAY OF COLored feathers were perched high in tall coconut palm trees, serenading Treasure Island with their sweet music. The crooning nightingales were actually lustful males, and, as lustful males often do, they were using their song to seduce the female nightingales by convincing them of their mating prowess.

The seductive birdsong, however, sounded like damnable white noise to Janus's ears. Shrill cacophony. Janus hated birdsong.

Janus had just led his black-clad crew of crowmen through Zeno's Forest. Profiting from Zeno's space-and-time transcending properties, the crowmen had transported themselves to Treasure Island. When they touched down on the island, they flew the rest of the way, winding up at the summit of Spy-Glass Hill.

Janus hated it there. But Treasure Island was the location of the portal. And the portal led to the place where the treasure lay in waiting—a treasure far more valuable to the Enchanter than any wooden chest brimming with the plundered booty of pirates.

Janus had brought six other crowmen with him. All six were dressed like Janus in identical black garments. Dark fedoras with creased crowns and downturned brims cast narrow shadows on their elongated, tar-black beaks. Each crowman wore a long, dark coat that hung to his black-feathered anklebones.

Janus had selected only masculine hunters like himself for this task. The male crow's propensity for extreme violence, along with its remorseless nature, was a necessary trait for achieving a successful outcome. Crowman Janus was determined to perform his task quickly and efficiently to impress the Lord of the Curtain. Janus's craving for power and position almost matched his lust for flesh and ants.

Janus's mission on behalf of the Lord of the Curtain was clear: remove the obstacle to the treasure. The obstacle, in this case, was the firstborn. This would clear the way for the Enchanter's top deputy, a thieving bastard buccaneer, to secure the treasure: the second-born.

The Enchanter's first deputy went by the name Blackbeard, though his scurvy face was nearly beardless aside from a slight outgrowth of stubble—more salt-and-pepper than honest black.

Blackbeard had special status among the Enchanter's minions because he was the one who, long ago, had opened up the first portal into the human world: the Kirriemeuir Cemetery.

The Enchanter's second deputy was the notorious marauder Captain Flint, the man whom Janus had come to meet—and to take measure of him.

Janus was the third deputy, but he hoped to rise in rank after today's task.

Flint's role was to reveal the hidden whereabouts of the portal so that Janus and Blackbeard could cross over and carry out their part of the operation.

Janus's *covert* mission was to also evaluate Flint and Treasure Island for signs of life and the green band of the color spectrum.

There were already rumors circulating about Captain Flint and the island. Rumors alleging that the red was dissipating from Flint's eyes, that the island was messing with his head.

Treasure Island had become a rare phenomenon—one of only two known locations in this world where there was any semblance of life. Strange occurrences of greenery had been reported there, despite the deficiency of the sun's green wavelength. Even the songbirds Janus found so insufferable were suddenly sporting colors.

No one knew why.

The only other place rumored to claim traces of life in defiance of the affliction was the island of Neverland.

The whole vibe of Treasure Island ruffled Janus's feathers. But the tall crowman had no choice about accepting the mission. He found the hut where Flint and Blackbeard were waiting for him. The six crowmen stood guard outside as Janus entered.

Captain Flint's face was decrepit and pale. Blackbeard's distinguishing features were a facial scar, scabs, and the salt-and-pepper prickly stubble that in no way justified his name.

Janus sensed treason from the get-go. He watched Flint switch out a perfectly good, stiff glass of blood for a tall bottle of rum, which he poured into a shot glass.

I'll fill a shot glass with your blood soon enough.

Flint slid the shot of rum in front of Janus and filled a second one for Blackbeard. He then poured a third shot for himself. Raised it. Toasted.

"To the treasure!"

Blackbeard clinked his glass with Flint's and said, "Aye, to the treasure."

Janus didn't toast. He just let his shot glass sit, unattended. He stared, silent and cold into Flint's bloodshot eyes.

"Cat got your tongue?" Flint mocked as he downed his rum. He swallowed and eyeballed Janus with contempt. "When was the last time you birds had a bath? Your feathers stink like rancid cheese."

Blackbeard winced at the testy comment. Janus sat there, calm and icy cool, angling the razor-sharp point of his long beak toward the empty shot glass. "Drinking rum now?" Janus responded. "Losing your taste for blood?"

Flint squirmed slightly as he answered, "Bit o' congestion in the lungs. Nothin' like a shot o' rum to warm the chest."

Blackbeard was obviously trying to ease the tension. "Liven up, lads. I says nuthin' wrong with a shot o' rum every now and then."

Janus's black eyes remained fixed on Flint. His beak angled up. "Cold virus growing inside of you?"

Flint squirmed even more. "Nah. Inhaled too much sawdust. Sanding a ship's hull early this morning."

Janus knew that if plant life was growing on the island, and if a cold virus was growing in the pirate's body, it meant Flint was already making choices.

The undead have no choices. Janus never chose. A bloodeyed followed the commands of the Red Spectrum obediently, staunchly, and blindly.

When that wretched feminine human had liberated their kingdoms from the full force of the affliction last year by destroying the scepter, choice had returned. There were those—like Janus and the wulves—who longed to return to the profane and savage taste of flesh and organ. Granted, alive or undead, Janus's diet had always included both delicacies, but his undead state intensified the hunger exponentially. In turn, that immensely magnified the renewed thrill of satiating a virtually insatiable appetite.

And so Janus had sought out the Enchanter, surrendering his will in exchange for the exalted sensation of gratifying vulturous hunger. The undead lived only for that moment. Habitual indulgence. Existing solely for immediate meteoric pleasure, never contemplating the consequences that lay beyond the moment. It was always about the moment, the fleeting rush and gratification of *now*.

The Lord of the Curtain had also rewarded Janus and his flock with something extra for choosing the way of the living dead: the power to walk upright, on two clawed feet, in the form of an anthropoid. Like those wretched werwulves.

"The portal. Where is it?" Janus asked Flint softly.

"What's your hurry?"

Janus tilted his head, his liquid-black, beady eyes still glued on Flint. He was growing impatient.

Flint pointed to a plant. "See that over there? Life. Quite a bit of that around here now. The Enchanter has an explanation for such an occurrence?"

Blackbeard winced again. He saw where this was going. And he was right, because Janus had had enough.

The Crowman thrust his head forward—*SWOOOOSH*—with terrible power and speed. He drove his long beak through Flint's chest and out the other side, impaling the dangling buccaneer like beef on a skewer.

No more chest congestion.

"Good god!" Blackbeard cried out. "What the hell didya do that for? The bloke's supposed to tell us where the damn portal is."

Two other crowmen wrenched, wrangled, and twisted the

dead captain's body from the beak-stake. They dropped him in the dirt for the vultures to feed on.

Blood pooled at the tip of Janus's beak. He set the tip over Flint's empty shot glass. Two gleaming teardrops of blood filled the glass. Janus raised it.

"To the treasure." He gulped it down and cawed in delight.

And here's to my coming promotion to second deputy, behind this beardless buccaneer.

"How will we find the portal now?" Blackbeard asked Janus.

"I already know the location."

"How? I thought only Flint knew."

"I saw the map."

"Where?"

"From the sky. Flying in. A corpse lay sprawled on the ground. Flint murdered the man. His name was Allardyce. His arms are pointing to the portal."

"And how, may I ask, did you know this?"

"Read it in the Great Book of Records. Before it was locked away in the Great Vault."

Blackbeard seemed impressed.

"The vault that touches stars?"

Janus nodded. "And you'll find the incident recorded in Treasure Island."

"The book in the human world?"

Janus nodded and then cawed in disgust.

Janus' plan was to lead his crew of crowmen through the portal and to the place where the humans resided. Janus's black-winged brethren—the regular crows who inhabited that mindless material realm—had homed in on the firstborn at a place called Hyde Park.

Janus nodded to his crew. There was only more thing to do before departing.

"Join us," Janus said to Blackbeard as he gestured toward a large mound of dirt.

It moved.

The pirate's face soured. "Thanks, but no thanks."

Janus winked a beady black eye. The crowmen attacked the large colony of yellow ants scurrying about their anthill to relish another one of those gratification moments. This was the supreme indulgence—excessively exhilarating, decadent, and pleasurable. They crushed the insects and smeared their fluids all over their black-feathered bodies!

The juices induced a heightened state of ecstasy. The crows writhed on the ground to absorb as much of it as possible, squirming in euphoria.

When the narcotic wore off, they were ready to ascend the portal to the physical plane where humans walked.

Humans, Janus thought disdainfully. He knew they were in complete denial about the existence of Janus's universe—the nonmaterial realm of sheer imagination.

Such arrogance. Such narrow-mindedness.

Human cynicism is nothing but a superiority complex. They have no basis to stand on, because humans possess the very same addictions as I do, the same choiceless existence as the living dead. So in what way are they supposed to be superior? Even the animals of their world are more intelligent. Animals know, instinctively, to run from fire. Humans always jump into real and proverbial fires, making their own lives more miserable.

They were also slaves to the Red Spectrum. Worse, they were blind to its very existence, which made them the best slaves possible: the slaves who know not of their own slavery or their taskmaster's.

Except for that worthless feminine creature of human blood.

He'd been told she was starting to wake up. And, she was the firstborn. The one obstacle to the treasure.

This was why the Enchanter had summoned Janus to the portal on Spy-Glass Hill, high atop Treasure Island.

She had to be disposed of.

The treasure was the second born. The younger sibling.

Which was why the Enchanter had summoned Blackbeard.

CHAPTER SEVEN

THE DAY SHOULD HAVE BEEN GRAY AND GLOOMY WITH LOW-HANG-ing, slate-colored clouds. And those overcast skies should've been crying with light rain.

Instead, the sun shone blindingly bright, and the air was crisp with the apple-cinnamon scent of autumn. England's skies were cerulean blue as Caitlin and Natalie, family, and friends stood at the gravesite of Harold Fletcher, next to the gravestone of Caitlin's mom, Evelyn Fletcher.

I'm an orphan, Caitlin thought.

The notion was surreal. The situation unfolding around her was unbearably nightmarish. The only thing that felt authentic was the numbing hurt and impending panic in her chest.

Untimely thoughts attacked her as she participated in the funeral rites for her dad.

What if I have a panic attack now? What if I have to flee? How embarrassing and inappropriate that would be!

And then came the guilt, which only amplified her anxiety. *How could I be worried about such things at my own dad's funeral?*

Instead of beating herself up emotionally, Caitlin realized her breathlessness and dizziness were not the result of a random anxiety attack—there was good reason for such overbearing emotions.

She was burying her father.

And so she allowed herself to grieve and to feel awful, and sad, and distraught, and hopeless and short-breathed for this one piercing day.

But then she chose to celebrate her dad's life instead. She blinked hard as salty moisture stung her eyes. She thought about his patience and his unconditional love for her and her sister.

Oh God, how he must have suffered when Mom passed!

But her dad had been more concerned about Caitlin and Natalie than himself. He had given Caitlin the necessary space to come to terms with the disappearance and subsequent death of her mom. For four years, he had waited for her to find the courage to confront the truth.

And he believed in me! Especially when that conniving Dr. Kyle had tried to portray me as some delusional, loony teen.

Natalie grabbed Caitlin's hand and squeezed it so tight her nails dug into Caitlin's palm.

Oh, dear God. Poor Natalie. She has no one but me anymore. And I have no one but Natalie. No one!

The casket was being lowered into the grave. Caitlin's chest tightened and she could no longer swallow her saliva. She shaded her eyes with a raised hand and glanced over the cemetery lawns, looking anywhere but at the casket.

Her heart jumped.

A strange-looking man was standing among the crowd.

A tall, narrow-framed man with a weathered, worn, corrugated face the color of concrete. He had long, scraggly hair and a rough, raw exterior. His deep-set, dark-rimmed eyes and menacing presence gave him a dagger-sharp edginess. So did the gold earring glinting in his ear. Danger shone from his piercing eyes.

Caitlin had no clue who he might be, but his deep-lined face made her terribly uncomfortable.

His eyes found Natalie.

Why's he staring at her?

Caitlin squeezed her kid sister's hand tighter.

The man abruptly directed his gaze to Caitlin.

She flinched and lowered her head. She shifted her eyes back to the casket.

The coffin was dipping below ground level, disappearing from view. Reality hit like a vicious body blow. Tears fell from her eyes. She clutched Natalie. The sisters wept in each other's arms. A couple of aunts or cousins from her mom's side of the family—people that Caitlin never really knew—came over to embrace the girls.

Caitlin swung her head around. Her eyes scanned the

cemetery grounds. She searched for an exit. A path out of the place.

She needed to run. Needed to find Jack. Alice. Her mom. She desperately wished she could see her dad one more time, to tell him how much she loved him and how much she appreciated his unwavering belief in her.

She looked back at the grave. Men in wrinkled suits wielding shovels scooped up dirt from a mound of deep-brown soil and tossed it into the hole. The thud of dirt striking wood made Caitlin cringe.

And then, an oddly warm feeling began to swirl in her chest cavity.

Her eyes hardened. She curled her fingers into fists. She could feel the knots in her stomach, and somehow she knew a violet-blue force was seething in her belly. It bled into her bones. Her fists tightened as her eyes narrowed.

Caitlin was going to hunt down the heartless being Alice had called the Lord of the Curtain.

He had struck her hard, ruthlessly, and without mercy. She knew it was related to threatening to expose Dr. Kyle. Yet, somehow she knew Dr. Kyle was a mere pawn, a puppet, working at the behest of the unseen entity. J. L. Kyle might be dangerous, but he was not the one in control.

She looked back at the man with the decrepit, stone-colored face. Her brow crinkled. Could that be *him*? Or was he just another henchman or puppet, like Dr. Kyle?

Perhaps she was just overreacting and being melodramatic. Who could blame her under these circumstances?

The strange man was now grinning at her.

She glanced over at a spare shovel wedged in a mound of dirt. A sharp and merciless shovel. A blunt instrument. A fatal weapon. The fingers on her right hand twitched. Her legs tensed. She leaned forward on the balls of her toes, verging on a first step toward the *weapon.*

She hesitated.

That man's corrugated, corpselike face—it looked as if it were in the middle of settling into rigor mortis. And she could *feel* his presence slithering across the lawn and passing right through her.

She stood her ground.

Patience. Now is not the time or place. Today is about honoring Dad and laying him to rest.

She could not defile this solemn moment with violence— especially not in front of Natalie.

The last clump of dirt landed in the hole, and Harold Fletcher was officially interred at Mount Cemetery.

Mrs. Kraggins, the social worker from Foster Home Services UK, gently escorted both girls toward a waiting car parked a little ways in the distance. Caitlin and Natalie had been placed into their emergency foster-care program until the court could appoint the girls a legal guardian. The only suitable relative hadn't been in the country for years. Caitlin, however, couldn't even think about problems like that—or her temporary living conditions—right now. It wasn't that it was just too painful and altogether intimidating. No. She knew she had to start formulating a plan. Focusing on a plan would keep her mind preoccupied.

Besides, by the looks of that disturbing man at the graveyard and the slimy nastiness of Dr. Kyle, she knew she was definitely dealing with a formidable enemy—a dark and malevolent force that had brought death into her life.

Mrs. Kraggins led Caitlin and Natalie along footpaths imprinted onto the fallen autumn leaves strewn about the Mount Cemetery lawn. The foliage crunched beneath her feet.

Waiting for Caitlin by the car was a warm and welcome sight: Barton Sullivan.

His eyes were soft and comforting and Caitlin deeply appreciated his being there. Barton embraced her and whispered in her ear.

"I feel gutted. I can't even imagine how you must feel. Anything you need, Caitlin, please, please, let me know."

Barton held her close. Then he kissed her gently on the forehead.

Other students from Kingshire had gathered around the car, each one coming forward to offer condolences.

The Banister twins, Alfie and Piers. Piper was there. Layla and Paige, as well. All three girls were dressed conservatively. No gloss. No Brazilian blowout-blonde hairstyles.

Piper approached Caitlin and hugged her, whispering in her ear, "I'm truly sorry for your loss." Piper wouldn't let her go, and Caitlin heard her sniffle.

Mrs. Kraggins placed her arm gently on Caitlin's back. "We must go."

Piper's eyes glistened with moisture as she released Caitlin, who smiled sweetly at her friends.

"Thank you all for being here." She turned away so they wouldn't see the fresh roll of tears.

Once the sisters were buckled safely in the back seat of the car, Natalie laid her head on Caitlin's lap. Caitlin gently caressed her, running her three middle fingers through Natalie's curly mane.

The car interior smelled of leather and pine, reminding Caitlin of her dad's car back in New York. Ever since she was a kid, her dad had hung pine-scented air fresheners on the rearview mirror so the car always smelled as fresh as a forest.

As they rode back to London, things grew clear in Caitlin's mind. She had gone to the Lewis Carroll grave weekly, for months on end, riding the train from Central London to Guildford. No one from *down under* had ever shown up.

Caitlin gritted her teeth as she observed her own eyes peering back at her in the front rearview mirror. Her mind was made up. She was going to go back to Lewis Carroll's grave as soon as she could. She'd start digging—all the way to Wonderland if she had to.

Somehow, she could feel that Jack was getting closer. She could almost hear unworldly commotion right now at Mount Cemetery. Something was in the air.

Her fingers twisted and tugged on Natalie's curly locks. Judging by her deep breathing, it seemed her kid sister had fallen asleep. The time had also come to tell Barton Sullivan her own story. They had become close friends. She could confide in him. She would need his help. He was strong and tough, and he really loved Jack. He had loved Jack from the very first day—when he popped Barton on the nose in the schoolyard.

Barton would believe her if she told him about everything that had happened beneath Lewis Carroll's grave.

Oh God—he'd better believe me!

Caitlin had also made a ton of new friends online over the last eleven months. Kids who loved her posts. They had embraced the ideas that she shared on how to overcome anxieties, fight fears, and conquer phobias.

Caitlin had been stunned when various newspapers and online news outlets had started running stories on the new friendships suddenly being forged in middle schools, high schools, and on playgrounds between kids from different cliques and distant social circles. The so-called experts could find no reason for this sudden new phenomenon.

But *she* knew. And it filled her with pride. Natalie had warned her that it was all going to her head, though. She had even called Caitlin a narcissist. She told Caitlin she'd better humble herself and get down from her high horse.

But she'd just figured the little twerp was jealous.

Caitlin had no doubt all her readers would trust her if she let them in on her secret. After all, they had initially thought she was out of her mind for suggesting uncomfortable random acts of sharing—and for doing them when anxiety most clutched them by the throat. They were dumbfounded when it had worked. She had been flooded with emails and appreciative comments. They had forced themselves to get out of their comfort zone, at Caitlin's suggestion, and befriend people who were the precise opposite of themselves. To talk to other kids and get to know them. It humiliated their egos, but she advised them they would have to do it if they wanted to heal crippling panic attacks. That was also working.

Well, the time has come to tell them everything.

Caitlin stroked Natalie's hair as a plan began to take shape in her mind. She would recruit an elite group to help her hunt down the Enchanter. She'd select kids who were suffering from anxiety because, along with human fear, that emotion proved to be the perfect stealth armor to conceal oneself from blood-eyed zombie predators.

She'd tell them how the blood-eyed had ruled a universe under the depraved leadership of the Queen of Hearts— who happened to be her mom, Evelyn Fletcher, under a spell. Courtesy of the Enchanter and his cursed red glasses.

The glasses.

Caitlin shifted in her seat. Those glasses had blinded her mom and given her psychic vision instead. But the perverse lenses had reversed reality in the mind of Evelyn Fletcher. That simple but deceptive reversal trapped her mom, who remained in character, and imprisoned her in Wonderland. What was sweet, the Queen of Hearts would sense as bitter. Wherever love overflowed, the Queen of Hearts sensed abundant hatred.

Caitlin's fingers strummed Natalie's curled strands as

Girl Wonder softly snored. Caitlin stared out the window. The pane fogged up.

What if I had never been able to help Mom last year? What if I had been unable to convince Mom to remove those cursed glasses? Oh God.

The memory of what she had said to her mom in order to trick her into taking off those voodooed glasses.

Oh God. It cut deep. Bone deep.

Now especially, after having just buried her dad.

But she'd *had* to speak truth, or her trick would never have worked. Her mom would have never felt the reverse emotions emanating from her daughter.

Which meant Caitlin had no choice but to locate her own resentment, animosity, and . . . *hatred.*

When Evelyn Fletcher had initially disappeared, Caitlin suspected her mom had walked out on her dad, abandoning the family. The hope that she might return never died inside her.

When she finally found out that her mother had died, *abandonment* proved to be the lesser of two evils. All the years of resentment and all that pain. And the burden of denying and suppressing the truth.

Last Halloween, in Wonderland, Caitlin had to summon the raw emotions born of that psychological trauma to *save* her mom. She had to spew forth her worst feelings like a snake secreting venom.

And it had to be the truth.

It had to be the truth!

That was the *only* way her mom could sense the opposite. But now, the wounding words she had uttered were returning to punish her.

"I hate you! Do you hear me? I hate you. I don't ever want to see you again. Ever! You are dead to me!"

The guilt crushed her.

And now her dad was gone.

A fresh bout of anxiety almost overwhelmed her when a stark truth touched her heart: *Natalie is all I have left!*

The doorway to that other world had also remained closed since Halloween night last year. Jack Spriggins, Alice, Snow, Cindy, Rapunzel—all had vanished without a trace. And yet, when she had woken up some mornings, she could have sworn she could sense their presence. But when she came to full wakefulness, those perceptions dissolved into shapelessness, the way a cloud form reshaped anew in seconds.

Caitlin warily nibbled the tip of her thumbnail. Then she jerked her thumb away from her mouth. She sat on her hands, full weight.

No way am I going to fall backward.

She shifted in her seat, exhaled, and looked out the window, eyes resolute, mind firm.

But then her shoulders slackened. She lifted her butt, freeing her hands, and bit away at the tip of her thumbnail, peeling off slivers to calm her nerves.

A gnawing feeling had been trying to surface in her mind—a feeling she had been trying to ignore since the funeral.

She wanted to see her mom again. She needed to find her dad, too, so she would at least be able to say goodbye properly. But a strange feeling told her that they both belonged to some other world now. Some other *kingdom* that she was not yet ready to understand. Some other reality that she was destined not to visit ever again.

She knew now with certainty: today was truly about letting go and facing the truth of their passing. Saying goodbye.

Goodbye, Daddy!

The heartbreak of her situation was now beginning to yield to horror. Everything that was playing out seemed to be leading to an inevitable confrontation between Caitlin and the Lord of the Curtain. The stakes were nothing less than life or death.

Alice had told her that he was the root of all cold, evil, and death. He was the nurturer of all the villains and monsters that wreaked havoc in stories. Zombified and pretty-as-a-peach Alice had warned Caitlin that he had crossed over to her world and that he was coming for her. He had struck his first blow—by taking her dad—and this punctured her heart.

She squinted as she gazed out the window, seeing nothing of the passing landscape because of the harsh realization forming in her mind.

She had grossly underestimated the threat and Alice's warning. She had allowed the passing of time to give her a sense of false comfort.

But now what?

The car was approaching Foster Home Services, a

nineteenth-century, two-story Victorian building that looked straight out of a Charles Dickens novel. The dirt and grime soiling its burgundy bricks looked to be equally as old. The sprawling front lawn, thankfully, showed signs of life—it was green and well kept, as were the gardens adjoining the building.

Natalie woke and lifted her head from Caitlin's lap. She sat up as the car began to slow. Girl Wonder seemed refreshed and perky and that made Caitlin happy.

"How long was I sleeping?" she asked.

"The entire way," Caitlin said.

"You mean we're here already?" Natalie responded in shock as she peered out the window. Then she saw the dingy, bleak building.

"Hey, Olivia Twist, it's a relic! Orphanages like these have been deinstitutionalized."

Caitlin gave her sister a quizzical look. "De . . . what?"

"Deinstitutionalized. Shut down. The things that went on in the old orphanages were dark and horrific. I heard about dozens of kids being buried in unmarked graves back in the old days. Today, orphans are placed with foster families in private homes. I suppose they only use this place for emergency foster-care cases. Like us."

The girls exchanged wary looks.

The car passed through the black, wrought-iron entrance gate.

The gate!

It triggered a memory.

Caitlin blew hot breath onto her hands.

Eleven months ago, when she and Jack had returned from that other world on Halloween night, they had shared a hug beneath a crescent moon at Mount Cemetery. The moment was lovely. They had been standing by a black front gate. Jack gave Caitlin a birthday present: a bottle of Elizabethan rose perfume. Natalie had snapped their picture from across the road.

Caitlin now remembered a faint sound she had heard at that very moment.

A crow's caw.

Oh my gosh! That was probably the moment. That's when it must've happened.

The Enchanter climbed out of the Lewis Carroll grave that night.

And he followed me home!

CHAPTER EIGHT

RECRUITS WANTED

JOIN AN ELITE UNIT OF WARRIORS TO
WAGE WAR AGAINST THE UNIMAGINABLE,
THE UNBELIEVABLE, AND THE
INCONCEIVABLE.
WE WILL BE HUNTING DOWN EVIL ITSELF!
AND THE SOURCE OF ALL FEAR AND PANIC.
CONSIDERABLE RISK—SOME MIGHT NOT
COME BACK ALIVE.
OR SANE.
ONLY THE FRIGHTENED SHOULD APPLY!
FEAR, PHOBIAS, ANXIETIES ARE
DEFINITE ASSETS.
OCD TOO.
THE MORE, THE BETTER!
TRUST ME.

ONCE UPON A ZOMBIE

CAITLIN TAPPED THE DIGITAL KEYBOARD ON HER PHONE, CHANG-ing the period after the word "me" to an exclamation mark. Then she posted her call to action on her blog and all her social media sites. She punched herself in the shoulder as a self-congratulatory gesture.

She had spent a few days planning this operation, while staying at the emergency foster home building. She found the exercise to be both therapeutic and motivational. It helped to distract her from her current living conditions, and the sense of purpose she gained from plotting to avenge her parents' deaths brought meaning to her situation.

This post would generate a humongous response, she knew. She already had over fifty thousand "likes" on Facebook. And ten thousand subscribers to her blog. A post like this would electrify kids. Her only worry was that she might not have the necessary time to go through all the applicants.

"Will you turn off your phone already?" Natalie shouted from her bed. "The light is keeping me up!" Girl Wonder pulled her thick blanket over her head and sank flat into the mattress.

Caitlin checked her phone: 11:37 p.m. She was anxious to fall asleep, eager for the dawn, and totally stoked about seeing the results of her posts.

She plugged her phone into the charger and then closed her eyes.

* * *

The alien sun was a scintillating fireball, burning lurid red and filling the sky with its powerful presence. A nebulous haze in the atmosphere prevented the sunshine from transmitting the full seven colors of the spectrum into this fantastical world. A moderate amount of the green color was being filtered out.

Which posed serious problems—though not for the alpha werwulf and his pack. His subspecies of lycanthrope were upright, biped creatures, able to verbalize thought into speech through the oscillation of their esophagus. Their eyes roiled with blood, and their jaws were frothy with saliva.

They were biological kin to the Big Bad Wolf of *Red Riding Hood* fame—and his carnivorous cousin, the other Big Bad Wolf, serial killer and stalker of piddling pigs. They were highly intelligent creatures with exceptional acumen.

But intelligence and consciousness did not equate. Intelligence was the processing of information related directly to self-preservation: how to hunt, kill, and eat. They could outthink their prey, navigate, and adapt to all sorts of terrain. They were adept at making tools and they built societies.

Consciousness, however, concerned powers of free will: the ability and willingness to resist primal reactions. These, of course, undermine the evolution of the mind toward becoming chivalrous, merciful, and magnanimous.

The undead have no resistance to basic instincts. They could care less about moral choices and willpower.

They just want to eat.

The alpha werwulf was on a mission. He'd been searching for the undiscovered portal that would lead to the soon-coming world of Eos.

The portal could be identified by a signature: *Crosthwaite.*

The alpha wulf found it in short order, and, as instructed by the Lord of the Curtain, he began preparations for the opening of the portal.

* * *

Caitlin woke before the alarm went off, even before the morning sun spilled through the blinds at the foster home. She lifted the picture of her dad from her chest and placed it on her nightstand.

She jumped out of bed, skipped her morning wash and teeth brushing for the moment, and grabbed her tablet from her dresser.

She eagerly climbed back into bed and propped up her pillow behind her back. She set the tablet upright on her chest, nestling it in a crevice that she formed with her wool blanket.

There were a gazillion messages in her inbox.

Yes!

Countless comments posted on her Facebook page.

Her feet wiggled excitedly beneath the blanket.

With wide eyes, she read the first one. The second. The third.

Her heart dropped in her chest, and her jaw dropped even farther.

Loon.

Deluded fool.

Ur the undead doofus.

Psycho.

Faker or wackadoo—choose one!

Read your shrink's file on u. Sounds like ur short a few garbanzo beans in that vegetable head of yours!

Haha! Jack and the Beanstalk? Totally bananas.

Zombies with blood in their eyes? Unhinged girl!

U r a certifiable wack job! Just say'n.

Living dead Rapunzel? Im thinkn ur the dead one—from the neck up.

Caitlin skimmed the rest of the comments. They were pretty much all the same, notwithstanding the various colorful adjectives that gave some comments their own crass distinction.

Dr. Kyle had leaked her confidential file onto her Facebook page. It included his private notes assessing her psychological profile and condition.

A preemptive strike!

He made it seem as though Caitlin had stolen all the ideas from *him* for her blog to gain popularity and to satiate her ego. Her file said that she was delusional, that she conjured up all kinds of far-fetched stories: about a portal to Wonderland beneath the Charles Dodgson grave and a zombified dead mother parading around as the Queen of Hearts. There were wild claims of blood-eyed zombies and famous zombie princesses, including Cinderella herself. Jack of the beanstalk was there, and his magical garbanzo beans that grew all the way from Wonderland to a graveyard in Guildford, England, instantly, because of some kind of magical soil. Caitlin's tale of climbing up the extraordinary, fast-growing beanstalk at the speed of sound was there too, and how she claimed to have used it in order to escape a degenerating, decomposing fairy-tale universe crawling with ghouls.

She stopped reading when her throat began to close. And her throat was closing because it *did* all sound grossly ludicrous when it was read with an objective mind.

The room began to whirl like a carousel. She mopped cold sweat from her brow with her sleeve. Held her stomach and tried belching to ease a wave of nausea.

Worse than all of this was a thought crystalizing in her mind with cruel clarity.

Suppose none of it ever happened?

Maybe that whole episode in the other world was a psychotic delusion. I dreamed it. Or hallucinated it. Because I'm not coping with the death of my mom. I've repressed the pain and buried the truth far too long—it eventually manifested as a nervous breakdown.

Maybe I've been losing my mind all this time, losing touch with reality.

Her eyes searched the bedroom. Examined the furniture. Floor. Ceiling. She leaped out of bed and inspected her room closely.

Uh-oh.

She smacked her palm against her mouth as her eyes widened in terror.

Am I even in a foster home?

Or am I really in the psych ward of some mental health institution? Have I suffered an emotional collapse?

The stark white walls were closing in on her. Her breathing became labored, her head heavy, legs wobbly. She plopped down on a chair. Massaged her thighs.

Fifty thousand high-school kids around the globe now thought she was out of her freaking mind.

Oh. My. God. They're right! I am out of my mind!

Perhaps Dad checked me into this institution. Maybe he never died. Or did Dr. Kyle have me committed? Maybe I dreamed him up as well. Maybe I'm having hallucinatory fantasies after losing my grip on reality. And Jack is still at my school. And he isn't even Jack Spriggins of fairy-tale fame! He's just a regular person.

Actually, I think he was! His real name was Jack . . . something. Jack . . . Jack . . .

I can't remember it!

Caitlin warily walked over to Natalie's bed.

Please, please, please be lying there!

Caitlin's hand slowly reached for the edge of the blanket. She pulled it back.

Empty!

I hallucinated my own baby sister!

Caitlin dashed into the hall. Her eyes flitted around wildly.

This place does look like some kind of sanitarium for the delusional.

She rushed back into her room and bee-lined it to the window: iron bars. She slid her fingers between the bars and slid the window open. It only lifted a crack.

She leaned down, nudging her nose against the narrow opening. She sucked the cold, predawn air into her lungs.

Then Caitlin crumpled to the floor. Her head drooped, and her limbs went limp, flopping to her side. She let her entire body slouch over.

I'm really alone.

She exhaled. She lifted her eyes to the ceiling and then slowly wagged her wrist back and forth, as if waving a flag of surrender.

I'm done.

No longer was she going to fight the panic. No longer going to chase after oxygen. No longer going to try to hang on to *normal* and to try to control . . . well, *anything!*

If she lost her mind, so be it.

She let go.

And it felt as though fifty-two tons of weight simultaneously lifted off her shoulders.

"Hey, Little Orphan Annie. Why you slouched on the floor?"

Natalie?

Caitlin leaped up. She seized her kid sister like a drowning person seizing a life jacket.

Natalie winced. "You're crushing my intercostal muscles."

"Where were you?" Caitlin cried out.

"Emptying my bladder. Why the freak-out? Because of Dad? Or because we're languishing away in some nineteenth-century orphanage instead of a nice, middle-class foster home?"

"Yessss!" Caitlin shouted with glee. She ran to the wall, kissed it, patted it, and danced with delight. "It *is* an orphanage! A beautiful, safe, nurturing orphanage!"

Natalie just shook her head and said, "Indeed it is." She waved a pamphlet. "I've been reading about this place. It's for children who are bereaved and grieving. Except, sweet sibling, you're neither bereaving nor grieving."

Caitlin yanked Natalie by the arm, pulling her close. She crumpled the pamphlet against her body and wrapped her arms around her sister.

"I think you just dislocated my shoulder. Have you lost it?"

"Totally! Kids across planet Earth now think I'm certifiably crazy. And I couldn't be happier!"

Caitlin squeezed her sister tighter, inhaling the raspberry aroma of her curly flop top.

Natalie managed to nudge her mouth free from Caitlin's smothering embrace. "You *have* lost it."

"I'd rather be sane and ridiculed than praised and outta my mind!"

"Too late."

Caitlin would've normally slam-dunked Natalie with an even snarkier comment, but she was too relieved to be angry. Besides, Caitlin had heard her little sister crying herself to sleep last night. She just didn't have the heart to snap back.

"Promise me something, Nat," Caitlin said as she let go. She put her hands on her sister's shoulders and stared intently into her eyes.

"Depends what it is."

"I'm serious. Will you promise me something?"

Natalie could obviously see the water welling in her sister's eyes. "Okay. What's the promise?"

"Always be careful. And always stay close."

Natalie nodded. "That's two promises. But of course." Natalie paused a moment. She replied, "Do something for me in return?"

"Sure," Caitlin said.

The expression on Natalie's face suddenly seemed odd, something totally unfamiliar to Caitlin.

Natalie went uncharacteristically silent. She simply stared into Caitlin's eyes.

This is, like, totally weird, because wordlessness and prolonged stares into her sister's eyes are not Nataliesque things to do.

Caitlin was about to crack a remark when she saw Natalie's lower lip quiver.

"Natalie, what is it?" Caitlin asked as her heart began to drum.

Her kid sister was struggling to hold back her feelings. Then a sliver of sadness touched the corners of her mouth; a slight crack of emotion showed in her full-moon eyes. Her words came unguarded, in a trembling whisper.

"Can you keep holding me, just for a bit longer?"

Caitlin clutched her sister. Natalie showed vulnerability and returned the embrace with uncharacteristic warmth, and this shattered Caitlin.

"Don't worry, twerp. I'm here for you. Always! And I'll hug you whenever you want."

Natalie's fragility was devastating. "Promise?"

Now Caitlin's voice quavered. "Promise!"

After a lingering hug, Natalie pulled back and wiped the wet from her cherry-red cheeks. Caitlin smiled at her. Natalie giggled.

"Know what else?" Girl Wonder said.

"What?"

"I find it kinda sad. And strange."

"What?"

"So many orphans. Kids who are parentless."

Caitlin nodded warmly. "In the world?"

"Well, that too. But I meant in stories. Oliver Twist. Peter Pan. Pip from *Great Expectations*. Little Orphan Annie. Tom Sawyer. Huckleberry Finn. Harry Potter."

Caitlin added, "Mowgli, from *The Jungle Book*."

Natalie's lip quivered again as the heartache overwhelmed her. "And now you and I. Caity-Cakes, I really never thought this would ever happen to us."

Caitlin wrapped her baby sister in her arms and pulled her close to her heart. Her body was shaking against Caitlin's with intermittent convulsive sobs and suppressed sniffles.

But this is good. This is very good. It needs to come out.

When Natalie's body finally calmed, Caitlin leaned back and planted a kiss on her sister's forehead. She handed her a wad of tissues.

Natalie smiled appreciatively. She blew her nose with a resounding honk that probably woke up all of England.

How does such a booming foghorn blare out of such a small nose?

Natalie unfolded the crumpled pamphlet. "By the way, you'll never guess who the managing director of this place is."

Why would I care?

"Okay, who?"

"Your therapist, Doctor J. L. Kyle."

Chills ran cold down the back of Caitlin's neck and shoulders.

No! No! This can't be!

Her fingers tugged at her collar, which suddenly felt like a noose.

Natalie's brow crinkled as she muttered to herself, "There's something peculiar about his name."

No—there's something peculiar about him! And he's dangerous.

Then it came from out of nowhere.

A feeling.

Inside Caitlin.

Something from somewhere else was suddenly summoning her. Something deep inside, calling to her from a faraway place, a distant land, an otherworldly kingdom. . . .

Except the summons was also coming from. . . .

Right outside the orphanage!

Caitlin moved swiftly to the window. She peered out between the iron bars. Dawn had broken, and standing in the street in the early morning light was. . . .

Oh. My. God!

It's him!

Jack!

He waved.

Then he pointed to his watch. Held up both hands. Flashed ten fingers.

He mouthed the words: *Halloween night. Mount Cemetery.*

Caitlin smiled. Winked. Fist-pumped the air.

I'll meet Jack at ten p.m.! At Mount Cemetery. October thirty-first. My birthday!

That was just four days away. Her bright smile was as sweet as ripened fruit fresh off the tree. She gave Jack the thumbs-up.

Finally!

Jack Spriggins nodded assuredly, then happily dashed off.

"Who's out there?" Natalie asked.

Caitlin was speechless. Giddy. Eleven long months had passed without a word from Jack—or anyone from that other world. Doubt had been creeping in. Only a few minutes ago, she had had the fright of her life, convinced that she *was* losing her mind—and had lost her sister.

But now Jack had shown up. And just in time. Caitlin was beside herself with anticipation.

So much had gone tragically wrong in her life these last few days. Her dad. Her confidential file leaked online. Her reputation ruined beyond repair. And now her imprisonment in an orphanage where the warden was Dr. Kyle!

Caitlin felt a welcome surge of hope from seeing Jack.

Perhaps the recent string of devastating misfortune is finally over. Maybe things are about to turn around.

"You girls are up early!"

Mrs. Kraggins had just walked into the room, a fresh smile upon her face. "And I'm glad. Because I've brought good news!"

Caitlin couldn't contain her grin. Another fist pump.

I was right!

"I didn't want to get your hopes up," Mrs. Kraggins said, "but for the last few days we've been working on your file and trying to find your uncle in Amsterdam, but to no avail. However, we did locate some cousins."

Yessss—I'm outta here!

"They're in California," Mrs. Kraggins continued. "And they've agreed to take you temporarily while we track down your uncle. Yesterday afternoon, the court appointed them as legal guardians. You'll both be on a flight back to America later this afternoon."

Caitlin thwacked her forehead, leaving a bright-red palm mark.

She glanced at the window where she had seen Jack a moment earlier. Then she shifted her eyes back to Mrs. Kraggins. Caitlin had to escape the orphanage before Dr. Kyle moved in on her. And she had to meet Jack on Halloween night.

Which means only one thing is absolutely certain, Caitlin realized with great fury and fierce defiance.

There's no way on earth I can move to California!

CHAPTER NINE

THE DOUBLE-DECKER BRITISH AIRWAYS A380 TOOK OFF FROM Heathrow Airport at 7:31 p.m., en route to Los Angeles.

Natalie had a window seat on the first level, near the back of the plane. She watched a few sitcom episodes. Ate dinner. Munched a few snacks, then slept.

Caitlin had the aisle seat in the same row.

During the last few hours, she had shifted restlessly in her seat, shook her head, and fought to stop herself from pulling out every one of her precious strands of cinnamon-colored hair. To stem the frustration, she began plotting how to get back to London to meet Jack on Halloween night.

She glanced at the entertainment screen in front of her. It was tracking the flight. The plane was halfway across the Atlantic Ocean.

Uh-oh.

The map triggered a barrage of disturbing thoughts that interrupted her strategizing.

This plane cannot land even if there's an emergency, because . . . there's no land to land on!

If she had to get off the plane, if she started freaking out and panicking . . . there was no way out of the flying tin can.

The double-decker airliner suddenly felt the size of a closet to Caitlin.

What if I need an emergency appendectomy? Or one of the engines blows, and we need to make an emergency landing?

On the ocean?

Far worse than the claustrophobic feeling of being imprisoned on a plane over water was the feeling of being totally and helplessly out of control.

Her breaths became short and clipped.

Oh God, this is not the time to start hyperventilating.

At least when she had a panic attacks usually, she was . . . *on the ground!*

Now she was panicking at forty thousand feet.

Everyone will stare at me if I start breathing heavy and perspiring.

This thought made her breathe heavily and perspire.

She glanced up at the oxygen mask compartment.

The plane jolted.

The dreaded *ding* rang through the cabin as the seat belt sign lit up.

I knew I shouldn't have looked at the oxygen compartment!

Life is punishing me. For looking at the oxygen compartment. I shouldn't have. Now I'm going to need it.

Life often punished her like this. So much so, she was afraid of not being afraid. Weeks before a flight, she would agonize. Darkness would swallow her the way it swallowed up the light in a closet when the door was shut.

But this is good, she thought. *Because the flights are never that bad when I agonize over them in advance.*

So it became a habit. A superstitious methodology for coping. If she was happy and calm and relaxed like her friends—like normal people were before a flight—the odds were the flight would scare the living hell out of her.

She'd fought to remain calm during the drive to Heathrow. And now the turbulence was happening.

I should've been more afraid. I should have worried more. I shouldn't have looked at that stupid oxygen compartment.

More bumps rattled the cabin. The aircraft dropped into another air pocket. Caitlin's tummy leaped into her chest.

"Flight attendants, take your seats," came the pilot's deep voice. Caitlin began rubbing a fingernail, resisting the irresistible compulsion to pick it till it bled.

Lord Amethyst Bartholomew!

She remembered that the sage caterpillar had revealed a great secret to her. But she couldn't recall it now. She was too busy breathing.

A shrill cry from a few rows ahead caught her attention. She wanted to lean out to see, but she was paralyzed in her seat, too scared to move a muscle. She'd be punished if she relaxed her body, so she remained taut as a high wire. That was how she would control the plane and her anxiety.

Her fingernails clawed at her armrest.

The crying from a few rows up intensified.

Somehow, Caitlin forced herself to lean into the aisle and sneak a look.

A little girl was in tears. She was around five or six. Her plush rabbit was lying in the aisle, a foot away from her out-stretched fingers. Obviously frightened by the turbulence, the poor kid likely wanted to hang on to that bunny for dear life. So did Caitlin.

Flight attendants couldn't help. They were buckled into their seats. The kid's mom was buckled into a middle seat.

Tears glistened on that poor girl's face.

The plane dropped again. Then it swerved right. Left. Caitlin peered out her window. Dark clouds flickered with electricity in the distance.

Caitlin undid her seat belt.

"You are *not* going to the cockpit," Natalie shouted, obviously woken by the turbulence. "It's just a storm and a few air pockets. Nothing to freak out over."

Caitlin rose, clutching the top of the seat in front of her. Then she stepped out into the aisle. She made her way toward the teary-eyed kid, rocking and bouncing as the plane shimmied.

"Please return to your seat immediately!" shouted a flight attendant sitting by the emergency exit.

As the airliner swayed and Caitlin wobbled, she managed

her way over to the rabbit. She kneeled, snatched it, and handed it back to the girl.

"Here you go," Caitlin said, gripping an armrest for support. "And there's nothing to be afraid of. It's just a storm and a few air pockets. Nothing to freak out over."

The girl sniffled and smiled thankfully. Caitlin winked, then turned to head back to her seat. The plane hit another air pocket, jolting Caitlin a good foot in the air.

She laughed aloud. "Totally crazy!"

She rushed back to her seat, buckled up, and experienced an enthralling sense of freedom that she had never felt before.

Like, who freaking cares if this plane bumps and bobs around like a buoy in a rough sea?

She had no control, so she just let go and allowed the magic of the violet-blue spectrum to fill her with calm, confidence, and the conviction that all was well on this flight. She told herself that was simply the way it was going to be.

Something wholly unexpected happened next: the air smoothed out, and the plane began cruising like a ship on calm waters.

I remember!

"Don't chase after the sunlight," Amethyst the caterpillar had told Caitlin. "Rather, chase the clouds that hide it."

Caitlin had helped another person when it was most difficult for *her*. She did it by charging right through the dark clouds of fear that were trying to smother her.

Natalie nudged her sister. "I forgot to tell you something."

"What?" Caitlin asked.

"I was having a weird dream about you. Just before the turbulence woke me up."

"And?"

"There was a girl. Dressed in lacy white. Calling for you. Standing by a black iron gate leading to some kind of weird or magical forest. She wanted to you to follow her. She said you were in mortal danger."

Turbulence—or even appendicitis at forty thousand feet—suddenly seemed positively trivial.

* * *

MOUNT VAEA, SAMOAN ISLANDS, THE SOUTH PACIFIC

Janus and the others had traveled up the portal from Treasure Island and emerged onto an island. They had been there for two days now, sleeping in the woods and feeding on reptiles, grasshopper eggs, even shark—courtesy of the South Pacific. They were waiting for the Enchanter to appear.

The island was the site of a portal called Robert Louis Stevenson. Stevenson was the creator of various worlds, including *Treasure Island* and *The Strange Case of Dr. Jekyll and Mr. Hyde.*

On the morning of the second day, Janus and his flock had stumbled upon an anthill. They quickly began to dig it up. What a glorious morning it would be for them if they struck pay dirt as they waited for the Lord of the Curtain.

After unearthing their find, Janus was more than pleased.

The colony contained more than a million restless ants whose sweet, golden color reminded him of a Samoan island sunset.

Janus had to calm his brethren for, in their feverish excitement, they had pulled off their long, black overcoats and begun to strip bare. Truth be told, Janus was also finding it difficult to control the primal urges bubbling like a volcano inside him.

But if the Enchanter appeared while they were indulging, that could prove to be a serious problem for—

Janus lost control!

He surrendered to the lure of the ant colony.

"Be quick," he instructed his crew.

Janus stripped down. With their sharp ebony beaks, the seven crowmen crushed hordes of ants, smearing their excretions and fluids all over their black-feathered arms and shoulders, then rolling onto their backs in orgiastic rapture.

The rest of their day passed without incident. The Enchanter finally arrived just after nightfall.

He appeared in the dense woods directly behind the tomb of Robert Louis Stevenson.

The Enchanter stood before Janus, not in material form but as an ethereal impression, a spectral shadow cast from the invisible part of the color spectrum: the infrared. The Lord of the Curtain assumed the visible part of the Red Spectrum only when necessary. He existed in the invisible part of the spectrum—the colors that couldn't be seen by the naked eye, in any kingdom or realm.

"What have you learned?" he asked Janus. His words

ONCE UPON A ZOMBIE

emitted no physical sound waves but reverberated directly in Janus's medulla.

Janus stepped forward. "The girl—the elder one. She grows stronger. Bolder."

The Enchanter shimmered a smile. "She is deftly competent, but I don't have to tell you that."

No, you don't have to tell me. Tell the one who calls himself Blackbeard. I would have had her by now. But I will show you how good I am. I will show you who should become the second deputy when this mission is accomplished.

The Enchanter waved a long, bony finger. "You are not to engage anyone of this world," he instructed. Janus nodded. "Focus only on the firstborn," the Enchanter continued. "Discretion is vital. And though you will walk among humans, parts of your anatomy will appear repulsive to their primitive perceptions. Be discreet. Favor the shadows. Above all, hide your head!"

CHAPTER TEN

CAITLIN AND NATALIE STROLLED OUT OF CUSTOMS AND ENTERED the arrival terminal, wheeling their luggage behind them. Cousins Cordelia and Harry Wannamaker were waiting there for them with flapping arms, broad smiles, and earsplitting squeals.

"Oh my! Caitlin, Natalie, how much you have grown!" Cordelia cried out as she wrapped her pudgy, freckled arms around them.

Cordelia seemed sweet enough, and she immediately reminded Caitlin of two fruits: a pear because of her wide hips and bountiful butt, and two bananas because of the yellow polyester slacks stretched tight around her thick legs.

Cousin Harry grabbed the girls' suitcases. "Welcome to California, young ladies! Now, stick close to your cousin Cordelia. Everyone follow me to the car. We'll chat on the car ride home."

Natalie shot an uncertain look at Caitlin that seemed to say, *Is this really happening to us?*

After navigating through the crowds in the terminal and finding their car in the parking lot, Harry piled the luggage, Cordelia, and the girls into his nautical-blue Prius. He promptly hit the freeway, meticulously obeying the speed limit posted along Interstate 110.

"Well, girls," Cordelia said from her position riding shotgun, "Harry and I are so delighted to have you as part of our family. The first thing we shall do tomorrow is to prepare a Halloween birthday party for Caitlin."

The thought of Halloween and missing Jack at the grave of Lewis Carroll renewed Caitlin's nervousness and anxiety. She took out her phone and texted Barton Sullivan.

So much to tell you, Barton. I'm in California now. Need you 2 go 2 the grave of Lewis Carroll. Guildford. Halloween night. 10:00 p.m. sharp. Jack will be there waiting for you. Yes, Jack! I'm going 2 try 2 get back by then as well. Hopefully a morning flight. I know you don't believe the garbage being said about me online. But do read in full detail what happened to me. I swear, it's all true. I'll explain tomorrow night. Jack can also explain.

Caitlin hit "Send" and—

THUMP!

The Prius swerved. Caitlin jolted left, jamming against Natalie. Cousin Harry kept his cool—thank God—and quickly regained control of the vehicle as honking cars and irate drivers mouthing awful words whizzed past them.

An object had struck the front windshield.

"Dear Lord!" Cordelia shouted. "Did you see that?"

Caitlin surely hadn't. But the splat of blood and black feathers sticking to the front windshield made it abundantly clear what they'd hit.

A black crow had slammed into the car. The suicidal bird had been blown off the windshield instantly by the blasting wind.

Caitlin was a bit freaked.

Harry shook his head in dismay. "That bird seemed to deliberately strike our car."

Cordelia turned to the back seat. "Are you girls all right?"

"Totally fine," Natalie said. "They estimate between fifty and a hundred million birds crash into cars each year in the United States alone."

Cordelia did not seem comforted by the statistics. "Well, in all our years of driving, this has never happened. And we've crossed this country by car on numerous occasions; haven't we, Harry?"

Harry was too busy watching the road to respond, obviously still frazzled.

"How far is Los Angeles from London?" Caitlin whispered to Natalie.

"About 5,400 miles. Why?"

"How long would it take for a bird to fly that distance?"

Natalie made eyes at Caitlin as though she were out of her mind. Then she said, "Assuming the average bird flies at twenty-five miles per hour, I'd estimate a hundred and eighty hours—or approximately seven days. Why? You think that drunken fowl flew here from the United Kingdom just to collide with our car on the freeway?"

Caitlin let out an awkward laugh. "Don't be ridiculous. Ha ha."

Natalie rubbed her chin. "They're highly intelligent, you know."

"Who?" Caitlin asked.

"Crows. As clever as the great apes."

Caitlin shifted in her seat.

"And their brains are unusually large," Natalie continued. "About the same size as a chimpanzee's—relatively speaking, of course."

"Thank you, *Natalie Geographic.*"

"And they have facial-recognition abilities."

"We've heard enough, thank you."

"They can remember and distinguish between individual humans."

"Oh. My. God! Why weren't you born with a mute button?"

"They're also into anting."

Caitlin's brows scrunched. "Anting?"

Natalie smirked. "Oh, so you *do* want me to continue?"

Caitlin ignored the snarky undertone. "Please answer the question. What's anting?"

Natalie was in her element as she babbled on. "Crows crush ants with their beaks. Then they rub the ant fluids and excretions on their bodies."

Caitlin's mouth shriveled like a prune. "Disgusting!"

"Not to crows. They love it. It's a stimulant. Like a

narcotic. It arouses ecstasy. They find it irresistible. The buzz seems to be triggered by formic acids the ants emit."

Caitlin plugged her ears with her hands and turned away from her sister.

Hopefully that will shut her up.

The rest of the car ride was uneventful—except for the part where Caitlin saw the Hollywood sign. Harry Wannamaker's Prius soon arrived in Glendale, then wound through a hilly subdivision and pulled onto their street.

The Wannamakers lived in a charming neighborhood and on a tree-lined street that featured single-family, Tudor-style homes and Spanish bungalows.

When the car pulled into the driveway, cousin Cordelia hesitated before opening her door. "Don't get out of the car just yet," she instructed. She took out a mini, high-powered flashlight from her purse and pointed the beam through the window. Her eyes warily scanned the driveway and lawn. She was clearly searching for something.

Natalie elbowed Caitlin, mouthing silently, *Are they a bit weird?*

Caitlin shrugged to say, *Possibly.*

"Cordelia, please," Harry said, shaking his head. He turned to the girls in the back seat. "She's paranoid. Some wolves were spotted in Northern California yesterday. First time in decades. And then someone reported seeing wolves in this area this morning. I think it's just a coyote coming down from the Verdugo Mountains. Nothing to be worried about."

The expression on Cousin Harry's face suddenly shifted

from unruffled to skittish as the blood on the car windshield began to dribble down.

"Everyone sit tight," Harry said, "until Cordelia gives us the all-clear signal."

Black crows crashing into cars in California?

Wolves on the prowl in Glendale?

What could possibly be next?

CHAPTER ELEVEN

CAITLIN THUMBED THE KEYS ON HER IPHONE AT SPEEDS THAT seemed to defy the laws of physics. She was calculating.

Three days left to get back to London.

Seventy-two hours before Halloween.

Four thousand, three hundred, and twenty minutes before her ten o'clock rendezvous with Jack at Mount Cemetery in Guildford.

Judging by the first day at the home of her cousins, Caitlin could see that the Wannamakers were kind and decent people. They would understand. And, therefore, they would help Caitlin get back to London—pronto. She'd have a heart-to-heart talk with them right after they returned home from their Wednesday-night bowling league.

"You sure you're all right staying home alone?" Cordelia asked.

Caitlin rolled her eyes. "I've been babysitting Natalie since I was twelve. Not to worry, cousin Cordelia. We'll be fine."

Cordelia set her bowling-ball bag on the floor and gave Caitlin a hug. "You have my cell number if you need anything. We're only ten minutes away. And Harry left a twenty-dollar bill on the dining-room table. In case of an emergency. And don't go outside. There's a wind advisory in effect. The Santa Anas are blowing in this evening."

As soon as Cordelia and Harry left, Natalie grabbed the TV remote and put on some PBS science and nature show featuring a gabbing scientist who promised to make the complexities of photosynthesis simple to understand. Caitlin smiled; she knew Natalie could have done a far better job of explaining.

She then sat on a La-Z-Boy chair and opened her iPad. She spent the next few minutes checking flights back to London. She searched for the best airfares and wound up shaking her head and huffing a lot.

How will I possibly afford the plane ticket?

The TV volume was too loud for her to be able to concentrate, so Caitlin powered down her tablet and wandered into the kitchen. She peeked through the screen of the open window above the sink. The backyard was dark except for a few moonlit trees casting irregular shadows that seemed to be moving. The winds were picking up. Tree branches swayed boisterously. Caitlin could hear whistling through the screen. The night air was crisp and she could smell roasted firewood billowing out of some nearby chimney. She closed the window and locked it.

The hallways were dimly lit, all the bedrooms as dark as the night. The Wannamakers were obviously frugal folks. Why waste electricity when no one was in a room? Caitlin stepped into the hallway. She was about to flip on the light when she heard a man talking to Natalie.

What he said chilled her blood. Something about the red light wavelength and the color spectrum and her life depending upon the red-band portion of the spectrum!

Oh my gosh—

Caitlin grabbed a knife from the kitchen and raced into the den. Natalie was absorbed in her TV show and still flopped on the sofa. The man's voice was coming from the TV.

"Will you lower that volume this instant!" Caitlin shouted.

"Chill, girl. Come watch—you'll learn something."

"What was he talking about?"

Natalie perked up and lowered the volume on the remote, apparently delighted that Caitlin was taking a shared interest in the show she was watching.

"Actually, it's pretty incredible," Natalie said. "Photosynthesis and quantum biology."

Wasn't that in my dream?

"What about it?" Caitlin asked.

"Did you know the red wavelength of light is the most efficient and powerful color for stimulating photosynthesis in plants? Life on earth depends on photosynthesis, which means the red side of the spectrum is critical for our existence."

How odd.

"But that's not the incredible part," Natalie said.

"What is?"

Natalie's eyes rolled to one side as she thought about how to answer. "How can I make this simple?" she muttered.

Her brows furrowed in concentration. "I know—I'll give you a riddle. Suppose you're driving a car. You have to reach a certain destination. But the destination is at the end of this crazy, tangled maze of roads with lots of dead ends and wrong-way signs all along the way. You'll only have enough gas to make it to your destination if you find the shortest route. If you drive into the maze blindly, the odds are totally against you making it to your destination because you'll run out of gas."

Caitlin interjected. "What are the odds of you getting to the end of this boring riddle before you run out of gas and I run out of patience?"

"Very funny. Now, here's the riddle: You can make *one* move before driving into the maze that will guarantee you arrive at your destination. What is it?"

"I have no idea, and I could care less."

"I'll give you two hints."

"How 'bout I give *you* two hints: one, I'm bored to tears; two, I'm bored to tears."

Natalie ignored the diss. "Here's your first hint, sweet sis: it's windy."

"Good, now blow away."

Girl Wonder persevered. "Hint two: there's a man in a uniform standing by."

"I love a man in uniform," Caitlin said. "But why not a woman in uniform?"

"You're stalling. You're too scared to try to solve the riddle. In case you flunk it."

Caitlin made an epic *Are you kidding me?* face.

"Then try it, Caity-Pie," Natalie dared.

"I'll humor you. I have one move?"

"Yep."

"And it's windy. And there is a man in uniform, right?

"Yep."

"Okay, twerp—the dude in the uniform is a pilot. He flies helicopters, and the spinning rotors from the copter are creating the wind. The pilot takes me up to give me *one* bird's-eye view of all the routes at once. I map out the shortest one. Then he—or she—lands the helicopter. I drive into the maze and make it to my destination in record time."

"Impressive—I'm proud to call you my big sister."

"I'm, like, so flattered. Now what does photosynthesis have to do with the red side of the spectrum?"

"I'm impressed by your curiosity as well. Okay, so photosynthesis works the same way as the riddle. It's called quantum biology. First, the red light of the spectrum excites an electron in a leaf."

"The electron corresponds to the car in the riddle, right?" Caitlin interjected.

"Affirmative. Now, there are many routes for the electron to travel to get to the part of the leaf called the reaction center; that's where the light is converted into energy."

Caitlin rolled her eyes. "I graduated grade school."

Natalie didn't miss a beat. "But there's only *one route* that allows the electron to make it there without running out of gas—or energy—along the way. The miracle of photosynthesis is that the electron *somehow* chooses the shortest route every single time. And scientists could never figure how this was possible. Until recently. So, you wanna know how?"

"Do I have a choice?"

"Always. Ready?"

"Like Freddy."

"Superposition."

Caitlin shrugged. "Is that word supposed to mean something to me?"

"It means an electron is not just located in one position or one place. An electron can exist in *all* possible positions, in *all* places, *all* at the same time."

"That's, like, totally nuts."

"Indeed. It's a freaky phenomenon, but it's a proven fact of quantum physics."

Hmmm. I'd like to superposition myself right over to London.

"Do you know what this means?" Natalie asked.

"Enlighten me."

"It means an electron can travel along *all* the routes to the leaf's reaction center simultaneously! So once it knows the fastest way, that becomes the de facto route that it travels. And—voila! Light is converted into energy. Plants can now produce the air that you hyperventilate on."

Cheap shot, twerp.

"All thanks to the red band part of the spectrum."

Caitlin's brows sharpened into points. "Superposition sort of reminds me of you. Everywhere I turn, wherever I go, you're always there."

Natalie winced. That one hurt.

Caitlin ran over to her and hugged her. "I'm sorry, Nat. I didn't mean that." She held her tighter. "I'm just frustrated and frightened and—"

Ding!

Doorbell.

Who'd be ringing the bell at this hour of the night?

"Pizza's here!" Natalie shouted.

Caitlin let her go and shouted, "Pizza? Who said you could order a pizza?"

"I'm ravenous."

"Who's paying for it?"

"Chill, cheapskate. Our new foster parents left a twenty on the counter, remember?"

Natalie skipped into the kitchen, grabbed the bill from the countertop, and scurried to the front door. Caitlin followed.

Natalie opened the door. . . .

Caitlin's eyeballs ballooned in terror.

It's him!

The intimidating man from their father's funeral was now

standing in the doorway. The man who looked like an undead pirate. Same wrung-out face, dark-rimmed eyes, and facial lines as deep as the Grand Canyon. His voluminous sway of gunmetal hair was in its own sort of superposition—scattered everywhere at once, defying even gravity. And he was wrapped in an oversize black houndstooth scarf. He stood there in the nippy night air.

Caitlin's heart leaped into her throat, rendering a scream impossible.

Natalie was sizing up the lanky fellow, pointing at him with a quizzical look. "Why is Keith Richards standing in our doorway?"

Caitlin shoved Girl Wonder behind her. She stuck out her chest boldly, put on the bravest possible face, and spoke in an unflappable, harsh tone—despite her pounding heart. "Who the *heck* are you to come knocking on our door at this hour of the night?"

The old man smiled, causing the crevices in his face to sink deeper. Wind and leaves whirled behind him.

"I'm your great-uncle, Derek. Derek Blackshaw. Brother and bandmate of your deceased grandfather, Robert "Bobby" Blackshaw, the second born in our family. Uncle to your dear mum—and my beloved niece, Evelyn—also the second born in her family."

His accent was unmistakably British, his voice scratchy in a bluesy kind of way.

"I'm Natalie—second born in the Fletcher clan," Natalie quipped. "And I don't suppose you brought a pizza?"

Caitlin shook her head. "What are you doing here?"

The man claiming to be her great-uncle smiled. Thankfully, it was a kind smile. "I've come back from Amsterdam to take you and your sister back to England. If you want to go back, that is. Been following your blog. Ever since your dad left to meet his maker."

This could be my ticket home!

"I saw you at the funeral," Caitlin said.

"Indeed, you did."

"Why didn't you come over and introduce yourself? You scared me half to death. I thought you were some zombie psycho." As the words left her lips, Caitlin winced. "Sorry. That came out wrong."

Derek Blackshaw's corrugated face cracked a knowing smile.

"Five decades of . . . um, well . . . let's just say *time* took a heavy toll."

Natalie nodded suspiciously and folded her arms. "Uh-huh. I suppose you mean five decades of ingesting various plant substances, alcohol, and tobacco extracted a heavy toll."

Derek Blackshaw's eyes lit up. "Which reminds me," he said, pulling a crinkled pack of hand-rolled cigarettes and a box of matches from a back pocket. "It's been a while." He popped the cigarette in his mouth, struck a match, and lit up as Caitlin and Natalie stared at him with contempt.

"Now, how about inviting your long-lost great-uncle inside?" he said, puffing leisurely in a cloud of smoke.

Caitlin politely stepped aside, but Natalie stood her

ground. She even stuck out her arm to halt his progress. "ID first." She opened her palm. "Driver's license or passport. Need to verify you're an authentic Blackshaw. And put out that disgusting cigarette."

He sneered at Natalie as he blew smoke from the corner of his curled mouth. "I heard about you. IQ off the charts. Arrogant. Precocious. Smart as a whip." He went from sneer to smile with a gravely chuckle. "A true Blackshaw to the bone—ha ha!"

"Half Fletcher, half Blackshaw," Natalie corrected.

Derek rolled his eyes as he presented his passport. He then pulled out an old, wrinkled four-by-five-inch photograph. "Might wanna have a look at this as well."

Caitlin snatched the photo.

"That's your mum," Derek said as Caitlin's eyes drank up the photo. "When she was twelve."

Caitlin's eyes misted over as she gazed at her mom. She knew the photo well. Young Evelyn Fletcher, née Blackshaw, was absolutely adorable. She had an uncanny resemblance to Natalie.

Natalie examined the passport meticulously, then fired off a few questions like a customs agent.

"What's your father's name?"

"Edward Junior."

"Mother's name?"

Caitlin stamped her foot. "Natalie, you're being rude."

Girl Wonder's eyes were glued on the passport as she responded. "I'm being thorough. You don't let complete strangers into your home without proper identity verification. Now, what's your mother's name?"

Derek chuckled and said, "Claradine."

Natalie's brows narrowed as if she were about to pose a trick question.

"And what was the family surname *before* it was changed to Blackshaw?"

Caitlin flinched. "*I* didn't know mom's family had another name before Blackshaw."

"Well, they did," Natalie confirmed. "And I knew about it. But if this person calling himself Derek Blackshaw doesn't know, it, I'm calling the LAPD."

Caitlin huffed. "Nat—enough! You're being totally offensive."

Derek Blackshaw straightened his shoulders and responded as if he were talking to a border patrol agent. "The name was Thatch. Edward and Claradine Thatch."

Natalie snapped the passport shut and handed it back to Derek Blackshaw with an assured nod. "We're good here. You are who you say you are." Then her face broke out in a wide smile. "Uncle Derek, so nice to finally meet you!"

Natalie flew into his arms.

Uncle Derek hoisted her up, embracing her in a warm hug while letting out a full, raspy laugh.

Caitlin's face went blank and her shoulders slackened. She wanted to hug him even though he reeked of tobacco and looked like an aging Hell's Angel. He was, after all, her mom's uncle. He was blood. Family. She so badly needed to hug family right now.

Uncle Derek set Natalie on the stoop. Her eyes were watery. Then turned to Caitlin. He opened his arms.

"Well, young Cait? How about a hug for an old fart of an uncle?"

She hesitated. But then a warm smile forced its way onto her face. She strode over and hugged him politely. Uncle Derek kissed her on the forehead, then took a long drag of his cigarette.

"Really?" Caitlin said. "That God-awful smoke is polluting your polluted lungs!"

Derek nodded. "And, therefore, you should learn from my mistakes, young Cait. As I've always said, 'Do as I say, not as I do.'"

"It was John Selden who said that," Natalie noted as she dried her eyes with her sleeve.

"Who the bloody hell is that?"

"Legal scholar. Lived five centuries ago."

Derek's face soured. "The hell with him."

* * *

Uncle Derek sipped a cup of lemon gingerroot tea that Caitlin had prepared for him. The two sisters were sitting around the dining room table with their uncle, eating the pizza that had finally been delivered and listening attentively to stories about their uncle and grandfather.

"Blackshaw was also the name of our band," Uncle Derek said. "Bobby—your granddad—played lead guitar. As well

119

as anyone, I might add. I played bass. The band was full of promise."

"Why did your parents change their name to Blackshaw?" Caitlin asked.

Derek cracked an amused smile. "Good question. My grauntie, Shirley Thatch, suggested the change."

"Grauntie?" Caitlin asked.

"Great-auntie—grauntie."

Natalie giggled. "So you're my gruncle—Gruncle Derek."

He chuckled. "I suppose you can say that."

"Why did Grauntie Shirley Thatch want to change the family name?" Caitlin asked.

Derek sipped his tea and responded. "The Thatch surname was a bit of a drag. Had its fair share of notoriety attached to it back in the day. Me mum didn't want to burden us with it. So she changed it to Blackshaw. Which makes perfect sense, when you think about it."

"Tell me about Blackshaw, your rock band," Caitlin said.

Uncle Derek leaned back in his chair and crossed his leg. "Blackshaw came to be in 1961. Liverpool. The beginnings of the Merseybeat. Had a helluva fan following by sixty-three. One year before The Beatles crossed the pond to America."

Caitlin's eyebrows popped up. "You played at the same time as The Beatles?"

Uncle Derek chuckled proudly. "Young Cait, would you believe that John Lennon once bought me and your granddad, Bobby, a pint of beer? True story. This was before

Lennon and his mates found their fame in America. John had caught one of our sets in a sweaty, cramped club in Hamburg. He really dug the way Granddad Bobby played the mouth organ."

"Mouth organ?"

"Harmonica. John loved the harmonica. Pinched one in Arnhem once. In the Netherlands. Played it on 'Love Me Do.'"

"Love me do what?"

"Never mind. Anyway, your gramps also played a mean harmonica." Derek reached deep into his pocket. He pulled out an old, worn instrument. "Been carrying this with me since my beloved baby brother passed in sixty-nine. It belonged to your gramps."

Caitlin's eyes lit up. "Can I try?"

Uncle Derek smiled as he passed it to her. She blew a few notes of music as she exhaled her breath. The sound was bluesy. Then more musical notes sounded as she drew in a breath.

"How cool! Hey, Nat! Wanna try?"

Natalie's face took on an expression like she had eaten a sour cherry as she declined. "Germs."

A gleam had sparkled in Uncle Derek's eye, but Caitlin sensed pain as well. "Gruncle, what's wrong?"

Derek laughed sadly to himself. "You know Blackshaw was *also* booked to play on *Sullivan*. A few months after the four lads from Liverpool."

Like Barton Sullivan?

"The Beatles' *Sullivan* gig opened the door for a lot of British bands."

"Sullivan?" Caitlin asked.

"*The Ed Sullivan Show*—an American variety program on the telly. Biggest bands played that show. Beatles. Stones."

Natalie rubbed her chin. "Anyone ever tell you that you look like Keith Richards?"

Uncle Derek's face curdled. "Now why would you say something like that?"

Natalie slouched. "Forget it."

"So your band played on American TV?" Caitlin exclaimed. "That's so freaking cool."

"Hold your horses, young Cait. Things didn't quite turn out as expected."

"What do you mean?"

Uncle Derek exhaled wearily. The lines on his face revealed years of regret. His glassy eyes betrayed deep-seated pain.

"Your granddad, Bobby . . . my transcendence-seeking second-born brother . . . got bloody wasted the night before we were to depart for America. Head trip. Fell over in a drunken stupor. Right arm shattered a nightstand. Broke his blasted wrist. A glass shard severed the radial artery. He started bleeding out quick. Pools of blood everywhere. Almost lost me brother. We missed the *Sullivan* gig, lost our record label, and Bob's your uncle."

"You mean Gramps—our granddad?" Caitlin asked.

Derek laughed. Natalie too. "No, young Cait. 'Bob's your uncle' is an expression. Like 'there you have it.'"

Caitlin smiled. "Got it."

"Anyway, Blackshaw had peaked by sixty-five. But after that fiasco, the band started going on the skids. Bobby's right hand would never again strum a guitar. Wrist does most of the work, you know."

Caitlin listened, mesmerized, as Derek continued.

"But then your granddad received a genuine miracle. Started strumming chords, plucking guitar strings left-handed."

"How did he manage to do that?"

"Like I said, it was a miracle. And me brother Bobby became the best damn guitarist I ever saw. Lord knows I saw them all. Had a child—your Aunty Gwen, firstborn and older sister to your mum. Poor old Gwen."

"I don't really remember her," Caitlin said.

"Course not. You were just a child when she died. Freak accident."

"What happened?"

"A few years back. Car accident. Flock of birds smashed her windshield on the motorway. Lost control of the vehicle."

Caitlin spiraled a lock of hair around her index finger. "What kind of birds?"

"Ravens or crows, if I recall," Derek said as he narrowed his eyes. "Why would you care what type of birds?"

"No reason. Just curious."

Caitlin and Natalie exchanged uneasy looks.

"Anyway," Derek continued, "the Blackshaw band got back on top after Bobby Gramps's miraculous recovery. Except Bobby never did give up his indulgent quest for altered states of consciousness—if you get my drift."

Natalie and Caitlin rolled their eyes in unison.

"My beloved brother bought the farm in sixty-nine. Just a few months after your mum was born."

Caitlin sipped her tea and then asked, "What happened to you?"

"Solo career. European tours. Small clubs. Playing the old hits. Had a blast. Hell of a lot of parties along the way. Chatting up all the young lovelies. Blackshaw had *loyal* fans." Derek laughed mischievously as the nostalgia gleamed in his eyes.

"You're a hedonist!" Natalie declared.

"Indeed I was. But it wasn't always about the partying." Derek pensively stroked the stubble on his face. "We were connecting to something back then. Call it love. Peace." He chuckled. "Does sound a bit lame today, don't ya think? But we felt something in those days. As if we were making contact with something outside this universe, where music was already composed. In full." The gleam in his eye intensified. "We felt like transistors in a radio. As if the finished song was being transmitted right *through* us. It simply poured out of our fingers as we played." He took a final swig of his ginger-root tea and shook his head.

"Problem was, for many bands, power and fame went to their heads. And then the tap turned off. Major drag. So they found themselves needing a bit of help to reach that *other* place where music comes from." He shrugged.

But it was a sad shrug. Probably intended for his younger brother, Bobby Blackshaw.

Caitlin massaged her chin as she eyed her gruncle.

Should I tell him what happened to me? This old rocker dude is such a crazy-ass oddball freak, it might just seem perfectly normal to him.

She pushed her hair back and planted her teacup hard on the tabletop.

"Nat, please clean up before Cousin Harry and Cordelia get home." She laid on a thick mock British accent. "Old Gruncle and I are going for a stroll. And lock the door after we leave!"

Caitlin grabbed Uncle Derek's hand and led him out the front door.

The winds had died down. The night air was cool but bone dry. Gruncle removed his cashmere scarf and wrapped it around Caitlin. She smiled appreciatively. Not a cloud obstructed the starlit Southern California sky. The street was bare, with only a few parked cars curbside. All the homes were quiet and calm. One nearby home was even burning a real fire in the hearth.

"Look," Caitlin said as she and her uncle strolled, "I'm gonna tell you something, but I don't want you to think I'm crazy or that I'm making this up. Because I think it might be related to my mom and dad. Indirectly."

Uncle Derek winked. "Shall we light up a spliff?"

She shook her head along with an eye roll. "Won't compare to what I experienced."

Aging rocker Derek Blackshaw seemed genuinely intrigued.

"Speak up, young Cait."

They rounded a street corner. "Do you believe in the supernatural? Like different dimensions not of this world?"

"I can't say I *believe* other dimensions exist—that's because I *know* they exist."

Caitlin broke a smile, and there was a sudden spring in her step. "Really? How awesome. Because I *know* they exist as well. I've been there."

Oops! Might've said too much too soon.

Uncle Derek turned and gave Caitlin a penetrating once-over.

"You say you've *been there?*"

Caitlin huffed.

Who cares—just spill the freaking beans!

"I was *totally* there."

"And where is *there?*"

"Beneath the grave of Lewis Carroll."

"You're referring to Mount Cemetery? In Guildford? Where your Bobby Gramps and your mum and now dad rest?"

Caitlin nodded firmly. "Yes! The grave opened up like a wormhole. It leads to another dimension."

Derek examined her with a probing eye from underneath his raised eyebrows.

Caitlin said, "You think I'm crazy?"

"Didn't say that. Your old fart of a gruncle experienced quite a few strange trips back in younger days. Saw a lot of unexplainable things. But what is it you want to tell me, young Cait?"

The words flew out of her mouth helter-skelter. "There's another universe. Where the fairy-tale kingdoms exist. But all the characters are dying—they're decaying into ghouls and zombies. Cinderella . . . all of them. And the crows. And my dad. He didn't just die of a heart attack."

Uncle Derek's piercing eyes glinted under the streetlight. He held Caitlin's gaze as she rambled on.

"He was murdered. Mom too. And I need you take me back to London ASAP so I can prove it."

Just then, a car passed them.

The screech of slamming brakes broke the calm of night.

Caitlin and Uncle Derek turned to look.

The vehicle had stopped.

Caitlin and her gruncle exchanged wary looks.

The backup lights lit up.

Uh-oh.

Tires squealed and burned rubber as the car screamed in reverse.

Caitlin clutched her gruncle's arm.

The vehicle shrieked to a stop alongside them.

"Caitlin Rose Fletcher, what on earth are you doing out here? And who is this man?"

Cousin Cordelia was shouting out the car window from

the passenger side. Cousin Harry leaped out of the vehicle and move quickly to stand nose to nose with Uncle Derek.

"And who might you be?" Harry asked, pushing Caitlin behind him.

"Derek Blackshaw. Brother of Caitlin's granddad, Bobby Blackshaw. Uncle to Evelyn, and in-law to your deceased first cousin, Harold Fletcher, may he rest in peace."

Harry's shoulders drooped, and his eyebrows arched. "Oh my! Please accept my apology. Have we ever met?"

Derek smiled. "If you danced at the wedding of Evelyn and Harold in London way back when, then most probably we have."

Harry extended a handshake. "Unfortunately we didn't make the trip to England at that time. Anyway, a pleasure to meet you." Harold turned to his wife, who was still seated in the car. "Look, Cordelia, the great-uncle of Caitlin and Natalie."

"Call him 'gruncle,'" Caitlin chirped.

Cordelia extended an arm out the window and shook Uncle Derek's hand.

"We were worried there for a moment. Please come on back to the house," Harry added. "We'll have a late-night cup of tea and get acquainted."

Derek smiled gratefully. "I'm afraid it's a bit late. I got here only a few hours ago. Still need to find a motel and get—"

Harry raised his hand, cutting him off. "Nonsense— you're staying the night with us. And I won't take no for answer." Uncle Derek glanced over at Cousin Cordelia. She nodded emphatically. He looked at Caitlin, who shrugged. Derek looked at the group and said, "Well, okay then. Much obliged."

"Hop in the back seat," Harry said as he got back in the car. Caitlin and Uncle Derek exchanged looks. Caitlin unwrapped the shawl-scarf from her shoulders and handed it back to Derek, who had opened the rear car door for her.

He whispered, "That's one far-out tale ya told. Let's continue this conversation in the morning."

* * *

The clock read 11:37 p.m. by the time Caitlyn and her cousins (Natalie was at the house already, tidying up), and Uncle Derek got back to the house. Cordelia made up the spare room for Uncle Derek. Caitlin was beyond tired. Uncle Derek definitely seemed jet-lagged.

The winds had picked back up. They howled outside as they swept the lawns, tossing up leaves and strumming tree branches.

To Caitlin, it felt cozy to be indoors. She was excited to snuggle under her comforter. She would wait till morning to bring up the subject of moving back to London with her uncle.

Everyone exchanged good nights and retired to their rooms.

As she had done every night since her dad's passing, Caitlin thought of her dad and mom and cried herself to sleep.

*   *   *

At 3:17 a.m., Caitlin was out like a light, deep in slumber.

A hand firmly cupped her mouth, waking her with a jolt.

A strange older man was staring at her!

What the—

His index finger pressed softly against his mouth. He muttered, "Shhhh!"

Her heart drummed in her chest.

If he were a burglar, he wouldn't have wakened her. If he were a serial killer, he would have killed her already. He had done neither. He had wakened her softly. And so Caitlin didn't try to struggle or scream—*yet.*

"Please listen," he whispered. "I'm here to help. You're in grave danger." He lifted his hand from her mouth. "The young lad Jack sent me to fetch ya."

Jack?

"Who are you?" Caitlin asked.

"I'm your great-uncle, Derek Blackshaw. The *real* Derek Blackshaw."

CHAPTER TWELVE

THE MAN CLAIMING TO BE CAITLIN'S AUTHENTIC UNCLE SLOWLY
lifted his hand from her mouth.

"You must leave this house quickly, I tell ya. Before
he wakes." There was pleading in his eyes. "His power is
unearthly."

The stranger's demeanor radiated a soulful gentleness,
the only thing keeping Caitlin from fainting from the shock
of his sudden presence in her room.

"Ya must listen," he said with great urgency. He spoke
with a British accent. "Ya saw me last when you was three
years old. I don't expect ya ta remember. But if ya don't trust
me now, you and your little sister will share the same fate as
yer mum and dad."

The old man handed her a picture. "That's you, in yer
mum's arms. You were eight months old. Now pack up, Caitlin,
and let's shove off." Indeed, it was Caitlin's mom holding baby

Caitlin. Caitlin also knew *this* photo well. She'd seen it dozens of times growing up.

The blood in her veins iced over as she suddenly considered the *other* man, the *other* Derek Blackshaw, asleep in the next room. He had been so convincing. She had to know.

"Who's the other man sleeping in this house?"

"Lord knows. A living human being he's not," the new Derek Blackshaw replied. "And he's most definitely not me." He checked his watch. "Hurry! Fetch a suitcase, and pack only what ya need."

"But what about Cousin Cordelia and Cousin Harry?"

"He's got no interest in them. It's *you* he's after."

Caitlin's left eye narrowed to a slit. "What was the family surname before it was changed to Blackshaw?"

New Derek Blackshaw froze. "Pardon me?"

"You heard me."

He tugged at his face impatiently and said, "No time for this, Caitlin Rose—not if ya want ta live. Name was Thatch. Now hop to it, before he wakes."

Caitlin's exhaled. "Okay. Where are we going?"

"Rendezvous. With Jack. The one who told me ta fetch ya."

Natalie squirmed under her duvet, then popped out from underneath.

"What's going on?" she mumbled, rubbing the sleep from her eyes. Those sleepy eyes quickly widened when she saw the strange man at Caitlin's bedside.

"Nat, don't freak out. This is our *real* uncle, Derek

Blackshaw. You'll have to trust me on this, because there's no time. Listen to him while I pack up our things."

New Uncle Derek exhaled a big breath as Natalie stared groggily at him. Caitlin quickly tiptoed out of the bedroom and down the hallway.

She opened a closet door a crack. She winced when it creaked loud enough to wake up all of Southern California. She leaned down toward the wretched, squeaking hinge and drooled a gob of saliva on it to oil the pins. She tried opening the door again. Sweet silence.

She swung it open and reached her arm in, pushing aside coats and sweaters. Grabbed a suitcase handle. Carefully pulled it out, mindful not to knock one of the wooden coat hangers to the hardwood floor.

A toilet flushed in the bathroom down the hallway, just a few feet away.

He's up!

Which meant he'd be out any second. One suitcase would have to do.

Caitlin scurried as soft as a mouse back to her bedroom, then closed the door behind her soundlessly. Her window was wide open, the sheer curtains flapping in the night's breeze. Natalie and Uncle Derek had already slipped out the window. She had to hurry.

Caitlin rummaged through the dresser drawers, packing clothes and undies for her and Natalie. Then she whipped on her clothes.

The sound of the bathroom door opening echoed in the hall.

He's out!

Caitlin's heartbeat hammered like a staple gun.

She made a beeline to the window and hoisted her suitcase onto the sill, where she noticed flecks of paint were peeling off. As she shoved her luggage out the window, the bedroom door flung open.

"Caitlin!"

She turned and swallowed hard to prevent her heart from leaping out of her mouth.

The *impostor* Derek Blackshaw stood in the doorway, his ragged face twisting in anger!

The knot in her throat was cutting off her air supply.

Derek stormed into the room. She was about to scream bloody murder when the rumble of a van engine shot through the window. Derek marched right past her and leaned his tall rock-'n'-roll frame out into the dark.

"Christ almighty, someone has just snatched Natalie!"

Caitlin's mouth fell open. She leaned back against the wall, pressing a closed fist firm against her quivering lips.

How could I have been so stupid, gullible, and naive?

Uncle Derek placed his hands firmly on Caitlin's shoulders. "Better tell me what's going on, young Cait!"

All she could do was jam her fist harder against her mouth. The world seemed to crumble around her.

First that inhuman creature had taken her mom. Then her dad. He'd almost taken Caitlin away from Uncle Derek a minute ago. And now he had taken the last living being on Earth still dear to Caitlin's heart—part of her blood and soul.

He abducted Natalie.

And it only happened because Caitlin had left her kid sister all alone with that monster.

Natalie's face was imprinted on her brain, seared into heart. The poor kid had appeared confused when she first woke up and saw that strange person in their bedroom. But the little twerp with the big brain suddenly also had a very rare look upon her face: innocence. And trust. Trust in her big sister, who had vowed to always hug and hold her whenever she wanted.

Caitlin's eyes welled up. Then she—

CRASH!

Was that the window by the front door?

A foul odor swept into the bedroom—the ammonia-like smell of earthworms writhing in the rain.

"They're coming for me!" Caitlin cried.

Derek pushed Caitlin toward the open window. "Run, young Cait! I'll stay and watch over Harry and Cordelia. *Go now!*"

She grabbed her phone, opened an app, and tapped buttons. *Two minutes—thank God!*

Caitlin scrambled out the window and hit the ground running. The temperature had dropped. She flew across the front lawn and ran up the center of the dark, bare road.

Her legs pumped, and she breathed hard as the street

sharply inclined. The Santa Ana winds had picked up, buffet-ing her, making it difficult to gain speed. Nevertheless, she kept her eyes glued to the road ahead.

High winds dusted up leaves and debris. Palm fronds fell to the road.

A terrible sound tore through the dark night.

A throaty and primal shrill carried on the wind.

The unearthly scream weakened her legs. She prayed the hard-driving winds were slowing down whoever—or *what-ever*—was coming for her.

She approached an intersection. The cross street sloped downward. This was tempting. But she purposely sprinted *up* the same rising road. A gust of wind propelled her forward.

She fell to the pavement, but broke the fall with her hands, scraping her palms bloody. She got back up. Galloped onward . . .

She checked her phone.

Less than thirty seconds.

She passed a second intersection. A blast of wind almost sent her into orbit.

Headlights *finally* appeared up ahead.

Uber!

She waived frantically. The vehicle pulled alongside her and stopped. She jumped in the back. "Turn around and drive the other way!" she shouted. "Someone's chasing me!"

The driver, a young Asian male in his early twenties—who she noticed was kinda cute—turned to Caitlin with suspicious eyes. He then turned back and looked out his front windshield.

Tall, dark shapes. Six. Maybe seven. Men? In long coats? *Flying upright?* Pursuing the car. Their garments flapped wildly in the wailing winds.

The driver needed no more convincing. He slammed the gas pedal. The car managed a 180-degree turn at a hellish speed and screeched off in the opposite direction.

Caitlin turned back and stole a look through the rear window.

Her injured hand left blood prints on the backrest. The road was empty.

Yes!

Oh no—

The dark shapes were back on the hunt. Gaining.

"Faster!" she screamed.

The car made a hard right. Rubber squealed. "I'm trying," the driver said, "These winds are fighting the car."

Caitlin looked back. They were opening up a greater distance. The terrible shrieks seemed to be fading.

The driver glanced back at Caitlin. "Where you going?"

"Just drive. If they catch me, they'll *kill* me."

The driver's knuckles were white.

He made a sharp left. *Screeeeech!*

The car barreled past a half dozen intersections. Then a sharp right turn. Then another. Caitlin checked behind her. The dark shapes were back on her trail.

How are they moving?

She chewed her thumbnail. She knew the driver couldn't drive like this forever. Eventually the car would run out of gas.

More shrills split the air. An unholy symphony of savage howls.

The car turned left. Right. Another right. Then a left.

Caitlin suddenly saw it.

Her eyebrows rose like two exclamation marks.

The *forest.* The polished *black gate.*

From her recurring dream.

She screamed, "Stop the car!"

The brakes slammed. The vehicle skidded to a halt. Caitlin pushed open the door. She slipped out. "Drive!" she shouted before slamming the door closed. The car sped off into the windswept night.

She hid behind some bushes, watching. . . .

Yes!

The dark shapes flew right past her, still in pursuit of the car.

Flew?

Caitlin's eyes shot across the road to the black iron gate leading into the forest. But this wasn't a forest like Zeno's Forest where she could transport herself across time and space in an instant. In fact, it wasn't a forest at all.

The place was Forest Lawn Cemetery.

In Glendale, California.

And someone she didn't recognize, dressed fashionably in white, was standing by the black-gated entrance as if waiting for her.

CONFIDENTIAL TRANSCRIPT OF
CAITLIN'S SECOND THERAPY SESSION

Dr. Kyle: I believe I have a comprehensive understanding of the universe you've constructed in your mind.

Caitlin: It wasn't in my mind. It was real. It happened.

Dr. Kyle: Tell you what—let's put aside all debate over whether or not this was an actual experience or a far-fetched flight of imagination. I'm more interested in the particulars of how this helped you—and some of your contemporaries that you shared your story with—cope with the tribulations of anxiety and OCD. I'd like to suggest some deep hypnotherapy.

Caitlin: I'm uncomfortable with that idea. Besides, you'll never hypnotize me. I'm not a willing subject.

Dr. Kyle: A small, painless injection of sodium pentothal has delivered extraordinary results in patients dealing with trauma and repressed memories. I've used it on a number of patients.

Caitlin: You want to stick a needle in me? Never! And let you inside my head? You're drea—Ouch! What's going on? You had no right to stick that syringe in me.

[Pause on tape]

Dr. Kyle: How do you feel, Caitlin?

Caitlin: Calm. Happy. A bit sleepy.

Dr. Kyle: I'm now going to take you into a deep state of hypnosis, so please listen to my voice carefully. Is that all right?

Caitlin: Yes.

Dr. Kyle: Do I have your permission?

Caitlin: Yes.

[Pause on tape]

Dr. Kyle: Before we begin, I want to make it clear that you will retain no memory of receiving the injection prior to this session. Is this well understood?

Caitlin: Yes.

Dr. Kyle: Excellent. Let's begin. I'm inclined to believe that the alleged zombie phenomenon that you've described has been a distraction. It's utterly irrelevant to your underlying issues. It is nothing more than a subliminal, unnecessary, psychogenic fabrication resulting from an excessive glut of zombie content on the telly, in the cinema, and in mass media. Do you agree with my professional opinion?

Caitlin: No. I believe that you are using that opinion as a distraction for your own self-denial because the truth frightens you. It lies outside the box that is your rational mind.

Dr. Kyle: Nurse, another injection—twenty-five milligrams.

[Pause on tape]

Dr. Kyle: What role does the fairy-tale zombie play in regard to your mental and emotional well-being and the fears that have afflicted you?

Caitlin: Maybe the fairy-tale universe is symbolic of the imagination, the human mind, and the characters correlate to our thoughts and desires. Specifically, the princess and prince characters might embody our true inner self and our deepest aspirations in life. The decay of these characters into relentless, flesh-eating ghouls might refer to the negative thoughts and relentless pessimism that hinder our dreams and stop us from realizing our full potential. Perhaps the fact that iconic fairy-tale characters are rendered as relentless zombies may be an allusion to the negative thoughts that attack us daily, trying to devour our happiness and destroy a well-balanced state of mind.

Dr. Kyle: In your psychoanalytical scheme that you've just laid out, what role does the one you've identified as the Enchanter, or Lord of the Curtain, play?

Caitlin: Perhaps the Lord of the Curtain refers to the hidden root of these negative thought attacks. Which might be our very own incessant selfishness, or, as my baby sister has pointed out—narcissism. I believe we live in a materialistic world because the soul has been sucked out of us by this incessant self-centeredness. For some of us, this manifests as fear, anxiety, and panic; for others, it becomes blind ambition, a quest for popularity, and indulgent self-gratification. But the common denominator behind all of this is that it's always about *me* instead of being about someone else. In truth, everyone is miserable most of the time. Even though they work 24/7 in their pursuit of happiness, they only achieve it maybe ten percent of the time.

Dr. Kyle: And what does the color spectrum symbolize? How can it help us?

Caitlin: It represents this whole dynamic as it relates to human nature and our character. The violet represents our highest aspirations. The red is our relentless desire to feed our selfishness, whether that expresses itself as fear or unending, blind ambition. The only way out of our misery is the green color, representing the willpower to resist selfishness—the red color and its constant focus on the *me*. The self. When we become fixated on the *me*, we are enslaved to the red, and we become as mindless as a zombie. The zombie phenomenon occurring in our culture is likely a reflection of these unwanted fears, insecurities, and anxieties that swallow us. It's a subconscious recognition of our addiction to selfishness and the red side of our nature. I believe we find our soul, we find our humanity, when we resist the redder angels for the better angels. No resistance against the red robs us of our soul. And without a soul, without consideration for someone other than ourselves, we become the living dead. Because life on Earth only occurs through pure sharing, as evidenced by the sun that ceaselessly shares its light—and therefore life—with our planet. In simple terms, when we get busy helping others, the violet end of the spectrum gets busy with us.

Dr. Kyle: Quite impressive. I'm pleased you seem to agree that your personal experience was merely the manifestation of deep-seated emotional issues, psychogenic in nature, as opposed to an actual, tangible experience that took place in some other hyperdimensional reality whose substance is made up of raw imagination.

Caitlin: They are one and the same, Doctor Kyle. I think everything that I just said went right over your head. You're failing to resist your own red side, and therefore you've been unable to grasp what I have shared with you.

Dr. Kyle: Let me remind you: when you wake from this hypnotherapy session, you will remember nothing.

CHAPTER THIRTEEN

IN CAITLIN'S RECURRING DREAM ABOUT A GLEAMING BLACK GATE leading to a forest, there was always a mysterious, white-clad girl waving her over. The dream had now become reality, because standing by the black front gate to Forest Lawn Cemetery stood a strange girl adorned in splendid white apparel, waving her arm.

"Over here!" the girl cried out when she spied Caitlin. Her words turned to steam in the cool air. Caitlin hightailed it across the road, praying that those awful dark shapes were still pursuing the car.

When she arrived at the gate, the girl smiled sweetly. She was beautiful, lit by moonlight, and wearing a white, long-sleeved lace top with a sort-of-long peplum. An elegant lace drop-pearl choker graced her neck, and her white skinny jeans—to die for—featured fashionable ripped slits above ribbed knees. White, quilted lace-up sneakers adorned her feet. Her hair was in stark contrast to her white outfit, though—it was as red as precious rubies.

The girl in white dispensed with formal introductions and simply said, "Come."

She took hold of a thick rope dangling from the high black gate and began to ascend the iron bars with graceful agility. She climbed up and over, then hopped down on the other side.

Caitlin's turn. She gripped the rope with both hands and wedged her feet between the bars. She began pulling with her hands, pushing with her legs, and scaling her way to the top. Once she climbed over the sharp top edge, she slid down the bars, landing inside the unlit cemetery.

"Please follow me," the girl instructed. She sprinted off into the dark. Caitlin went after her.

They raced across the pitch-dark parkland that was Forest Lawn. A span of unreachable stars speckled the night sky. The whistling winds were behind them now, giving them added lift. They sprinted past tombstones . . . swaying trees . . . more tombstones. . . .

"Who are you, and how'd you know I'd be here?" Caitlin called out, breathing fast and heavy.

"I'm of the South. Lady Glinda."

The good witch from Oz?

The air was dry and nippy as the girls galloped across the dark lawns. Leafy windblown tree branches hissed like waves upon the sea. They crossed a narrow roadway and cut across another tract of land. Then the girl called Glinda finally pulled up to a stop by a large tree. Caitlin skidded to a stop next to her, panting. She hunched over, hands on her knees.

After catching some gulps of air, she glanced up.

Next to the thick tree was an unusually broad headstone.

Carved into the rock was the name L. Frank Baum, the author of *The Wonderful Wizard of Oz* and its sequels.

A hole gaped open where Baum's grave should have been. Glinda approached it. A rich yellow light suddenly began to swirl into a golden whirlpool in the hole. Twirling airborne particles glistened like magic dust as leaves, twigs, and other debris started to get sucked down the golden funnel.

Another shrill echo in the distance, followed immediately by the awful earthworm smell.

"They've found us," Glinda said breathlessly. "Please hurry down that hole—now."

"But what about Natalie?"

"She's somewhere down there. Hurry."

Caitlin didn't need to hear anything more. She jumped in, feet first, and was instantly swallowed up by the vortex of golden glimmer. Glinda followed right behind. As Caitlin descended the twisting portal, she glanced up. The top of the grave was sealing shut, locking her and Glinda inside.

For the first time in her life, she was relieved to be in a claustrophobic environment.

After about thirty long seconds of plummeting through a spiraling, hyperdimensional tunnel awash in a warm honey-amber color, Caitlin touched bottom in a surprisingly soft landing. She kneeled over to catch her breath. Beneath her feet was a road of gleaming gold bricks.

Of course!

The air was pleasantly warm, as if it were spring.

Thud!

Glinda touched down.

Caitlin glanced up at her, still too winded to speak. She smiled appreciatively and huffed and puffed rapidly.

Glinda returned the smile and said, "You're safe. For now."

Caitlin exhaled a jumbo-size breath as her lungs recuperated.

"You're the Good Witch of the South?"

"I prefer the title Sorcerer of the South. *Witch* is fraught with negative connotations."

"And you're wearing makeup." Caitlin said, realizing that Glinda looked young and healthy and tanned.

Glinda winked. "Well done!" She pulled a tissue from a pocket and wiped it along her forehead. Beneath her golden, flesh-toned makeup was bone-white flesh. She wiped the rest of her face clean with the tissue, and a zombified Lady Glinda emerged. Silvery-milk complexion, concave shadowed cheeks, and recessed, dark-rimmed eyes. Her lips were like the hearts on Valentine's Day cards. But instead of ruby red, they revealed themselves to be a pale shade of purple. She looked as if she were suffering hypothermia, though of course she wasn't. She was suffering from a living death. Her eyes were like double sapphires. And yet, despite her ghoulish features, her countenance remained almost regal.

"Someone abducted my sister," Caitlin said. "I think it was the Enchanter. I absolutely need to find her. Can you help?"

Glinda waved a finger. "It wasn't the Enchanter."

"I don't understand."

"You're being hunted. The episode at your house was a setup designed to separate you and Natalie." Glinda suddenly flexed her back, as if involuntarily. Her keen eyes scanned the skies.

"They're on our trail. We need to get off this road."

Glinda cut a quick detour off the yellow brick trail and headed straight into a dense and tangled rose thicket. "They won't follow us through here."

Of course not. Who would?

Caitlin certainly wouldn't venture willingly into the brush.

This is a thicket from hell.

Razor-sharp thorn bushes and prickly trees snarled together so tightly, it was like traipsing through a maze of barbed wire. There was not a single turn or opening that allowed them to dodge the thick cluster of claws, spines, and thorns. It felt like the devil's fingernails scratching at them as they squirmed past.

"Elbows and arms inward," Glinda said.

Ya think?

Caitlin took a breath and went for it. A few strides in, her arms were already pinpricked and scratched bloody.

Glinda picked up a long, sharp-edged piece of wood and started hacking her way through.

"Who's after me?" Caitlin asked as she wiped thin lines of blood from her forearms. "And who kidnapped my sister?"

"Since you left this place last year, things have changed—and most certainly *not* for the better."

A hooked thorn snagged Caitlin's collar. She twisted out of its grasp and said, "What do you mean?"

"The Enchanter's blood-eyed crows—they're the ones hunting you."

Caitlin shook her head. "Impossible! That was no flock of birds chasing me. Those *things* were tall and upright—they walked on two legs, like humans."

"No, no. Those *things* chasing you were *not* human. They're crows. Some of the crows are . . . *different* now."

"Different?" Caitlin echoed. "How?"

Glinda looked back at Caitlin as she slashed her way through the spiked bramble. A repugnant look crossed her face.

"Good gracious. The Enchanter—he did terrible things to them. Mutations. Bad magic. The crows grew torsos. Arms. Legs. And their heads . . . oh my, their heads . . ." She cupped her mouth with her hand.

"What about their heads?" Caitlin asked.

Glinda shuddered. Then she shook her own head and waved her finger as if to say, "Let's not go there."

Hooked thorns and needles continued to snag Caitlin's top and jeans. She unfastened the barbs one by one, careful not to cut up her arms and knees more than they already were. She finally squiggled out of the prickly shrub.

She crouched low, taking cover behind Glinda as she continued hacking through the bush.

"Why are these crowmen after me?" Caitlin asked.

"To stop you from preventing the encounter."

"What encounter?"

"Between Natalie and the Lord of the Curtain."

"Nat? Why's he after *her*?"

"I'll explain later. First, there are things you need to know to protect yourself."

Caitlin felt like she was drowning in brushwood. "I'm listening."

"These crowmen can fly—and without wings! Even though they walk upright like you and me. That gives them a great advantage."

Caitlin laughed, but it was a nervous laugh. "I witnessed that firsthand."

"Seven crowmen were sent to hunt you down," Glinda continued. "They're unafraid of practically everything. Fearless. Heartless. Especially their leader—Janus. There's almost no one who can stop Janus."

"So I'm doomed?" Caitlin responded in despair. "Condemned?"

"Oz and all the kingdoms, including the imminent worlds, are doomed if we don't stop this," Glinda said. "I'll do whatever it takes to protect these places."

Thorns bit at Caitlin's ankles, and bristles lacerated her arms.

Does this thicket have a foreseeable end in sight?

"There is someone who might be able to help you," Glinda said. "He's only one in all the kingdoms who stands a chance against the crowmen."

"Who?"

"A dear friend of mine. He's the only one that scares the crows."

Caitlin's brow wrinkled as she whispered Glinda's last three words to herself. Her eyes lit up. "You mean . . . Scarecrow?"

"I do," Glinda said, blinking her long lashes. "But he's a *living dead* Scarecrow now. And his eyes are *half* blood-eyed."

The thorny thicket from hell finally gave way, and they stepped into a merciful clearing.

Caitlin's arms and legs loosened up as she and Glinda quickened their pace.

"Half blood-eyed? Why?"

"He's full zombie. A dreadful ghoul, inside and out. But his brain—"

Caitlin remembered that Scarecrow had received brains from the Wizard in the original Oz book.

"His brains make him very smart," Glinda said. "Which makes him smart enough to use his dark desires only for good. And so he willingly drinks her brew."

Her? Whose? What brew?

"And he never sleeps," Glinda continued. "So he will always be on watch for you. But I must warn you—Scarecrow scares *everyone*. He gives off odorless pheromones that make you tremble with terrible fright whenever he's close."

If I could bottle his scent and sell it as deodorant in high school, I'd make a fortune.

Caitlin raised her eyes to the sky. The moon was a bow-shaped, lit ember fixed in a dark purple firmament. The last time she had bathed in that same moonlight, she had been sailing aboard a ghostly pirate ship with Jack. Now Jack and Natalie seemed as remote and unreachable as the moon. Her chest muscles tightened as she recalled Natalie's face just before she'd been taken. Finding Girl Wonder and getting home safely seemed about as likely as running full tilt back through that thorny thicket without getting a scratch.

She shifted her glance to Glinda.

"You said it wasn't the Enchanter who took my sister."

"It wasn't."

"Then who?"

"Pirates."

Caitlin's hand clasped her mouth. "How do you know that?"

"It's written it in the Great Book of Records."

"What's that?"

"An ancient manuscript that continues to write itself. It tracks and documents all the events that occur in all the king-doms, and all the worlds, as they happen. In real time."

Facebook on steroids.

"Is that how you knew I'd be arriving at Forest Lawn when I did?"

She winked.

"According to the Great Book of Records, a pirate crossed

over to your world from Treasure Island a short time before Natalie's abduction," Glinda said. "It was Blackbeard."

"Blackbeard? But he was a real pirate—not a storybook character."

The dirt trail curved right, leading them back to the winding road of yellow bricks.

Glinda nodded to Caitlin as she picked spines and bristles from her white lace top. "Point well taken. But Blackbeard was written up in *Treasure Island*. And he was also recorded in the tale of *Peter and Wendy*."

"So?"

"The moment his name was published in a book, he entered our Great Book of Records and was conceived in our world."

A fascinating notion.

"Two more questions, if that's okay?"

Glinda smiled warmly. "And two more answers—go!"

"I thought the Good Witch—er—the Sorcerer of the South was an older woman. I totally mean that as a compliment. You're so young looking and beautiful."

"How kind of you. Goodness and youthfulness go hand in hand. That being said, I'll be one hundred seventeen next June."

"Whoa! That's like, insane. You look twenty!"

"And your second question?"

"I thought Glinda always wore a formal gown."

The Sorcerer of the South caressed her white lace top with the backs of her fingers, then ran her palms along her silky white skinny jeans.

"Formalwear is not suitable for the apocalypse. I'm more agile in this attire. Now, we must go. The crowmen are coming, and Scarecrow's waiting. Follow me down this road of yellow brick."

"Where're we headed?" Caitlin asked.

Glinda made a crooked face that said, *Really?*

Caitlin winced. *To the Emerald City, of course.*

* * *

The thin, sharp blade of a knife punctured the earth a few hundred feet east of L. Frank Baum's resting place. As the knife stabbed repeatedly, gouging out a plot of ground at Forest Lawn cemetery, the figure doing the knifing shoveled away the dirt with his other hand. Finally, he unearthed what he was looking for.

He had a large duffel bag swung over his back. He slid it off his shoulder and loaded his find into the bag. Then he moved around, digging up more places in Forest Lawn until he had half-filled the bag. He decided to dig some more and fill the bag once he crossed over. He knew time was running out.

He swung the hefty bag back over his shoulder and lugged his way over to the burial site of L. Frank Baum. He carefully set the duffel bag onto the grass.

He took his knife and stabbed the ground above Baum's grave. The blade punctured the surface without resistance. Clods of soil fell through an existing chink in the grave. He carved out a larger hole, and the portal reopened as a cone of pumpkin-orange light shot out of the grave like a concert floodlight.

The knife diligently dug up the dirt. He hacked out a sizable opening, one big enough for his frame to fit through. He climbed into the hole, bag over his shoulder, and proceeded to plummet through the honey-colored, hyperdimensional wormhole that had connected mythical dimensions, wondrous worlds, and ordinary families for centuries.

CHAPTER FOURTEEN

CAITLIN STRODE RESTLESSLY ALONG THE YELLOW BRICK ROAD, keeping pace with Glinda while being mindful not to trip over the uneven pavers. Her steps became more deliberate as she thought about her kid sister being abducted and duped by the despicable impostor Derek Blackshaw—who, as it turned out, was really the notorious pirate Blackbeard.

Caitlin subconsciously balled her hands into fists. Her stride down the crooked yellow brick road morphed into a soldierly swagger. She held her head high and her back firm and straight.

A profound sense of bravado tingled along her spine. A tenacious sense of mission began to fill her.

"What else has happened since I left?" she asked Glinda.

"Well, if you must know, Goldilocks is now eating bears, Riding Hood is lunching on wolves, and Hansel and Gretel are terrorizing the witches of the north, south, east, and west. The whole wretched world is upside down and inside out, and it worries me to no end."

How could this be happening again? I destroyed the scepter.

And then, without warning and for no apparent reason, Caitlin's courage and daring flowed away as quickly as if someone had siphoned it out of her.

Her hands turned clammy. Her body shivered like a caffeinated Chihuahua's, even though the air wasn't cold.

An unexplainable glut of anxiety seized her in the chest. Irrational panic grew in her throat, causing it to constrict. Her body quivered in petrified fear of nothing she could see or hear or explain. The intensity of her illogical fright bordered on imminent hysteria.

"Behold! Guess who's nearby?" Glinda said. She appeared calm, but her voice fluttered and her hands shook.

"Scarecrow?"

"Well done. You'll get used to the shivering. Just don't react to it. It's not coming from inside you. The scentless pheromones that come off Scarecrow are putting it there. If you react and accept the fear as your own, it'll awaken *real* fear inside you. Then it will grow like a worthless weed."

Before Caitlin could fully process what Glinda had just told her, her eyes found him.

Just up ahead. Standing square in the middle of the yellow brick road.

The Scarecrow.

The last time she had seen him was at the Queen of Hearts's castle during the masquerade ball, but it had been hot, crowded, and steamy. She had never really gotten a good look at him. Now she did.

Tall and broad-shouldered, Scarecrow was garbed in gunny cloth and denim, overstuffed with straw, and fastened together with thick, twisted rope.

Be brave.

As she approached, she saw that his cloth-skinned face was bleached pale and his cheeks were sunken like a dead man's corpse and menacingly shadowed. His eye sockets were as black as jet, except for a blade-thin, ghostly red glimmer that lit his eyes. His face was held together by zipperlike stitches that crossed his lips, cut into his cheekbone, and crept diagonally down his chin.

Two long and narrow sticks of rotting timber ran horizontally across his shoulder blades, broadening his physique. A battered burlap hat tipped downward over his brow. He was utterly mean and nasty-looking.

I said, be brave.

Scarecrow fixed his glimmering ruby gaze on Caitlin.

"Listen carefully," he hissed, wasting no time on introductions or small talk. His inhuman voice sounded like a saw blade cutting steel. "These crowmen lack a moral compass. They maim without conscience, murder without pity." His razor-thin pupils pulsed, blood red, to the cadence of his voice. "Compassion, mercy, penitence, atonement—alien concepts to these mutants."

Caitlin's knees involuntarily knocked together like swinging coconuts. She couldn't help it.

No wonder this dude scares the crows.

His vocabulary reminded Caitlin of Natalie. She wondered which of them had the bigger brain.

Scarecrow slid the rope fastened around his left wrist farther up his forearm, which tightened the long cuffs of his canvas glove. "There are seven crowmen who walk upright—full-bodied, like yourself." He slid the rope up on his right forearm, tightening the other glove. "The rest of the crows form regular flocks and fly. They're in constant telepathic contact with the seven, however. Specifically with their leader, the one called Janus." Scarecrow's scarred mouth grew tight. "There is no darker, soulless creature than Janus." His eyes narrowed. "Except for the Enchanter. He *created* Janus."

The sound of his words scraped her eardrums like sandpaper.

"How does all of this connect to Natalie?" Caitlin asked.

"Eos."

Her brows curled like question marks.

"Eos is a future kingdom," Glinda revealed. "An imminent world still in the making, still embryonic, but soon coming. It will be a world of ceaseless sunlight—a realm of perpetual regeneration and existence. A kingdom that will never know night or death, because the shine of seven new orbiting moons will equal the luminosity of its sun."

Glinda's spoken words were not just vapors or sound waves. Caitlin actually *tasted* the flavor and quality of each word when Glinda's voice touched her eardrums as she spoke of Eos. Her flesh tingled with each lofty syllable. Each letter was like a savory ingredient in a recipe for some kind of intoxicating, utopian kingdom.

"The stories destined to emerge in that world are so glorious, so enchanting and dream-worthy, the words to describe the ineffable joyance they will produce have not been formed yet."

Scarecrow interjected, his face hardening.

"The Enchanter plots to infect this new universe; change its destiny. Like mutating the seed of a great tree to make all its branches and fruits sickly and diseased. His plan is to birth a *defective* new kingdom. A realm of unnatural darkness, which will give rise to other kingdoms bearing dark moons, dark suns, and dark hearts."

"What has this got to do with me?"

"Nothing," he said.

Caitlin flinched.

"It has to do with Natalie."

"Why?"

"I'm unable to answer *why* questions."

"Huh? Why not?"

Scarecrow remained silent. Caitlin realized that was another *why* question.

Glinda gestured with an open palm to the straw man. "The vial."

He reached into an inside pocket and retrieved a large glass vial sealed with a cork stopper. The vial was filled with a glistening, pearly-silver fluid.

"Scarecrow only answers questions dealing with *how, what, when, where,* and *who,*" Glinda said.

Caitlin threw up her hands. "But I need to know *why* this involves Natalie. Who can answer the *why* questions?"

Scarecrow spoke: "The wisest in Oz."

Caitlin pointed at him. "But that's you—the smart one with the big brain."

Scarecrow waved a gloved finger. "And I'm smart enough to know a simple truth: information resides in the brain, but true wisdom lives in the heart. The brain can only tell you how. Only the heart can tell you why."

Caitlin instinctively pressed her palm against the left side of her chest and said, "The Tin Woodman?"

"Kudos," Glinda said. Scarecrow nodded.

"Then let's go find him," Caitlin said.

Scarecrow held up the vial of silver fluid.

"We're all decaying," Glinda responded. "Decomposing because of the affliction. However, tin doesn't rust. But it *does* melt."

Caitlin's eyes brightened like the blush of dawn. "You mean . . . that's him? Inside the bottle? Like, a liquefied zombie?"

Glinda grinned. Scarecrow's red-slit eyes pulsed.

Glinda pointed to the worn, weathered yellow brick road that still lay ahead. "You may ask questions along the way."

Just when Caitlin thought this world couldn't get any weirder, it had. Thankfully, she was fixated on finding Natalie and didn't have the energy to contemplate the inherent strangeness of her situation.

And with that, Caitlin and her two cohorts began their journey down the jagged amber road that turned, twisted, and led far off into the distant horizon.

* * *

The figure with the large duffel bag detoured to Treasure Island via Zeno's Forest. He took the portal to the Samoan island and Mount Vaea, where Robert Louis Stephenson lay buried. He began digging up that burial ground area, too, and loading up his duffel bag some more.

Once full, he went back through the portal to Treasure Island and began tracking his target—the firstborn Caitlin Fletcher.

CHAPTER FIFTEEN

"DOES THE LIQUID TALK?" CAITLIN ASKED AS THEY WALKED briskly down the brick road. "I mean, how do I address questions to a test tube of melted tin?"

Scarecrow turned to Glinda. She nodded and winked.

Scarecrow popped the cork stopper from the spout of the vial. He strode over to the center of the road and poured out the contents.

Hot tin liquid pooled on the bricks like fluid quicksilver. Then it began to congeal, thicken, and amplify in volume. From the gelatinous, expanding goop, the form of a body began to rise up. It solidified rapidly into a highly polished Tin Woodman whose eyes were nickel silver and flecked with red.

"You may ask the *why* questions to Tin Man," Glinda said to Caitlin.

Except she couldn't at that particular moment. She was

staring, wordless, and squinting her eyes in response to the way the light glinted off the man made of tin.

It took a moment for her to regain the power of speech. And when she did, she spoke in a voice filled with awe. "So very nice to meet you."

Tin Man bowed his head graciously.

"Please, can you tell me *why* Natalie is connected to Eos?"

"The Lord of the Curtain has chosen her," Tin Man said. "If they should meet physically in person, she won't stand a chance. She'll succumb to the red-band path of light. When you're that close to the Enchanter, his power is overwhelming. Your presence in this realm protects your sister. This is what has prevented a physical encounter thus far. But Natalie may willingly choose to meet him, of course."

She'd never do such a thing!

"How did the Enchanter get so powerful?" Caitlin asked.

The man of straw responded to this *how* question. He nudged the brim of his burlap hat upward with a finger. "A sunlit room grows dark when you close the curtain. But the sun still shines. The presence of the curtain simply manufactures a new dimension of palpable darkness."

Amethyst, the green-tea-drinking caterpillar/butterfly, had said something similar to Caitlin.

She remembered and nodded. "I think I understand. But what's your point, straw man?"

"There's a curtain that hides a great truth."

Hmmm. Like the curtain that hid the "great and powerful" Wizard?

"What truth?" she asked.

"Happily ever after."

"Not following you."

Glinda pointed to the horizon. "Speak as we walk. The crowmen are advancing."

Caitlin picked up her step as Scarecrow continued. "Happiness is the only reality. The singular truth. But the Lord of the Curtain has cloaked it. The Enchanter managed to conceal a world ablaze in light simply by hanging up a curtain and creating a dimension of darkness on the other side. Within this darkness all misery is born. *Happily ever after* gives way to *woe ever more.* Only because we walk on the dark side of the curtain."

Caitlin was lapping up the answers like a thirsty puppy, but answers led to more questions.

"But I don't see any curtains. Where are they?"

Scarecrow's eyes pulsed as his brows sharpened. He pointed to his head.

In the mind?

"He's so powerful that he can do that?" Caitlin said.

A bloodcurdling shriek from Janus and the crowmen reverberated far off in the distance.

Grave concern crossed Glinda's face. The Sorcerer of the South said, "The Enchanter has no self-generating power. None at all. The only strength our nemesis acquires is what we hand over. We give the Enchanter our own sparks from the violet band. That's how this nefarious being sustains existence and wields power over us. "

"Oh my gosh—*we* give him the power? How?"

Glinda signaled to the straw man with the big brain. "Pay attention," he said. "The Enchanter conjures up illusions around you, illusions born of the darkness that *he* fabricates. This is done for one purpose: to trigger a robotic, reflexive, reactionary response from *you.*"

"That's a lot of *R* words. Perhaps be a tad more specific?"

"You become a slave."

"To whom?"

"To everything in front of you. Everything around you. Everything you see and hear. You respond obediently each time the Enchanter stimulates a rash response arising from the red band. And that's when it happens."

"What?"

"Each reaction transfers a spark from your Violet Spectrum to the Lord of the Curtain. All those twinkles, shimmers, and waves of violet become the very life force and power of the Enchanter. And he stockpiles it. Like a backup generator."

"So my fear feeds him?"

"Like flesh to a shark."

"My anger?"

"Blood to a bat."

"Jealousy?"

"Dung to a beetle."

"Gross! But I get it."

Caitlin had a hunch. "I haven't seen Jack Spriggins, Rapunzel, Snow White, Alice, or any of the others since last year."

Glinda, Scarecrow, and Tin Man smiled slyly as Caitlin

continued. "Then I had a dream about Jack. In it, I hadn't seen him in ten years. But he told me he had been near me all along. I thought maybe the Enchanter had altered my glasses. But it wasn't my glasses, was it?"

Scarecrow nodded. "No."

"How did he get inside my head?"

"You opened the door."

"How?"

"When your blog went viral. You invited the Enchanter to draw a curtain over your mind. Which made you see the opposite of light."

She shook her head. "I let the popularity go to my head?"

Scarecrow nodded.

"Vanity?"

He nodded again.

"Arrogance?"

Nod.

"Pride?"

Nod.

"Ego?"

Instead of giving a nod after this last word, Scarecrow smiled wistfully and waved a finger. "The human ego—the ultimate spark. The very root of the Red Spectrum."

How freaking depressing.

"But I'm not an egomaniac."

"The phenomenon called *ego* is not what you presume. The Red Spectrum also incorporates diametrically opposed, inverse explications of all those other egocentric emotions."

"You lost me at *also*."

"Ego includes the flip sides of all those traits."

"I thought ego meant that I think I'm, like, totally wonderful."

Scarecrow shook his head "The Enchanter is far more clever than that. The Red Spectrum is only about triggering a reactive emotion. And the ego refers to *all* possible reflexes. Shall I elucidate?"

"Please do."

"The ego is the dominating voice in our head that says, 'I can do no wrong.' But the ego also says, 'I can't do anything right.' The red band triggers emotions that convince us to think 'I'm the absolute best there is.' But it also makes us tell ourselves, 'I'm the worst there ever was.' It will conjure thoughts that declare 'I can never lose,' and then the inverse notion: 'I can never win.' Feeling that we are unstoppable winners or inevitable losers are both red-band reactions—opposite emotions with one single common denominator—a reaction! That's how the Lord of the Curtain traps us. And with each reaction, the ego expands. And as the ego expands, the curtain thickens and illusion grows more powerful. Without a will to resist this onslaught of reactive emotions, true reality gradually recedes behind an ever-thickening curtain. The Enchanter's power and control magnifies. Welcome, therefore, to the world of ghouls and zombies."

Tin Man chimed in, "And that's *why* you could no longer perceive the beings that dwell in other kingdoms."

Natalie was right—it was my narcissism.

Caitlin's heart suddenly ached for her sister.

"Wait a minute! Then why can I see you now? And why was I able to see Glinda at Forest Lawn?"

"Pain," Tin Man replied. "Pain's ultimate purpose is to draw back layers of curtain."

"What pain?"

Tin Man's silver head tilted to indicate disbelief, as if Caitlin should be able to figure that one out on her own.

She did. The devastating loss of her dad. The anguish she had experienced when she thought she was losing her mind at the orphanage. The shame she had felt when her reputation was ruined. And, worst of all, the abduction of Natalie, for which she felt totally responsible.

With that much chaos clobbering you, that much tragedy wounding you, there's no room for the ego to shine.

A wooden signpost caught her attention. Carved into the wood was a single direction: West.

A nervous flutter arose in Caitlin's chest. She dropped the last thread of conversation as she picked at a fingernail.

"Um . . . I see we're now walking westward," she noted to Scarecrow.

He grinned and replied in his staccato, saw-blade voice, "We are."

The yellow brick road had come to an unexpected end. At the outer edge lay a vast and dying field.

Caitlin loosened her collar. The widespread, parched grasses were dotted with decomposing daisies and decaying poppies. Caitlin's mouth went dry.

"I thought we were going to the Emerald City?" she asked Scarecrow.

"Detour."

"Doesn't a certain one-eyed, wicked witch live in the West?"

Glinda suddenly issued a firm command.

"Seize her!"

Tin Man snatched Caitlin's left hand.

What the—!

Scarecrow snagged her right.

The sky darkened.

Caitlin glanced up.

Endless flocks of blood-eyed black crows were sheathing the sky.

With her free hand, Glinda plucked a shiny object out of her left eye.

Oh my gosh!

Then she popped another object out of her right eye.

Contact lenses!

Glinda swiveled her head toward Caitlin. Her naked eyeballs glistened like fresh blood.

Oh my—!

Scarecrow and Tin Man tightened their grip. Caitlin locked her knees. Stiffened her legs. She flailed her arms to wrench free. Not a chance. Scarecrow and Tin Man were too strong.

"Move on," Glinda commanded.

Scarecrow and Tin Man began hauling Caitlin forward.

"Where you taking me?" she screamed at Scarecrow.

"I think you already know."

"But *why?*" she shouted at Tin Man.

"You'll know soon enough."

She was being dragged against her will across the scorched field. Her eyes bulged in stark horror. She dug her feet into the dirt to try to slow them down, but to no avail. They marched, westward-bound, heading toward the one-eyed Wicked Witch, with Caitlin screaming, scuffling and thrashing wildly the whole way.

Talk about a reaction to the red band.

CHAPTER SIXTEEN

A GRIMY, RANCID, RAG-GAGGED NATALIE WAS BOUND TIGHTLY BY leather constraints. She was strapped to a large wooden wheel, arms stretched above her head, legs pulled as tight as piano strings, her body locked upside down in the six o'clock position.

Natalie knew precisely what this diabolical contraption was: a medieval torture wheel. And the wheel had been positioned so that blood was pouring into her brain and the backs of her eyeballs. The putrid rag stuffed in her mouth did its job well by preventing her from screaming for help. Not that there was anyone who could have heard a scream anyway, since her forsaken cell was subterranean.

She surveyed her prison from her bottom-up view. The walls and floor were plank wood. No windows. A few jugs of water were piled up in the corner, maddeningly just out of her reach. That was the extent of the amenities in the underground dungeon.

The cell was also chilly, but she felt warm, as if she had a low-grade fever. There was nothing to do but wait till she passed out or that kid-snatcher came back to spin the immoral spinning wheel right-side up.

The memories of Wonderland and her bizarre experience with her sister last Halloween had come flooding back to her when that nefarious impostor, posing as Uncle Derek, forced her down the grave of L. Frank Baum. He had put a bag over her head when they touched the bottom of the portal, and then he took her God-knows-where. She had fallen asleep— or was put to sleep. When she woke up, she found herself mounted onto the Gothic torture device.

Natalie was stunned that she had gone an entire year without remembering the otherworldly kingdom and the extraordinary events that had taken place there.

Did Caitlin remember?

Her sister had never talked to her about it. Perhaps that was because Natalie had never brought it up, having repressed all her own memories. Obviously, she would've never believed Caitlin even if her sister had tried to broach the subject.

Natalie could only remember particular parts of the experience. She recalled diving into the glimmering portal that mysteriously opened up at Lewis Carroll's grave on Halloween night last year. She had been enthralled by the opportunity to explore what she thought might have been a genuine wormhole leading to another dimension. But her zeal and motivation for diving into the glowing grave weren't just about intellectual curiosity. If other dimensions existed, if other worlds were just as real her world, perhaps that meant the death of her mom was not really the end of her being. Energy never dissipates. Atoms never die. For Natalie, it was also about hope.

She also recalled meeting the authentic princesses Rapunzel, Cinderella, Snow White, and Sleeping Beauty. The memory had surfaced clear and bright, but she still wasn't sure whether she had been more fascinated by the tangible existence of fictional literary characters or by their shocking decay into the living dead.

And who could forget those carnivorous Venus flytraps? And the awesome experience of teleporting through Zeno's Forest—which to her mind offered irrefutable evidence of the space-time continuum being a persistent illusion, as Einstein had theorized.

The very last thing she remembered was climbing a mountainous wall of stone on the perimeter of the Queen of Hearts's castle.

The last memory she had of Halloween was of waking up at Mount Cemetery in Guildford with a relentless craving for beef kabobs and hummus.

A wooden door swung open with a resounding *bang*, breaking her train of thought. A pair of upside-down black boots clunked on the wood floor as they stepped toward her in the derelict dungeon.

The boots approached the wheel. The contents of her

stomach suddenly swirled as the rack spun, whirling her right side up.

The impostor Derek Blackshaw stood before her. He untied the gag and pulled the stinking rag from her mouth. He stank of cheap rum, stale blood, and unwashed clothes.

His black hair was as greasy as an oil spill and pulled into a ponytail. His unshaven face was bloodless, battle-scarred, and nail hard. The stubble on his face had been salted and peppered by the hands of time. Definitely not a face to mess with. Nevertheless, Natalie nodded knowingly as she peered at him with scorn.

"You're the Enchanter. The one Rapunzel said had cursed the Queen of Hearts and made such a despicable mess of this place."

His bony fingers rubbed his chin. He narrowed an eye and sneered, "I says you ain't as clever as you think you are," the man replied. He leaned in close to Natalie. The rum and blood on his breath were so robust, she could taste them on her own tongue.

"I also says when I'm done with ya, it'll be a name you'll never forget." His eyes were pools of crimson liquid, his grin as cold as a cadaver.

"And what is this unforgettable name of yours?"

He stroked the waxy stubble on his face. "Blackbeard."

"The pirate? Ha! I think your name should be *Nosebeard*! You have more whiskers coming out of your nostrils than on your chin."

His eyes flared.

Natalie struggled to free her arms but the leather straps burned into her wrists. "Get me out of this contraption. I'm not afraid of you."

He cracked a knuckle and snickered. "Only the dead have no fear."

Don't say it!

She couldn't help herself.

"Well, I'm not dead, and I'm *still* not afraid."

He cackled with heartless glee. "Not yet. But ya can avoid yer fate by choosing ta become *undead.*"

She rolled her eyes, feigning condescension. "Now why would I do a ludicrous thing like that?"

Blackbeard raised a sharp eyebrow as he pointed a dirty fingernail at her. "How would ya like ta become a real princess, little lambkins? Rule over yer own kingdom?"

Natalie's nose scrunched. At this particular point in their interaction, she had been expecting more dastardly threats— not the offer of a royal coronation.

Blackbeard tapped his head with a finger as he continued. "And ya get ta dream up all the laws of nature inside that presumptuous head o' yours."

Silence hung like a cobweb in the air. And then Natalie's eyes lit up with a compelling curiosity.

CHAPTER SEVENTEEN

THE GRIND, CREAK, AND CLATTER OF A WINCH, A PULLEY, AND IRON chains startled Caitlin. A footbridge had begun descending. It lowered down across a deep, waterless moat. The footbridge led to a medieval castle, gloomy and char-grilled gray. The castle's spiked towers and walls of stone were chipped and scarred. The Gothic fortress loomed large, like a precipitous, haunted mountain before Caitlin and her captors.

Scarecrow and Tin Man twisted Caitlin's wrists as they hauled her across the wooden walkway into what was presumably the abode of the Wicked Witch of the West.

Indeed it was. The hideous hag was already waiting for them in the vaulted entranceway of her stone castle.

Caitlin squirmed.

The wretched, withered old woman really just had one eye—dead center in the middle of her forehead, like a Cyclops—and it was immensely repulsive to look at. If the

Oz books were to be taken literally, Caitlin knew that eye was also telescopic, giving her far-ranging vision.

The eyeball itself was excessively bloodshot, with multiple broken blood vessels and red retinal veins from hemorrhaging. She was definitely a bona fide blood-eyed, just like the savage ghouls Caitlin had encountered last year in Wonderland.

But why were these mortal enemies—Glinda, Tin Man, and Scarecrow, who in the stories worked *against* the Wicked Witch—suddenly forming an unholy alliance *with* her?

"Come close, dearie," the wicked old witch summoned with a wave of her decrepit hand.

Not a chance.

Tin Man and Scarecrow pulled Caitlin near her. The old woman stank of oregano. She ran two frigid fingers through Caitlin's hair. Caitlin shivered from the cold touch of dead flesh on her forehead.

"I've had my *eye* on you for some time, child," the wicked one said.

Could that explain the feeling I've had of being watched?

The witch leaned in close to Caitlin—too close—examining her with that single eyeball as if the hag were peering through a microscope and examining some kind of exotic specimen.

The witch's breath was scentless and cold on Caitlin's face.

"I need your help, blessed dearie," the witch said.

Caitlin's eyebrows jumped a tier.

The witch smiled. Her teeth were crooked, sickly yellow, and stained brown from rot. "Your assistance is required if we're to restore some semblance of free will in our kingdoms."

A wide-eyed Caitlin swiveled her head to Scarecrow. Then Tin Man. Then Glinda.

"That's why you all dragged me here? This old witch needs *my* help?"

Glinda nodded. "You would've never come knowing you were to meet a blood-eyed, one-eyed crone—especially if you knew *how* you were going to help."

Caitlin bit her thumbnail. "I'm listening!"

Scarecrow and Tin Man released Caitlin's hands.

"The Wicked Witch initially pleaded for *my* help," Glinda said. "I was surprised, to say the least. We've been adversaries since birth. And she has enslaved so many creatures for so many generations."

"What changed?"

Glinda nodded to her wicked counterpart.

The hag sighed in self-pity. "Alas, I had always been the slave master in these parts. Then suddenly *I* was the one being held captive!" She shrugged. "Retribution and restorative justice, I reckon."

"Who's holding you captive?"

The witch's brow narrowed in anger. "The Red Spectrum. Lord of the Curtain. Look here, dearie—I never vowed to walk the undefiled path of Lady Glinda and the Southern witches. But even the option to do so has been cast away," she hissed. She pointed her pale, bony finger at Glinda,

Scarecrow, and Tin Man. "The option has been blotted out for all of us. Our will has been predisposed. The privilege of choice revoked. We're imprisoned by hunger, shackled to the cravings of a perverted appetite. And worst of all, dearie, we're undead! Beyond recall. Even water won't bring the end for me!"

Caitlin shook her head. "I don't get it. I destroyed the scepter. Your will to resist should've been restored."

Scarecrow wagged a gloved finger. "The destruction of the scepter only restored part of the green frequency— enough to heal our eyes and return us to a less-extreme state of decay. We only got up to the same levels as the royal-blooded maintained during the original affliction."

Caitlin's brows furrowed. "I know that. So what happened?"

"The rebellion happened."

"What rebellion?"

"After you left last year, the Lord of the Curtain was neutralized. But there were some who longed to return to the full-blooded eye. They were craving the instant rush of red. They surrendered their wills. Voluntarily. And so the Enchanter grew stronger again. About a month ago, a full blood-eyed rebellion broke out. All the wolf species. Others. It grew like an epidemic. The Enchanter grew even stronger."

"But you're *all* blood-eyed again."

"We *chose* to be."

Caitlin shook her head in bewilderment. "Why in the world would you willingly choose to become a walking corpse if that's what you had just fought *against*?"

Glinda shot a look at the Wicked Witch and said, "Prepare the cauldron."

Cauldron? Cauldron of what?

The Wicked Witch winked her one eye, then disappeared into the bowels of her fortress.

Tin Man swiveled to Caitlin. "You cannot change what you don't have. To weaken the overall red band spectrum, we needed to access it, make it part of us. Then, the idea was to weaken its influence within us. By doing so, we hope to lessen its dominance over the kingdoms and, in turn, diminish the influence of the Enchanter. And so we fight a terrible, dark war that rages inside us."

His eyes smoldered red. He leaned in close to Caitlin.

Ugh!

She could almost taste the saliva drooling from the corners of his mouth. "Every moment, an unholy hunger burns within us. Even now, it's impelling me to attack you without mercy. But I fight it because I know each victory, large or small, over the hunger dims the red and weakens the enemy." He paused for moment without taking his eyes off Caitlin. Then he said, "There are others."

"Others? Who?"

"A select few that chose to wage this war alongside us," Scarecrow said. "A few who willingly forsook their will to become one of the blood-eyed, living dead in order to defeat it."

"How many?"

"Including myself, six. But we need a seventh. A human. You."

"Why seven?"

Scarecrow turned to the man of tin.

"Our world mirrors yours," the Tin Man said. "Seven continents. Seven seas. Seven days of the week. Seven notes of music. Seven colors in a rainbow. The number seven is woven into the fabric of all worlds. Ergo, if we want to change reality, we will need seven people to effect change."

"What type of change?"

The straw man nudged up the tip of his burlap hat a tad.

"Mastery."

"Over what?"

"The influence of the red band spectrum."

"How does one do that?"

"Resistance."

"Armed resistance? Like a rebellion?"

His finger tapped the top of her head. "No. We discussed this. Mind resistance. We must resist red band reactions."

Caitlin nodded. "Yes . . . of course. Which is why we need the Green Spectrum—the will to resist."

Scarecrow wagged a finger. "Forgetting what we already learned and repeating the same mistakes is also a byproduct of bowing to the Red Spectrum."

Caitlin shrugged sheepishly. "I get it."

Glinda patted her on the back. "Well done. This is the only way to restore balance."

Caitlin's face suddenly soured. Her shoulders slumped. And she felt a sudden warming around her. She also felt feverish and flushed on the inside.

Glinda lifted Caitlin's chin with her fingers. "What is it?"

"Restoring the color spectrum. Changing worlds. It all sounds so poetic, but it's so not practical. I mean, how can just seven people impact a world if billions of others stay the same?"

Scarecrow smiled sagaciously. "Intelligent question. But you just answered it."

"I did?"

"Indeed. You said 'billions of others stay the same.' Which means zero change has occurred among the multitude. I'll reveal a sweet and precious secret to you; please pay close attention. It is the *degree* of change that influences worlds. Therefore, if seven change a little and a billion changing nothing at all, which group do you think influences the kingdoms more?"

Caitlin's eyes brightened as if a great truth had been revealed. *Wow! The positive actions of a few can far outweigh the negative behavior of billions!*

"The Lord of the Curtain is the one who blinds us to this truth. He hides it behind yet another curtain. Each one who attains even the smallest victory, each individual who manages even bare-minimum resistance to the reactions born of the red band impacts all the kingdoms, whether they know it or not. They sustain kingdoms. And now you know this, Caitlin. But with that knowledge comes accountability."

"And that's why we need to be blood-eyed," Caitlin said. "To register change each time we resist those disgusting, undead impulses. But now that you're blood-eyed," she continued, "how do you even have the strength to resist? The Green Spectrum is still impaired, right? I mean, isn't that the major problem here? What makes you different from the crowmen?"

Scarecrow beamed his blade-thin, cherry-red eyes at her. Saliva continued to foam around his mouth. "The witch's elixir," the straw man replied. "She cooked up a special broth that gives us just enough will to resist. That's why I'm *half* blood-eyed—I harness enough evil to ignite the red, and also just enough to give me a chance to resist it. Like I am doing right now." His eyes flared. "Not easy sometimes."

Caitlin bit her bottom lip. "Is *that* what the witch is brewing in her cauldron? For me?"

Glinda took her hand. "It's the only way."

Though her fingers betrayed her nervousness by twisting the ends of her burnished auburn hair, Caitlin knew she had to do what she had to do. No matter what.

Scarecrow took her other hand. "Ready?"

The words got caught in her throat. So she nodded firmly, and then balled her fists.

Scarecrow and Glinda escorted Caitlin deep into the damp darkness of the witch's castle.

CHAPTER EIGHTEEN

THEY QUICKLY ARRIVED AT THE COOKERY—A HOT, STEAMY, STONE kitchen replete with rancorous aromas that almost made Caitlin lose her dinner for a second time. She inhaled the pungent smell of oregano mixed with what seemed to be rotten fish, foul meats, moldy cheese, stale dog food, and . . . *dirty laundry?*

Hanging from the gray stone shelves were large steel stockpots, oversized frying pans, and cast-iron skillets. In the heart of the cookery, a black cauldron bubbled over a pile of flaming coals. Some kind of repugnant, stinking mishmash was simmering inside it. The witch stirred it with a wooden ladle while tossing in fresh eyeballs, half a dozen or so wolf snouts—*or were they dog snouts?*—plus several strips of raw liver, and some soft, fatty globules of who-knows-what.

Better that I never know what.

Scarecrow gestured to the cauldron. "Ingredients for the brew. The eyeballs are from eagles."

"Why?" Caitlin asked.

Tin Man said, "Eagle eyes. They help us see."

"See what?"

Scarecrow wagged a finger to emphasize his answer. "To see that negative thoughts and dark impulses are really just the cunning provocations of the Enchanter."

"I thought they came from the Red Spectrum."

"Same thing. The Enchanter and the Red Spectrum are one. The point is to recognize that any thought that makes you unhappy does not stem from your true essence. When you see this false truth, you won't adopt it as your own. You'll be less tempted to follow their marching orders."

Caitlin reluctantly leaned over the cauldron and peeked inside. Eagle eyeballs were floating atop the bubbling surface, but quickly melting into the mix.

Major yuck!

"How can I tell if a thought comes from my essence or the red spectrum?" she asked.

"Your own thoughts include other colors. Only the Enchanter's prompts are strictly red. For instance, Natalie grossly misbehaves."

"What else is new?"

God, I miss her.

"When I tell you that, you feel the need to reprimand Natalie," Scarecrow said. "The Enchanter incites pure red anger so that you'll react blindly to his command. The result is that you lose your temper with your sibling."

Caitlin felt a pang of guilt. She longed to hug Girl Wonder again.

"There is no green color to restrain the anger," Scarecrow said. "No violet to sweeten your judgment with some compassion and sisterly love."

Stellar point. And to think that shameless Dr. J. L. Kyle plagiarized all of this for his own profit. No wonder his book made the bestseller list.

"How about the livers?" Caitlin asked.

"From shark and swine," Scarecrow replied.

She knew to turn to Tin Man to ask *why*. He elaborated. "The liver is the seat of all anger. The witch's brew injects us with a diluted dose of anger to build up our *immunities*."

Caitlin smiled. "Like a vaccination."

"Bravo," Glinda said. "It helps us control rage and resist cannibalistic cravings."

"And those disgusting wolf snouts?"

"Not wolves," said Scarecrow. "They're from foxes."

Tin Man smiled. "A devilishly sly and cunning creature. Helps us outwit the negative thoughts. Outfox the Lord of the Curtain's provocations."

The Wicked Witch gestured to Glinda.

"Are you ready?"

Glinda's eyes came alive with wild passion.

Caitlin rocked back and forth on the balls of her feet. She

could sense some kind of primal urge radiating from Glinda like atomic heat.

"Look, I'm not gonna chicken out and bail," Caitlin said, "but will this hurt?"

"Very much," the man of straw admitted.

Truth also hurts.

Glinda's eyes throbbed a feverish red as she closed in on Caitlin. She ran her fingers through Caitlin's auburn hair, brushing away long locks from her neck and shoulders.

Caitlin's breath quickened.

Glinda took Caitlin's hand and held it warmly, caressing the soft, fleshy part on the backside with her thumb. Glinda was being kind, thoughtful, and doing what she could to ease whatever god-awful nasty thing was going to happen next.

Suddenly Glinda bit into the warm flesh of Caitlin's neck. A tremor shivered through Caitlin's body.

Is she a zombie or a vampire?

Warm blood trickled down Caitlin's shoulder and chest. She missed a breath when her heart skipped. She felt a bit panicky. There was no turning back now.

Glinda opened a bite wound on her own wrist next, and drew blood. She rubbed her glistening red wrist on Caitlin's neck wound in a circular motion. Caitlin noticed that Glinda's blood felt cold as it intermingled with her own warm blood.

"I'm sorry if this hurts," the Good Witch said, overly contrite. She was obviously trying to disguise the perverse pleasure she took in tasting her friend.

So far it had been no worse than a shot of Novocain at the dentist—the bite felt like a mere prick of a needle.

She realized fast that she had jumped to conclusions.

Her senses initially came alive. At first, she felt a strange, intimate, uncanny connection to every cell in her body.

Cool!

But then her insides began heating up as if she were being nuked in a microwave.

Owww!

She furiously rubbed at her arms with the palms of her hands. Then she shook her arms vigorously to try to blow off the heat rising to the surface.

Her skin began to cool again. Then her flesh tingled as a devastating hunger engulfed her. Her growing appetite was devoid of any mercy or compassion.

The Wicked Witch dipped her ladle into the simmering, stinking cauldron. The hag poured the thick, gooey liquid into a ceramic cup. "Drink quickly, dearie, and leave not a drop."

Caitlin's organs burned like molten rock as her eyes welled up with blood. The surface of her skin split and fractured into thin tributaries. Her flesh quickly became as pale as a bleached white bedsheet. It felt like acid was being poured over her cracked skin.

The thought of tasting pink flesh and fresh blood suddenly became palatable to this ordinary fifteen-year-old girl. Her salivary glands drooled; saliva pooled in her mouth. A moment later, she wanted to attack someone—anyone—and ingest the vital fluid in their veins. Along with the entrails in their belly.

This is absurd, depraved, grossly immoral. And it's—

She was losing control—succumbing to a vile, bottomless pit of hunger. The blistering pain of splitting skin and scarring flesh, however, paled in comparison to the shame of losing her decency.

Before she lost all her humanity by acting on these abominable new urges, Caitlin chugged down the witch's brew. Its lumpy texture and gamey taste on her tongue triggered a gag reflex. When she had swallowed half the cup, her body began to heave and retch and sweat profusely. Her heart palpitated against the wall of her chest. She wiped cold perspiration from her brow with the back of her forearm. She squirmed and jiggled her arms as gobs of sweat puddled in her underarms.

Worse than gym class!

She clutched her abdomen with both hands.

Ugh.

She began to rub her stomach with small, circular motions. The abdominal muscles were contracting on their own, preparing to expel the contents of her stomach.

Worse than the worst-ever stomach flu! Yep, I'm going to royally puke all over the place.

"If you throw it up, my dearie," the witch warned, "you'll need to lap it up again."

Harnessing whatever remained of her free choice and mental powers, Caitlin willed the vomit back down her throat, then chased it with another chug of the witch's brew. She hadn't noticed until that moment that her left hand had spontaneously snatched poor Glinda by the neck. She was on the verge of strangling and chowing down the fictional Good Witch of the South.

But, thankfully, her blood-red vision began paling to a soft shade of pink. Her appetite was deescalating, along with the obscene cravings.

Strange.

As her hunger subsided, she began feeling something new . . .

Is the word droll? Tart? Cheeky? Whatever.

She opened her fist, releasing Glinda from the death grip. She wiped more perspiration from her brow. She desperately wanted to slip her top off to wring out the sweat. But she feared that might produce a tidal wave.

Lady Glinda was most gracious about it all. She smiled.

"I, like, almost killed you," Caitlin said, mortified by her homicidal behavior.

Badass bitch, I am!

Glinda had the decency to caress her hand and apologize for the discomfort she'd caused by biting her neck.

"Feeling better, dearie?" asked the old crone of the western horizon.

"Hell yes!" Caitlin responded, surprised by the newfound zing in her personality and vocab.

Scarecrow's manner suddenly became no-nonsense. Stern. He fixed his eyes on the Wicked Witch. "We're done?"

"As the day is," she replied.

"Good." A steely-faced Scarecrow looked like a card sharp ready to show his hand. He fixed his scarlet gaze on Caitlin. "Now, a dire warning."

I knew it!

Caitlin glowered. "Outrageously uncool, straw man! You purposely waited till I drank the poison before sounding the warning alarm. Foul play, dude."

His head tilted. "You'd rather I *not* reveal the cosmic secret of how a zombie comes to be?"

Cosmic secret? Origins of zombies?

She perked up. "On second thought, you obviously have my best interest at heart. A solid strategy. Now pipe up, Scarecrow. Where do zombies come from? From the get-go."

The Nataliesque, wannabe-hipster wit warmed Caitlin's heart as she heard herself say the words. It was as if a small part of Girl Wonder was giggling inside of her, poking at an untouched part of Caitlin's innermost being.

Her arms twitched slightly—a response to a phantom limb-type ache, which made her want to lift her arms and hold her sister.

How ironic.

In this grotesque state of partial inhumanity, she felt she knew Natalie a little bit better; Girl Wonder's flippant remarks and attitude aroused resiliency and buoyancy when the heavy waves of pain came crashing down and you needed to stay afloat.

Scarecrow's eyes intensified as he responded to Caitlin. "It's called the Pleasure Effect."

"Love it already. What is it?"

"The mechanism by which one devolves from a normal benign being into an abnormal, ghastly ghoul. I'll be deftly simplistic in my explanation."

"I'm all ears—go."

"You desire a penny's pleasure."

"I'll assume the penny's only a metaphor and doesn't take inflation into account. Continue."

"You earn a penny, and reap pleasure when you spend it."

Caitlin fanned herself. "Oooh—I'm breathless already."

"The primary problem concerns the pleasures reaped from the red band of light. There is an aftereffect. An upshot directly related to Red-Spectrum pleasure."

"Repercussions," Caitlin said. "I get it. Break it down."

"Pleasures reaped from the red band have a strange effect on one's previous cravings."

"What kind of effect?"

"Severe inflation."

"Like when my stomach bloats due to excess flatulence?"

Did I just admit that publicly?

"Yes—but I'm referring to the expansion of one's original desire."

"How big an expansion are we talking about? Big-Bang big, or a small bloat of gas in the belly?"

"*Double* the size of the original desire."

"Jeez."

"It makes you feel half-empty after experiencing pleasure, because the craving has doubled. So you require two pennies to sate your desire."

"Your point?"

"You're forced to go out and earn two pennies to reap pleasure."

"I see where you're going."

"Once again, the pleasure doubles your desire—"

Caitlin nodded. "And now I'm lusting after four pennies' worth?"

"Correct. And the doubling continues. The pleasure quickly becomes quicksand."

"Yikes."

"Each new round of increased pleasure inflates your desire twofold, leaving you half-empty again."

"Like chasing wind on a hamster wheel. Or splurging on a dial-up modem or eight-track cassette player. Waste of time. No scenario where we end up jumping through hoops of happiness."

"Except this is not some sort of Sisyphean task," Scarecrow said.

Must look up Sisyphean task.

His tone turned bleak. "It's far more dangerous than that."

Now comes the dire warning!

"As the doubling continues," Scarecrow said, "your expanded craving compels you to take increasingly drastic measures to fill it."

"Such as?"

"Your best friend becomes popular. You're jealous, desperate to ascend the social ladder. You engage in outlandish behavior to fill the craving and steal your best friend's thunder. It works. You capture the spotlight. But the pleasure you feel eventually wears off, because the pleasure effect has doubled your desire for popularity. Now you feel twice as insecure as you did before, but you don't understand why."

I wonder what his office hours are?

"You become consumed by a superficial need for fame and celebrity, lost in some illusionary fantasy that has you dreaming about a KFC gig."

"Cashiering at Kentucky Fried Chicken?"

Scarecrow shook his head. "No. A guest spot with Kimmel, Fallon, or Colbert."

"That was kewl, Scarecrow."

Home sweet home!

"Thank you; much appreciated."

Scarecrow nodded and continued. "This process permeates every part of your existence. Some yearn for wealth. They dedicate their time and effort to stealing away someone else's business. Then they're compelled to defraud and embezzle—whatever it takes to fill the void. Some commit murder to usurp a victim's entire existence, to replace them in this world."

"Like some kinda weirdo, homicidal doppelgänger syndrome?"

"You might say that. And so, to make a long story short—"

"Too late."

"If left unchecked, it does not take long for you to graduate from stealing your best friend's boyfriend to eating your best friend's gallbladder. And *that's* how a zombie is born."

"Totally crackers. Desires gone wild. My math teacher talked about this once. Double a penny each day for thirty days—you wind up with over five million bucks. Exponential growth. The perks of compound interest."

Scarecrow wagged a finger. "Think about it, Caitlin. If people react to the red band thirty times in a day . . . therein lies the tragedy. So many of us roaming the various worlds half-empty, half-hollow, half-fulfilled. Eventually, all the kingdoms are overrun with flesh-eaters. The emptiness inside and the futile pursuit of red-band gratification is the cause of it all."

"Okay—I want off the hamster wheel."

"Resist the lure of the red band—*not* because it doesn't arouse pleasure. It does. But because it comes with a cost. The pleasure never lasts. The very pleasure you reap leaves you desiring twice as much as before."

"So a pleasureless existence is the life that awaits us?"

"You forgot."

"I did?"

"Yes. When you resist red-band reactions, light from the Violet Spectrum shines. Violet has no side effects. It's permanent. And it includes solutions to any and all your problems. But the only pathway to the violet band is by resisting the red. Do you now understand the dire warning?"

She drew a breath, then exhaled long and hard. "Each

time I give in to one of my compulsions, they'll double in strength. One step forward—two steps back. Instant gratification equals double greediness."

Scarecrow nodded grimly. "You must remain vigilant at all times. Keep your focus inward. Reaction is now your enemy, as much of one as Janus or the Enchanter."

"How do I manage both?"

"Mentally, you need to be in two places at the same time. No one ever said life was going to be easy. At least, not in our universe."

Tin Man and Glinda smiled poignantly as they gathered beside Scarecrow, shoulder to shoulder, arms around one another.

"Welcome to our life," Glinda said.

Welcome indeed.

Caitlin was now one of them.

A half-blood-eyed, half-walking-dead corpse who was half under the hypnotic influence of darkness. And she was really standing in the cookery of a medieval castle belonging to the authentic Wicked Witch of the West. She nearly did in Lady Glinda to boot.

Certainly not what Caitlin had planned when she had woken up that morning in Glendale, California.

CHAPTER NINETEEN

JANUS CAUGHT THE SCENT OF HIS PREY STRAIGHTAWAY, BY DETECT-ing the alteration of a human's blood. He and the six other crowmen congregated on a hillside and homed in on their prey's location: the Wicked Witch of the West's castle.

"She's ours now," Janus said.

The crowmen pressed their black fedoras tightly onto their black-feathered heads. They buttoned their long black coats and rose straight up into the sky, red fire pulsing in the pupils of their bubbling, tar-black, liquid eyes.

* * *

Caitlin's new acute senses detected a sudden vigilance in Scarecrow's demeanor. His eyes glimmered like a red cherry on an ambulance, confirming that he was worried about something.

"Wat up now?" she asked.

He departed the cookery urgently, without responding. Caitlin chased after him. He dashed out of the castle and began to scan the skies, eyes afire.

His fingers balled into fists, and he began snorting like an angry bull ready to gouge.

"What's happening, Straw Man?" she asked.

"We need to leave! Now! He found you—they're coming."

"Who's *he*? *They* who?"

"Janus. The crowmen. I need you to stick two fingers down your throat."

"Do what?"

"You'll have to vomit up the contents of your stomach after all."

"Excuse me?"

"Crowmen trace the scent of digestive fluids easier than bodily flesh. They're hunting you. We need to keep them tracking to this location while we go another way."

Glinda rushed out of the castle, clearly distraught. She was carrying some sort of fine antique magnifying glass. The handle was mother-of-pearl with brass mounts. The circular magnifier lens was oversized and set in an ornate baroque frame inlaid with semiprecious stones. "They're on the way. We haven't got much time."

How does she know that?

The straw man turned to Caitlin. "We need it now."

She had never willingly poked her fingers down her throat before. She hated throwing up. More than crowded elevators.

More than strips of slippery anchovies on top of her Caesar salads. But they were coming for her. Scarecrow was growing impatient. And Glinda had just warned that time was running out.

Caitlin took two fingers and warily inched them down her throat.

She gagged, but nothing came back up.

"Deeper," Scarecrow said.

"Don't think so."

Scarecrow held her hand as if to comfort her. Caitlin rolled her yes. "I appreciate the gesture, but your touch is making me shudder."

Scarecrow squeezed tighter. Somehow, as if worming through her layers of fear, Caitlin felt a welcome glint of warmth radiating from the straw man. Beneath all the petrifying straw, Scarecrow must've been the sweetest creature in their world.

She took two fingers and tried again, forcing them deeper down her throat.

She gagged. Then heaved.

"Ta-da!" Caitlin sang when she was done. The decorative splat of vomit was bountiful.

Come and get it, crowmen!

Caitlin wiped her mouth. "I'm ready. Where to now?"

Scarecrow's eyes gleamed like red gemstones. "The Twin Mountains of Velarium."

Her eyes brightened. "Is that where Natalie is?"

"No."

"But I thought we needed to find her to prevent an encounter with the Enchanter. Surely I need to find her first."

"Searching for her will be like looking for a needle in a haystack."

"That's almost punny," Caitlin said, pointing to his body made of straw.

Scarecrow pressed the point. "We haven't the faintest notion where Blackbeard is holding her. Which one of a thousand kingdoms should we search first?" he asked rhetorically.

"So why go to this Velarium place?"

"According to legend, the Twin Mountains of Velarium are said to be the home base of the Lord of the Curtain. And the source of his very power."

She threw back her shoulders. "Are you kidding? You want me to walk through Evil Incarnate's front door and be like, 'Honey, I'm home!'"

"Yes."

"Only bimbos and dimwitted dudes in movies willingly walk into a house of horrors."

Tin Man addressed the query. "Darkness must be destroyed at the seed level."

"That's a bit abstract—extrapolate."

"I'm a Tin Woodman."

"Got that part."

Tin Man pulled out his ax. He walked over to a small orchard of apple trees adjacent to the drawbridge and pointed to a branch. "Poison apple," Tin Man said, pointing to a dangling fruit.

"Nah, I'm good."

"Poison apples are plentiful and quite famous in our world, as Snow White can attest."

The Tin Woodman swung his silver ax with a mighty thrust, startling Caitlin with his power and precision. He cleanly lopped off a branch, then held it up.

"I just eradicated a deadly apple from the tree, treating the symptom by dealing with a branch. Yet, the tree is *still* filled with countless branches dispensing a panoply of poisoned apples." He crouched and touched the ground beneath the trunk. "But if I dig it up by the roots, I can destroy the entire tree in one fell swoop."

She smiled. "Got it. We're going to destroy the root of a mountain."

"No—the root of the Lord of the Curtain."

"How?"

"By destroying the root of all darkness," Scarecrow replied. "The dark power in ourselves. That's the reason we became half blood-eyed in the first place."

Caitlin shook her head. "Way too dangerous. How do we possibly visit a mountain of unspeakable evil, destroy parts of ourselves, and live to tell about it?"

"One of the twin mountains is an ancient volcano. Violent. Vicious. Spews out blazing, blood-red fire and crimson lava. Legend says it's the place where baby dragons come to kindle their first flame."

"Now I feel better."

"The other mountain sits directly above the Well of Velarium."

She silently mouthed *Well of Velarium* to herself. Then she said, "Like a Jack-and-Jill type of well?

"Yes. Have you ever wondered why Jack and Jill climbed *up* a hill to fetch water when well water is usually found belowground?"

"Can't say I have. But now that you mention it—"

"It's a code. A cryptic reference to the mythical Dipping Pools of Velarium supposedly located atop the mountain summit. They're filled with precious, violet-colored waters. This is the water newborn fairies come to suckle to draw their enchantment—at least they used to."

"What's their connection to the Well of Velarium below the mountain?"

"According to ancient legends, the Well of Velarium is really a vast underground reservoir, a near-boundless ocean of untouched, pristine waters flowing hundreds of leagues below the surface of our world."

Should've brought a bathing suit.

"This sparkling underground sea is connected to the Dipping Pools on top of the mountain."

Caitlin narrowed an eye and wagged a finger. "I detect a recurring pattern here. Red fire from a volcano. Violet waters flowing atop and below a mountain. Two colors that just happen to lie at opposite ends of the color spectrum. And the elephant in the mountain is . . . the missing green."

"Precisely. Through an untold number of underground arteries, including those directly beneath our feet, these violet waters flow. They're connected to every single of body of water in our world."

"Fascinating."

"Indeed. There's more."

The cold, immortal cry of the crowmen shook the skies.

Glinda pulled a silver wristwatch from her pocket. She checked it.

"Need to leave forthwith!" She was emphatic.

The Wicked Witch hurried out of the castle, a flask of witch's brew in one rickety hand, a folded umbrella in her other. "Filled to the brim," the Wicked Witch said as she handed the flask to Lady Glinda. "Fare thee well, my former and most worthy adversary," the old crone said. "I hope next time we meet you're clear-eyed, I'm wicked-eyed, and we're old-time mortal enemies once again."

Glinda handed her the ornate magnifying glass. "Keep this with you. And guard it well until she arrives."

The wicked old woman smiled knowingly.

Until who arrives? And what's with that fancy magnifier?

"I'm off on a witch's sabbatical," the hag said with a snicker. "I'll be back once those beastly crows come and go." She popped open her umbrella with a *whuuuump* and immediately achieved liftoff, soaring into the skies. She flew concentric circles above her abode, cackling like the notorious hag she longed to be again, then disappeared into the low-hanging clouds billowing in the eastern skies.

"Our turn to depart," Glinda said as she led the way.

Caitlin kept pace with the group as they ditched the old crone's castle. She scurried up alongside Tin Man.

"You said there's more. Tell me."

The foursome crossed a wooden footbridge and then headed down a long, dry, sandy trail. The air was chalky and the land low and barren. A river channel hugged the trail line. Caitlin saw a lonely sign affixed to a wooden post: Zeno's Forest: 1 League South.

Beneath that was a warning: Beware of Quicksand.

Caitlin kept her eyes glued to the ground in front of her as Tin Man continued.

"The Twin Mountains embody fire and water," he explained. "Naturally, fire and water are opposite forces. They cannot combine without destroying each other. An abundance of water will extinguish fire. Likewise, excess fire will evaporate water. They're wholly incompatible."

Like Piper and Barton.

"I get that. So?"

"Their opposing spirits are the source of all darkness."

"Why?"

"The lack of green. No balance. Which leaves only extremes—extreme hunger, extreme violence, extreme darkness."

"Sounds extreme," Caitlin replied.

"But there's a great secret," Tin Man said. "A secret that reveals a unique way to bind and unify the essence of fire and water without letting one destroy the other."

"Merging fire with water? Some feat. Spill the beans."

The crows' screams returned to the skies.

That was, like, way too fast!

She figured they'd located her spewed stomach stew at the castle. Probably polished it off quick as a blink and renewed their hunt.

Caitlin ignored the caws and listened attentively. It wasn't often that one learned the clandestine methodology for combining fire and water.

"Take an empty crystal goblet," Scarecrow said. "And fill it with water. Then set the goblet over a hot flame. The fire infuses the water with its essence, swiftly bringing it to a boil. Two opposites have thus merged energies. All by virtue of the goblet."

"Nifty. Where's our goblet?"

"You are it."

"Me?"

"Yes."

"I'm a goblet?"

"You're a vessel; you hold both ends of the spectrum inside of you. Fire and water. You can become the mediating power that merges both sides to bring balance."

"How?"

"By resisting the red. And the more red, the greater you need to resist. And that is how we will drain the Lord of the Curtain of his power. And then Natalie's encounter with the Lord of the Curtain will not be fatal. We must get you there before they meet."

"And what if—"

Caitlin felt a slurping suction on her left foot.

Her leg quickly sank ankle deep into a patch of quicksand.

One heartbeat later, her right foot sank into a second patch.

Wait.

There were no "patches." The entire ground beneath her was moving like liquid sand, and Caitlin was standing—or sinking—dead center in the middle of it.

Scarecrow had already managed to leap into the air and land securely outside the range of the quicksand.

Nice footwork.

And Tin Man had liquefied lickety-split. He skimmed across the sinking ground to safety and reconstructed in seconds.

Boy, he's quick!

That left the two girls calf-deep in the drink.

Glinda grabbed Caitlin's hand, as if that could prevent them from sinking to their knees in the sucking muck.

"Don't move a muscle," Glinda said, "or we'll be swallowed whole."

Scarecrow wrapped his legs around the trunk of a tree, then laid down on the ground, his body fully stretched out.

Sluuuurrrp!

"Hurry!" Glinda shouted. "We're sinking fast."

Tin Man reconstituted himself, then kneeled down and set his ankles in Scarecrow's hands. The straw man tightened his grip.

Splosh!

The girls continued to sink farther.

"Gotta titanic problem here!" Caitlin shouted. "Pun intended!"

Tin Man sprawled on the ground and reached his left arm toward Glinda's right. They interlocked fingers. Glinda gripped Caitlin's hand harder.

The daisy chain was in place. Which was a good thing, because both girls were waist-deep in watery sand.

Scarecrow pulled . . .

Tin Man tugged . . .

Glinda squeezed . . .

Caitlin prayed . . .

This daisy chain was so tight, with everyone pulling with such enormous strength, that nothing happened—and that's because Scarecrow's straw arm had come unstuffed. It flew right out of its socket.

Caitlin and Glinda were now neck-deep in muck.

The mud was hot and scratchy from chest to chin. Caitlin noticed, though, that it had an almost-sweet aroma.

"Only one thing worse than sand in your shoes and undies," Caitlin said with minimal facial movement. "Sand in your throat and lungs!"

Though her sentiment was glib—a result of the ghoul in her bloodstream—she was trembling like cold Jell-O, panic-stricken at the prospect of being buried alive.

Hot, liquefied grains rose above Caitlin's chin. They began pressing just below the overhanging curl of her bottom lip. It took unimaginable willpower for her to not flail her arms and kick her legs hysterically in an attempt to tread and stay afloat.

Glinda began spitting out sand grains. Caitlin tasted gravel on her tongue, and granules crunched in her back molars.

The time had come.

She and Glinda prepared for the inevitable.

They drew a gargantuan gulp of air into their lungs and held it tight.

And then the two girls were submerged, vanishing beneath the pool of milky quicksand.

Caitlin's world turned as dark as mud.

CHAPTER TWENTY

THE PASTY, BEARDLESS, RUM-SMELLING GHOUL CALLING HIMSELF Blackbeard had unfastened the leather constraints and taken a curious Natalie down from the torture wheel. He had retied her to a wooden stool in the center of her subterranean cell. He sat down directly in front of her.

"Tell me more," Natalie said, thankful she was chained upright to a chair as opposed to strung upside down on an unspeakably uncomfortable medieval contraption. Her head was still spinning like a Ferris wheel and the contents of her stomach were still jouncing from all the spinning.

The warm, feverish feeling also returned.

Have I caught the flu?

Blackbeard gave her a wide smile. The only thing not decomposing on the living-dead buccaneer were the gold molars that glinted in the back of his mouth.

"A bona fide princess, you'll be," Blackbeard said. "Governor

of yer own world, I tell ya. Yer own rules. Controlling ol'
Mother Nature herself. The laws of the kingdom, too."

"What world are you referring to?"

"Eos is the name."

"Eos? Like the Greek goddess of the dawn?"

Blackbeard's face contorted. "Don't know squat about any
goddesses. All's I can tell ya is that this will be a blessed world
of brightness. No darkness, I tell ya. No sickness either. A
happy, merry world full of fun."

"Is this a world or a theme park?" Natalie said.

"Keep runnin' a sassy mouth, and you'll talk yourself into
one helluva mess o' trouble."

"Noted. So what's so special about this world?"

"Ya control everything with your mind. A realm where
your dreams come true just by thinkin' about 'em."

Natalie rolled her eyes. "Telekinesis, psychic power—pure
bunk."

A wily grin lit Blackbeard's face. He stroked his salt-and-
pepper bristles as if considering his next words. Then he
nodded with resolve.

"Bunk, ya say? Okay, little bird, I'm gonna reveal a long-
kept secret ta ya," Blackbeard teased. "A secret no one—in
any world, in any kingdom—knows. And when I says no
one, I mean *no one*! I learned it from the Lord of the Curtain
himself."

Natalie shrugged." And what is this ancient, enigmatic
secret that no one, but no one, knows?"

"Mind over matter!"

Did he just say "mind over matter?" Hmmm. Now that's a rather intriguing turn of phrase coming from the mouth of an old, undead, grammatically challenged pirate.

Natalie cast a curious eye at her captor.

"What about mind over matter?" she asked.

"I says ya already have it."

"Is that what *ya* says?"

"Don't mock my speech, ya pint-size bag o' wind." His eyes hardened. "I'll grab ya by the ankles and swab the crapper with your mop o' curls."

"Eloquently put."

"Now you've gone too far. Back on the rack ya go."

"Wait!"

"What?"

"I have to pee."

Blackbeard shifted squeamishly. He grunted. "I'm in the middle of interrogatin' ya."

"You're not interrogating my bladder."

He went silent, as if giving consideration to her comment. He got up abruptly, without word, and left the cell. Natalie's forehead wrinkled as she stared quizzically at the door. A minute later, it reopened. Blackbeard reappeared with a sullied, empty pail in his hand. He tossed it on the floor in front of Natalie.

"Use this." He untied her hands. "Ya got two minutes." He left again, locking the wooden door behind him.

She fanned herself with a hand. Then she fluttered her top to release the heat coming off her skin.

Natalie didn't have to pee. Even if she did, there was no way she would crouch over that filthy, unhygienic bucket and risk contracting some infectious disease. She massaged her wrists, stretched out her arms, and exhaled long and hard. She was still dizzy from her Ferris-wheel-on-steroids tilt-a-whirl. The room was rocking.

She had less than two minutes to devise and execute an escape plan.

CHAPTER TWENTY-ONE

EVERY BONE IN CAITLIN'S BODY SCREAMED IN FRANTIC DESPERA-tion for air; every cell pleaded for her to somehow reach the surface. But she knew if she struggled, she'd sink lower. If she remained calm like a good girl, she'd suffocate in minutes.

Damned if you do, and damned if you don't.

Probing fingers brushed the bottom of her foot.

Oh my gosh! Someone's down there! Yes! Please help me!

She felt a sharp tug on her ankle.

No! No! No!

The hand was trying to pull her downward, deeper into the quagmire.

Oh God—no!

She jerked wildly and wrenched her foot free. But she dropped even lower into the gravel soup in the process. She kept her eyes closed. Airtight. Hermetically sealed. She knew those coarse granules of sand would scratch her eyeballs. She floundered in darkness.

Is it Glinda pulling at me? Is she trying to help me suffocate quicker, to get this over with?

Another fierce tug on her ankle almost dislocated her knee. This time the hand wasn't letting go.

This can't be happening!

But it was. Caitlin was being dragged down deeper into the quicksand, each yank of her leg distancing her from the surface . . . from safety . . . from air!

The only thing sinking faster was her last glimmer of hope.

Downward, deeper, and lower she sank as the hand pulled and the pressure of the liquid sand increased. She was dropping to unspeakable depths, descending into the suffocating grains and darkness. She knew with total certainty that she'd never see the surface of the sand pit again.

Her legs and feet touched some kind of mucky, round opening. It felt like a cylindrical vent or a ring-like hole.

Oh no!

She was being pulled into it.

Stop!

Caitlin was now horizontal—on her backside, being dragged along into what felt like a narrow passageway.

The gritty consistency of the quicksand began to thin out as she was towed along.

Her body bumped against mucky walls, burrowed through thinning sands. Her lungs throbbed in protest—the result of holding her breath for so long. She desperately craved one quick suck of air.

Sticky walls of mud gave way to rocks slimy with moss. Her fingers rubbed against slippery stone as she moved along.

The wet sand continued dissolving, and the passageway soon turned swampy. Marshy. It diluted further until the cavity became cold, clear, and watery.

The environment surrounding her now seemed to be liquid, as opposed to granular. She took a chance and raised an eyelid—but just a crack.

Clear water—yes!

She opened both eyes. Someone was ferrying her and Glinda along by the ankles.

The currents of fresh water flushed the sand grains from her eyes, washed the mud deposits from her ear cavities, and rinsed the granules of clay from between her toes.

If I could just sip a bit of oxygen!

Caitlin glanced over at Glinda. Her face had turned pale blue from lack of air, and her bloated cheeks looked ready to burst. She offered a tentative smile. It brightened when the mysterious person tugboating the girls abruptly swam upward, heading toward the surface. Chips of jeweled sunlight flickered like glitter above them.

Caitlin was moments away from having to involuntarily gasp for air. Which meant water rushing into her lungs. And drowning.

Splash!

The girls' heads crashed through the surface of the water. They frantically gulped fresh air.

"Are you both all right?" the Little Mermaid asked.

A speechless, breathless, and dumbfounded Caitlin could only nod deliriously.

After a few heaving breaths of oxygen, Glinda and Caitlin swam to the shallows and then straggled onto the sunny banks of the creek they'd been in.

They dropped to the ground, rolled onto their backs, and spread out their arms and legs. Their chests rose and fell rapidly as their lungs lavishly inhaled oxygen. Then exhaled, inhaled, and exhaled again.

"I'm going back to tell the others where you are," the Little Mermaid said. "Sit tight."

Caitlin leaned up. Before she could call out, the Little Mermaid had vanished beneath the river with a flourishing flap of her purple fin.

Caitlin laid back down again, recuperating in the warming rays of the sun. She took hold of Glinda's hand.

The emotional stress of the ordeal began to give way to giddy relief.

"I'd say that was pretty freaky!" Caitlin declared.

Glinda chuckled through grateful tears and sobs. "I didn't see that one coming."

Why would you have?

Caitlin picked granules of sand from her belly button. She rolled a single grain back and forth between the pads of her thumb and index finger. She stared at it up close.

She still had no clue what she was supposed to actually do once she reached the mythical Twin Mountains of Velarium—the place where evil lived, violent volcanoes erupted, and the ruthless Red Spectrum ruled.

How will I possibly topple the Lord of the Curtain, find and rescue my sister, and get the hell out of this place alive? I'm one person. Okay, there are six others helping me. But I'm the one designated as the goblet. A homeless, motherless, fatherless, orphaned goblet.

But she still had a sibling. The thought brought fresh tears to her eyes.

Oh, Natalie!

"You okay?" Glinda asked as she sat up on the river bank.

I don't even know.

Caitlin shrugged at Glinda. Could she—would she—be able to confront and somehow overpower the mountain of evil and the monster known as the Lord of the Curtain?

With her index finger, Caitlin flicked the lone grain of sand off her thumb.

Suddenly the idea of sinking away into quicksand seemed the easier proposition.

CHAPTER TWENTY-TWO

BLACKBEARD OPENED THE THICK WOODEN DOOR AND ENTERED THE cell. Natalie was standing by the stool, staring at his scabbed face. She was holding the pee pail. It was half-full.

"Quite a load o' piss ya got there," Blackbeard said. "How big is that bladder o' yours?"

"I haven't been able to go to the bathroom since I got here."

He scowled. "Well, be careful with that bucket."

Natalie started toward him. His eyebrows arched.

"Where ya goin' with that?"

She lifted the pail to her chest, left palm under the bottom, right hand gripping the rim.

Blackbeard's face reddened. "Hold on—"

She hurled the pail at his face.

His batted his arms to block what he knew was coming.

SPLASH!

Too late.

Flustered and soaked, he snarled. "Aaaarrrgggggggghh!"

Natalie ducked past him and hotfooted it out of the cell. She fled down a skinny passageway that ended at the base of a short wooden staircase, steep as a ladder. Daylight spilled in from above.

Yes!

She climbed, step after step. Reached the landing. Escaped outside. Sprinted into the free and open air.

Behold freedom!

Suddenly, her eyes bugged out. Her shoulders sagged like a faulty parachute. And her mouth went slack-jawed. She felt as though the ground beneath her feet had just fallen away.

She was standing on the deck of a ship. A pirate ship. Sailing on a shoreless sea. She whipped around, searching every direction. The horizons were landless—nothing to the west, east, north, or south! No other ships were out there. And there was no sun in the sky, only rainclouds on the verge of opening their floodgates. The air was salty, subtropically humid, and slightly fishy-smelling. The only sounds she heard were windblown sails, breaking waves, and the lingering wails of distant seagulls.

Atop the ship, the skull and crossbones flag flapped in a light southerly wind.

And then thunder clapped. The skies opened. Lashing rain fell like crystal pins.

"Pretty, ain't it?"

Natalie turned. Blackbeard stood behind her, eyes

transfixed by the open sea and rain-swept skies. The view clearly touched him.

Natalie began to tremble, but not from the cool sting of rain. She was thinking of Caitlin.

So this is what it feels like. Neurosis. Phobia.

She realized there was no getting off the boat. There was no one to call. Nowhere to run. No place to swim to if she jumped overboard. She loosened her collar and started nibbling on her pinkie nail.

Blackbeard shoved her from behind. "Back inside ya go before we catch cold."

She had to tamp down the uncomfortable feeling gathering inside her, a feeling teetering on unbearable cabin fever. A disturbing sense of being vulnerable and totally out of control of her situation. If she'd been tied up and stuffed in a box locked inside a dark, cramped closet located in the basement of an old, abandoned house, she would have felt the same strong unease that verged on panic as she had felt upon seeing the wide-open sea. Equally harrowing. Like two sides of one coin called phobia hell!

She couldn't let Blackbeard know how vulnerable she was, or that all these bleak, unbidden thoughts were cropping up in her mind. She stiffened her back and flexed her arms.

The old pirate shoved her back into the cell. He followed behind her and locked the door.

He pointed his finger at her sharply. "I says yer darn lucky that was jug water in that bucket and not yer warm, yellow piss."

She mocked him. "And I says yer darn lucky I don't got mind over matter right now, 'cause then I'd use my *mind* to reposition that *matter* that is your head right up your scrawny, hairy, zit-abundant butt. Then, when folks saw ya flounderin' down the street, they'd stop and say, 'Hey, what's the *matter* with that guy?' And then other folks would respond, sayin', 'Ahh, pay no *mind* to 'im. There's nothin' the *matter* with the guy. He's just one, big, dopey, dumbass butthead.'"

Inside, Natalie was laughing herself silly at the dorky, lame, dim-witted remark.

Her claustrophobia and agoraphobia dissipated—for the moment.

And so it happened that this was one of the rare occasions in the life of Natalie Fletcher where it felt absolutely awesomely delightful for her to . . .

Just. Let. Go.

And act her age!

CHAPTER TWENTY-THREE

CAITLIN SHRIEKED WHEN AN ANONYMOUS, COLD FINGER POKED the bottom of her foot.

"Aaaahhhhhhhh!"

She bolted upright. She was sweating profusely, swinging her arms, and kicking wildly as if she were drowning in a pitch-black sea. Her eyes were still shut.

"It's just me," Scarecrow whispered. "You fell asleep. Open your eyes."

The trauma of the quicksand caused a reflex response when she felt Scarecrow's fingers fiddling with her foot. It was an innocent effort to rouse her from her slumber.

"What's happening?" Glinda mumbled as she, too woke up, yawning and stretching her arms and torso.

They were still on the sandy shore by the creek. Scarecrow lent a gloved hand to Caitlin and helped her to her feet. Tin Man did the same for Glinda.

"I take this as a good sign," Scarecrow said.

Caitlin looked at him, clearly confused.

"The Well of Velarium," Scarecrow explained. "You managed to find one of the underground water arteries. It saved your life. Which suggests the Twin Mountains and the Dipping Pools are real."

"*She* saved our life," Caitlin said. "The Little Mermaid."

"I trust you're refreshed now. We need to keep moving."

"I'd like to take a sick day."

"There's much we need to discuss," Scarecrow said.

The straw dude is right. I have questions that need answers.

Tin Man pointed a silver finger eastward. "The trail picks up over there."

Caitlin picked a sand grain from her tooth. "Let's go. And watch out for quicksand."

The foursome found their way back to the trail without incident. Caitlin renewed the conversation that had taken place prior to her being buried alive.

"As I was saying . . . how is all of this gonna play out? How do I—the goblet—combine fire and water to take down the Enchanter?"

"You already have the fire inside you," Scarecrow said. "You're blood-eyed. Once at the mountaintop, you'll immerse yourself into the hallowed waters of the Dipping Pools of Velarium. The violet waters will cleanse all traces of the darkness from you. As the darkness dies, the Enchanter will weaken. But first you must become an empty vessel—empty of fear, doubt, hesitation, uncertainty. And most important of all. . . . " He paused.

She made eye contact with him. "I'm listening!"

"Selfishness."

Her eyes narrowed sharply. "Did my sister tell you to say that?"

Scarecrow's stitched-up mouth broke into a slight smile.

Caitlin ignored the grin. "You said you heard about these fantastical twin mountains in a legend."

"Yes—an old one."

"Then how do you know the place even exists?"

"A few throughout the ages claim to have found it."

"Like who?"

Scarecrow went silent. A baffled look crossed his face as he shrugged.

Boom—I just stumped the big brain! Who's your zombie now?

Scarecrow turned to Glinda, who took the cue.

"Dear, dear Caitlin. I'm almost certain the Twin Mountains exist."

Almost?

"They're recorded in one of the Great Books of Records and—"

"Wait! Did you just say *one* of the Great Books of Records? Like, there's more than one?"

"Well, yes . . . sort of . . ."

"Sort of? How many Great Books of Records are there? And do they all mention the Twin Mountains?"

"That's a bit complicated to explain at the present moment."

Scarecrow gamely interceded, perhaps trying to save face as a result of his prior mental lapse. "According to my calculations, if you piled all the existing Great Books of Records one on top of the next, they would touch the stars." He perked up. "I can calculate how many books that'd be, if you'd like?"

Lady Glinda rejected the offer with a dismissive wave of the hand. "We're getting ahead of ourselves. No need to overwhelm her with information at this point." She sidled up to Caitlin and interlocked arms with her.

"To be perfectly frank, sweetie, there is a fifty-percent chance the Twin Mountains are real. If they're not real, the Lord of the Curtain will be able to continue blocking the light forever, the kingdoms will drown in darkness, and this conversation will be moot."

Why be subtle? Tell it like it is.

"Something doesn't make sense," Caitlin said. "Why would the Dipping Pools be unaffected by the broken spectrum?"

Tin Man stepped in beside her. "They sit at the summit of the mountain. And the summit stands higher than the firmament—above the clouds and *curtain* impairing the rays. Therefore, the Dipping Pools capture the full spectrum of the sun. The same holds true for the feminine waters in the underground oceans. The Well of Velarium lies beneath—"

"Hold on a sec. Did you just say *feminine* waters?"

"I did."

"What does that even mean?"

Scarecrow took up the baton. "Two types of water exist in our world—masculine and feminine."

Kinky.

"Masculine waters fall from the skies," Scarecrow said.

I think they call that rain.

"The masculine waters are collected in the Dipping Pools, at the summit. Feminine waters, on the other hand, rise from underground oceans—the Well of Velarium—deep below the mountain."

Male on top. Some things never change.

"Then what happens?" Caitlin asked.

"Something extraordinary!" Scarecrow replied. "There's a network of channels inside the mountain connecting the Dipping Pool to the Well of Velarium. When the masculine waters flow into the feminine waters below, magic happens!"

Mating waters—this gives new meaning to the term "hot springs."

"You mean, like, the Earth moves?"

"No. After their union, the coupled waters begin to shimmer violet. This signifies the unleashing of profound restorative forces. The underground violet oceans nourish all the aboveground streams, rivers, lakes, and seas. These regenerative waters are what produce our enchanted kingdoms. And because these healing waters saturate our world—in the atmosphere, as rain, fruits, and drinking water—no one ever dies here."

"Well, they sure do now. So what happened?"

"Long ago, the Enchanter siphoned off the masculine

water supply in the Dipping Pools. He literally separated the masculine and feminine waters, causing them to lose their curative powers."

"How did he manage that?"

"The Lord of the Curtain is able to hang curtains that dim or filter light and create illusions, as you know. But one thing he *cannot* do is change the structure of our world without human intervention. He found someone."

"A human?"

"Yes."

"Who?"

"Blackbeard. Long ago, the thieving marauder swore allegiance to the Enchanter. He's the one that dammed the water channels inside the mountain. Then he built a special valve that cuts off the water supply from the summit, separating the masculine and feminine waters."

"And that was the end of violet underground oceans and everlasting life?"

"Worse. The Enchanter siphons off violet from our essence."

"How?"

"Our reactions. They nourish him. Feed him. And because we can't access the green band, we have no ability to resist, even if we want to. Each time we react to the red band, our desire doubles in intensity, and then our next reaction generates double the amount of violet for this fiend. He's constructed the perfect system of darkness, of slavery. Our everyday actions exponentially strengthen his existence while weakening ours. The Enchanter's plan is to usurp all the violet from the entire universe: all the worlds, all realities, and every dimension."

"That's a lot of places. How's that possible?"

"The Mount Velarium volcano—the second of the Twin Mountains. Inside that volcano are countless portals and endless tunnels that interconnect countless dimensions and endless worlds."

"Wormholes?"

"Yes. The Enchanter needs a human with a mind powerful enough to control all realities—by controlling the most powerful world of all."

"Eos?"

"Precisely."

"So he needs Natalie and her big brain."

"Correct."

"So there's no hope?"

"There's you."

"Right. I'm the goblet."

"The Dipping Pools are said to be flowing with violet waters. This is where he stores the violet power he's stolen from us. The plan is to use that power against him."

"How?"

"You. The goblet. You have both fire and water—the red and violet forces—inside of you. Right now, the red is dominant because you're half blood-eyed. This imbalance connects you to the Enchanter. Each time you resist, you weaken your red, and you weaken him by association as you restore balance within yourself. But the ultimate purge will be the Dipping Pools. The waters will purify you of all the dominating red power. And that will drain him. First, you'll dip into the pools seven times to purge that walking-dead force from your being. The nail in his coffin will be the *draining* of the Dipping Pools. Only a living human hand can turn that valve."

Caitlin lifted her hand and inspected it, wiggling her fingers.

Scarecrow continued. "Right now, you have a hand, but it's not living. You're an undead human. After you purge the ghoul from the bloodstream, you'll be able to find the valve and open it."

"Where's this valve?"

Scarecrow shrugged. "We don't know. We'll figure it out when we get there."

The plan crystalized in Caitlin's mind.

"I get it," she said. "The Dipping Pools! The separation of the male and female waters. The curtain in the sky impairing the green spectrum. He's hijacked control of the earth and sky, the waters of the world, and the light of the sun."

Scarecrow's eyebrows narrowed. His eyes flamed red. "You understanding nothing!"

I do? I mean, I don't?

"You've got it completely backward. Your grasp of our dire situation is woefully upside down. The opposite of the truth."

Caitlin's mouth went dust dry. She grabbed on to Tin Man as her knees weakened and her leg muscles became jelly.

"Everything that you perceive with your eyes, all that you discern with your senses—none of it is the cause of anything! Not the scepter. Not the separation of the waters of Velarium."

Stop speaking, straw man! My head is turning like a carousel on steroids.

"It's only a reflection," Scarecrow said. "A subsequent shadow. A branch. An effect. An automatic consequence of a *prior incident* set in motion long before. The prior incident is the true cause. It's the first domino that was tipped over, which then set off a chain reaction of tumbling dominos."

A shiver crept down Caitlin's spine. Her salivary glands seized up, and her bones rattled like fallen bowling pins. The looming question weighed heavy on her like a backpack of bricks.

"Do you know what the prior incident was?"

Scarecrow winked his pulsing, red slit of an eye at Glinda.

She said, "Yes. I read about it in the Great Book of Records."

There was a long pregnant pause—until Caitlin broke it. "Well?"

Glinda winked at Scarecrow, who tilted the brim of his battered burlap hat low over his brow. He set his blade-thin, ruby eyes square on Caitlin.

"October 31, 2002," he said. "The birth of Caitlin Fletcher. Firstborn daughter of Harold and Evelyn Fletcher. Your arrival was the first domino tipped. The root cause of this entire calamity."

CHAPTER TWENTY-FOUR

BLACKBEARD HAD A GOOD, LONG WHEEZY CHUCKLE AFTER NATALIE finished her rant on buttheads and mind over matter. "Good god, lassie! Ya can ramble on longer than the mighty Mississippi."

After his laughter died down, he sat her back on the stool.

Thank goodness—mercy! No torture wheel!

Blackbeard got straight to the point. "Like I told ya, kid— ya *already* have the ability to control everythin' with yer mind. Ya just never knew it till now."

"When do we walk over the hot coals?"

Blackbeard went to the torture wheel and gave it a spin, as if to warn her about her dissing him or giving him more back talk. Natalie's eyes rotated as she watched the spokes whirl.

"How did I acquire this telekinetic power?" Natalie asked,

nervously watching the wheel spin from the corner of her eye.

"You was born with it," he said. "Everyone has it. Jus' that no one knows the secret about how to use it."

Her brow furrowed. "So why can't I put my hand through this wall?" She slapped an open palm against the wood-paneled wall. "See? Solid. Not a dent."

Blackbeard cackled with glee. "Ha! Ya proved my point, missy—mind over matter!"

She rolled her eyes. "Gimme a break. How's that proof?"

"I'll tell ya. I says ya believe that bleedin' plank o' wood is more powerful than yer mind. Right?"

"Duh."

"It ain't. Not even close." He narrowed his eyes and leaned forward until he was so close his nose hairs almost touched her face. "But ya *believed* it was, *before* ya tried to put yer hand through it. And because ya believed it was, yer mind made it so. Yer crooked presumption passed the power over to the damn wall! Just like that. Presto! Mind ruling over matter! And that's why ya couldn't pass yer hand through it."

Apparently this cadaverous buccaneer is out of his mind.

She folded her arms. "That's utterly ridiculous!"

He sneered. "Back on the rack ya go." Blackbeard snatched her by her underarms and hoisted her onto the torture wheel. The old pirate fastened her four limbs to the four leather straps, positioning her like da Vinci's *Vitruvian Man.*

He leaned in close, going nose to nose with her. His breath

still reeked of cheap rum and stale blood. And this time, a few nose hairs did tickle her cheek.

Ugh!

"Now listen up, smart-arse. Ya just said 'that's ridiculous.' Right?"

"Your hearing's up to par."

Blackbeard tightened a wrist strap.

"Owww—you're hurting me!" Natalie cried.

Perhaps it's time to tone down the sarcasm.

Blackbeard wagged a finger in her face. The tips were rust yellow and stank like tobacco. "Can't help yerself, can ya, lambkins? First ya say it's ridiculous, 'cuz ya doubt what I'm sayin' and ya just can't believe it's true."

He pulled down hard on one of the wooden spokes, sending the wheel into a spin. The blood in Natalie's head went for a rollicking ride, round and round in her brain.

"Then ya gotta talk back like some hard nut 'cuz yer concerned for yer safety, worried for yer life. So ya pretend to be a barracuda to hide the fear flutterin' like windblown sails in yer belly. Then ya go and throw fake piss in my face, tryin' to escape. And all's I'm tryin' to do is reveal a great secret to ya." He stopped the wheel, but that didn't stop Natalie's vision from whirling like a windmill in a windstorm. Blackbeard then cruelly spun it again—but this time in reverse.

Whooooooooooooooaahh!

Her stomach spun like wet laundry in a dryer, and her head felt moments from exploding.

"And yer fightin' me the whole time like a bloody naysayer,"

Blackbeard ranted. "That's all ya do, naysay and naysay. And this is why a half-pint like you can't get what I'm tryin' ta tell ya."

His blurred face circled by, over and over, as she spun like a human roulette wheel.

"And this is why ya can't control yer mind the way ya'd like to. It's yer doubt, little bird. Yer problem ain't with mind over matter. Yer problem is the doubt in that noggin o' yers. Now I'll tell ya why."

Blackbeard finally stopped the unholy twirling contraption. He gave Natalie a moment to catch her breath and regain her balance and bearings.

The undead buccaneer retrieved one of the jugs of water sitting on the floor by the wall. He moved to her and held it to her mouth. "Drink."

She gulped a few hearty mouthfuls. He pulled it away.

"Thank you," she said.

"Will ya listen now?" Blackbeard asked.

The water had made her queasy, though, and she was still too dizzy to answer, so she nodded.

"Okay, now I'll tell ya the big secret," he said with glee. "Shine the light of a lantern through a sheer red curtain— what color comes out the other side?"

"Red."

"And Bob's your uncle!" Blackbeard said, pleased as rum punch. "Ya see, the only way to control the world is to control the mind of the people living in that world. Ya need to manipulate the mind in order to hijack it and pirate all of its power."

"The Enchanter?"

"Yep. The undisputed Lord of the Curtain."

"How does he do it?"

"Just told ya. Alls ya need to pilfer the power of the mind is a curtain."

"What kind of curtain?"

He winked. The pirate seemed pleased that her curiosity was stirred.

"The mind shines *certainty*, same as the lantern shines *light*," Blackbeard said.

"Certainty about what?"

He almost hugged her. "Atta girl. Now yer askin' smart questions. Certainty in yer mind's ability to control matter. I'm referrin' to yer conviction. Yer trust. Got it?"

She nodded.

"Good. Now, what ya don't know is that certainty is yer birthright, little lambkins. You was born with it. Ya always had it."

"I've *always* had the power to manipulate matter?"

"Yep. And not just you, kid. Everyone. In every kingdom. In every world. But if ya slip in a thin curtain of doubt, yer mind shines *doubt* instead of certainty out the other side. Are ya gettin' this?"

"I think so."

"Ya think? C'mon, pop tart, it's simple. Don't make me spin ya on that rack again. Same way the lantern goes red when ya hang up the red curtain, yer certainty turns to doubt when it passes through the curtain of doubt in your head. Happy becomes sad. Calm turns to fear. Yer natural-born optimism becomes pessimism. If yer mind is tricked into believing that the wall is superior, the mind will use its own power to *make it superior*. Done! Blindsided. Now ya doubt yer command over the world. Ya doubt yerself. And ya give away all yer power."

Blackbeard squinted as he waved his grubby finger at her.

"And ya know what's happenin' the entire time, lambkins? Yer doubt makes ya feel so dang smart when yer right, so darn clever when ya taste it. But it's a sucker punch, I tell ya. All your boneheaded cynicism. All that thick-skulled skepticism. It's only the curtain distortin' yer thoughts and foolin' ya. Put there by the Lord of the Curtain. But it sure tastes flippin' good when ya feel—don't it?"

Is my mind really self-sabotaging its own power?

If all this is true . . . the freaking Lord of the Curtain is a genius!

Natalie's doubts had *always* tasted delicious. They made her feel smarter, bigger, better, when she proved someone else wrong. Or when Caitlin complained that she always sucked the joy out of a situation by pointing out all the potential problems. Her mind found it easier to believe the worst and was quick to embrace a negative notion over a positive one. Always compelled to expect the worst instead of the best, the bad instead of the good. She had never stopped to wonder—until right now—why pessimism was such an easy state of mind to attain, while an optimistic view was so dreadfully difficult to achieve. Was it really all a clever con designed to keep her in the dark, powerless to matter, subservient to the physical world? She had never considered that a cynical outlook could be rooted in something external. A projection into her mind by some devious force—or a filtering curtain. A simple curtain that was blocking out the light of truth and only allowing the darkness of doubt to shine through.

"So that's it? We're all prisoners to the pessimism of the Enchanter's curtain?"

Blackbeard smiled craftily. "Yep, unless. . . ." His pause was as scheming as his smile.

She was definitely curious to know what that *unless* meant.

Could this world actually offer a way to banish all worry, skepticism, and anxiety?

And that's when she felt a painful twinge in her heart, an ache that almost brought her to tears.

Caitlin's fears.

Her anxieties.

Her big sister had built a world of torment all around herself because she empowered her fears believing in their tangible existence. And Natalie had never been sensitive to the pain Caitlin had felt, or to the dark force that she had surrendered herself to. Of course, that was *if* what Blackbeard had just said was true.

Aha—there's the doubt again!

Wow. Remarkable. Extraordinary.

If she believed that Blackbeard was misguided, if she doubted his words and was certain that none of what he had said was true, her mind would manufacture a reality in which

Blackbeard *was* wrong, and that all this mind-over-matter stuff was certifiably untrue!

Self-fulfilling prophecy on steroids!

This could drive one to madness.

I have to find out.

"Unless what?" Natalie asked the pirate.

A gleam lit Blackbeard's eyes as he spoke in a whispery tone thick with intrigue.

"Unless there's a way to free ya from the dark, devious force of the Red Spectrum."

No more curtain?

Nothing to limit the pure, raw, consummate power of the human mind?

Blackbeard cackled. "Ha! That mischievous gleam in your eye tells me ya wanna know more."

She knew she had to play it cool. Nonchalant. He couldn't know that she was so psyched that she was ready to blow a gasket. She responded with a calm, affirming nod.

"Atta girl. But first you nap. I need ya well rested. Lemme fetch ya a blanket and mat." He got up to leave, but then stopped. He turned and pointed a sharp finger at her. "Better not be any piss in a bucket when I get back. Ya hear?"

That reminds me. . . .

"Actually, I really do have to pee now."

"Good god, yer a handful. Bucket's in the corner. Help yourself."

"What about some food?"

He chuckled. "Don't think you'll eat the ghoul's grub that

I eat. Lemme check the galley. I might have a bit o' cheese and some porridge for ya."

He left, locking the wooden door behind him.

Natalie sat there on pins and needles, anxiously eyeing the filthy, unhygienic bucket that was probably crawling with all kinds of germs and pathogens linked to all kinds of infectious diseases. She muttered to herself, "Here goes nothing!"

CHAPTER TWENTY-FIVE

CAITLIN, GLINDA, TIN MAN, AND SCARECROW HAD HIKED ACROSS jagged rocks and broken stones, trekked around felled logs and weathered boulders. Then they crossed a parched land-scape of rotted buttercups and dying daisies. And throughout the entire stretch, a contemplative Caitlin had been as silent as the hushed passage of time.

Suddenly, she asked, "What does my birth have to do with this whole zombie affliction?"

Scarecrow put his arm around her as they walked. "The Lord of the Curtain needed another human to help him, but not just *any* human. He needed someone with a level of fear and anxiety never before seen in human history. Someone who had *never* activated their own free will to resist fear. Someone robotically enslaved to believe negative thoughts."

"Sounds like someone I know."

"Indeed it does. The Enchanter can harness that robotic mind by gaining control of one of the mark's possessions."

"My wand." Her dumb toy wand, which had acted as her security blanket. She always took it with her to help cope with her fears.

"Exactly. And because it embodied your inability to express your free will, he was able to transform that wand into the scepter, which robbed our world of *our* will by creating the curtain filtering out the Green Spectrum. That left the Red Spectrum unfettered, free to rule over our thoughts and command our actions."

Glinda nodded. "And the zombie affliction was born."

They had just arrived at the entrance to Zeno's Forest.

The ominous, blue-tinged woodlands buzzed with new life. Caitlin did not remember seeing so much of it the last time she was there.

As they stood on the edge of woods, Caitlin heard familiar sounds: the *pitter-patter* of small animals scrabbling up trees, the whisper of swaying branches.

She felt a twinge in her chest as she remembered the perplexing laws of motion that governed the mystifying place. They reminded her of Natalie. According to the weird laws of motion in the forest, the farther one's destination was, the quicker the arrival would be. Which meant if you were set on traveling to a distant kingdom, light years away, you'd get there bright and early the next . . . *moment!*

Totally bizarre.

Likewise, the shorter the distance, the longer it would

take to reach one's destination. Which meant that if your true objective was to travel a mere centimeter, it would take eons to arrive.

For that paradoxical reason, Zeno's Forest was used *exclusively* for commuting to unimaginably faraway worlds.

But the real technology underlying Zeno's Forest lay in one's own conviction, one's own certainty in the desired destination—and the capability of the forest to be able to transport you there lickety-split. If you doubted your destination or questioned the efficacy of the laws governing the wooded terrain, you could get stuck for eternity among the trees. Ugh!

And with that dreadful, doubtful thought in her mind, and without a word of warning, Scarecrow seized Caitlin's hand. The trio was suddenly hurtling through the time-transcending, space-bending forest.

Streaks of blue, brown, and green moved past Caitlin in liquefied walls of blended color as if she were jetting through some kind of psychedelic, transdimensional tunnel. Scintillating flashes of fruity orange, citrus yellow, and lime green colors brought spots to her eyes as she held them open. She didn't want to miss a moment. The old Caitlin would have slammed her eyelids shut. She would've mobilized every muscle in her body to keep from looking. But not now. Not this time. Now she absorbed the wonders of the hyperscreamin' mode of travel—all of which ended mere seconds after it had begun.

Whoooooomp!

She tumbled to a stop by rolling into a cold bank of snow not too far from Scarecrow. He hurried to her side, offered her a hand, and pulled her to her feet. Her palms were cold and clammy.

Caitlin glanced at her surroundings. They had landed in a towering, mountainous region that appeared to be some sort of mythical, magical snowscape—like an otherworldly rendition of the Swiss Alps.

Having trekked through so many realms of gloom and gray, the sudden blinding white of snow and brilliant glare of ice invigorated her senses. Except, neither Caitlin nor her companions were properly dressed for such a high altitude. Her stomach knotted, and she quickly fell short of breath.

"How high do you think we are?"

"Two thousand, one hundred thirty-seven meters," Scarecrow said.

"How can you be so precise?"

The straw man pointed to a sign that read: Altitude 2,137m.

The cold touch of air moved through the woven fabric that covered Caitlin's skin, raising goose bumps. Her teeth were already chattering and her limbs trembled as she reclaimed her footing. She was calves deep in snow.

"We must hurry through these parts," Scarecrow said, "or the cold will have our last breath of air."

A frigid wind scraped across Caitlin's cheeks like sandpaper. Despite shivering, she was still able to marvel at the mountain's densely powdered snowfall, tree trunks shellacked in ice across a snow-drifted landscape, brilliant blue frozen lakes, and magnificent naturally formed ice sculptures that could have been displayed in a museum of modern art.

There were soft curtains of snow breezing along the mountain ranges. The skyscapes between the white-capped peaks were not the usual dreary haze found elsewhere in the dying fairy-tale universe. They were milky white from the teeming snowflakes carpeting the air.

Caitlin walked over to the edge of a soaring mountain ridge. The view from the great height was breathtaking: a veritable oasis of virgin snow and blue ice that was surely cold as death yet as alluring as fresh, homemade vanilla ice cream.

The next closest mountain ridge lay about a hundred meters directly across from Caitlin. In between was a steep, fifty-meter drop. A death drop, no doubt.

Caitlin peered over the edge. Her stomach churned and she became light-headed.

A steamy thermal hot spring bubbled at the bottom, circular in shape. Its circumference filled the entire gulf between the two mountain ridges. Fiery sparks ignited on the surface of the hot springs when snowflakes landed in the simmering water. The larger the flakes, the more luminous the flashes.

And then there was the bridge connecting the two mountains.

The bridge!

The bridge that was heartlessly narrow and diving-board thin.

The bridge made of pure ice. Slippery ice. Crystalline ice. Slabs so transparent you'd surely be convinced you were walking on air—if you dared cross it.

Those thermal, flammable hot springs continued boiling away beneath the bridge like volcanic lava sizzling in the bowels of hell. Not only would the fall kill you, the acid springs would incinerate you on contact.

Has anyone ever had the courage—or stupidity—to attempt crossing such a perilous bridge?

As if reading her thoughts, Glinda pointed to a squiggly, bright yellow line of ice trailing off back into the mountains behind her.

Frozen pee. Apparently *someone* had considered crossing, but they'd gotten cold feet. Caitlin was grateful they wouldn't have to contemplate such a treacherous challenge.

"We need to cross this bridge to reach the Twin Mountains," Scarecrow said.

A freight train derailed in her stomach.

"Not a chance," she declared defiantly as she waved a finger at it. "It would be sheer suicide to try to cross that . . . that *horizontal popsicle!*"

"Should've brought a pair of skates!" Glinda said. Apparently she wasn't keen on slip-sliding across the oversize icicle either.

Caitlin scanned the terrain. "There must be another way to get to the other side."

Tin Man brushed away a shimmer of snow and gestured toward a deep cleft in the rock, farther down the ridge they were standing on.

"There's a portal inside that cleft," Tin Man said. "You're free to use it to return home."

Home?

"Just enter the portal," he continued, "and you'll be transported back to your world. To Copenhagen, Denmark. The grave of Hans Christian Andersen."

How freaking tempting is that?

Caitlin could still catch a train to London and meet up with Jack at Mount Cemetery in Guildford. She could call Barton and enlist his help as well. She could return with an army to help extract Natalie from this vile place.

But then again—

"What happens to Natalie in the meantime?" Caitlin asked through chattering teeth.

Scarecrow removed his battered burlap hat. He calmly shook off the snow that had accumulated around the brim. He planted the hat back on his head, angling the brim downward to shield his eyes from drifting snowflakes. He spoke in a sardonic tone. "You can return next Halloween, when the portals reopen."

Caitlin sighed.

Suddenly, red band urges attacked.

An ungodly hunger seethed in her belly. The whiteness of her environment suddenly glinted maroon. Her senses intensified as she felt the redness overcome her—a certain animal instinct of survival and untamed urges—the kind she might even enjoy if she thought she could control it.

But then the worst possible urge overcame her. She felt the desire to close her heart and do the unthinkable. To take a life. To tear the living flesh off the bones off a dying creature, or—she struggled to resist the vulgar notion—to consume another human being. She could feel it clawing in her stomach. Ravenous, insatiable. An inhuman yearning. The moral line between decency and depravity began to blur.

She had witnessed Glinda feeding in secret when they had first left the witch's castle. Crouched behind bushes, gnawing on a rodent. Glinda was struggling. And yet she had managed to be tender and restrained when she'd tasted Caitlin's blood. With stark horror, Caitlin realized she would not have been able to reciprocate the tenderness.

"Witch's brew!" she cried out.

Glinda pulled out the thermos and handed it to her. Caitlin gulped down a single swig, then waited for the nausea and hunger to pass.

She took a deep breath as the white returned to the snowscape. Her eyes locked with Scarecrow's.

"Let's go get my sister."

Scarecrow tightened his gloves. "The bridge will only hold one at a time," he said.

"We'll draw straws," Glinda said. "Short goes first; longest goes last." Scarecrow picked a handful of straw from his shoulder and held it in his gloved hand. Everyone but Tin Man reached forward and pulled a straw.

Scarecrow drew the shortest, Glinda the longest. Caitlin's straw was smack in the middle.

Tin Man suddenly began hypermelting, a rather miraculous feat considering the frigid temperature. He pooled into a silver puddle of liquefied tin. Scarecrow set the glass vial on the snow, turning it on its side. The silver fluid moved to fill the vial, moving quick, like liquid mercury.

Scarecrow corked and pocketed the vial. He backed up a few meters and then did something utterly insane.

Scarecrow ran full tilt, with reckless abandon, toward the bridge.

Seriously? Is he out of his mind?

The man of straw glided across the narrow tract of ice at full speed. He displayed balance, dexterity, and skill worthy of a world-champion snowboarder.

He slid off the other end of the bridge and onto the next ridge, landing softly in the snow. He rose up and dusted off the white flakes.

He made it look so easy.

"Do not—I repeat—do *not* attempt that!" Scarecrow shouted with a stern face.

Oh really?

"My agility and proficiency with movement far exceeds everyone else's. My brain was able to instantly calculate wind velocity, surface interaction friction, acceleration, drag, and other influencing factors involving kinetics and kinematics. This allowed me to adjust my approach accordingly. Attempt your own crossing with unrestrained care and caution."

No kidding.

Scarecrow poured the vial of silver fluid onto the snow. Within moments, Tin Man reconstructed himself out of the pool of silver.

"Guess I'm next," Caitlin said.

Glinda glanced up at the sun. Then she surveyed the snowy mountains and checked her wristwatch. She turned to Caitlin.

"Mind if I go next, sweetie?" Glinda said.

Caitlin was in no hurry to cross the icicle. "Be my guest."

Glinda blew hot breath on her hands and rubbed them together vigorously. She got down on all fours and said, "Pardon the ungraceful posture."

She began to crawl, slow and purposeful, over the narrow belt of ice.

Luckily, the winds were velvet soft. And somehow, Glinda seemed to keep her traction on the slick surface. But then the beautiful Sorcerer of the South burst into tears.

Caitlin quickly saw why.

Glinda's undead skin was sticking to the ice, leaving a fresh trail of frosted blood prints—fingertips, palms, and kneecaps. Despite her pain and whimpers, Glinda crawled onward, bravely and bloodily.

Two more crawling strides forward, and again a palm got stuck to the ice. But this time she couldn't detach it from the surface.

Then came an ominous rumble: the kind of rumble that portends imminent disaster.

Scarecrow saw it first. He pointed to the high ridge on the adjacent mountain.

Everyone looked. Everyone heard.

Avalanche.

The heaving roll and tumble of ten million tons of snow on the neighboring mountain sounded like warring gods of thunder. The effects of that avalanche sent turbulent gusts of snow barreling in their direction.

Glinda began rocking her hand gently, back and forth, to and fro, to loosen it from the ice. Then she yanked with all her strength, and her hand tore free—but the snow winds came hard and fast.

There she was, stranded thousands of meters high, out in the open air, balancing on a tenuous, slippery slab of ice.

The first blast of snow blew by.

And just like that, the wind gust carried Glinda right off the bridge.

She fell like dead weight, plummeting through the air.

She splashed into the hot springs below in a violent combustion of colored flames.

Caitlin watched, slack-jawed, as the terrible blaze quickly died and the bubbling hot springs calmed to a simmer.

Scarecrow wailed. Tin Man howled. Caitlin gasped.

She was gone.

Red bubbles of hot gas rose from the springs.

Just then, something compelled Caitlin to peer over at the adjacent mountain ridge to her right.

Her eyes widened.

Perched high atop a thick tree branch, a mysterious dark shape with a duffel bag was watching her prepare to cross the giant icicle bridge.

Who is that? And is that a body bag over his shoulder?

"Caitlin, hurry!" Scarecrow cried out.

She had to shut down the shock and sorrow of Glinda's demise. She had to focus on finding Natalie. She had to cross the bridge—now.

When the last gust of snow from the avalanche brushed by, she inhaled a full breath of mountain air and held it deep in her belly. Then she delicately stepped onto the narrow block of ice.

Her toes curled under to help her feet grip the slick surface.

She raised her arms for stability.

To maintain her balance—and her wits—she didn't dare look down.

She heard the repressed sobs of Scarecrow and Tin Man as they urged her to continue. The mere fact they were encouraging her onward, still focused on the mission, was revelatory to Caitlin. Their commitment to her well-being and care for her safety filled her with the strength to persevere through her shock.

She glided on her front foot and shoved off gingerly with her back foot, sliding her way forward. Arms spread wide. Tilting left. Angling right. It was like walking a high wire, which would've been easier.

Something Natalie had once told her sprang to mind.

Slipping on ice was second to traffic accidents as a cause of accidental death.

And that's when her left foot slid out from under her.

She wobbled. Flung her arms in a desperate attempt to regain balance. She teetered on the edge of the bridge . . .

A crosswind buffeted her back up and she managed to find her footing.

She stole a quick glance at the mysterious figure perched on the tree to make sure he was not coming after her. The figure glanced upward. She raised her eyes to see what had caught his attention.

Crows were winging across the sky.

Thank God—not Janus!

A black bird suddenly dive bombed, kamikaze style, into the thermal springs below her. The crow vanquished in a plume of black smoke and red flames.

"Oh my gawd! That crow killed itself on purpose!" Caitlin cried.

"Keep moving!" Scarecrow shouted.

More red bubbles filled with hot gas began to rise from the hot springs. They floated upward. The ones that rose high enough reached the underside of the bridge and burst in puffs of red steam that reeked like a backed-up septic tank. The bursting bubbles began melting the bridge.

More birds began dive-bombing into the springs, causing more hot gas bubbles to rise and melt more of her ice bridge. Droplets of ice fell back down into the spring, igniting more sparks as they struck the surface—and causing even more hot bubbles to rise. And as more hot bubbles rose and burst, the melting process accelerated.

"Hurry!" Tin Man screamed. "They're trying to melt the bridge."

Each step made Caitlin's heart stop. She anticipated an inevitable collapse. She was barely a quarter of the way across. She shook her head bleakly. It didn't look good. No matter how gentle her movement, each step forward sounded like jumbo peanut shells cracking under her feet. The sound of fracturing ice echoed off the hillsides like mocking laughter daring her to take another step. She felt destined to suffer the same fate as Glinda.

A strange feeling urged her to glance behind her toward the cleft in the mountain. The cleft that could lead her to the grave of Hans Christian Andersen. And back home.

A million glittering snowflakes swirled by the cleft's entranceway, forming a shimmering apparition. The shape of a young woman crystalized in the cell-like particles of snow floating in the air. She was a beautiful woman in a long, flowing, royal white coat trimmed in luxurious blue fur. A tiara glinted atop her head. Strands of white pearls bejeweled the lapels of her coat.

Through the blur of wet snowflakes, her complexion looked cadaver pale. She had gorgeous high cheekbones and smoky black circles around her eyes. Her lashes were frosted, and her irises were a crystalline violet, indicating royal blood.

The Snow Queen?

She blew a kiss to Caitlin and summoned her with a gentle wave.

"Come home, Caitlin. I'll take you!" Her voice was like a ribbon in the wind.

Caitlin's insides twisted like braids. She could continue crossing this perilous bridge and risk falling, or she could return home and risk losing Natalie.

Hairline cracks were veining along the ice.

The sheer weight of her body would shatter the bridge in a matter of moments, seconds.

More like nanoseconds.

Her body would splash into the springs and the liquid would disintegrate her flesh and bone.

Was it from a movie? Or a TV show? Caitlin couldn't remember, but she recalled a technique that might delay the collapse of the bridge.

She lay facedown gently on the ice, spreading her arms and legs to distribute her weight across a wider area.

But don't touch the ice with your flesh!

Her body burned from the cold.

She tenderly shimmied forward.

She caught sight of something out of the corner of her eye.

Another crow.

This one was not on a suicide mission. It flew in at a low angle, homing in on her.

The flask.

She pulled it out and swung it hard at the bird when it swooped by.

A good hit!

Unfortunately, it was also a good hit for the crow. The crow had stabbed her left eye with its beak.

The flask of witch's brew fell into the spring. Another flash of fire.

Caitlin's eye stung with the bite of barbed wire.

Ice cracked behind her. Pieces of the bridge began to fall away.

Keep moving forward.

She snaked along the melting surface. Polar-cold puddles were seeping through her clothing, soaking her neck to toe.

She slithered past the midpoint. Shivering. But steady. Skimming forward.

I can do this!

And then the bridge began to splinter in *front* of her.

The mockery cut like arctic wind.

You gotta be kidding!

She stole a peek back at the cleft. A cruel gust of wind burst the Snow Queen's apparition into a shower of random snowfall.

Mockery has no mercy.

She heard the final fatal cracks, like the roll of a snare drum capped off by a cymbal. *CRASH!*

The icicle bridge was no more.

Crystal shards of ice rained down into the hot springs like gleaming daggers.

There was horror in Tin Man's scream. "Caitlin!"

Blasts of cold air pressed hard against her face as she plummeted toward the boiling waters.

I'm so sorry, Nat. I tried.

The dark figure on the tree had already knotted a rope to his branch, already wrapped the free end around his wrist. With a dagger in his teeth and the duffel bag still strung on his back, he took a daring leap off his tree branch.

He swung across the gulf—*swooooooooosh*—and snatched Caitlin clean out of the air.

Thuuuump!

They landed atop a soft drift of snow on the next ridge.

Scarecrow ran over to where the man had set Caitlin down in the snow.

"Use the knife to take the eye," Scarecrow instructed the man.

"Who the hell are you?" the man responded.

Scarecrow's eyes sizzled red. "Take the eye—*now!*"

The man drew his blade and moved it swiftly toward Caitlin's face.

"Aaaah!" she screamed. "What are you doi—"

Before she could finish her sentence, her eyeball had been severed from its socket.

Oh my gosh—they're butchering me!

Caitlin's cold cry reverberated across the mountains.

Green, puslike fluid oozed around her eye socket.

She had one eye left, and with it she recognized the face of the man who had cut her eye out.

She gasped.

Derek Blackshaw! *Gruncle* Derek Blackshaw!

It felt as though her entire world had just fallen out of its orbit.

"It's poison," Scarecrow said. "Venom from the crow. A few more minutes and it would've seeped from your eye cavity to the brain, eating away at it until the skull became an empty shell."

"Toss the eyeball," Scarecrow said to Derek. "It's toxic."

Gruncle Derek threw it into the hot springs, where it spit up a thin blue flame and a burst of smoke. He wiped the blade of his dagger in a drift of snow, the rivulets of blood icing up.

He grabbed the back of Caitlin's head with one hand, her forehead with the other. He titled her head downward. "In that case, if you prefer living, hold still, young Cait."

The remaining globules of green mucus poured out of her socket, pooled on the chilled ground, and formed a top layer of frost.

Derek grabbed a fistful of wet snow. He packed it inside Caitlin's vacant eye socket to freeze the area. Combined with her state of near-shock, which had an analgesic effect, Caitlin's pain became manageable.

Scarecrow pulled the bandana off Derek's head. He handed it to Derek, along with his own suede glove. "Patch it."

Caitlin felt like she was having an out-of-body experience as she watched her Gruncle Derek ponder a moment. He gave Scarecrow a reassuring nod. He took his dagger and cut a circle of suede from the glove's backside, then punched two holes on opposite edges. He threaded the bandana through the suede. Then he wrapped and tied it around Caitlin's head, fashioning a makeshift eye patch.

She was emotionally numb.

"Well, young Cait, it's a drag ya lost an eye, but ya look like one helluva swashbucklin' pirate now."

She was shivering cold. "H-how d-did you g-get here?"

"Followed ya after those bloody winged fiends left the house. Chased ya all the way to Forest Lawn."

"I s-suppose you b-believe me n-now."

"Never said I *didn't* believe you." Derek turned toward Scarecrow.

"And who are you?"

"Scarecrow."

"That's bloody blatant. But what's under that Halloween mask?"

"Straw."

"Are you off your chump? Okay, Mr. Straw, what's your interest here?"

"To help Caitlin."

"Help her what?"

"Live."

"That goes bloody double for me as well. But why are you made up like a walking dead Scarecrow? And who was the poor lass that lost her life?"

"We've been infected by the blood of the living dead. We're from Oz. The girl we lost was Glinda."

Derek's eyes widened as he cast a haunted look at Tin Man and Scarecrow. "My deepest condolences. So you're the genuine article. From the Land of Oz."

"T-told you so," Caitlin said, trying her hardest not to think about what had just happened to her eye.

"How many times must I tell ya, young Cait? I never said I *didn't* believe you."

Gruncle Derek turned to Scarecrow. "I take it my great-niece is also infected, which explains her pasty complexion."

"Yes," Scarecrow said. "Now, please take Caitlin and go with the Tin Man." His nostrils flared as he snorted like a fiery bull. "I'll take care of the crows."

The mountain ranges resounded with a perverse symphony of caws. A black ocean in the snow-swept skies swarmed above.

This is Hyde Park all over again.

Hundreds of thousands of black birds began to descend like a mile-wide, sky-obstructing meteor.

Seven large, distinctly humanoid shapes led the flocks of birds.

"Janus," Scarecrow whispered to himself. He shouted at Derek and Tin Man: "You're out of time!"

Derek swung the duffel bag from his back and passed it to Tin Man. "Careful with it, mate. She's heavy." He lifted a shivering Caitlin, cradling her in his arms.

The last time she had been held like that, she was around Natalie's age. Ten or eleven. Her dad, Harold Fletcher, had carried her in from the car after she'd fallen asleep in the back seat. Her dad had done that quite often. Her eye grew moist.

"W-what's in that d-duffel bag?"

Gruncle smiled. "A few conveniences."

Scarecrow had turned toward the legion of incoming crows. He gallantly raised his arms in preparation for battle.

Derek fled behind a galloping Tin Man, dashing over crunching snow, Caitlin nestled tight in his arms. The snow was still packed tight in her eye cavity, numbing the pain.

She glanced back.

Scarecrow's arms lashed at the air in a methodical pattern. Sizzling blue arcs of lightning flashed from his fingertips, and blazing red firestorms shot from his eyes like jumbo Roman candles on the Fourth of July. His saw blade-cutting voice screeched out a bone-rattling war cry.

"Yawwwwahhhhhhhhhhhhhhhhhh!"

A *scare*crow indeed.

The straw man battled valiantly, bombarding murders of crows with pyrotechnics. Colorful explosions lit the heavens. The skies were aflame with recurrent flares of burnt orange, neon purple, and lime green. The shots hissed, whistled, and fried the fowl to a crisp.

Despite the dazzling aerial detonations, and despite the incineration of battalions of birds, Scarecrow was vastly outnumbered. Hundreds of crows managed to breach the "firewall" in ghastly fashion; many offered themselves as a sacrifice to the flames, allowing Janus and his crowmen to pass through narrow air pockets in the colorful combustion.

Tin Man and Derek Blackshaw picked up their pace, tracking along a narrow trail that disappeared down the side of the mountain. The last thing Caitlin saw back on the ridge was Janus and his crowmen rolling on the ground in a cloud of smoke, dampening their flaming garments.

Tears trickled from Caitlin's eye. Poor Scarecrow. He was shriveling beneath a monstrous black wave of fiery feathers. Throngs of smoky crows flitted about, their beaks full with straw.

My God, that man of straw just saved my life.

And Gruncle Derek just saved my life.

And poor Glinda lost her life!

I'm alive, and yet there is so much death around me!

So much death . . .

Caitlin succumbed to exhaustion and fell into a feverish slumber.

CHAPTER TWENTY-SIX

THE TEMPERATURE HAD BEEN GRADUALLY WARMING AS THE FOUR-some slogged to lower altitudes. Caitlin's fingers kept grop-ing for an eyeball no longer in its socket. Instinct. She had to settle for fidgeting with the suede eye patch while coping through the trauma of losing an eye.

Despite the thawing environs and milder climate, she was shivering, still wet from ice melt and frigid from skin to bone.

"We're l-late for the m-movie," she said. "M-mom's already there, and D-dad is decorating the apartment f-for the p-party. I think we're all invited. B-but not squirrels. N-no, not squirrels. S-squirrels and c-crows eat n-nuts and earth-worms, n-not party sandwiches."

Gruncle Derek still cradled Caitlin in his arms. He smiled at her solemnly. Then he called over to Tin Man, "Need a fire, fast. She's delirious—close to hypothermic shock."

The woodman made of tin cut a sharp left off the trail.

He led the group into woodsier terrain, where knotted willow trees stood dead or dying. They reached a small clearing and came to rest.

Tin Man drew his ax.

He swung mightily, severing thick, dead branches from a lifeless willow.

He collected the chopped firewood and leaned the logs together in a triangular shape. He gathered dry twigs, tangled brushwood, and other flammable tinder and built a small pile of kindling at its base.

Gruncle tossed Tin Man a box of matches. Tin Man struck a match and lit the kindling. The dead wood caught fire quickly, and in no time they had a crackling-good bonfire.

"The woodman and I will go keep an eye out," Derek whispered in Caitlin's ear as he gently set her down by the fire. "And my apologies for the unintended pun."

"I don't want to die alone in the woods," Caitlin said.

"You're not dying today. Now undress and dry your clothes. Keep close to the flames. Thaw your flesh; warm your bones." He unwound the long scarf from his neck and laid it like a blanket over Caitlin. Gruncle's eyes were flickering like lit candlewicks. He kissed her on the head.

He got up and went over to Tin Man. They whispered, but she could overhear their conversation.

"We lost a flask of witch's brew in the springs," Tin Man said. "It controls our appetite. When her hunger returns, there will be no way to restrain her. Or myself."

Derek's forehead creased. "If she dies of hypothermic shock, hunger will not be an issue."

* * *

A pack of fifteen werwulves loped along the moonlit land. The air was sand-dune dry, and choruses of crickets sang to the stars.

A spectacularly oversized moon was bright and full, gleaming gold like a comb of fresh honey. The lunar orb dominated the sky, looming an astonishing one hundred leagues in radius. It looked like a whopping moon pie that eclipsed the alien sky and filled the horizon.

That's the way the moon always appeared in these parts. There was no other place like it—not in any other kingdom, not anywhere, for this was where the Man in the Moon lived, along with the cow that leaped over the lunar sphere on occasion.

The lunar influences were heightening the werwulves' senses. The blood flow in their veins quickened, and their appetites magnified.

But the wulf pack wouldn't eat just yet. Finding the emergent portal was the priority for the group, as it was for all the kin-wulves hunting down the six other portals in neighboring kingdoms.

Werwulves were nearsighted creatures, but their long-range vision was sharpened by the full moon's influence. The pack's eyes smoldered red as they fixed their gaze upon the horizon.

These highly intelligent, biped carnivores had been searching for two days already. The pack stalked along weed-choked grasslands, led by their alpha male. As the mammoth-size moon crept along the horizon, one of the wulves caught sight of a rustic cottage off in the distance, the only cabin they had seen for leagues.

That had to be it.

The dwelling of the Man in the Moon.

Ribbons of moonlight revealed a cowshed adjoining the cabin—a good indicator they were in the right place. The cow that jumped the moon would be inside, which meant the portal would be inside that shed as well.

The werwulves discharged urine, staking claim to the territory and using the scent to mark the terrain for future navigation.

As they trekked toward the cottage, the alpha detected a worn metal sign fixed to the cowshed.

A spill of milky moon glow illuminated the name on the sign: Wolvercote.

The werwulves broke into a sprint, howling praise at the moon and signaling the news to their kin-wulves—and to the Lord of the Curtain.

One more of the seven budding portals to the nascent world of Eos had been uncovered. The ravenous pack would wait in the cowshed until the portal opened.

And then their invasion into Eos would begin.

Meanwhile, they would hope some stray animals or perhaps a couple of drifters should happen to pass through the area, so at least they would have something to eat while they waited.

*   *   *

Caitlin raised her eyelid. Buoyant spits of fire fizzled in the air amid the hissing sounds of burning wood and crackling bark. The maroon glow of dusk was sinking heavily into the horizon, casting shadows from thick willow trees.

Her clothes had dried in the campfire. They were warm and toasty, making her as comfy as a quilted mitten. She nestled cozily by the bonfire next to Gruncle Derek and the Tin Woodman. She felt her strength returning. She gently touched her suede eye patch. The pain in and around her eyeless socket still throbbed, but not as intensely as before.

Thankfully she wasn't hungry yet, but she was as thirsty as—

Whoa!

The trunk of a knotted willow tree suddenly seemed to have moved within a millimeter of Caitlin's eyeball. The bark was so close she feared it would scrape her retina.

Whoa! Whoa!

A split-second later, clusters of thick willows looked as distant as the furthest horizon.

What the—

Her remaining eye apparently possessed some kind of power-zooming focus.

One moment she beheld a wide panorama of the willow-treed landscape, then she zoomed in on a microscopic focal point, a macro close-up so extreme she felt she could practically have sucked acetylsalicylic acid from the willow bark.

Her lone eye seemed to possess a mind of its own. And all the rapid telescoping brought on a bout of nausea far worse than her worst-ever case of carsickness.

"Something's totally weird with my eye!" she said.

Tin Man leaned over and placed his metal hand on her shoulder. His touch was warm, soothing, despite the chilly turgidity of the tin.

"It's the witch's brew," he said.

"What's the connection?"

"Scarecrow answers the *what* questions."

He's unstuffed and unreachable at this moment!

She rephrased the question. "Okay, *why* is there a connection between the witch's brew and my auto-zooming, runamok eyeball?"

"Eye of the eagle. In the witch's brew. That's how the Wicked Witch developed her telescopic eye. When it influences *both* eyes, its power is balanced. If it concentrates into one eye, it's an . . . overload. Takes a bit of time to harness it. But you'd better hurry."

"Why do I see a funky translucent haze around you?" she asked.

"White or red?" Tin Man replied.

"White. Why?"

"Another side effect of the witch's brew. It's similar to an aura. White indicates truth is present. Red indicates deception and falsehood."

She smiled. "Built-in lie detector. Should come in handy."

"Are you getting hungry?" Tin Man asked worriedly.

Caitlin shrugged, hoping that by not admitting the inevitable she would delay it.

"I'm growing hungry as well," Tin Man said. "I suggest we get moving."

Derek shifted his body, settling into a more comfortable position by the fire. "Why the urgency? We're finally catching a bit of rest and relaxation."

Tin Man shrugged coolly. "I suppose we can sit here and sing campfire songs till the crowmen come and kill us. Or we can wait till our hunger returns—and then we can kill each other."

"Much prefer campfire songs," Derek noted. He pulled out his harmonica and played a few bars of the blues.

"Anyone have a favorite?" Derek asked.

Tin Man perked up when he heard the harmonica music.

Strange.

"What's your pleasure?" Derek said.

Tin Man didn't respond. Instead, his silver eyes danced and blinked like lights on a circuit board.

Then his whole face lit up like an oversize LED.

"I do have a song request," Tin Man announced.

Derek nodded. "Bloody good. Let's have it!"

"Play C and B sharp."

Derek rolled his eyes. "Do me a favor, Woodman."

Tin Man explained. "There are rumors coming out of Neverland and Treasure Island—reports about new plant life. Vegetation. I've been contemplating this phenomenon for some time. An intriguing notion has just occurred to me. It could be the nightingales of Neverland."

"You mean songbirds?" Derek asked.

"Yes. Treasure Island also has a sizable watch of nightingales. I wouldn't be surprised if their birdsongs were composed of the musical notes C and B sharp."

Derek smiled. "Impressive. Ever thought about being an ornithologist?"

Caitlin interjected, "Why are those musical notes important?"

"The frequency of the seven musical notes equate to the seven wavelengths of color."

"I never knew that," Caitlin said. She sat up, excited by where Tin Man was going with this.

"The C and B sharp notes just *happen* to correspond to the color green," Tin Man said.

Caitlin fist-pumped the air.

Nice work, brainiac.

The Tin Woodman continued, "Perhaps this is the nightingales' way—or nature's way—of crying out. Of compensating for the lack of the green wavelength in the sun's rays. It's the only logical explanation as to *why* a delicate bloom of life has occurred on those two islands. "

Caitlin jumped to her feet. "Tin Man, I don't give a whoop-de-doo if you think you don't know *how* to get us to Neverland. This is *your* world, kemosabe. Find a friggin' way."

"I can only tell you *why* we need to go there," he said

matter-of-factly. "I cannot tell you *how* to get there. It would be a case of the blind leading the blind. By the way, my stomach's growling."

"Mine too," she said.

Not good.

"And I'm thirstier than a salmon in the Sahara."

Panic time.

"Tin Man, do something! Wing it if you have to. We can't just—"

"Caitlin, I already told you, even if I attempt—"

Derek interrupted the back and forth with another riff on his harmonica. Then he leaped to his feet. "Young Cait, keep your hair on. Tin Man, put a sock in it. And both of you, calm bloody well down! I know you're both hungry. And I know those black-feathered fiends are hunting us down right now. But I know something else as well."

"What?" Caitlin asked.

The campfire flames twinkled in his eyes like glowing twin embers. His grin was downright wicked. "I know how to get to Neverland."

Jeepers creepers!

Gruncle Derek waved a finger, admonishing both of them. "But never, ever, tell a soul what I'm about to tell ya."

CHAPTER TWENTY-SEVEN

OLD EX-ROCKER GRUNCLE DEREK REFUSED TO ELABORATE ON HIS mysterious secret till he fully established his whereabouts and charted a course to their destination. Getting there was a priority.

"Where are we headed?" Caitlin asked as they traveled over a wide stretch of rough grassland rife with tangled weeds. The moon was still visible in daylight in these parts— but more impressive was its monstrous size and nearness to the horizon.

"We need to find Dead Man's Cove," he said. "If we make it there by noon, we can hitch a boat ride to Neverland."

"So how do you know all this?"

Something distracted Uncle Derek before he could reply. A hesitant look crossed his face as he pointed dead ahead.

A murky river, fairly wide and relatively calm, loomed in the distance.

"That there might be the Dragon Bite," Derek muttered. "If it is, we'll need to cross it and follow it till the river meets the sea. There we'll find Dead Man's Cove and our ship."

"I'm parched," Caitlin said. "I need to drink something first."

"It's all grassland, young Cait."

"No. I see a cabin. Way over there, to the left."

Sure enough, there was a rustic cottage with an adjacent cowshed. It was the first dwelling they had come across for some time.

"They gotta have running water, or a well," Caitlin said.

Derek's eyes lit up. "That's good. I've been through here many times. That place belongs to the Man in the Moon and the cow that jumped over it."

Caitlin rolled her eye. *The Man in the Freaking Moon? Leaping cows from nursery rhymes? Is he serious?*

"Are you serious?"

"As a surgeon with a scalpel. Because it means that river up ahead *is* the Dragon Bite."

"Well, I'm heading over to the moon cow first—to milk it dry. I won't make it anywhere without something to drink."

Caitlin started off toward the cottage.

"'Ang on a minute," Derek called out. "You're looking at a ten-minute footslog. And another ten back. We'll miss the last ship."

Tin Man wagged a finger. "And if you drink the cow's blood, your cravings will double."

How did he know I was going to do that?

"And then we end up hungry instead of thirsty."

"Then we're really in a pisser," Derek said. "Our man of tin is right. Let's keep at it." He summoned her back with a wave. Caitlin huffed grudgingly and followed them onto the trail toward the river.

"Why's it called the Dragon Bite?" she asked Tin Man.

He offered a deferential bow and hand wave, ceding the *why* question to Gruncle Derek.

"Bloody creek is crawling with Alligator Snapping Turtles," Derek said. "Big bastards. Heads ugly as dragons. Prehistoric. Jaws quick as a cobra. Catch a bite, and you'll need a crowbar to pry open its bleeding jaw."

Derek massaged his chin as they approached the river's edge. The water was murky and the river channel was narrow and curvy. Acres of tall pines canopied the other side for as far as the eye could see.

The air smelled damp and earthy, but also slightly sweet thanks to the fruity fragrance of nearby honeysuckle vines.

"Ready to ferry 'cross the Mersey?" Derek asked.

"Oooh, me first!" Caitlin shouted, raising her hand. Her brows then sharpened into two daggers. "Are you freaking crazy? I just got dragged *out* of a river. And this one's poop brown and thick as a turd. We'll never see those turtle dragons coming."

"Snappers aren't fond of humans," Gruncle said. "They tend to keep away. I think we're good to cross."

"I'm only half human."

He shrugged. "Good point. Still gives us a fifty-fifty chance of getting out unscathed."

Gruncle Derek and Tin Man exchanged wary looks. Derek hoisted his duffel bag onto his shoulders. "Okay, Tin Man. Move your tin arse."

Tin Man and Gruncle tentatively waded into the Dragon Bite River.

They held their arms high above the surface, out of biting range; their eyes scanned the river right to left, left to right, ahead, and then to the rear.

Caitlin shook her head in dismay as she watched them. Then she flapped her arms, rattled her legs, and exhaled, going through motions of a swimmer loosening up before a race. Gruncle and Tin Man were already waist-deep in the river.

She reluctantly followed them into the turtle-turd soup.

The river was unexpectedly warm. It smelled like the bathroom at home after Natalie had binged on chili dogs.

Caitlin eyed the water for sudden ripples or air bubbles— indications of incoming dragons.

"Tell me what's really going on," Caitlin shouted ahead to Uncle Derek as she waded out of the shallows and into deeper waters. "How do you know all this?"

"You must swear silence," he hollered back.

"You have my word," Caitlin said.

"Young Cait, you're not the only Blackshaw descendant to cross over into this world. I've been here many times."

Oh my gosh!

"Really? Why?"

"Started with me baby brother—your Bobby Gramps."

"What happened?"

"Remember I told you about our band and gig in America?"

"Yeah—Bobby Gramps got good and wasted the night before. Fell and hurt himself. Nearly died."

"Yup. Suffered a career-threatening injury. Lost the use of his guitar hand."

"Right. But you said it healed. He learned to play guitar with his other hand."

Derek glanced back at Caitlin, smiling and proud. "Best damn guitarist there ever was."

Tin Man stopped abruptly.

He fell silent and signaled with a raise of his arm. Caitlin and Derek froze.

A subtle breaking wave passed in front of them, as if something was swimming beneath the surface.

Caitlin chewed her lip. She saw air bubbles.

Tin Man gave a gentle half-turn back, nodding to Derek and Caitlin.

"Snapper!" he whispered.

The trio stood motionless in the river. The ripple passed them and moved up the river channel.

Tin Man pointed forward, indicating it was safe to continue.

Gruncle picked up where he left off. "Do you know what a pact with the Devil is?"

"Duh! Selling your soul."

"Well, me brother ransomed his."

"To the Devil?"

"To the one they call the Lord of the Curtain. That fiend had paid a *visit* to Robert 'Bobby' Blackshaw."

"How?"

"Only a human can open a door to the other side. Me brother opened one such door, one night in Scotland."

"You mean while indulging in one of his bad habits?"

He nodded sadly. "That slimy serpent promised to heal me brother's hand—bring him renown and fame—provided he ransomed his soul and birth order."

"Birth order?"

"Your grandpa was the second born. Your good old Gruncle Derek is the firstborn. The Enchanter and Bobby Gramps struck a bargain: new hand and newfound fame in exchange for the souls of the second-born descendants of Bobby Gramps."

Caitlin felt a chill on her neck. "My mom was the second child in her family."

"That's why the Enchanter snatched Evelyn from Mount Cemetery in Guildford on Halloween night. Came to collect his ransom. That inhuman ghoul-maker needed another real human. Specifically, he needed a human mind. It's the only thing more powerful than he is. His bargain with Bobby got him that."

"Why would Bobby Gramps do such a thing?"

There was a crack of heartbreak in Derek's eyes. "He

wouldn't. Me brother had a generous heart. A nurturing spirit. He was soft like a baby's blanket."

"So what happened?"

"Deception. Thought he was only ransoming his *own* soul. In his desperate state, the poor bloke never read the fine print on his bargain. According to the deal, if he died before his thirtieth birthday, his line of second-born descendants would also be ransomed. Your grandpa died two years shy of his thirtieth birthday. Ever since, he's been enslaved somewhere in this world to that bloody Bugger of the Curtain. Me brother will never know peace unless I can find him."

Caitlin bowed her head. "Natalie is the next second-born ransom."

"I don't have to tell ya, young Cait, that we need to end this. So listen good—"

Tin Man stopped again, arm up, a finger pressed to his lips. "Shhhhhh."

A ripple of water with air bubbles . . . another alligator turtle lurking beneath the surface.

Yesss!

The snapper turned and swam upriver.

Caitlin gestured for her gruncle to continue.

"The only person who can protect or liberate a ransomed second-born and break the Devil's bargain is a firstborn child."

A cascade of emotions engulfed Caitlin, and scattered thoughts swirled in her head.

Derek continued. "Remember the question you asked me that night in Glendale, when we first met?"

"A question about what?"

"Your Grauntie Gwen. Your mom's older sister."

"I asked you what kind of birds struck the car that killed her. You said it was either ravens or crows."

"It was crows, young Cait. You understand now? The firstborn protects the second born. Also the third and fourth. 'Cuz the firstborn is the seed of all the children born into a family. And when an apple seed sprouts, the seed always remains part of the apple tree, nourishing it. Once Gwen was removed from this world, your mum became vulnerable to the Enchanter. All it takes is one face-to-face meeting with him. He is too overpowering to resist. Natalie is the second born. You're her protector—while you live."

"Oh my God, it's all on me now!"

"Quite right, young Cait. But it's *also* partly on your Gruncle Derek."

She grimaced, embarrassed that she was only thinking of herself and Natalie. She had totally disregarded the painful ordeal her Bobby Gramps and gruncle had already been going through all these years.

"And that's why I've been coming here," Derek went on. "To find me brother and emancipate him from this wretched covenant."

"But that was, like, over fifty years ago!"

"Yup. Went searching for him after he passed in sixty-nine. Because I knew his second-born child would also be next. Your mum. But it's been like looking for a needle in a haystack. Countless kingdoms to search."

"I don't want to spend fifty years of my life looking for Natalie."

Derek didn't respond to her comment. He simply continued wading across the river in silence. The sudden quiet was like a blow to Caitlin's gut. It almost winded her. But Gruncle Derek's next comment was the real knockout blow.

"I'm quite prepared to spend the next hundred years searching if I have to . . . because, well . . . I luv me brother, and that's what siblings do."

Caitlin's eyes no longer searched the river for snapping turtle dragons.

She was too busy searching inward.

CHAPTER TWENTY-EIGHT

THE WERWULVES MOVED BY THE LIGHT OF SUNFIRE REFLECTING
off a sterile moon. The lunar globe generated no light of its
own—it was forever dependent on the daystar for its light,
just as the undead wulves were reliant on the Enchanter for
their red-band luminance.

The roaming, fanged carnivores were of the Slavic species: tall, two-legged, and vertical in posture. Hunger propelled their every movement.

They were known for their supernatural speed, even when
chasing their prey on two feet. They were gifted with clair-
voyance and familiar with the ways of sorcery.

These wulves garbed their bodies in black leather, believing in leather's occult capacity to arouse the arcane forces
that swirled in the sunless, starless, bleak regions of space.

This species was also of princely blood; they were descendants of shape-shifting human royals who had once ruled

over distant kingdoms. But they now preferred to manifest as werwulves, and embraced the cold breath and blood of the living dead.

Vestiges of their human ancestry were still incarnate in their anatomy. Their facial features, for example, looked like a genetic fusion of man and wulf.

The Slavic pack of wulves was in pursuit of the Pantheon portal, their gateway into Eos. They had recently heard about the recent Wolvercote discovery from their kin-wulves. And just hours ago, in quick succession, more portals had been found: Patcham, Headington, Lazerev, and La Madeleine. Along with Great Crosthwaite and Wolvercote, that made six.

This pack would be the one to secure the final, seventh site.

After Wolvercote was found, the Lord of the Curtain had dispatched a hundred more wulves to that site—and a thousand more to the other portals.

The impending incursion into Eos would be a large-scale invasion. Lethal. The anticipation bathed the tongues of the wulves in salty saliva.

They homed in on the Pantheon portal efficiently, their second sight facilitating its quick discovery.

Now they waited for the human creature to open up all seven portals.

CHAPTER TWENTY-NINE

"BLOODY HELL!" DEREK BLACKSHAW'S PAINED WAIL SENT A SHIVER down Caitlin's spine. His body twisted in the river. "Damn dragon turtle's got me ankle."

A swirl of blood rose to the river's surface.

Tin Man disappeared under the water. Derek winced, his face anguished and pale.

A moment later, that dragon turtle was rocket-launched out of the river. It soared into the sky like a fired missile.

Tin Man splashed back up to the surface. "He'll bother us no longer."

Gravity soon brought the alligator turtle splashing back into the river, dead as ash. It floated on the back of its shell.

Caitlin grimaced. Never had she seen such an ugly creature in all her life. The head was hideously reptilian and pre-historic, like something out of a Japanese monster movie, its

skin ridged like an alligator's. Its fangs were still red with
Gruncle Derek's blood.

Derek wiped sweat from his brow. His breathing came
hard and heavy.

Luckily, the river met the sea just up ahead. Caitlin could
see wooden docks and the tall masts and sails of various ships
docked at Dead Man's Cove.

The trio picked up its pace, her gruncle in obvious pain as
they silently waded through the water.

They reached the shoreline. Derek staggered out of
the river, Caitlin and Tin Man in tow. Gruncle's limp was
severe. He pulled up his pant leg to check the bite. The wound
appeared to be deep, down to the bone.

He hobbled over to a tangle of dead trees, then broke off
a long, sturdy branch and used it as a cane.

"I'll be fine," he said. "We must find a boat straightaway."
Leaning on his cane as he limped, Gruncle Derek led the way.

The twinge in Caitlin's heart turned doubly painful, and
she got choked up.

Watching her gruncle persevere like this made her sad.
And watching him hobble with the cane stirred the memory
of Jack. He had also needed a cane last year, when his tibia
bone had broken through the surface of his skin. The memory of a wounded Jack and Caitlin sailing on a moonlit sea,
sharing their first kiss, now seemed like a lifetime ago.

The smell of dead fish suddenly hit her full in the face.

They had reached the wharf. Seagulls with glowing
red eyes plunged beneath the waves that lapped against the

seawall, emerging with beaks loaded with squirming, black-eyed fish. The fish seemed unaffected by the Red Spectrum. Slatted wooden planks stretched across logs that protruded vertically from the ocean floor. Ships, one more ominous-looking than the next, were tied to these moorings. There were three-masted carrack ships, brig warships, schooners, two-masted brigantines, fluyt cargo vessels, and galleons.

But, like everything else in this world, the ships were in a state of decay. Their sails resembled bedsheet ghosts—disembodied specters billowing in the shore breeze. The wood of the hulls appeared to be rotting and worm-infested. Caitlin hoped they weren't to the point of being unseaworthy.

"What kind of ship are we looking for?" Caitlin asked.

"Pirate ship. Brigantine."

"With real pirates?"

"If they haven't shoved off yet."

"Is that safe?"

"Ha!" Her gruncle laughed. "Sometimes the safest place is in the company of armed and dangerous men."

Derek led the way down the dock. He stopped by a ship bearing two masts and ragged, ghostly sails. Caitlin counted at least ten cannons emerging from its sides. Sure enough, the skull and crossbones flapped in the wind atop the boat.

Is this the Jolly Roger?

Derek slapped the side of the wooden vessel.

"Ahoy!"

"Wait," Caitlin said. "Do you know these guys?"

Before Uncle Derek had a chance to answer, a head-kerchiefed, mustached, toothless man slid down a rope dangling from the ship's mast. He landed on the deck before them. He was pale, and his eyes were bloodshot.

"Blimey, mate," said the toothless man with surprise. "S'good to have you back."

"Good to see you," Uncle Derek said. "Meet my lovely young niece, Caitlin. Caitlin, Billy Bones."

"Nice to meet you, Miss Caitlin," Bones said as he strode down the plank to shake her hand.

Caitlin nodded with a smile and shook. "Likewise."

Bones's hand was Eskimo cold.

"Any member of the Blackshaw clan is a friend and crew member of mine. Come aboard." He pointed to Caitlin's missing eye as she climbed the plank. "Nice patch. We'll make a buccaneer of you yet." Bones's curious eyes found Tin Man.

"And the silver lad?"

"The Tin Man, from Oz," Derek said.

"Shiver me soul," Bones said as he shook Tin Man's hand, "Come aboard, mate."

Tin Man smiled. He tailed Caitlin as she boarded the vessel. Derek began hobbling up the plank last. Bones saw the limp.

"Gout?"

"Nah. Caught a bite in the river."

"Snapper?"

"A bloody ugly one."

"Better yer ankle than yer arse!"

Derek smiled as he reached the deck. "Don't suppose this vessel will be sailing anywhere near Neverland Island?"

Bones slapped the mainmast. "That's *exactly* where she's headed." He winked and said, "You know, they party every night on that island. Some good tail there."

Derek gestured toward Caitlin, scowling at Bones.

The pirate cringed. He cleared his throat and said, "Lemme fetch ya some biscuits and rum."

"I'm in desperate need of water," Caitlin said.

"I'll fetch a mug o' that, too." Bones scurried off.

Caitlin rubbed her stomach as nasty, gnarling sounds burbled in her belly.

Uh-oh.

Her hunger was beginning to surpass her thirst. But she wasn't going to mention that to her gruncle or Tin Man. No point. If they didn't make it to Neverland in time, she and Tin Man would go completely blood-eyed and, as Gruncle Derek would say, Bob's your uncle. No reason to agonize over it and heighten tension during the boat ride.

Gruncle Derek, meanwhile, was surveying the main deck. He inhaled a lungful of air and turned to Caitlin. "I'd tell ya to catch yourself a whiff of this ocean spray, except it stinks like dead trout and undead pirate."

Caitlin sort of envied the undead pirates. They weren't blood-eyed or even half blood-eyed. They were *normalized* ghouls, like the royal-blooded princesses. They could get by on somewhat regular food—like biscuits and hot spices—whereas Caitlin's palette was limited to entrails with a side order of cartilage.

And she was getting hungry.

CHAPTER THIRTY

Natalie slowly raised her eyelids, then stretched her limbs and body from head to toe. She had just woken from her nap. She smiled because it felt more like she had woken from a long, heavy, mesmeric sleep. She felt refreshed, recharged, and just really, really good.

Until she realized something about the floor. . . .

And the space around her. . . .

Nothing was moving. Or swaying.

Which meant she was no longer on the water.

No longer on a boat.

Then where am I?

She bolted upright. Her eyes strained as they swept her surroundings. She was inside a dark cavern—a bare-bones bunker with gray walls of rock. The only object in the room was a heavyset red quartzite slab of rock. It was flat on top, about knee high, and set in the center of the space.

And the only source of light was a thin band of recessed lighting running the length of the curved walls. The source of the light seemed to be pale-blue sunlight seeping in from somewhere.

She heard soft humming, barely audible. She couldn't identify its source.

The air temperature seemed pleasant enough, perhaps a touch on the cool side. And the air smelled like fresh ozone and fresh summer rain—sweet and pure with a subtle hint of musk.

A murmur of warm air erased the light chill around her.

She rubbed her arms to warm them.

Then she had second thoughts about that.

She had an eerie feeling.

She wasn't alone.

She scrambled for a door.

She circled the room, palming the walls and searching for an exit. The walls were completely smooth. There was no door. Anywhere. Only walls. And that thin band of faint blue light.

But it wasn't electric light. It was indeed a razor-thin crevice in the wall where sunlight was leaking in.

There were no windows.

No obvious way for anyone to enter or exit the space.

It felt like she was trapped in a child's riddle.

What kind of room has no doors or windows?

A mushroom.

Lame.

She thought perhaps that zombie pirate had fed her hallucinogenic mushrooms, and now she was in the middle of some kind of loopy, paranoid, delusional head trip?

She remembered another riddle.

A girl is trapped in a room that has no doors or windows. There's only a basement. But the walls and floor are not breakable. And yet she manages to escape. How?

Hmmm.

She tabled that riddle and moved on to a different riddle that she recalled.

She smiled.

This one might provide a way out.

I'm all alone in a house that has no doors or windows. I have to get out. Where am I, and what am I?

Easy . . .

A baby chick in an egg.

Bingo! That's it!

Natalie hauled ass, running full force into the wall.

BAM!

Ouch!

The walls were bone solid.

I think I dislocated my shoulder.

Just as she was about to go into full panic mode, she heard footsteps.

They were coming from . . . everywhere.

Huh?

The sounds were bouncing off the circular walls, making them impossible to source.

She knew she had to get out of there.

How did that other girl in the riddle escape a room without doors or windows and with unbreakable walls?

Natalie's face broke into a smile gradually and triumphantly. And after checking to see if her solution to the riddle was correct, her jaw dropped to the floor in horror.

CHAPTER THIRY-ONE

THERE WERE SIX PIRATES ON THE SHIP THAT CAITLIN COULD SEE, and they were all scurrying around preparing the boat for launch. One of them, the muster gunner, went by the name of Crabbit and he had long dreadlocks that were almost as long as Caitlin's hair.

But where was the captain?

"Who's commanding this vessel?" Uncle Derek shouted boldly, as if reading Caitlin's mind.

As if on cue, the door to the hull swung open and the captain emerged. He wore a three-cornered hat with a feather and a shirt with billowy sleeves that spilled from under a leather, lace-up vest. A heavy leather belt harnessed a long sword that hung over black leather pants, which hugged the shape of his muscular legs. His face was chiseled, with a strong jaw and nose. Dark eyes dripped danger, but in a sexy, rock-star kind of way.

And there it was, at the end of one sleeve, in place of a normal hand: a gleaming, polished, iron hook.

"Behold!" Gruncle Derek said. "Our notorious master and commander, Captain Jas. Hook."

Caitlin's knees went weak. Even in the body of a forty-something-year-old, he oozed charisma. Unkempt hair fell perfectly into grungy place, and shaded spectacles rested on exactly the right spot on his nose. He seemed the type that didn't give a damn what anybody thought about him, and by that, he set the bar. His confidence stirred something in Caitlin.

Captain Hook approached her and Derek. With lively eyes and an impish grin, he removed his hat and bowed like they were royalty.

Then he glanced up at Caitlin. His smoldering eyes were like doubled-barreled cannons taking aim at Caitlin's virginal innocence. She was square in the crosshairs.

"Captain Jas. Hook at your service, milady. How can I please you?"

His voice was saturated with charm, as if his vocal cords had been dipped in sugar.

"That's my kin, Hook!" Derek warned.

Hook's eyebrows arched as his eyes rolled to Gruncle Derek. "Oh. I beg your pardon, Blackshaw. My apologies." His eyes shifted back to Caitlin. "Well, then, let me say that it's a genuine honor to meet you, my fair young maiden."

Caitlin's jaw locked. His very presence and deep eyes stirred her insides like a sorcerer stirring his magic potion.

She nodded and curtsied.

Did I just freaking curtsy?

The captain stuck out his hook, and Caitlin shook it. It was smooth and electric warm, but the tip was a sharp spike.

"And who's our metallic guest?" Hook asked as he eyed Tin Man. "Wait, don't tell me . . . 'tis the woodman of tin who gained a heart?"

Tin Man smiled and said, "'Tis I. And I believe prior to your captainship of the *Jolly Roger*, you were formerly boatswain under the command of the infamous Blackbeard?"

"Aye," Hook replied with a nostalgic gleam in his eye. He extended his arm. "Well, me hearty from another kingdom, let tin meet iron so we may formally exchange pleasant greetings."

Tin Man reached out his silvery-white hand and shook the iron hook.

"Welcome aboard the *Jolly Roger*. Make yourselves comfortable."

The captain then nodded to the group. "What's your business on Neverland?"

"Quick detour," Derek said. "The Tin Woodman thinks the song of the nightingales there might heal some of their blood-eyed affliction."

"Aye—a precious blessing that would be. And if it does?"

"We're off to the Twin Mountains of Velarium," Tin Man said. "If they exist."

"Of course they exist," Hook declared. "And someone has clogged up the water arteries inside that mountain. Which is why my crew and I, and all of you, are pasty-skinned and gluttonous as ghouls. There's your proof of their existence."

"Some say Blackbeard is the one that dammed the water," Tin Man said.

Hook's eyebrows went crooked. "I've heard the same. That blasted buccaneer wittingly gave himself over to the Lord of the Curtain. That's where Jas. Hook draws the line. One thing to plunder a man's ship and loot his treasures. It's a whole other thing to pilfer his pancreas and loot his liver just to fill your own belly. Uncivilized, it is. Even ruthless freebooters have a moral code. For that reason alone, I'll sail you to the Twin Mountains myself."

"We need to find the shut-off valve and drain the summit," Tin Man said. "But no one has ever been to the summit to see where it's hidden."

"On the contrary," Hook responded. "That young, crazy bloke Peter Pan has. Before the affliction, Pan flew there often to swim and partake in Lord-knows-what other activities in the Dipping Pools. I'm certain he could provide a map to where this shut-off valve is hidden."

"Where do we find him?"

"The roguish lad throws a party practically every night. We'll be dropping anchor on the north side of the island. Make your way to the south side. You'll find him there. But forewarn your young maiden, Blackshaw—since the rise of the affliction, Pan and his merry mates have become quite the sordid bunch." Hook slid his good hand inside his coat pocket and drew out a small brass spyglass.

"Now, if you'll excuse me, I shall give the command to hoist anchor."

Hook paced away down the deck with authority, looking the undead sailors up and down, scrutinizing their every detail, while Tin Man, Caitlin, and Gruncle Derek took seats on the floor of the bow.

Captain Hook took command of the wheel and the *Jolly Roger* shoved off, speedily sailing away from the dock at Dead Man's Cove and toward the open sea.

CHAPTER THIRTY-TWO

NATALIE STARED, WIDE-EYED. HER MOUTH HUNG AGAPE.

She had solved the riddle. She felt shell-shocked.

The girl had escaped out of the room because, in addition to having no windows, no doors, and no breakable walls or floors, the room also had no ceiling.

Duh. The girl obviously escaped via the roof, or lack thereof.

When Natalie initially looked up after nailing the riddle, there was nothing but blackness where the ceiling was supposed to be. But then a bright purple light started flashing rapidly above her, like a warning. What made her mouth fall open was the distance to the flashing purple light.

As it flashed, the purple light began moving higher and higher still, until it reached an elevation so high it winked out of view. She figured it had reached to around twenty thousand feet. Perhaps thirty thousand—as high as the double-decker A380 she had flown to Los Angeles in from London.

Which is, like, more than a hundred times longer than my soccer field at school.

This made her feel as if she was looking up at the purple light from an abyss.

How did I get all the way down here? How will I possibly ever get out of here?

And where is that nefarious kidnapper who calls himself Blackbeard?

She screamed at full volume, throwing her voice upward.

"Hellloooo!"

The sound died fast. It did as much good as standing on a sidewalk and trying to call out to someone sitting above in a passing airplane.

Another soft breath of warm current circulated near her, erasing the chill in the air.

And again she had the creepy feeling she wasn't alone.

Wait. It isn't just a feeling.

She somehow *knew* she wasn't alone.

Who else—or what else—is in this room with me?

A grinding sound broke the silence. It groaned like a winch or a hand crank being turned . . . like someone was hoisting chains.

A deep, low rumbling began throbbing into the room, vibrating in her chest. Something big and heavy was moving.

I hope it's not hungry.

Whatever it was, the chains were pulling it along.

A dragon?

No.

A large part of the wall started receding.

There's a hidden door—the wall itself!

Natalie stepped away from it.

"How ya doin', lambkins?" the gravelly voice resounded in the room.

Blackbeard!

She was almost delighted to see him walk in. She shook her head and replied, "How am I doing? Well, the porridge was yummy, the cheese hard and moldy, I went wee-wee, but this time I almost filled the bucket with my real pee, and then I fell asleep. So how did I get down here?"

"I carried ya. Yer actually light as the feather in me captain's hat."

"You're not wearing a captain's hat."

"That ain't my point."

"And where am I?"

"Center of the universe."

That stopped her in her tracks.

"What's that supposed to mean?"

"Ain't supposed to mean anything other than what I just said. And I says yer standing in the center of the universe."

"Like, with planets and galaxies orbiting around me?"

"Yup—something very close to that."

"What do you want from me?"

"Nuthin'. The Lord of the Curtain wants to meet you. There are plans for ya. Royal plans."

"You mean that duplicitous offer to become a bona fide princess and ruler over the so-called Kingdom of Eos?"

"Aye." He seemed pleased that she remembered.

"No thanks. Not interested. I just wanna go home. And I'm not gonna meet that Enchanter dude either."

Blackbeard cackled. "Ha—more'n likely ya already did."

Her brows scrunched together. "What do you mean?"

The pirate's eyes went blade thin, his gaze cutting right through her. "Look, I didn't wanna scare ya none. But the Enchanter's here *now*. Been by yer side all along. On the boat, too. Standin' right beside ya this instant. Touchin' yer curly locks. Lookin' in yer pretty eyes."

Icy shivers ran from her neck to her toes.

Oh my gosh! The pockets of warm air, the feverish feelings . . . it was him!

"Why can't I see him?"

"The Enchanter ain't a *him*."

"Huh? You mean he's a girl? Or rather, *him* is a *her*?"

"Ain't no *her* neither."

"We're out of options here."

"The Lord of the Curtain is *everything*—and *everywhere!*"

"Why can't I see him—or her—or *it?*"

"The Lord of the Curtain is the red band in the sunlight. The red in the rose. The red in the rainbow. The red in yer blood. Can be visible or invisible. The Enchanter decides. The Enchanter can also be in two places at once. Or three places. Or four. This too much for ya, lambkins?"

Actually, it wasn't. It was fascinating but also frightening. Fascinating because the pirate was referring to the visible color spectrum—the red frequency. But it was frightening because it apparently involved the invisible part of spectrum—the infrared band.

Which is why she felt warmth but couldn't see him—or her—or, rather, it.

What chance do I stand against an invisible power? And does this mean that pervert saw me pee in the bucket?

She knew infrared light could also pass through physical objects.

This is a hugely unfair advantage, in addition being creepy to the bone.

She recalled a part of her conversation with the pirate back on the boat. "You said there's a way to get rid of the Red Spectrum? Your words—not mine."

His tobacco-stained teeth flashed as he smiled. "Now we're talkin'."

From the inside pocket of his long, burgundy-leather coat, Blackbeard pulled out a golden metal box, perfectly square. Purple-blue light escaped from the corners of the box, while white light leaked out from the thin crevice between the lid and base.

"What's inside?"

"Yer destiny."

CHAPTER THIRTY-THREE

Captain Hook steered his infamous brigantine ship over a light, choppy sea. From the deck of the *Jolly Roger*, Caitlin saw it in the distance, through the salty air, looming larger by the minute.

The legendary island of Neverland.

Her lone eye's telescopic power continued to intensify. Far distances had become sharper, more vivid.

She smiled as she considered where the vessel would soon be docking: the mythical Neverland from her childhood books. She wondered if it was really populated with sprites and fairies—notably Tinker Bell—and all the other colorful characters she had read about in the stories of J. M. Barrie.

Even in her half-zombified state, she still had not gotten used to the idea that these were all authentic places with tangible people—if you defined *authentic* and *tangible* as real things in a universe whose very building blocks were made of unbridled imagination.

She gazed ahead as Neverland drew near.

Snaggletooth mountains rimmed the island, rising out of the sea like the backs of giant serpents. While most of Neverland appeared burned-out and brown, there were places where plants and trees bloomed in a riot of iridescent color. Tin Man was right—new life was spurting in patches. A grand profusion of wildflowers clustered around the bases of the largest trees—trees that boasted green leaves and bore fruit. But apart from these few tracts of life, the rest of the landscape remained barren.

Caitlin's major concern was that they might not make it there in time to find the nightingale songbirds. A glaze of red was already beginning to shimmer over her vision, as if someone had inserted a red gel over her spotlight of an eye.

The sinful hunger was rising.

Which meant Tin Man was feeling the same way.

Which meant Gruncle Derek was in grave danger. The entire crew of the ship was in imminent danger, in fact. Imagine the shock at Neverland if the *Jolly Roger* arrived crewless and with decks awash in blood—Hook, Bones, Crabbit having vanished into thin air. Or, more accurately, inside Caitlin and Tin Man's digestive tracts.

A crazed Caitlin and manic Tin Man would be the only ones left on board, well satiated, picking morsels of food from their teeth, and primed to devour all the inhabitants of Neverland next. Her mind swam with all these ghastly thoughts and images, which seemed straight out of a low-budget horror movie.

Hey—where is the Tin Woodman?

Caitlin suddenly realized he was nowhere to be seen.

"Kill the lamps," Hook called to his crew as he leaned toward a setting sun. "We're ten minutes from anchoring."

Ten minutes too long!

First mate Billy Bones heaved the serrated mast to help the tattered sails catch the southern wind. Mr. Crabbit flung his tangled black dreadlocks out of his face and extinguished the gas hurricane lamps that hung from the posts. The southern wind filled the sails and began pulling the ship behind the rocks.

Tin Man suddenly emerged from the stairwell leading to the lower deck. He was accompanied by two buff and burly buccaneers with barrel-size bellies. They were cradling a set of thick iron chains—complete with manacles and iron collars.

Caitlin gulped. Her throat tightened after she swallowed. She knew what those weighty chains were for.

"We won't reach the island in time," Tin Man warned.

The two big pirates dropped the hefty chains at her feet, and they hit the deck with a ringing clank.

Gruncle Derek's eyes were suddenly wrought with grief. He watched Caitlin offer her up arms and legs. Tin Man sat beside Caitlin and did the same. The two strapping pirates proceeded to tangle the chains around their bodies and limbs, manacling their hands behind their backs, shackling feet by the ankles, and bolting the iron collars firmly around their necks.

The metal collar was cold and smooth against Caitlin's throat.

Gruncle Derek strode over to the ship's rail. He leaned against the edge and gazed at the reddening horizon.

How weird. How odd.

A new feeling was stirring inside Caitlin. It wasn't from the rising impulses of the Red Spectrum. Nor was it related to the crippling, claustrophobic chains that had rendered her immobile.

It was something else.

A raw hurt.

But not for herself.

She was hurting for Gruncle Derek.

It clearly caused him pain to have to watch her suffer, so he was forced to turn away. And the thought of being bound and chained like this would once have been an unthinkable, inconceivable nightmare for Caitlin. But the anguish she was now feeling was actually empathy for her uncle, and it exceeded the torment she felt at her own situation.

But then that hurt began to yield to a longing that rose from the pit of her abdomen. Her eyes felt as if they were hemorrhaging.

Tin Man's eyes also shone red. He grappled with his chains, shaking and flinging his body around in a futile effort to break free. His arms and legs were bound so tight he looked like a silver herring out of water, flapping about on the ground.

Caitlin was also succumbing to near madness as she tried to break out of her manacles. She almost broke her own wrists in desperation. She battled to retain her will to resist as foamy saliva dribbled from the corners of her mouth.

The next few minutes were misery, as she was unable to either service her hunger or move a limb.

And then the rolling deck of the *Jolly Roger* stabilized.

"Drop anchor!" the captain shouted.

The ship had arrived at Neverland Island.

The sun kissed undulating waves and they sent back a reflective, warm glow as they lapped against the sand dunes on the perimeter of the island. With the anchor safely down, the crew prepared to disembark.

Bones and Crabbit made their way over to Caitlin and Tin Man. Each pirate wielded a long metal pole with a grappling hook fastened to its tip. They snagged the chains around their necks. Then they carefully steered them off the *Jolly Roger*.

How demeaning!

But Caitlin was still grateful she was chained, because she knew if she hadn't been, she would take a life.

With both legs shackled at the ankles, she waddled down the plank. She whipped her head around almost robotically in search of someone to bite. Tin Man was growling like a rabid dog, his nose and mouth frothing with creamy-white foam.

She felt her humanity slipping away as she chomped at the air. And yet, because of those remaining strands of higher morality still inside her, she had the surreal feeling that she was watching her beastly body from afar.

Thank goodness for that long metal rod! It keeps the crew just out of my reach.

The island air was salty and clammy. Sea mist began to bead into droplets on Caitlin's brow and roll underneath her eye patch. A nagging itch in her eye socket intensified with the moisture.

Gruncle Derek briskly trotted down the plank and onto the sand dunes ringing the island. He cupped both hands behind his ears to amplify his hearing.

"Bloody good! I hear the song of the nightingales. Follow me."

"Hold on, Blackshaw," Captain Hook called from the deck of the *Jolly Roger*. "We'll meet you back here at the ship when you're ready to sail again. Meanwhile, the crew and I are off to partake in a wee bit of gallivanting."

Fins flapped in the lagoon adjacent to the *Jolly Roger*. Flirtatious giggling followed as a dozen or so alluring mermaids surfaced above the water and waved at the buccaneers.

Hook and his sea-roving robbers winked and waved back, and then unashamedly stripped down to their skivvies. They leaped overboard and splashed into the sea, swimming eagerly toward the lagoon and the promise of inexpressible pleasure.

"Find the damn songbirds fast," an anxious Bones called out, obviously keen to join his captain and crewmates.

"I heartily concur," Crabbit said.

CHAPTER THIRTY-FOUR

BLACKBEARD OPENED THE GOLDEN BOX. LIGHT POURED OUT. IT was so bright Natalie had to cover her eyes with her hands. When her pupils adjusted, she spread two fingers to take in the contents.

"A tiara?"

He winked. "Aye. Bejeweled with diamonds and sapphires. Magical stones."

"Who's it for?"

As if she didn't know.

"Certainly not I," he said. "But be warned."

"About?"

"Its power. Set this on yer pretty little skull, and the Red Spectrum vanishes like a ship over the horizon."

"Isn't that supposed to be a good thing?"

"If ya know how to use it."

"What do you mean?"

"Hold still."

Blackbeard gingerly lifted the polished diamond-and-sapphire tiara out of the golden box. Each stone glinted like star fire in a glittering sky. The tiara's twinkle and dazzle made the adolescent girl—who still secretly adored princesses and princes—completely giddy. The cerebral part of Natalie was also thoroughly taken by its breathless beauty, but only because she could fully appreciate the physics underlying the gems' internal dispersive reflection of light.

Blackbeard held the shimmering tiara reverentially over her head. "Ya ready?"

"Not really."

He set it gently upon her mop of curls. He twisted the two edges of the crescent-shaped tiara around some ringlets to secure it on her head.

"Bucket!" Natalie screamed in panic as her body temperature soared. Her head felt as heavy as an anvil. "I'm gonna throw up!"

The room began spinning far faster than she had experienced on the torture wheel. It felt like severe vertigo. As if she were home from school, bedridden with the flu, with a 105-degree fever. Suddenly, she stood up, inducing one of those horrible fainting-spell head rushes.

Natalie dropped to the floor.

Before she collapsed, she had the presence of mind to sit on her butt, arms extended, palms flat on the floor to stabilize herself.

"Don't panic, lambkins," Blackbeard said. "The red fever is just breakin'."

Perspiration pooled on her body, cooling her. She almost steamed because of her high temperature.

"I don't like this feeling!" she moaned.

"Ride it out, kid. It's worth it."

Do I have a choice here?

Natalie did ride it out. The profuse sweating cooled her body down, then it dried up as the fever broke. She began to feel wonderfully refreshed.

And then Natalie lost her mind.

There was no other way to describe it. It was as if a new mind had been downloaded into her brain—but her own identity was still intact. She felt like a perfected version of herself, one without any emotional baggage or complex hangups. There was no more pain or worry or uncertainty or fear. Nothing but unceasing calm and serenity and gentle peace of mind. And the most utterly remarkable phenomenon of all was that she was experiencing unspeakable happiness and euphoria for no good reason at all. As if jubilation was the default emotion for her operating system, as natural as breathing and as ever-present as oxygen.

The strangest part of the experience was a newfound realization, devastating in its truth. It was awakened by the stark contrast between her present awareness and her pretiara life.

She never knew until that very moment how much pain and grief she still had inside her. Pain and sorrow, repressed and unresolved—due to the tragic death of her mom, the sudden passing of her dad, and the emotional anguish her sister, Caitlin, had endured all those years. She thought she had cried it all out at the orphanage. But she realized now that was just total denial, a coping method to try to get past the bereavement as quickly and painlessly as possible. Her quips, comebacks, and her sassiness—sometimes they made positive contributions by making others chuckle and smile, but mostly they were defense mechanisms, distractions to conceal her own uncomfortable emotions.

She suddenly wanted to collapse onto the floor and let out the pent-up, inconsolable sobbing that she had subconsciously repressed—except the new feeling of contentment inside her would not allow it. Not in a suppressing kind of way. On the contrary. She had transcended the memory of the pain through a kind of enlightenment. This new awareness prevented any lessening of the uninterrupted happiness now coursing through her veins, filling her body, and saturating the depth of her soul.

And there was no more self-doubt about anything. Everything seemed possible. This was an extraordinary state of mind to possess, and—dare she say—a rarefied, superior level of consciousness. She knew she was now endowed with perfect conviction about what she could do—and what she would do next.

She walked over to the wall of solid rock. Her heart fluttered in anticipation.

She gazed into the rock . . . reached out her arm . . .

With the bare tips of her fingers, she tenderly caressed the surface. She couldn't contain the giddiness over the certitude of what she knew she would be able to do, and a giggle fell out of her mouth on its own.

And then she did it: she moved her five fingers right through the wall.

She passed her entire hand right through the rock, as easily as if she had been gliding it through water—but with even less resistance. There was less drag than water would have created. The wall somehow felt smoother than air.

She wasn't sure which was the more surreal and sublime feeling: her hand disobeying the rules that apply to physical matter, or her stunning conviction in its ability to do so. Her mind was suddenly the ultimate source of joy, and she was at a loss of words to describe how that felt.

The freaking pirate was right.

Mind over matter exists.

It always has.

I've always had this ability.

Now, her mind was unobstructed by the baggage of rational, skeptical, cynical, and doubting thoughts. The high-cal diet—of cynicism, skepticism, and egoism—was no longer being fed to her mind.

The tiara was neutralizing all red-band emotions. Filtering them out.

She moved her wrist through the wall . . . her forearm . . . her elbow.

Her eyes welled up with tears. It had become as clear as

transparent crystal that the wall of seemingly solid rock was as nonphysical, nonmaterial, and intangible as her own thoughts.

It's pure thought.

Blackbeard pulled her arm out of the wall. He gently lifted the jeweled tiara from her head.

He smirked as he pulled a pipe from his inside breast pocket and lit up. He puffed and exhaled, the tobacco smoke clouding around him. Natalie inhaled the spiced, woodsy aroma, and the scent brought her back to the corporeal world, back to her bodily senses.

"And that, little lambkins, was only a small taste," he said.

I cannot fathom anything more transcendent than this.

Natalie stared into his eyes. The internal dam finally broke, and the roll of tears and inconsolable sobbing came on strong. She really had no choice at that point but to yield to her pent-up emotions, so she ran into Blackbeard's arms. She didn't care if the sea-robbing scoundrel rebuffed her, strung her back on the rack, or killed her.

Because she needed to hold someone. Anyone. To cope with the tidal wave of grief that had been so layered deep inside her for so long.

CHAPTER THIRTY-FIVE

CAITLIN SLID HER SWEATY FINGERS BETWEEN THE IRON NECK COL-
lar and her throat. She pulled at its hinge. Of course it was
impossible to loosen, but just the gesture of attempting to
stretch it somewhat curbed her growing hysteria.

*Or is this neurosis being triggered by my creeping descent into
the world of the living dead?*

Bones and Crabbit led her and Tin Man into a dense
thicket of pines. They all followed Gruncle Derek, who was
tracking the song of the crooning nightingales.

There was no life where they walked, no movement except
for a low, billowing fog that obscured the forest floor they
trampled across.

And there's no fleshy food!

The spiritless stretch of island finally began to change
color, from listless gray to patches of lush green. Signs
of life accompanied the sweet song of male nightingales

broadcasting carnal desires to the females in the branches above.

Caitlin felt a pleasant tingling as the birdsong filled her. Her chest began to lighten.

The yearning for flesh—and Billy Bones—was diminishing.

Whatever was acting on her might not have been as potent as the witch's brew, but it sure tasted better.

Tin Man's deranged demeanor also softened to a soothing calm. His eyes shifted in color from lurid red back to nickel silver. The foamy secretions ceased seeping from his mouth.

Gruncle Derek broke into an impromptu Irish jig. "Bloody marvelous! It's working! Tin Man, you're a blessed genius!"

It took only minutes for civility to return to Caitlin and Tin Man, as the magic of the nightingale songs aroused sparks in the green band, giving them the ability to resist and diminish the cravings.

Bones and Crabbit unhooked their chains from the rods and unlocked their manacles. The two pirates then scurried off, eager-eyed, in the direction of the lagoon.

"Good luck, mates," they shouted in unison.

Caitlin massaged her neck and wrists as she watched the sun fall below the horizon. Dusk had set in. Now she had to find Peter Pan. He was the only one who could map out the location of the shut-off valve. Which meant he was their last—and final—hope.

Derek pointed to the south. "We head that way—to the far

side of the island." The group hustled on, tracking through shrubs and bush, past coconut palms and silver pine.

Night fell, swallowing the twilit sky as Caitlin's crisp, long shadow dissolved into the darkness.

A hazy, orange glow flared up in the distance.

Sparks from embers flew into the air like flitting fireflies, then quickly extinguished into coils of smoky trails.

A blazing bonfire and circles of lit torches raged on the beach up ahead.

Caitlin, Tin Man, and Gruncle Derek strode toward the flickering flames as the roar of revelry and rowdy partying grew louder. So did the beat of drums and notes of lilting melodies.

Caitlin walked along the sea's edge. Frothy night waves lapped up onto the sand, creating a curved line where wet met dry. The dry sand was soft and clung to the damp soles of her feet, while the wet sand was smooth and firm underfoot and made for a smooth walking surface. She alternated between walking on the wet and dry. The sensuality of this simple act took her mind off her traumatic close call with descending into a permanent living death.

Thick, humid air began to fill her lungs. It had an almost narcotic effect. The rhythmic drumming could be felt, pulsing, through the ground. Although they were still a distance away and the scene was obscured by thick reeds, Caitlin's telescopic eye allowed her to see the frenetic bobbing of heads and the impact of shoulders slamming into shoulders on a crowded dance floor of uneven sand. The movements were so vigorous, they kicked up a cloud of sand that rose to the knee. The music that carried them forward came from a drum circle—the innermost ring around the fire, where children and teens danced with tongues out. Some wore war paint and iridescent feathers. It appeared that one ghoul was somehow dancing while levitating three feet in the air.

Is that who I think it is?

They made it through the reeds and to the gyrating wall of dancers. But how were they to find Pan?

"Can you locate him?" Tin Man asked.

Caitlin's eye stared intently into the crowd, zooming and refocusing and scanning. . . .

Her concentration was broken by a harsh and jagged voice.

"Names?"

A young man about twenty years old stepped in front of them. He crossed his arms and blocked their path. He wore a vest woven from dead vines and a pair of shredded board shorts. Apart from the open vest, he was shirtless, muscular, and wiry in a zombie-surfer kind of way. Caitlin couldn't help but focus on the three hairs that sprouted from the middle of his chest.

"We're here to see Peter Pan," Derek announced with confidence.

"Ha," said the boy curtly. "Only the inner circle gets to Pan."

Tin Man muscled his way forward. "Excuse me," he said haughtily, "but we're on the list."

"Is that right?" The boy pulled out a clipboard and squinted at it intently. "Your names?"

Caitlin thought fast. She stared at the clipboard. Even though she could only see its back, it was as if her new eye could see right through it. She could read the names as clear as day.

"This is Jack Frost!" Caitlin said, pointing to Tin Man.

The boy sneered at him. "Since when is winter-white frost the color of silver?" he said.

Tin Man's eyes flared red in anger.

You sell it, Tin Man!

"When the color white is lacking the pigments found in the Green Spectrum," Tin Man said, "white becomes silver."

"And I'm Goldilocks," Caitlin interjected.

The boy narrowed his eyes. "So I suppose golden-blonde hair becomes auburn red when it lacks green pigments too?"

"Totally." She gestured to Gruncle Derek. "And this is Robin Hood."

Derek nodded.

The boy laughed and said, "Robin Hood, or Robin Hood's grandpa?"

"Just check the list," Caitlin said.

Surfer boy ran his finger down the sheet of names, muttering to himself as he found each one. "Jack Frost . . . Gold ilocks . . . and . . . Robin Hood. Okay, go on in." He gestured toward the fire. "Pan's in the center ring."

Caitlin, Tin Man, and Gruncle Derek strolled past the bouncer and into the first ring of the drum circle. Torchlights encircled the drummers, their flames setting the night sky ablaze as if it had been full of a legion of fire-breathing dragons. The torches were made from thick bamboo poles pitched in the sand. Lit bulrushes were set inside the hollow of the bamboos like wicks. They scented the air with the sweet, tangy smell of roasted animal fat. Caitlin's mouth watered. The savory smoke whetted her palate. She sighed, grateful the island's songbirds had tamed her hunger.

She moved among the partiers and drummers, absorbing the sights. She was right about the identity of the dude dancing in the air. He was performing some kind of mystic Arabian dance atop a flying carpet. An engagingly ghoulish Aladdin. His magic lamp was hooked to a belt that held up his shredded Arabian pants. He wore a tattered, open vest that revealed a smooth boy's chest smeared with red war paint.

Caitlin grasped Derek's hand tightly and made her way toward the innermost circle. Hot, humid wind blew across her face; the muggy weather made her clothes cling to her flesh.

The crowd was thicker there, dense with revelers. Bodily smells from sweaty boys cavorting all about filled her nose with a carnal essence she had never experienced in the prim and proper hallways of Kingshire Academy. Her hips began to move, and her knees bent in time with the hypnotic rhythm. Her body begged to dance, almost as if the hedonistic environment compelled her to do so involuntarily.

As she moved to the beat of throbbing drums, she passed a living-dead Ivanhoe and encountered a dancing, dead Romeo and Juliet. She stopped. She watched in awe as the star-crossed, living-dead lovers incorporated poisoned potions and plunging daggers into their performance.

First they circled each other, each reaching out a tender hand to touch the other's bleach-white face. Then Romeo pulled a glass vial from his pocket, took a swig, and fell to the sand, his face contorting, his body convulsing. As he lay writhing on the ground, Juliet pulled out a dagger. She drove the blade into her own chest. She collapsed too, and then smiled sinfully as Romeo sprang to his feet and helped her up to do it all again.

Gruncle Derek, meanwhile, had taken notice of a particular pirate pawing three girls.

"Well, I'll be jiggered," said Derek. "That's Long John Silver's new second-in-command—Israel Hands—with his filthy hands all over those three poor wenches."

"The wicked stepsisters of Cinderella," Tin Man noted.

I miss Cindy. I miss everyone.

Adjacent to the pawing pirate was a pint-size Tom Thumb. He was nibbling at the fingers of pint-size Thumbelina, teasing her with tender kisses and small bites.

Suddenly, a high-pitched battle cry rang out above the dancers.

Caitlin swiveled and found Gingerbread Man—needless to say, he looked good enough to eat.

He was balancing on a tall rock and beating his chest. Each blow sent crumbs and icing into the frenzied crowd.

Caitlin, Tin Man, and Gruncle Derek shoved their way

through the sea of slamming shoulders to reach the inner circle. The crowd grew denser. Caitlin climbed onto a rock.

She scanned the party grounds, then zoomed her eye dead-center on the innermost circle and its ring of torchlit drummers.

She found him.

The indisputable Peter Pan.

CHAPTER THIRTY-SIX

BLACKBEARD SEEMED FLUSTERED, AWKWARD, AND DEFINITELY uncomfortable as he held a weeping Natalie in his arms, her face buried in his shoulders.

He coughed. "Um . . . er . . ."

He cleared his throat. "Uh, look 'ere, little one. I says this tiara can dry all that wet from yer eye. I'll just set ya back down on yer feet, and we'll put it back on yer skull."

Natalie only squeezed him tighter. "I don't want to stop crying!"

He groaned. "Jeez, lass. I don't want ta have ta break yer pretty teeth or nuthin', but I can't give ya the comfort ya need. I'm tryin' to give ya somethin' priceless, I tell ya."

He wrangled her arms loose, unwrapped her legs, and then set her down on the floor.

Natalie wiped her soaking-wet face with both sleeves, one arm after the other.

She sniffled. "And what would that be?"

"The feelin' ya had when the tiara sat on yer skull."

"Yeah, well, now that it's *not* on my head, that memory is gone. All those feelings have been extinguished. So I'm not interested. I feel like it wasn't even real. Probably a trick. Like hypnosis or something."

Blackbeard snatched her by the shoulders and spun her around so that her back was facing him. He tied a bandana around her eyes, blindfolding her.

"What are you doing?"

"Givin' ya another taste." He positioned her hands behind her back. Roped them together.

The grinding pull of chains grumbled again, and the moving wall reverberated against her eardrums.

He's taking me out of here . . . but to where?

"Let's go." He pushed her from behind to get her moving. "Walk!" He set his grubby hands on her shoulders, directing her.

He led her out of the cavern, guiding her as they walked on what felt like cushions of air. It almost felt to her as if the gravitational field had been altered. He made a sudden right turn . . . then went straight . . . he turned her to the left . . . another left . . . straight. Finally, they curved in a half-circle. Then he spun her around twenty or maybe thirty times, so that she was beyond disoriented. She wobbled onward through more twisting routes.

Then something changed in a terribly strange way.

She walked about twenty more paces, and then her bodily

senses suddenly became so acute it defied description. She felt as if all the molecules and cells composing her body were augmenting all her faculties and powers of perception. These molecular, cellular impressions told her that she had entered what felt like a vast cosmic bubble the size of a sun. It seethed with celestial activity and teemed with both corporeal and disembodied intelligences.

They were floating toward the precipice of infinity.

How she knew all this, she could not say. But she was willing to admit to herself that the strange sensation might be nothing more than a mere fabrication of her own mind.

And I'm not even wearing the tiara!

Her skin tingled as if pricked by a million needles. Otherworldly sounds sent shivers down her spine. She heard a shrill, high-pitched tone accompanying a primordial bassy drone, haunting and grave. Flyby whirring and whooshing sounds evoked images of shooting stars, meteor showers, and other interstellar phenomena. Barely audible voices in various alien tongues seemed to be whispering across distant galaxies and through myriad spatial dimensions, amid the reverberating ringing of the spheres.

The aroma of ozone and fresh rainfall intensified, and she felt as if every pore in her body had been gifted with the sense of smell. As she absorbed all this, trying to make sense of it, Blackbeard lowered her head gently and helped her to step through a hatchlike opening.

The sounds, scents, and cosmic sensations vanished like a bursting soap bubble.

The atmospheric vibe in the new space was shockingly different—and familiar.

Robins chirping. Soft winds murmuring. And through the texture of the blindfold, she saw either the dim light of dawn breaking or the evening dusk.

The buccaneer slipped off her blindfold and untied her hands. The idea that she had arrived at a familiar place went swiftly out the window.

Natalie was standing in a dimly lit, fantastical forest. The trees were some kind of exotic species she had never seen before, and they smelled as sweet as marzipan. Some trees were double trunked, each sprouting its own set of limbs and branches. Some trees were even triple trunked. Other trees featured concentric coiled branches that reminded her of spiral galaxies, and some had branches growing in patterns that evoked fractals or snowflakes. There were trees bearing long branches that were braided, double braided, triple braided, and even quadruple braided. The sunlight refracting through the forest canopy painted the trees custard yellow, gingerbread brown, and kale green.

Wow!

And then there were columns of sinister-looking trees whose menacing branches reminded her of the arms and spindly fingers of bad men who did bad things to little children.

This was some kind of alien forest—alien even compared to Wonderland and all the places Natalie had visited the year before.

Natalie and Blackbeard moved deeper into the woodlands.

The forest floor was damp and soggy, but the air smelled of nougat.

Blackbeard put his arm out abruptly to stop her. "Shh," he said. "Hear that?"

Natalie heard a faint rustling. "What's that?"

"Signs of undead activity," Blackbeard said.

He lifted her over a muddy puddle and set her safely and cleanly on the other side, then pointed. "Over there."

The terrain took on a different smell. The sweetness was gone. The dusky smell of a dank basement entered her nose, or maybe it was more like the damp smell of the old camp trunk her dad had pulled out of storage after ten years. The smell grew stronger and more putrid as they crept along. Then a new smell wafted over. . . .

Wet dog!

Blackbeard stopped again and held perfectly still. He must have smelled it, too.

A faint, guttural growl rumbled beneath a pair of red, glowing eyes that moved toward them in the dim light. Slowly advancing, the eyes grew larger, brighter . . . and then they narrowed. A husky figure some seven feet high appeared before them, silhouetted by the reddened glimmers of moonlight. She saw a head and neck covered in patches of thick, winter-white fur, ears pointed up like a German shepherd's. But the rest of him. . . .

All werwulf!

CHAPTER THIRTY-SEVEN

THE SEVEN-FOOT-TALL WERWULF HAD A FACE THAT WAS HALF man, half wolf. He stood upright, on two feet.

"A White Wulf of Wyndonham," Blackbeard whispered, apparently unnerved by the creature.

Its narrow eyes shone arterial red. And the werwulf was decaying. Torn segments of rib cage and thigh exposed bare bone—bones that were ghost white, with tendons and surrounding tissues of ivory white. Its flesh was a bleached white, and patches of matted, arctic-white fur clung to him.

"Why so stark white?" Natalie whispered.

"Long ago, the first of this species swallowed the sun in their kingdom. They've been white ever since."

What does that even mean?

A rustling in the woods corralled their attention. More eyes appeared among bushes and trees in a flash, like pairs of

ONCE UPON A ZOMBIE

fireflies bobbing and hovering, methodically forming a circle around them.

"Leave this to me, peewee princess, ya' hear?"

Princess?

"Yes. Princess," echoed a deviant voice from behind the brushwood. "Don't you worry your pretty little princess head. We'll take *good* care of you." The tone dripped sarcasm.

The seven-foot-tall werwulf deferentially receded as the talking werwulf stepped out of the brush and into a beam of moonlight falling through an opening in the trees.

His appearance was chillingly perverted. He brazenly wore a red-hooded cloak over his bone-white, hairy body. "Three guesses where the caped hood on my back and the blood on my tongue came from." He quirked the upper left corner of his mouth and licked his pale lips with a long white tongue, dotted red with fresh blood drippings.

The cloaked wulf burst into a leering laughter.

The circle of werwulves in the woods followed suit, moving closer in a maniacal frenzy of baleful laughter.

The red-caped werwulf gave Natalie a leering once-over. He scanned her from top to bottom, his eyes hungrily sizing up her meaty parts. The right side of his mouth curled next, so that a twisted smile formed across his face. He winked, smacked his lips, and blew her a kiss. He grinned. Glossy white fangs glistened in the moonlight.

She stepped back and saw nine other sharp-fanged grins behind him, glowing like neon, popping out of the darkness.

The smiles crept closer.

Natalie's back stiffened.

Gimme the freaking tiara.

All nine werwulves stepped out of the shadows and joined the alpha werwulf in the pool of moonlight. They too were ghost white, as if they'd been born dead and bloodless.

Natalie stood motionless.

Blackbeard stood behind her, his big hands clasping her shoulders; they barely came to his waist.

Tiara, please!

He leaned into her, his whiskers scratching her neck as he whispered in her ear, "Ready for another taste—before they taste you?"

"Yes indeedy."

She kept her eyes glued on the talking werwulf. She felt the tiara crown her head.

Her eyes closed, as if by themselves.

Fear left her and was swiftly replaced by serene calm. Senses she never knew she had awakened, heightening her powers of perception.

She *saw* the universal laws permeating this once-enchanted universe, laws pertaining to the violet shimmer of the color spectrum.

This new awareness gave her clarity.

Blackbeard whispered in her ear, "Hurry it up. The wulves are creeping closer; their ugly snouts sniffing us like bloody hounds."

In her mind's eye, she saw a perfectly shaped skull made of rock, hollow and glowing with embers of consciousness.

She envisioned a glowing ball of pearlescent blue and white fluids swirling together inside it, and bands of red dissolving into nothingness. She focused on Caitlin and how she could aid, assist, and support her—most importantly—without a desire for anything in return.

Next, Natalie committed to sharing the indescribable power that she had tasted the first time she wore the tiara with everyone she'd meet for the rest of her life. She wanted to share it all, without condition. She wanted to be pure.

And then her body began to shake.

And quiver.

Steadily increasing vibrations.

Her skin began to burn so hot, it almost felt cool.

She opened her eyes. The werwulves had arched their backs, spines protruding through hairless, fleshless blotches on their backs. They were about to pounce.

Suddenly, the wulves began yelping wildly. They were fraught with fear. They began howling at the sky and appearing generally discombobulated. The wulves seemed unable to make sense of what their leering eyes were seeing.

What those ravenous eyes saw was . . . nothing.

Nothing at all.

Because Natalie had vanished. Leaving not a speck of scent behind.

And the bewildered pack, the fabled White Werwulves of Wyndonham, were reduced to growling at the vacant spot where Natalie should've been. The wulf pack was too flummoxed and frightened by this baffling, otherworldly occurrence to take further interest in Blackbeard, and so they fled into the woods.

But Natalie was still there. She had been standing in the same spot the entire time, watching everything unfold.

She had simply altered her wavelength by accessing the power of the tiara and the violet band of the spectrum. She had managed to accomplish a feat long dreamed of by human-kind but never before achieved.

She had fabricated a cloak of invisibility.

To accomplish this, Natalie had altered the violet wave-length engulfing her, courtesy of the tiara, and transformed the visible violet end of the spectrum into invisible ultraviolet.

CHAPTER THIRTY-EIGHT

THE BOY WHO COULD FLY WAS CLAD IN A LEATHERY, OLIVE-GREEN tunic with veiny leaf skeletons woven into the fabric. His suede leggings were the color of cayenne pepper. Twined, leafy jungle vines rode up his legs and belted his waist. And he wore the funkiest, rustic brown, pointed-toe, high boots that Caitlin had ever seen. Unquestionably, the authentic Peter Pan was far cooler and edgier than the traditional pop-culture renditions that Caitlin was used to seeing—even without the ghoulish attributes.

A string of lava-stone beads and braids fell at his temple, and a brownish-green bandana wrapped his forehead.

Pan was definitely one of the walking dead: pale silvery skin, cheeks recessed above the jawbone, and overshadowed eye sockets that encircled almond-shape eyes which shone like two chips of emeralds.

But it was the long, straggling, surfer beach hair that

really stood out—it was a flowing, mangled mess more tangled than the snarled branches of driftwood on the nearby beach.

The whole look gave him a Steven Tyler-type rocker vibe.

Pan sat on the tallest of a circle of bare rocks. The Lost Boys—presumably Tootles, Nibs, Curly, and the rest—were seated on a few of the shorter rocks. Caitlin wasn't sure who was who.

A glowing ember near the bonfire floated toward Pan. The spark flashed brighter and brighter, then faded to a dim glow . . . then turned brighter and brighter again . . . and back to dim. Finally, it lit up like a blinding camera flashbulb and then went completely dark.

"Lovely light show," Pan said, winking at the Lost Boys. "Ain't that right, fellas?"

Caitlin, Tin Man, and Gruncle Derek edged their way into the center ring.

Pan had noticed the trio's arrival. He immediately homed in on Caitlin. His provocative leer was so piercing, she awkwardly crossed her arms over her chest.

"Who do we have here?" Pan asked. "A lost girl who managed to fall out of the pram?"

The Lost Boys thought that to be a hilarious remark. They merrily repeated the line, and interjected catcalls, hooting, and hollering.

Pan shot them a look. "That's enough, fellas!"

They shut right up.

"Well, well," Gruncle Derek said with a snicker, "they certainly know who's boss around here. Don't they, son?"

"Indeed they do, gramps," replied Pan with a grin.

The ember lit up again and shot over to Caitlin. It clearly wasn't just a random spark from the bonfire. Flitting about Caitlin was a perfectly formed girl—undoubtedly undead—with silken, shimmering gossamer wings.

Tinker Bell!

She glowed like a tiny Christmas bulb.

She fluttered closer to Caitlin's face, inspecting her eye.

Without question, Tink was the most adorable ghoul Caitlin had ever seen. Her pearl-ivory complexion and deep-shadowed dimples accentuated splendid angular cheekbones. And she thought that delicate button nose was sweeter and positively cuter than a Love Heart candy.

Caitlin blinked and cheerily introduced herself. "I'm Caitlin."

"Whoop-de-do," Tink snapped back in a sharp tone that rang out like a bell. "Now tell me something I don't know." She was the size of a silver dollar—small enough to drop in your pocket, if only the petulant pixie would stay there.

"Yup," Pan said, overemphasizing the last letter. He hopped down from his rock and strutted over to Caitlin. "The impolite sprite is quite right. We know exactly who you are, my lovely. And I also know *what* you want. The question is this: Do you know what I want in return for giving you what you want?"

Pan had the gall to pucker his lips, close his eyes, and lean forward.

"He's a hedonist," Tinker Bell blurted out. "Do yourself a favor and turn around now."

"How inelegant, Peter," Caitlin said. "Such unattractive, adolescent behavior. It's typical of a boy-child."

He winced as if shot by an arrow.

Caitlin had blatantly lied—she found Peter Pan to be extremely attractive in a part bohemian, part biker kind of way. But she wasn't going kiss to him on his terms.

Wait—are there other terms?

"And what is it you think I want?" she asked him.

Pan shed the wounded look and regained his swagger.

"You'd like to banish the Enchanter from inside your head, sanitize the blood from your eye, and rescue your little sis. And to do all that, you need to take a swim on a mountaintop. In the Dipping Pools of Mount Velarium, to be precise. Then you must find the hidden shut-off valve in order to empty the pools dry. Which is where I come in. Now tell me, my lovely Cait—is Peter on the right track here?"

He winked over at Tinker Bell and gave Caitlin a self-satisfied smile.

"You're impossible," Tink declared. "And incorrigible."

"But lovable," he said.

Tink turned to Caitlin. "I'm his indentured wish-giver," she said. "So this is what I have to contend with every day."

Pan was certainly maddening. But Caitlin detected an

innocent boyish charm lurking somewhere beneath the bravado.

"Why are you ghouled out?" Caitlin wondered. "Couldn't you have flown to the top of Mount Velarium and bathed in the Dipping Pools to cure yourself?"

Caitlin saw an unexpected trace of despair in his eyes. Even Tinker Bell's light dimmed a tad.

"Flight restrictions," Pan said. "I can't seem to reach an altitude higher than one hundred thirty-seven inches off the ground—a mere eleven feet. Won't get me past the foot of the mountain."

"Why's that?"

"Haven't a clue." Pan rubbed his chin. "Hey, maybe ask the silver chap. If that's who I think it is, perhaps he can shed a bit o' light."

Of course—the Tin Woodman answers why *questions.*

"Well?" Caitlin asked.

"Human, fairy and elf flight require a formidable combination of fairy dust and happy thoughts," Tin Man said. "Fairy dust is in ample supply here. But the aforementioned happy thoughts are actually based on one's ability to resist the red band, and to banish the worry, fear, pessimism, and self-centeredness that infect our normal thought processes. Peter's problem is that he's currently consumed by decadent, hedonistic thoughts because of the impaired Green Spectrum."

Tinker Bell wagged her finger. "Told you so."

"He's still able to fly," Tin Man added, "but his limited

will to resist the red band has limited the heights that he can attain."

Everyone suddenly jumped, startled by an unexpected crack of thunder. Isolated storm clouds were converging directly above the island from seemingly out of nowhere. These were end-of-the-world storm clouds: roiling, heavy, and threatening.

"The Enchanter," Tin Man muttered nervously.

The drumming stopped, and hushed murmurs circulated among the shadows—frightened voices whispered the lore of the Lord of the Curtain.

"We must sail now," Gruncle Derek warned, "before the winds pick up and the seas turn rough."

A faint and distant caw arrived on a breath of wind.

Tin Man turned to Caitlin. "Janus!"

More murmurs erupted as Janus's name elicited more whispering.

Despite a valiant attempt to keep them squared, Caitlin's shoulders sagged upon hearing Janus's name. The nearby air seemed to warm and brush over her. She felt flushed, as if coming down with a low-grade fever.

I'm so totally frustrated. There's no logic to any of this—and apparently no justice in the world. Like, why is this monster so relentless? He never stops. He's always on the attack.

Janus circumvented or toppled every obstacle with an ease that suggested a grossly unfair, illogical imbalance in the universe. She, on the other hand, had lost her eye trying to do just one hard thing. All it took was the sudden bite of a bird and a simple swipe of a knife—goodbye, eyeball. Her dad had been taken swiftly and suddenly. Her mom had vanished in a flash. And after three years of being an official missing person, her mom had turned up dead. Murdered. Why couldn't she just as easily have turned up alive? Caitlin felt like she was flipping a coin a thousand times and always ending up with tails.

She fanned herself with her hand.

Life just isn't supposed to be this way. And yet it is.

So many nights, when she was just a kid, climbing into bed without getting tucked in by her own mother, the dread and the dark thoughts had come to her mind easily, relentlessly. Why didn't a tidal wave of happy thoughts overcome her in the same way? And that awful, endless list of nasty side effects that those prescription med TV commercials cited, one after another. Why did the mere mention of a particular disease or the side effects from meds cause her to agonize and believe that she must be coming down with a virus or experiencing unpleasant symptoms? Why wasn't feeling terrific and being hopelessly happy and feeling all-around super healthy just as easy a state of mind to fall into as worry and hypochondria were?

Why is my life skewed so disproportionally toward gloom and darkness?

Who fine-tuned and calibrated human existence so unfairly, unjustly, and underhandedly?

Caitlin recalled the years when her mom was missing; her OCD had intensified. Young Caitlin had to pace through the apartment every single night before bed and count all the corners in the ceilings of every room, then check all the knobs on the stove to make sure the oven wasn't on, and then check all the closets to make sure serial killers weren't hiding inside, and then look under the bed, and then close all the dresser drawers tight because if one was sticking out just a tad she'd obsess about it. And if she didn't follow this entire routine exactly, she would obsess about *not* having done it all night long and all the next day, and then she would panic because she couldn't get rid of *those* obsessive thoughts. So to prevent those thoughts from driving her to insanity, she had to cancel out the compulsion to think about that nightly routine by performing the nightly routine through a waterfall of agonizing tears because she was trapped in a maze that had no exit.

Where the hell are my parents? I want my mom and dad! I want to see them now! Right now!

She willed them to appear with all her heart, with every fiber of her being.

Nothing.

Zilch.

Ultimately, death was indifferent to the weeping of orphans and deaf to pleadings of the bereaved.

The warm air passed. The feverish feeling lifted. Caitlin was programmed to easily sink into that familiar place of deep dread, depression, and hopelessness, but she just couldn't allow that to happen this time. Not now. Not today. In fact, *because* everything was so out of whack, she couldn't allow herself to be just another tossed coin that turned up tails.

I will be heads!

And then, something spoke to her from a place still unscathed by the cynical, irrational, unfair, sullen world. She could feel there was an answer.

Somewhere.

And it was probably an exquisitely simple answer.

But for now, until she found it, perhaps some small measure of darkness and a whole lot of imbalance served a deeper purpose, a hidden reason that might soon become apparent.

She breathed.

Fully.

Deeply.

Lusciously.

She released the ache, the frustration, and the anger. She firmed her resolve to find Natalie and vanquish her share of darkness. She vowed to learn to understand her life a little bit more than she did right now.

CHAPTER THIRTY-NINE

"KILL THE LIGHTS!" PAN CRIED OUT. "DON'T WANT JANUS AND those bird-men spotting us from the air."

How ironic, Caitlin thought. *Now we're the ones turning off the lights and generating darkness!*

The Lost Boys doused the bonfire with buckets of seawater while others buried the burning bulrushes in the sand, snuffing out their firelight.

Caitlin gritted her molars. Then she grabbed one of the fiery torches, spun it upside down, and plowed the flaming wick into the sand.

She extinguished the firelight. She fabricated her own small curtain and used the power of darkness against the source of all darkness—the Lord of the Curtain and his assassin henchman Janus.

I won't make it easy for them.

The repulsive cawing of the crowmen grew louder, closer.

"Man the ship," Derek called to Caitlin and Tin Man. Derek put his hand on Pan's shoulders. "We need that map, son. The one marking the site of the shut-off valve."

Tin Man interrupted. "Caitlin can't board the *Jolly Roger.*"

"Why the hell not?" Derek asked.

"She'll never see the Twin Mountains. The inclement weather will slow the ship. The crowmen will catch up to us and kill her. Then kill us. It'll be a slaughterhouse at sea."

Gruncle Derek rubbed his head with both hands, sighing heavily. Then he turned to Peter. "Look 'ere, son. I need ya to fly young Cait to the Twin Mountains."

"Already told you—I can't reach the top."

"You don't have to. Just get her to the foot of the mountain. She needs to get out of here."

"What's in it for me, gramps?" Pan replied.

Gruncle Derek's face reddened. "I'll withhold my knuckles from your face for trying to steal a kiss from her earlier."

"You don't scare me, geezer."

Caitlin balled her fists and walked to over to Pan. She held one up to his face. "It'll be *my* knuckles that slam your nose if you don't help us, you self-indulgent ingrate."

An incensed Tinker Bell joined the fray. "For once, Peter Pan, get over your infantile self-love and demonstrate a shred of chivalry." Her words tinkled in the night air.

Pan bristled. And he fumed. And he grumbled. And then he seemed about ready to acquiesce. He gave a nonchalant shrug to Tink.

"Sprinkle a bit of dust on the lass."

Thunder shook the trees. The wind picked up.

Tinker Bell spattered a dash of glittering, golden fairy dust on Caitlin. Unbound from the laws of gravity, the magic dust particles hovered around her like fine mist. They smelled like orange sherbet.

Caitlin rubbed her tummy as her insides went topsy-turvy as if she'd embarked on a carnival ride. She became light-headed as she inhaled the fairy dust and it sparkled in her one eye. Then she began to feel bouncy, buoyant, and light on her feet. Gravity had lost some of its hold on her.

Pan promptly led everyone away from the party area and down toward an empty, narrow strip of beach.

"Why do we need both fairy dust *and* happy thoughts to fly?" Caitlin asked Tin Man as they trailed Pan. She was looking for some assurance that she'd make it safely off the ground.

"In our world, everything is made up of thought," Tin Man said. "Gravity, too. The gravitational thought-force is excessively self-centered. It only thinks to take. It does not impart. That's why gravity draws in everything to itself. And that's why it's so difficult to escape its stingy pull."

"I get it," Caitlin said. "So what's with the fairy dust?"

"Fairy dust is made up of trillions of unimaginably small, microscopic mirrors. A mirror reverses an image as it reflects light. For instance, if the Wicked Witch stands in front of a mirror and points west with her left arm, the left arm of the witch in the mirror points east—the reverse direction."

Caitlin grinned. "This is good. Keep going."

"The trillions of mirror particles that produce a small cloud of fairy dust achieve the same effect. They reverse gravity from a pulling force into a pushing force. They reflect a positive thought-field cloud around you. Combine that with your own waves of positive thoughts, and it amplifies the overall fairy-dust effect. Gravity now becomes your source of *propulsion.* Your thoughts and fairy dust become the fuel. And that is how you achieve flight."

That was, like, a totally wicked, freaking awesome elucidation of fairy dust aerodynamics!

They trotted onto the beach and Peter offered his hand to Caitlin. "Okay, my lovely. Hang on to your knickers and take my hand. And if you try to kiss me even once during the flight, you'll be flying solo."

Is he for real?

"We'll be flying on a low-altitude trajectory," Peter explained, "so keep your noggin down—if you want to keep it, that is."

Caitlin smiled warmly. "Thank you, Peter."

"I'm proud of ya, son," Gruncle Derek said.

Peter shrugged off the comments, but Caitlin saw a tiny crack in his aloof veneer.

"Tin Man and I will head to the *Jolly Roger,*" Gruncle Derek said. "We'll meet up at the Twin Mountains. Now give your old fart of an uncle a hug, young Cait, and be careful."

Peter awkwardly kicked the sand about with his boot as Caitlin and Derek wrapped their arms around each other.

After their embrace, Caitlin adjusted and tightened her eye patch.

Peter offered Caitlin his hand again. "C'mon, lass—those big black birds will be here right quick."

She gingerly took hold of it. His hand was unexpectedly warm, at least for a living-dead ghoul.

"Hold tight," he said. "I know the route, so I'll lead."

Caitlin gulped. She followed that with a hearty chug of night air to fill her lungs.

She and Peter began trotting along the sand, tailwinds at their back.

Before she could even exhale, they began to lift into the humid air.

Oh my gosh! My feet are no longer touching ground!

She was suddenly a good six feet in the air, moving straight ahead.

The sensation was exhilarating. Her torso and legs suddenly swung back, leveling out behind her.

Oh my gawd! I'm flying!

This was better than flying in a dream.

She extended her other arm like a wing and aligned her legs tight together, pointing her toes to optimize her aerodynamics.

Her hair tossed wildly in the strong breeze. The rush of balmy air brushed against her face. Headwinds whistled in her ears.

"Ready?" Peter shouted.

"For what?"

"This. . . ."

Caitlin lost her breath as they shifted gears, accelerating quicker and climbing another five feet in the air. They reached their cruising altitude of 137 inches above the sandy coastline of Neverland.

"Duck!" Peter screamed.

Caitlin lowered her head as they dipped below a large flock of flapping seagulls.

Bird droppings plopped on her head.

Guano'd!

She glanced ahead, marveling at the night sky and horizon.

Uh-oh.

She slammed her eyelid shut and dipped her head sideways as they flew through a mass of mosquitoes.

Buuuzzzzzzzzzzzzz!

A billion bugs whizzed by her ears.

She opened her eye and glanced ahead again, spitting a few bugs out of her mouth. Then she felt all her blood and bodily organs shift backward as another burst of acceleration kicked in.

The coconut palms whipping by began to blur as the pair picked up speed. Then the trees vanished.

She looked down. The beach had also vanished.

She glanced back. They had left Neverland behind and were now heading out over the vast open sea.

Oh no.

Deep ocean waves churned below. An ocean of stars twinkled above.

They flew through pockets of warm air. She suddenly realized they could be flying for hours with no land in sight . . . which meant no place to touch down if a panic attack struck. No safe place of security or comfort to hide in, to calm down and ride out the anxiety. *How come the anxiety I feel over a hypothetical anxiety attack is just as bad as the panic attack itself?*

Peter Pan and Caitlin began to lose speed.

"You got the collywobbles, Caitlin?" Peter shouted. "'Cuz we're losing altitude—fast."

"Collywobbles?" It was hard to breathe and get the word out.

"Unpleasant thoughts, the willies. 'Cuz if you do, and you believe those dreadful thoughts in your head are yours, they surely will be. And then you'll be dunking in the shark-infested sea below instead of in the Dipping Pools of Mount Velarium. But if you know it's all being sent by the Enchanter and you endeavor to reject the unhappy thoughts, that, in and of itself, will meet the criteria of a happy thought. See my point?"

"Sounds simple but not easy."

"Trying is ninety-five percent of battle, missy. Now, I can already feel the cold spray of ocean on my bollocks, so please, my lovely, snap to it."

She imagined the Lord of the Curtain floating in a skull-shaped storm cloud, speaking into a smartphone. As he spoke from the cloud, his words began to stream and download into Caitlin's mind, manifesting as her thoughts and her feelings of dread.

It's him. It's not me. So why react to it? Why be afraid? Let go.

But now she was too frightened to let go.

Because if it didn't work right away, she'd start thinking that she was wrong.

Then the anxiety will become worse, and there'll be no escape from this torment!

Wait!

Could that also be him? Trying to outfox me? Could all my doubting be him streaming into my head?

Including my doubts about my doubts?

Instead of trying to stop or transform all the negative thoughts, she let them float in her mind. She refused to validate them, though, or to invest sweat into them, or claim them as her own. She batted them away, like she was swinging a ping-pong paddle, knowing that it was only the Enchanter serving up all the balls full of doubt, dread, and distress.

Caitlin had actually loved playing ping-pong with Girl Wonder in her younger days. She realized she and Natalie hadn't played ever again after moving to London.

Caitlin decided to let go of trying to control her breathing. She let go of agonizing over the possibility of hyperventilating, fainting midflight, and falling out of the sky.

Focus on helping, assisting, and aiding Natalie and Eos! Focus!

An exultant sense of freedom began to overwhelm her from out of nowhere. She peered to her right . . . left . . . glanced upward . . . then below . . .

The wide-open expanse of space that had been tormenting her agoraphobic tendencies had inexplicably merged with her mind. That was the only way she could think to explain it. It manufactured an indescribable oneness, a feeling of connectedness with the universe. She felt in control of everything, along with a clarity. Everything was perfect and safe. The vast, unknown ocean in the middle of nowhere, far from everything familiar and safe, along with the unbound and starlit sky high above, became the sources of her exhilarating freedom. The same sweet comfort and security she felt at home, in her bed, snug under the covers, was with her right here, right now. And the feeling was so profound, it almost seemed worth going through the pain just to arrive at a better place.

Caitlin and Peter regained speed . . . altitude . . .

She was truly flying now . . . Gliding smoothly over the sea, beneath the boundless beauty of a storybook night sky.

Her legs stuck together.

Arms angled back like jet wings.

I can't wait to get there!

To the Twin Mountains of Velarium.

To confront the evil.

And to make a difference—to myself!

"Is there a shortcut?" she shouted to Peter.

"Yes. But we'll need to veer right."

She let go of Peter's hand.

She was flying on her own. Solo.

"I'll lead," Caitlin shouted to Peter. "Be my wingman."
She increased her speed.

Peter Pan fell into formation behind her.

"Where do we veer right?" Caitlin shouted.

He called out, "Second star on the right, then straight on till morning!"

Whoooooooooosh!

CHAPTER FORTY

THE ODDEST, MOST UNSETTLING SENSATION NATALIE FLETCHER had ever experienced occurred when she raised her hands to look at them . . . and they weren't there. She next glanced down at her torso and legs—and they weren't there either.

Invisibility was a fragile, vulnerable, surreal state of existence because it hovered tenuously on the thin edge of nonexistence. She thought she was in danger of losing herself completely, disappearing into some cosmic tear in the fabric of space-time where her consciousness would vanish into nothingness as her physical body had done.

But during that confrontation with the sun-swallowing white werwulves, the tiara had performed wonders on her imagination.

She now understood: a ray of light made the world visible, but the ray of light itself was invisible. An intriguing phenomenon.

For instance, outer space was as black as pitch even though the sun's rays shone through it to illuminate the earth from a distance of ninety-one million miles.

Hmmm. Why was that ninety-one million mile sun-kissed route blacker than black? Even though the endless, streaming light was shining along the entire route?

The answer was deftly simple: there was no physical object in space to *reflect* the light. The Earth shone because the atmosphere, mountains, and lakes reflected the invisible light rays.

Light itself is invisible because it has no mass. It generates no friction and thus no reflection. There's nothing physical about light. And physicality corresponds to the material body. And the material body is all about knee-jerk reactions. Knee-jerk reactions are the embodiment of selfishness. It's all about *me*, and *I*, and *myself*, and the *ego!*

Selfishness embodies the body!

Just like the red band of the spectrum.

Violet light is all about sharing and goodness and calm and giving and harmony. A galactic shift from one end of the spectrum to the other—a vast gulf that must be traversed in order to acquire the traits of light. One has to move from selfishness to selflessness.

Normally, this would be an impossible task, but the tiara made the impossible possible by neutralizing the influence of the red band of light.

Natalie knew that if she could eradicate all the reactionary egocentric whims within her own mind by tapping the power of the tiara, there would be no more spiritual mass, which meant no more physical mass.

Presto.

Violet goes ultraviolet, becoming the invisible part of the spectrum.

And that was basically how Natalie Fletcher managed the fantastical feat of making her physical body disappear into thin air.

Blackbeard, meanwhile, had been keeping one eye on the wulves and one eye on the spot where Natalie had been standing before she achieved her mastery over visible matter. When the werwulves scattered, he had quickly lifted the tiara from her head. And though that tiara induced euphoric feelings associated with the pleasures of the violet end of the spectrum, Natalie was still as happy as a cat in a creamery to have her observable body back again.

And now the two of them were back inside the cavern, sitting by the red quartzite boulder, and using its flat top as a table. Blackbeard sat directly across from Natalie, a look of destiny in his eye. Her destiny, she presumed.

"The world can be yours, kid," he said. "Alls ya hafta to do is help us *build* the world."

"Eos?"

"Aye."

"How?"

Grinning and keeping his eyes tightly fixed upon her,

Blackbeard pulled a dagger from his belt. He flashed the blade's edge in front of her, catching a glint of light seeping in from the crevice in the walls. He pulled a bronze skeleton key from another pocket and set it on top of the boulder.

Looking pleased as rum punch, he wedged the fine edge of his dagger into a thin slit that formed a circle on the flattened top of the boulder. The circle was a hidden door panel flush with the surface of the rock.

He lifted it up with a flick of the knife.

Hisssssss.

Green mist rose like colored steam from the hidden compartment.

So this is where the humming noise in the cavern has been coming from.

The soft sound rose in volume when the lid popped.

Blackbeard picked up the skeleton key, winked a red-speckled, bloodshot eye at Natalie, and slid his hand into the hidden compartment. His arm jiggled as if inserting the key into a lock.

Click.

He gave his forearm a half turn.

Snap.

A latch released.

The humming grew louder. He pulled out his arm.

Something was moving inside the boulder.

A polished, black, metal frame in the shape of a perfect hexagon rose from the boulder.

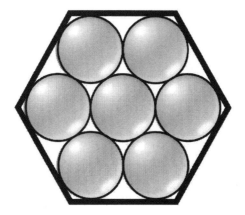

Fitted snug inside the metallic hexagon were seven perfect, translucent quartz globes like crystal balls, as smooth
as glass. Three were positioned on the left side, three on the
right, and one was fitted into the middle. It reminded Natalie
of a rack of billiard balls except it was hexagonal and not
triangular.

The seven orbs suddenly began to shimmer.

Each one glowed one of the seven colors of the rainbow.

And there was a distinct hum ringing from each one.

Each sphere played one of the seven notes on the musical
scale. The whole contraption looked like some kind of alien
technology.

Perhaps it's some sort of a remote access control panel.

"What is it?" Natalie asked.

"The most valuable device in all the world. The master
key that opens doorways."

"To where?"

"Other worlds."

"Which worlds?"

"All of 'em. Right now, it's set to open the seven portals to Eos."

"How does it work?"

"Alls ya gotta do is press each of the seven round keys. Seven portals will open. The Enchanter will then 'ave access to the world. So go ahead. Push 'em."

"Why don't you do it?"

"Only a living human hand can open doorways."

"Why would I want to unleash that curtained creature into some other world? So he can wreck it, like he did this world?"

"Either that, lambkins . . . or yer sister, Caitlin, dies."

Natalie's heart stopped.

That was the first time the pirate has even mentioned Caitlin— and when he did, he threatened her life!

"She's the firstborn," he said. "While she lives, she gives ya some protection. So I can't force ya to open the gates. Ya need to choose to do it. For yerself. But if ya won't, she dies. And then ya lose that protection. And then I *can* force ya to open them."

Natalie snatched the metallic hexagon from the boulder.

She raised it above her head. It was heavy, like a jug of milk. Maybe a bit heavier.

"I'll smash it unless you give me the tiara. I'm getting out of here."

Blackbeard chuckled. "Ya don't have to threaten me, little

lambkins. I'll give ya the tiara. 'Cuz yer never gonna make it outta here."

Why not?

Still holding the hexagon above her head, Natalie gestured with her chin toward the wall that opened like a door. "What's really behind there?"

He seemed pleased by the question. "Tunnels."

"What kind of tunnels?"

"Don't matter none. You'll never figure yer way out."

She lifted the hexagon higher, as if preparing to toss it.

"I said—what kind of tunnels?"

"Sort o' like Zeno's Forest, but located in the interior of the kingdom. Like being on the inside of a ship instead of on deck."

"How many tunnels?"

He chuckled. "It's a maze, lass. Impossible to figure yer way out, I tell ya."

She wouldn't have to figure her way out if she had the tiara—she could walk through walls and crosscut all the tunnels and escape.

She made a threatening gesture with the hexagon and said, "How many tunnels?"

"I says yer not as clever as ya think ya are." His eyes narrowed. "There's millions of 'em. Tunnels all tangled and twisted, leadin' to a hundred thirty-seven million doors, leadin' to a hundred million firmaments and a hundred million worlds and a hundred million faraway realms that you'd never imagine in a hundred million years. That enough for ya?"

His face became cruel. "But only one tunnel leads directly outta this place. How d'ya like them odds? Now put that thing down and I'll give ya the tiara. Ya can make yer choice: open the seven portals, or walk outta this place with yer tiara and roam about for eternity."

"You're bluffing!" she said.

But she knew he was right. It was impossible. She had sensed the unfathomable depth of worlds on the other side of that door when she had passed through a tunnel on the way to that wulf-infested forest. It would take countless lifetimes to cut through that many tunnels.

Blackbeard reached into his inside coat pocket and retrieved the tiara. He set it on top of the boulder. "All yers," he said.

"Step back," she instructed.

Blackbeard backed up a few feet.

"More."

He took a few more steps.

"All the way to the far wall."

He retreated farther until his back pushed against the rock.

She carefully returned the hexagon to the top of the boulder, keeping her eyes locked on Blackbeard. His left eyebrow curved.

She picked up the tiara . . . raised it . . . but then she hesitated.

Whatever this tiara really was, it might have had the power to make her happy and euphoric and giddy, but she'd be consigning herself to a lifetime of wandering through endless worlds, alone. Lost like a windblown autumn leaf drifting aimlessly along the ground. There would be millions of wrong choices at millions of intersections.

"What happens if I open the portals?"

"I'll answer ya. 'Cuz ya have to make this choice on yer own. If ya open up them gates, the Enchanter will be able to secure Eos at the moment of its birth. And then you will become supreme monarch of that kingdom, I tell ya, establishing the very laws of nature."

He started to amble toward her. "Don't worry, ya can keep the tiara. I'm not gonna break yer teeth or nuthin'. Look, there's no point in ya gettin' lost in a maze for eternity; not when ya could rule a world filled with happiness for all eternity."

He placed his hand inside the hidden compartment in the boulder.

"What are you doing?"

He fiddled. "Just watch."

The cavern began to hum at a different frequency. Blue, orange, purple, and green lights flashed and shimmered as a hologram materialized.

The hologram was a mirror image of the hexagon.

Seven new congruent circles formed before her eyes, followed by another perfect hexagon taking shape around the circles. Then another seven circles issued forth, producing another hexagon, and then one after another, after another. The pattern began to expand exponentially.

She was witnessing the perpetual genesis of new worlds, the formation of a cosmic honeycomb.

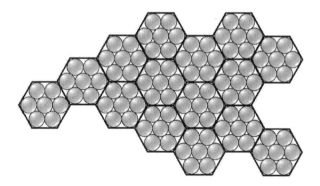

Suddenly, the holographic view zoomed in on one of the hexagons. Natalie saw that it was a hexagonal maze.

The expanding honeycomb was an evolving universe where each hexagonal world included a maze. The symbolism was striking—and tantalizing to Natalie's mind. These were all predetermined designs and destinies, and yet, within the design there existed choices every step of the way. Order and potential chaos coexisted, both dependent upon the act of choosing.

And now Natalie had to make her choice: try to escape by entering into that mysterious honeycomb maze comprising millions of worlds, knowing the tiara would keep her contented as she traveled like a windblown leaf . . . *Wait!*

A leaf.

Photosynthesis.

In a single flash of perceptual clarity, Natalie suddenly knew what to do next.

"I've made my choice," she told the pirate.

A broad grin filled Blackbeard's face as he gestured to the hexagon contraption. "Well, little lambkins, good for ya. Go ahead, start opening doors."

But instead of activating the seven colorful orbs in the hexagon, Natalie set the tiara upon her head. She shut her eyes.

And then she vanished.

As did the grin on Blackbeard's face.

CHAPTER FORTY-ONE

CAITLIN WAS CLOCKING SIXTY MILES AN HOUR OVER THE OCEAN and it was sheer exhilaration.

Kickass. Awesofrickintastic. Nothing else comes close. Period.

Normally adrenaline was the culprit and co-conspirator behind an anxiety attack. Now it was producing such a heady rush that it seemed to her like it must have come from an illegal substance.

Note to self: stock up on fairy dust should I ever get to go home.

She contemplated the *trippindiculars* of human flight: her mind willing forth her speed and altitude, the wind pressing hard against her face. Jetting untethered to terra firma, unbound from solid ground.

The cool spray of seawater invigorating her senses while triggering small gasps of air as it splashed her face. The blurry ocean whizzing by below. Starlight fixed in the firmament above. Moonlight making the sea look like honeyed syrup and its golden reflections like segments of mandarin oranges.

Her legs and arms tweaked her aerodynamics . . . a twitch of the shoulder here . . . a shift of the waist there.

But then, without warning, the thrill of flying began to wither. The songbirds' beneficial effect was tapering off and Caitlin's hunger was returning. The calm seas were also turning rough. The stars faded behind an overcast sky.

"You see that?" Peter asked.

She did.

Whitecaps. Up ahead.

"Those waves are a good fifteen feet high," Peter said. "We'll never clear them."

"Then we go through them."

"You're mad. They'll knock us right out of the air. If we plunge into the sea, we might lose our fairy dust. And I'm not too fond of sharks. I say we turn back."

As her hunger rose, her patience waned.

"Stop whining. No going back. If I fall in the ocean, I'll swim there."

"Persistent little bird. And a tetchy one."

Caitlin suddenly dropped in altitude, until she was practically skimming the surface of the sea.

"What the hell are you doing?" Peter shouted.

She began bobbing her head into the water. Once, twice . . .

A few more quick dunks . . .

She regained altitude. A sunfish squirmed in her mouth. It

stank like slime. Nevertheless, Caitlin bit down hard, sinking her teeth in.

Peter pulled up alongside her.

"That's a mola mola you're eating."

"Wanna bite?"

His tone sharpened. "No one ever warn you about pleasure escalation? Your desire doubling when you're blood-eyed? Toss the fish—now! Or soon you'll be nibbling on my thigh."

Too late; Caitlin was already spitting out fish bones.

Before she had a chance to belch up a seriously smelly fish burp, the fifteen-foot-high waves were upon them.

"Here we go!"

Caitlin and Peter smashed into the first cresting wave.

CRASH—whoosh!

Caitlin managed a breath in the trough between the crests.

Then another crest. *CRASH—whoosh* . . . catch a breath in the trough . . . *CRASH—whoosh* . . . catch a breath in the trough . . . *CRASH—whoosh* . . . catch a breath in the trough . . .

This went on for three hard, pounding minutes. As they finally found calmer waters to cruise over, Caitlin and Peter Pan were huffing and puffing, their bodies battered and beaten up by the slamming waves.

"You were right," Caitlin said.

"I'm always right—but about what?"

"I'm *doubly* hungry."

"Not good. Do me a favor: Don't react—to *anything*! It'll just escalate."

Caitlin suddenly spotted a blurred object jutting out of the sea, far off in the distance. It reminded her of two witch hats, side by side.

Instead of using her telescopic eye to zoom in and examine it, she increased her speed to reach its position quickly. She accelerated to seventy miles per hour . . . eighty . . . *swooo oosh* . . . she jumped to a hundred twenty.

Headwinds pummeled her face, making her eye water. Surging air whistled as it whipped through the crevices in her patch.

"Whoa, girl!" Peter cried out. "Even I've never gone this fast."

He always makes everything about himself!

At their accelerated speed, Caitlin and Peter were soon making their final approach to the citadel of grim darkness: a craggy, mountainous island. The two witch hats turned out to be exactly what Caitlin had expected: the towering Twin Mountains of Velarium.

Caitlin and Peter came in for a vertical landing—helicopter style. They touched down on the haunted island. The landscape was chock full of eucalyptus trees—tall centurions that emitted an eerie blue haze and a pleasant menthol-pine scent tinged with a faint note of honey.

"The leaves on the trees—they have a golden flicker," Caitlin noted.

"Eucalypts are gum trees," Peter Pan said. "They mine

minerals from deep underground. Through their roots. The glitter on those leaves is actually gold."

Note to self: stuff my pockets with fairy dust and eucalyptus leaves before leaving this place!

The delightfully inviting eucalyptus aroma coming off the trees—which cleared Caitlin's nasal passages, allowing her to sniff Peter's blood better than before—made a stark contrast with the foreboding ghost-gray mountains whose spiked points seemed sharp enough to impale bodies.

Caitlin glanced up toward the peak, but there was no summit in sight. The mountains were a milieu of gloom and granite. Their jagged slopes and ridges reached into the clouds, conveying an ominous warning: *Climb up—if you dare!*

Caitlin's face hardened as she took in the steep climb she'd have to brave and the dizzying heights she'd have to scale to reach the summit and Dipping Pools.

"That's totally crazy. Impossible!"

"I told you—no strong reactions!" Peter warned.

Caitlin exhaled in exasperation. A moment later, she fell to the ground, writhing in distress. She curled up into a fetal position.

Peter kneeled beside her. "What is it?"

Her words were strained. "You're right again. I reacted. I got mad when I saw the climb. Whatever is inside me doubled again. The hunger. Other desires. You're looking more appetizing than a tostada right now. Feels like I'm losing control."

Peter helped her to her feet. He seemed as nervous as hell—for his own life, no doubt.

"Stay calm," he said. "I'm going to take a quick survey of the place. Maybe there are some steps or trails that lead up this mountain. Hang tight."

Peter flew off.

Caitlin couldn't blame him for finding an excuse to get away.

And then she smiled at the sick humor of it all. What if the immortal Peter Pan, the boy who never grew old, was suddenly eaten like a hamburger and eradicated from existence forever? What would the world say about that?

She figured J. M. Barrie was probably rolling in his grave.

CHAPTER FORTY-TWO

A SINGLE PHOTON, OR WAVE OF LIGHT, EXISTED IN A SUPERPOSI-
tion, just as the excited electron in a leaf was in a superposition in the process of photosynthesis.

All of which was good news for Natalie. Because she was
now ultraviolet. Which meant she could superposition herself
to simultaneously travel every single possible tunnel route in
the hyperdimensional, intergalactic maze *instantly*. And just
as the excited electron in the leaf chose the fastest route to
the reaction center in a leaf, Natalie could choose the fastest
route—in fact the one and only route—out of this place.

She wasted no time.

When she vanished in the cavern before Blackbeard's
eyes, she made the shift to a wave superposition. The sensation of being in 137 million places at the same time was a bit
disorienting.

Ya think?

But the tiara and that glorious violet light freed her from fear and prevented her from losing her grip on reality—or her sanity.

She had identified the correct exit tunnel—or it had identified itself to her; she wasn't sure yet. So she shifted back from ultraviolet to visible, material form. Her sudden reappearance in the cavern a split second later shocked Blackbeard even more than her sudden disappearance had.

But now she knew exactly where to go when she bolted from the cavern.

Thankfully, the human brain's most important function is to filter out unnecessary information. If not for this filter, the mind would be under constant sensory overload.

Imagine absorbing 137 million worlds. Natalie was grateful for sensory gating.

But there was still a residue, an impression, that had remained behind. It was like the milky film on a glass after your pour the milk out.

Her hyperescape had become a hypermemory, slowed down into fleeting flashes of recall. She remembered whipping through endless tunnels at dizzying speeds but purposely not trying to find out anything about the vast worlds that waited on the other side of each doorway, for there was no time. She had to focus on one thing: choosing the correct tunnel. She had and she now blazed through the one that led to freedom.

She rocketed through the twisting tunnel, bypassing other inviting options and tempting detours which were made more irresistible by closed hatch doors that happened to show up at various intersections. Of course, she plowed straight ahead in the same tunnel, opening those hatches and bypassing the alternate routes until she finally reached the final—seventh—hatch out of the cosmic labyrinth.

That was easy enough!

When she came to a stop, she found herself standing outside under overcast skies, and breathing in mild, fresh air that had a tempered layer of cool crispness beneath it.

Yesss! How refreshing is this!

She swiveled to her right to scan the landscape . . . turned to her left to behold the opposite horizon . . . spun ninety degrees to look out across. . . . The unexpected sight knocked the wind out of her lungs.

The screams came on their own.

Over and over and over, inflaming her vocal cords.

And then she ran.

CHAPTER FORTY-THREE

CAITLIN'S WILL WAS WEAKENING WITH EACH PASSING MOMENT. Her resolve dismantled piece by piece, the way a child breaks down a Lego creation by pulling apart the building blocks.

Within those in-between, empty spaces, awful thoughts clouded her mind. Urges that brought twinges of guilt because she no longer loathed their depravity. Her independence was dissolving like ice in spring. Something inside her was dimming her decency. She felt like someone was layering soft blankets, one by one, over the lit lamp of her soul, and intended to keep adding them until the last sliver of light was snuffed out. Shame included.

She struggled to retain even a few sparks of humanity.

A bitterly cold wind blew by her, snarling, alive, pregnant with otherworldly wickedness. This was no ordinary current of air.

Janus is near! He's found me!

A fierce scream interrupted her thoughts.

She did an about-face, toward the sound. It seemed to have come from Mount Velarium.

There was nothing there.

Her eyes shifted . . . to its twin.

The Velarium volcano.

Caitlin was paralyzed by what she saw, unable to process the reality unfolding in front of her.

Natalie!

There was her sister, running toward her from the base of the volcano.

"Caity-pieeeeee!"

* * *

When Natalie saw Caitlin, the adrenaline surge in her body felt like a dam bursting. She started running wildly toward her.

But Caitlin started frantically waving her off. "Stay there! It's too dangerous."

Natalie skidded to a stop. "What?"

"I'll hurt you."

Caitlin suddenly looked past her sister. She screamed, "Watch out!"

Natalie turned. Blackbeard also hurtled out of the open hatch at the base of the Mount Velarium volcano. He came charging after Natalie.

She took off, but her feet got tangled up in her frenzy to escape. She tripped, then tumbled to the ground.

Blackbeard moved in fast, grabbing her by the wrists. He

held her tight so that she couldn't squirm loose and lifted her to her feet.

"Thought ya outsmarted me? Ha. Know what ya just did? Ya just opened up the doors to Eos."

Huh?

"What are you talking about?" Natalie asked incredulously. "I never touched the hexagon."

"Course not. That contraption was a diversion. Ya ran through the *real* hexagon. The tunnels. The seven hatches that ya opened to get out? Those are the *real* doorways that needed to be opened."

Natalie felt sick to her stomach.

"The Lord of the Curtain devised this deception to get ya to *choose* to open the doors. And choose ya did. With all yer heart and soul. It was all staged, kid. The encounter with the white wulves too. They'd 'a torn yer throat out otherwise. Ya had to locate your power, so we set ya up. But ya can still be a princess."

Peter Pan was flying faster than an arrow shot from a crossbow, whipping through the air just above ground level, sleek and straight.

He dipped.

He cut into Blackbeard at the knees, hurling him hard to the ground. Natalie spilled out of his arms and rolled along the dirt like a log.

The tiara flung loose from her head.

A black crow descended from the sky. It was clearly diving toward Natalie.

With its long beak, the bird scooped up the tiara and took off into the skies.

Peter circled back. He grabbed Blackbeard by the collar and hauled him to his feet. Ever so gently, Peter pressed the blade of his long knife to the pirate's throat just below the Adam's apple.

"Blade's sharper than a razor, bloke. Forged and sharpened it myself. A feather-light flick o' the wrist and your head tumbles off like a coconut falling from a palm."

Natalie came to a dusty stop. She spit dirt out of her mouth, scraped it off her tongue. She wiped dirt from her clothes. She saw Blackbeard held at knifepoint.

Peter Freaking Pan?

Six crowmen came out of the clouds, upright and flying swiftly overhead.

"Natalie, run!" Caitlin screamed.

One crow veered away from the flock.

Natalie ran.

That lone birdman came in for a landing, touching down clean and smooth, then bursting into a swift sprint on two feet without missing a beat. He made a beeline toward Natalie.

Natalie pumped her legs hard, galloping like a stallion. She glanced back. The monstrosity was gaining on her. Getting closer.

She pumped her legs. It wasn't even a race.

The creature was on her like a leopard on a doe. He snatched her by the arms and ground to a halt.

The crowman stank like worms.

"Lemme go!" Natalie screamed. Its claws were a vise around her arms.

The bird was about to fly off with her when a voice called out.

"Crowman!" Peter shouted as the creature secured his hold on Natalie. "I'll behead your lord's number-two man. And then you'll hafta answer for it."

"The boy's right," Blackbeard said. "Hang on a bit."

Natalie sighed in relief. They were locked in a stalemate. She just got a stay of execution.

Blackbeard muttered to Peter, "Makes no difference, flyboy. When Janus kills the big sister, baby sis loses her protection. Then she's ours."

CHAPTER FORTY-FOUR

CAITLIN WATCHED WIDE-EYED, BLOOD-EYED, AS POOR NATALIE was captured by the crowman and Peter held Blackbeard in a strategic standoff.

And now, the soulless creature that had been hunting her down since Glendale had come to take her life.

The crowman known as Janus dropped from the sky.

Whooooosshh.

He landed within spitting distance of Caitlin. This was the first time she had gotten a close-up look at a crowman. The experience was far from pleasant.

Janus's body was covered in black feathers that laid together as smoothly as satin, from malformed head to clawed toes. He was tall, with anvil shoulders above a broad chest. His ankle-length coat was black, as was his cocked fedora. The brim sat low over beady eyes that were cauldron black and wet like fresh paint.

But his head! Good lord, his head.

His face was a mutation of humanoid and crow, a monstrous abomination of nature.

A large black beak—meat-hook sharp—protruded a good three feet from his face. His brow ridge was prehistoric. And his immense, concave cheekbones made his face a horrific Neolithic mashup of caveman and carnivorous bird of prey.

Caitlin glanced at the sky. Churning storm clouds hinted at the terrible violence to come. Thunder crackled as the humidity-charged air filled her nostrils.

As her hunger rose again, she sensed waves of blue-violet light flowing out of her, ascending skyward. In her mind's eye, she saw the shoreline of the Dipping Pools of Mount Velarium rising.

Her rational mind was crumbling like crisp autumn leaves under the feet of passersby. Her body began to shiver as it became drenched in icy sweat.

Then the unthinkable happened.

The last slivers of white in her eye washed over in red.

Her will was gone.

Her muscles hardened until they were as firm as dried cement. The blood in her veins surged with fresh adrenaline. She felt as if she could have lifted the whole mountain over her head.

She whirled toward Janus.

Ha!

The big crow was far less imposing than a mountain. He

was a quick meal, fast food. She would have him now and be done with him.

But Janus moved first. He lunged through the air . . . seized Caitlin by the throat.

He was going for the quick kill.

His clawed hands choked the air out of her lungs. She laughed an airless laugh. Soundless. She stared hard into his icy black eyes. She was calm, serene, and as ravenous as a black hole!

Her violent hunger triggered tactics to help her end her impending strangulation.

She balled her fists.

Crossed her forearms in an X.

Then she exploded her two upper limbs outward, breaking his choke hold. Her right fist swung around with fierce velocity, landing a crushing blow to Janus's rib cage.

Snap!

She wheeled right, firing a punishing elbow uppercut to the beak.

Crack!

His black-feathered head snapped back.

His wings sprang open like a parachute.

Whumppp!

They flapped like devil wings. The stench of urinary ammonia hit Caitlin like a punch.

Janus's liquid black eyes began leaking giant tears—or was it black blood?

He's injured!

Black droplets rolled down his cheeks like boiling tar. His demon breath blew hot and she could smell the bitter aroma of charred liver on it. He cawed like a hellhound, belting out a song of the underworld.

Their battle dance was underway.

They circled each other slowly, sizing up the competition. A roll of thunder shook the ground. Sullen clouds pressed down from the skies. The darkness engulfing the dancers made the black shade of night seem like an orange-pink sunrise by comparison.

The crowman planted a thought in Caitlin's mind: *"Thank you!"*

It was said in all earnestness.

"The pain magnifies my power, deepens my quest to drain you of your last gram of blood!"

Janus struck his head forward with cobra speed.

Caitlin shifted left.

Not in time.

Janus impaled her on his scissor-sharp beak.

Her body dangled in the air, skewered like a piece of meat. Her legs pedaled, but she went nowhere.

Bright red blood pooled around the entrance wound on her belly and seeped out the exit wound on her back.

My blood is warm—I'm still human. But I'll die on this stake! Unless . . .

Caitlin gripped both edges of the beak with her hands. She pushed. Her stomach wrenched. Her torso squirmed. Her whole body bled its way backward as she scooted it along the beak. Blood smeared it with dark-red varnish. She felt the sickening sensation of the spike sliding through her belly, bypassing her entrails.

She shrieked, crying out her determination as she steadily maneuvered herself off the murderous appendage. With a final shove, her body disengaged.

She fell to the ground, hard.

Janus whipped his head from side to side. Blood sprayed from his beak.

She rose back up, her left arm protecting her belly wound. Her blood was turning cold. She was losing her true self, her spirit, her soul.

Janus speared his serrated claw at her remaining eye, intending to blind her.

She danced right.

He swiped with his other claw.

She swerved left, dodging the second blow.

The crowman shot straight up, skyward. He disappeared into the grumbling storm clouds.

He's fleeing?

Janus burst through the other end of the billowing gloom, and tore an arced path above a mountain peak.

He suddenly froze, midair. Upright. Standing motionless in the sky like some sort of demon god. He flung the fedora from his head, tightened his long black coat. His bat-black eyes began boiling red. And then Janus hurtled through the air like a bullet shot from hell.

Caitlin was dead set in his crosshairs.

Her telescopic eye calculated his speed, his time of arrival down to a nanosecond. She leaped.

Whoooooooooooosh!

He just grazed her.

Then he hit the ground hard, tumbling in a flare-up of dust and debris. As he struggled to his feet, Caitlin leaped onto him.

This ends now.

She wrapped her legs around his neck.

A triangle choke hold.

She twisted her body, sending Janus into a crocodile death roll. Again, and again, and again . . . On the final roll, she slammed him to the rock-hard ground.

I have him now!

His neck was locked between her wringing thighs.

The blood in her eyes flashed like torch fire. Her craving for Janus's blood was vampirelike: a primal and terrible yearning she had never before experienced. A yearning she loved. A yearning she despised and feared.

Two more crowmen dropped from the firmament. There was murder in their basement-black eyes.

"About bloody time," Derek Blackshaw shouted as he hit the ground after them, swinging from a centurion tree. "Now get on with it, you ugly bastard fowl!"

The crowmen closed in on Caitlin like a pack of hyenas.

"Stand down, or I'll snap his neck," Caitlin warned as she tightened her squeeze.

The crowmen's eyes darted about, flitting covetously. Their blood-hunting beaks poked at the air.

"What the hell are you waiting for?" Derek called out.

The crowmen inched closer, as if teasing their prey.

"I'll do it!" Caitlin shouted. She bent Janus's neck back, showing she was ready to bite his throat out.

Scarecrow swung down from another tree. He was stuffed with fresh straw and black crow feathers.

The woodman made of tin trailed behind them, emerging from another tree.

"Eat him and you'll become him!" Scarecrow shouted as he hit the ground.

"The Enchanter *wants* you to win," Tin Man warned. "Because he wins either way!"

There is but one victor in war: war itself!

Caitlin wrestled with her own primal instinct, her visceral reaction to her dire situation. Her instinct screamed, *Kill him. Now!* Her intellect understood that darkness has one goal: to breed. The Tin Woodman was right. She frantically searched her being for some lingering remnant of humanity. A spark. A glimmer.

There was none.

She had become powerless to resisting the red band of the spectrum.

Another voice spoke: *The sun still shines when a curtain is drawn and the room goes black.*

Was her humanity still shining somewhere inside?

Caitlin cried out: "Where?"

The curtains, Caitlin! Behind the curtains!

The curtains were the reactions generated by the red band. Pulling back a curtain took a strong measure of will, a glint of green.

She had none. Her self-control had been vanquished. The chance to choose lost, like a stone skipped into the sea.

An enchanting sound suddenly filled the distant skies: Birdsong, growing louder by the second.

The nightingales of Neverland!

Caitlin glanced overhead. The mass of songbirds eclipsed the sky; feathered troubadours arrived by the hundreds of thousands.

Another resounding chorus began to fill the firmament, but this time from a different direction. A hundred thousand *more* nightingales were arriving, probably from Treasure Island.

The skies teemed with a sea of brightly colored wings. It looked like a million gallons of freshly spilled paint splattered across heaven's canvas in hues of orange, pink, purple, and blue. Their melody lit up emerald sparks inside Caitlin. She began to hope it would be enough to allow her to express choice again.

Defeating darkness with darkness yields greater darkness.

If I win, I lose.

Choose!

Caitlin had always drawn curtains as a response to crippling fears when they attacked—the excessive regard for her own life, her own discomfort. Nothing else mattered in a moment of panic.

She wanted to kill Janus to save herself.

That was the normal reaction.

Solutions were found in the violet.

Resist the red.

A sliver of light tinseled in her eye.

She summoned a wavelength of green kindled by the birdsong. Caitlin unlocked her legs, releasing Janus from the throes of death.

The crowman leaped to his feet.

Two more crowmen dropped from the sky and gathered next to their leader.

Gruncle Derek moved in a bit closer. He shrugged. "Took long enough. Now make your move, you blasted black-eyed birds!"

The six crowmen spread their wings. *Whuuummmp!*

"Perfect," she heard Gruncle say as he swung the duffel bag off his back. It thumped on the ground.

There was a sudden commotion. Caitlin whipped her head around to look left.

Blackbeard had broken loose from Peter Pan. He was charging like a bull toward Natalie, who was still in the claws of the crowman. The galloping pirate had Peter's dagger in his own hand. He raised it high as he zeroed in.

Natalie squirmed and twisted, struggling to escape.

Blackbeard leaped in the air, knife poised to strike.

Natalie closed her eyes and braced for impact.

The pirate came down hard, plunging the dagger and then twisting it as it punctured—

Natalie howled in horror.

Janus and his five winged henchmen moved in on Caitlin for the final kill.

Gruncle Derek upended his duffel bag and poured out its contents.

Ten million yellow, crazed ants scurried out in erratic, bustling zigzags!

The crazed ants incited a blood-curdling symphony of caws from the crowmen!

Caitlin shook her head stunned by a realization. It had become as clear as freshwater in her mind: the *undead* really have no choices. Vulturous cravings commanded their behavior.

She watched it happen before her very eye: Janus and his crowmen groaned with terrible anguish at feeling compelled to turn away from her, then moaned with ineffable rapture as they turned to the horde of ants and surrendered themselves to the insidious pleasures of anting!

"Bloody addicts is what they are!" Derek muttered.

The crowmen crushed the ant colonies and smeared their narcotic fluids over their wings—a vulgar display of unrestrained indulgence.

Derek Blackshaw waved his hand in contempt. "This piss-colored infestation should keep those junkies occupied for a while."

Caitlin's heart shattered as she looked over at Natalie.

Back in the orphanage, she had given Girl Wonder her solemn promise to hug and hold her whenever she needed comforting. That brainiac twerp had come running to her, arms wide, but Caitlin had been forced to wave her off.

Now it was time to keep her promise.

CHAPTER FORTY-FIVE

Caitlin and Gruncle Derek swiftly jogged over to Natalie and Blackbeard. The crowman who had just held her lay dead, black blood pooling around the dagger that Blackbeard had plunged into his chest.

Caitlin threw her arms around a visibly shaken Natalie. Her curly mane of hair was sprayed with the blood of the dead crowman. The girls wept in each other's arms.

"Are you okay?" Caitlin whispered in Natalie's ear.

"I am now." She squeezed her big sister tighter. Then she whispered in Caitlin's ear. "Your eye? Is it—?'

"Shh," Caitlin interrupted. "It's no big deal. I'm just glad to have you back."

Gruncle Derek went straight to Blackbeard. Both men let out hearty laughs as they joined in a warm embrace, giddy like drunken men. They slapped each other on the back and danced about.

Caitlin and Natalie turned to look.

They know each other?

The nightingales still sang out, and Blackbeard's red-chipped eyes had turned lagoon blue—without a trace of scarlet. Whatever spell Blackbeard had been under, the song of the nightingales had broken it.

"Can you believe it?" Natalie said to Caitlin.

"What?"

"I think that's actually Bobby Gramps." She was pointing to Blackbeard. "He killed the crowman. His eyes changed from bloodshot to sparkling blue. I watched it happen."

Natalie ran into Blackbeard/Bobby Gramps's arms to test her theory. He hoisted her up in his arms.

The wheels were turning in Caitlin's mind. Her mom had been under a spell that deluded her into believing she was the Queen of Hearts.

Derek smiled at Caitlin as he gestured to Blackbeard/Bobby Gramps. "He's me long-lost brother."

Scarecrow next came trotting over and Caitlin was glad to see him.

The straw man laid an arm around her shoulders as he pointed to the base of Mount Velarium. Caitlin warmly patted his hand.

"You made it!" she said with a smile.

He gave a thumbs-up. "A bit of stuffed straw, some stuffed black feathers—works wonders. Now, please listen. We haven't much time. Follow the trail of stairs—over there, at the bottom."

Caitlin couldn't concentrate on Scarecrow's instructions. She had sensed something she couldn't put her finger on during the entire journey. Suddenly, the thought crystalized in her mind. It concerned Gruncle Derek. And it strangled her heart. She turned to him.

"You're dead. You died a long time ago. Like my mom." Derek seemed taken aback. "No, no," he replied. His white aura turned red.

"You're lying," she said. "You're dead—and now you're one of the *un*dead."

He winced, caught red-handed and fibbing like a bad poker player. After a lingering awkward silence, a sweet and somber smile came to his lips. He took Caitlin's hand and patted it gently as he sighed.

"My dear, dear Cait."

Her eye watered as she continued, "That's why Foster Home Services couldn't find you."

He shrugged sheepishly.

"You never *flew* to California from Amsterdam to get me and Natalie. You came to the house in Glendale after climbing out L. Frank Baum's grave at Forest Lawn Cemetery."

His brow furrowed. "Almost got mowed down by a bloody groundskeeper."

Derek brushed away the fresh tears from her cheeks. "There's something else you need to know," he said.

Her shoulders sank.

"Better brace yourself, young Cait."

"Please," she replied in a trembling voice, "it's hard for me to breathe right now. Just tell me everything and get it over with."

"Your good old fart of a gruncle . . . well, I'm not really your uncle." His aura gleamed clear white.

Oh my gosh! He's telling the truth!

Derek then patted Blackbeard on the back as he held Natalie. "And this is *not* your grandfather, young Cait. He's *not* Bobby Gramps."

Natalie's eyes suddenly bugged out. She nonchalantly squirmed out of his arms and said, "Leg cramps. Need to stretch."

Caitlin was trembling. "Now you're really freaking me out. Who are you people?"

Derek set his hands on Caitlin's shoulders. The warmth radiating from his eyes made her weep. "I'm your grandfather, Caitlin," said Derek as his eyes moistened. "*I'm* Bobby Gramps!"

He raised his hands from her shoulders.

She froze, struggling to process the full extent of what she had just heard. And then she let go of all her earlier misconceptions and flew into his wide-open arms. Bobby Gramps and granddaughter Caitlin held each other, weeping and embracing and making up for many years of lost hugs and missed time.

Caitlin attempted to rein in her emotions, sniffling and wiping her eye on her sleeve. "Why didn't you just tell me when you knocked on our door in Glendale?"

"And say what? Hello there, Caitlin Fletcher; I'm your

long-dead grandfather Robert 'Bobby' Blackshaw, whom you've never met before? I'm back from the grave to warn ya of an impending apocalypse?"

She laughed as he went on. "I had to first find out what you knew. I was about to tell ya during our stroll that night in Glendale, but Cordelia and Harry pulled up. I was gonna tell ya the next morning, but those black-feathered anting addicts came knocking on the door."

Caitlin smiled at her gramps and then turned to the pirate. "So you *are* the real Blackbeard?"

He winked. "Well, sorta."

"What's that supposed to mean?"

"Well, first ya gotta know that your Bobby Gramps—that old undead rock 'n' roller—he's also me baby brother."

Her jaw dropped. "So you *are* brothers? You mean—"

"Yep, *I'm* your genuine grand uncle—Gruncle Derek Blackshaw, the firstborn. Pleased to meet ya, Caitlin. Last time I saw ya, ya was six months old and bundled cute as a doll in a blanket, I tell ya."

"And that's why you both had photos of my mom. But why the Blackbeard identity?"

Derek chuckled. "Because me, your gramps, you, and the little lambkins over here—the whole damn lot of us—are all the living descendants of Edward Thatch. The original Blackbeard, a bona fide buccaneer. The Thatch name was changed to Blackbeard"—he winked—"because it was quite an embarrassing name at the time, if ya know what I mean."

Caitlin shook her head. "Wait, what you meant to say

is that the Thatch name was changed to Black*shaw*—not Black*beard*?"

Gruncle Derek laughed. "Same thing, lass."

"Huh?"

"Me mom—Shirley Thatch—changed the notorious family name. But she still wanted to honor her ancestor, Blackbeard. So she chose the name Blackshaw. Why? I'll tell ya. The word for *beard* in Old Norse is *shaw*. So *beard* becomes *shaw*, and Blackbeard becomes Blackshaw . . . and Bob's your uncle!"

Caitlin smiled. "In my case, Bob's also my grandpa. And both my Blackshaw relatives are dead—whatever *dead* means—because lately I've spent more time with people who are supposedly dead than with people who are supposedly alive. Yet I've never felt so alive as I have among the dead and undead."

"This is getting creepy and convoluted," Natalie said. She ambled over to her new Gruncle Derek and smiled sweetly. "You can hold me again, if you'd like." New Gruncle Derek lifted Natalie up in his arms and said, "Guess I was pretty rough on ya while I was under the red-eye spell?"

Natalie smiled wickedly. "I think I was rougher on you. I threw a bucket of pee in your face." Derek's teeth almost fell out of his mouth.

"My beloved brother liberated me by offering himself in my stead to the Enchanter," Bobby Gramps interrupted. "The bastard was happy to oblige. I tried to stop Derek, but he wouldn't listen. And me, being a second born—I couldn't free him. I needed you, Caitlin. Anyway, the clock is ticking for the living hands of a true firstborn Blackshaw to turn the valve on top of that mountain. Now remember, young Cait—your sister, Natalie, will be most vulnerable at the summit."

"Why?

"Where you find the most potential for violet light you find equal potential for darkness. That mountain peak is also like a beacon for the Enchanter's power. Now, I don't think that bastard will try to make physical contact with her while you're present. So you've got to keep Natalie close by at all times. Perform your task quickly and then hotfoot it outta there."

"Hey—how do we even get back home?"

"The volcano. Through its mouth."

"Are you serious? That's like willfully jumping into the mouth of a fire-breathing dragon."

"It's not a real volcano," Natalie said. "It's some kind of world builder. I can't explain it fully yet, but I do think it can get us home."

Praise heaven, a rare miracle: Natalie Fletcher cannot explain something!

"It *will* get you home," Peter Pan said. "I've used it myself. Many times. It'll work. I'll explain when I meet you at the summit."

"I thought you couldn't fly that high."

"The nightingales gave me new wings, my lovely. I think I just might be able to make it."

Caitlin exhaled a long breath. There was nothing to really say and zero time left to ponder the family tree or the way back home. There was only one monumental task still to be completed.

"Those stairs will lead you up the mountain," Bobby Gramps said, "to the Dipping Pools. Once there, dip *seven* times to purge the godforsaken ghoul from your blood. Then turn those valves to drain the pools—and drain away that bastard's power."

Caitlin walked over to the foot of the rock stairs. She traced the trail of steps with her eye—all the way up Mount Velarium and into the clouds. She had to lean back so far she almost fell on her butt.

Caitlin smiled at her gramps, her Uncle Derek, Scarecrow, Tin Man, and Peter Pan. She didn't want to say goodbye. She just wanted to focus on the task at hand. So she smiled and winked at them. She took Natalie by the hand and they began their journey.

After climbing up the first few flights of stairs, Natalie stopped. She turned and glanced back at the scene. Caitlin did, too.

The crowmen were still on their backs, wings spread wide, writhing on the ground in a heightened state of euphoria.

"They seem so content," Natalie said with a sigh. "Their dopamine and endorphin levels must be off the charts."

Caitlin tugged at Natalie. "We need to keep climbing."

"Eos would be like that," Natalie muttered, paying no attention to Caitlin.

"What did you just say?"

Natalie shook off the thought. "Nothing. Let's go, Caity-Cakes."

Caitlin cast a suspicious, narrow eye at her sister.

And then both girls began their long ascent up Mount Velarium.

CHAPTER FORTY-SIX

THE HARD-BREATHING FLETCHER SISTERS HAD MADE IT ABOUT A third of the way to the summit of the towering geological beast known as Mount Velarium. The stairs they'd been climbing were constructed out of old, worn rocks, hand carved from the serrated mountain itself.

Like, probably a thousand years ago, Caitlin thought.

Some steps were narrow and smooth, others chipped and jagged; some sections of the trail were slippery steep, while others rose in a manageable incline. All along the trail, boulders of various sizes served as low railings—though from the looks of most of it, there was no way the "railing" was high enough to prevent anyone from actually tumbling off the mountainside.

The chorus of nightingales had become a faint, distant lullaby echoing up from the base of the mountain. The melody still seemed celestial and resplendent—and thankfully still audible enough to infuse Caitlin with effulgent sparks of the Green Spectrum. This gave her just enough strength to resist the cold compulsions born of savage hunger.

Caitlin's calf and thigh muscles cried out in pain with each step up the rocky slope. Natalie breathed heavily as she huffed her way up the trail. Their pace slowed as the elevation rose and the air thinned out.

During the last half-hour, the girls had crisscrossed the entirety of the gray mountain face. There was something oddly familiar about it that gnawed at Caitlin.

It concerned the mountain's unusual shape and contour. Large sections of granite protruded outward. Other sections arced inward. There were clefts, cloves, and curves—as if it had been hewn by design rather than by nature.

A heavy rumble interrupted her thoughts.

Mount Velarium began to quake.

"What's happening?" Caitlin asked.

Natalie shrugged. "If this were the other mountain, that rumbling would suggest an impending volcanic eruption."

The stone steps beneath their feet and along the mountain trail began to fracture. The quaking sent jagged chunks rolling into a full-on rockslide, a thundering avalanche of dagger-sharp stone, rock, and rubble.

Caitlin snatched Natalie by the collar. She hauled her sister beneath a slight overhang to shield them both from the rain of rocks.

Natalie screamed in pain. A plummeting stone had clipped her on the head. Blood dribbled down over her forehead.

Caitlin slammed her own eyes shut. She pinched her nostrils and summoned whatever was left of her will to resist.

"Get rid of the blood—now!" she screamed at her sister. "Rub it into the ground."

Caitlin heard Natalie fussing about.

"I'm wiping it off with my hand now." There was urgency and fear in Natalie's tone. She was not stupid. She knew the risk. "Now I'm wiping my hand into the dirt. . . ."

"Good. Next, rip some fabric from your shirt," Caitlin instructed. "Tie it like a bandana over the cut to clot the bleeding."

The seductive scent of blood snuck past Caitlin's front line of defenses. It slipped through her fingers into her nostrils and invaded her every cell as if by osmosis, stirring violent hunger.

"Okay, done," Natalie said.

Caitlin opened her eyes. Unplugged her nose. She couldn't help herself.

"You look like a dog," Natalie said, appalled, as Caitlin dropped to her knees to lick the bloody dirt off the ground. She sucked on clods, slurping up the drops of blood that sifted through.

Caitlin didn't care. When that metallic tang of blood touched her tongue, she breathed deeper, calmer. It tamed the monster and protected her sibling. If it was degrading to be crawling on all fours and lapping up blood-tinged dirt with her tongue, so be it.

Then she remembered what Scarecrow had told her about desire. Fill a dark desire and it would be satiated for the moment. *But then it would double in size.* Which meant she didn't have much time before her compulsion for flesh and warm blood would be back. There was no telling what she might do.

They had to get out of that place fast—and summit the mountain.

Thankfully, the rockslide ended quickly. Caitlin leaned out from under the overhang to survey the damage to the soaring mountain trail. All the stone steps had been pulverized to dust. There was no way up the mountain—and no way down. The sisters were trapped.

Prickly heat began radiating from the granite. Mount Velarium was warming up!

Caitlin used her telescopic eye to zoom out wide. . . .

She surveyed the mountain as if from a distance.

Her palm smacked over her mouth in dismay. To her horror, she realized that she and Natalie had *not* been climbing an ordinary mountain.

"What's wrong?" her sister asked.

Shock paralyzed Caitlin.

Natalie shook her. "I said, what's wrong?"

"It's a head. Oh God, we are climbing a man's head!"

"Who's *head*?"

"It almost looks like my therapist—Doctor J. L. Kyle!"

"You're delirious!" Natalie said. "Altitude sickness. This isn't Mount Rushmore." Natalie suddenly crinkled her brow. "Wait a sec . . . J. L. Kyle, you said?"

"Uh-huh!"

Natalie massaged her chin as if the motion could help her brain percolate. "Something odd about his name," she muttered. She continued mumbling to herself as her eyes roamed over the landscape. Her brows suddenly lifted into orbit. "It's an anagram!" she shouted. "Doctor J. L. Kyle! It's the exact same letters as Doctor Jekyll."

The hairs on Caitlin's neck became needles on her skin. The mountain began to darken like night. The granite beneath their feet seemed to be . . . softening. The girls stepped back from the wall. The rock face began to swell, ripple, and wave. Finally it arranged itself into a sort of black curtain.

"Get me off this mountain!" Natalie cried out in an uncharacteristic display of panic.

The surface of Mount Velarium had indeed become a flowing black curtain blowing in a whistling wind. The air abruptly settled and the curtain came to rest. The impression of yet another face showed through, contoured underneath, as if someone's head were beneath it.

The curtain then began to thicken and solidify and harden back into granite. It silhouetted a new, frightening sculpture of a head—one bearing the face of consummate evil.

The words fell out of Natalie's mouth. "Doctor Jekyll and—"

"Mr. Hyde!" Caitlin said in astonishment.

This new head boasted beastly sharp cheekbones, a fiendish, crooked nose, deep-set sinister eyes, and the irregular-shaped forehead of a monster.

Natalie squeezed Caitlin tighter. "This is getting freakier by the moment."

"Don't react to it," Caitlin said. "The mountain is just trying to scare us."

"Chalk one up for the mountain," Natalie said in a quavering voice.

The girls remained huddled under the overhang.

Now what?

As Caitlin held Natalie tight, she could sniff the blood coursing through her sister's neck veins.

Please, no!

The cravings returned—this time doubly strong.

As if answering the girls' prayers, an object abruptly dropped out of the sky. It hung in the air, dangling in front of them.

Could it be?

Caitlin and Natalie exchanged wary looks.

A braided rope.

A braided rope of blonde hair.

A braided rope made from silken, golden-blonde hair.

An expectant smile lit Natalie's face. "Do you think—"

"Don't say it!" Caitlin interrupted. "Words have power."

There was no need to inject doubt into the words that left their mouths and tempt fate again. Caitlin pulled Natalie by the arm and led her to the rope. "Twist it around your arms and waist and follow me," Caitlin instructed.

The girls fastened the rope around themselves and began to climb. Their feet propelled them up the rock face, their arms pulled them up the rope, bicep and shoulder muscles flexing. Slowly, they began hauling their bodies upward.

The winds abruptly kicked up. A steady, rising air current produced an updraft, giving Caitlin and Natalie added lift. Then the braided rope began reeling itself in as if attached to a winch, accelerating their ascent even more.

The girls spidered up the mountain, feet scuttling along the vertical face, trying to keep pace with the lifting winds and the rope as it coiled itself back up. They weren't so much scaling the mountain as gliding up it.

"How easy is this?" Natalie exclaimed.

Caitlin shouted, "I told you to watch your words."

Caitlin glanced up warily. Sudden storm clouds appeared out of nowhere and began to churn above them.

"Figures," Natalie said regretfully. "We're heading right into those cumulonimbus clouds."

"Cumulo *what*?"

"Thunderclouds. Lightning. You know, *BOOM-CRACKA-BOOM!*"

Caitlin peered down toward the base of the mountain.

Bobby Gramps, Gruncle Derek, Tin Man, Scarecrow, and the rest of the group were now the size of dots.

She planted her eye back on the granite wall in front of

her. Even at close range, she could detect how grotesque Mr. Hyde's features were below the veneer of Mount Velarium.

The most dangerous part of the ascent was quickly approaching—the part where they would have to enter the cyclonic storm clouds and dodge the purple lightning zigzagging inside them.

Lightning bolts lit up the mountain like strobe lights, followed by booming bursts of thunder that palpated the air.

"Hang on!" Caitlin cried as they were lifted into the turbulent condensation.

Caitlin's hair frizzed as humid air currents whirled about, and her damp clothes clung to her body like Saran Wrap. Natalie's mound of curls puffed up like foam. A furious tempest suddenly whipped up, stretching their lips back and causing their cheeks to flap like leaves on a tree.

It would almost be funny—if this weren't a life-or-death situation.

Another vein of lightning hissed through coils of cloud, sizzling just past the girls in a blinding flash of heat. A few inches closer and they would've been charred to a crisp. The sun-hot lightning bolt evaporated the moisture from Caitlin's clothes instantly, leaving her desert dry.

Freaky!

Another thunderclap almost burst her eardrums.

And then, rather suddenly, the chaos of the cumulonimbus clouds gave way to calm air. A clear and cool, star-jeweled sky emerged as the girls were elevated above the violence of the storm.

The hushed, summer-scented summit of Mount Velarium came into view.

"I can hear it!" Caitlin cried with hopeful excitement. "Flowing water. The wellsprings of Velarium! Oh my God, they're real! And the aroma! It's insane."

The retracting rope slowed to a stop. The rising air currents died down.

The girls had come to rest at the summit.

And just as Caitlin had hoped, a perspiring, long-haired, beautiful ghoul was standing there waiting for them.

"That was one heavy payload," Rapunzel quipped as she gathered up her braided locks.

CHAPTER FORTY-SEVEN

"I've been hiding out on this malignant mountain for months waiting for you," Rapunzel said as she wrapped her arms warmly around Caitlin and Natalie. After they exchanged hugs, Rapunzel smiled delightedly. She took a good, long, loving look at Caitlin. She tilted her head when she saw the eye patch.

"What happened to your eye?"

"Lost it. Bitten by a crow."

"My goodness."

"I'm okay. How did you know we would be coming?"

"Glinda, bless her soul. She read it in the Great Book of Records a few months back. Thankfully, I got up this mountain before the rebellion broke out."

"But it hadn't happened yet. So how could she have known?"

Rapunzel pressed a finger to her mouth. "Shhhh. We can't

talk here. All I can say is everyone is where they're supposed to be. Especially you. Peter Pan is cruising the skies as a lookout and waiting for you. After you dip in the wellsprings and regain your full humanity, he will show you where the shutoff valve is."

"Is everything all right?" Caitlin asked.

"Of course," Rapunzel assured her. Her aura was redder than a pomegranate.

"You don't truly believe that," Caitlin said.

"It's what I truly *hope*," Rapunzel confessed. "Just stay close to Natalie. Don't leave her alone. And get out of this place as fast as you can after you're done."

Before Caitlin could say another word, Rapunzel kissed her and Natalie on the forehead. She whispered something in Natalie's ear.

Rapunzel then cast her braided cable of hair off the summit's edge, snagging it on a lower ridge. She swung off the mountain peak and vanished into the darkness below.

The brevity and blur of the encounter with her dear friend left Caitlin breathless and melancholy. There was so much for them to talk about. But she had to push the sadness away. She had to keep moving.

"What did Rapunzel whisper to you?"

Natalie shrugged. "She told me to remain strong and steadfast in the mind."

"Let's find those wellsprings," Caitlin said. She began to gallop across the summit in the direction of the flowing waters and lovely smells. The air was fresh and crisp.

The neighboring volcano was rumbling and spewing fire.

"I can't hear the songbirds anymore," Caitlin said.

She accelerated her pace, and Natalie sprinted full tilt to keep up with her. The wound on her head must have reopened, because blood began to soak through the bandana.

Ungodly urges began bubbling up inside Caitlin. She was eyeing her kid sister as she ran, contemplating doing terrible things to her. She tried shaking off the cravings.

The girls rounded a large boulder the size of a house.

Caitlin's heart began to pound as her predatory instincts intensified. "Just one small bite," she shouted. "I won't hurt you. But I need a bite. I'll stop at one bite."

Natalie shot angry eyes at her. "Get a hold of yourself, sister. I already have the Enchanter to contend with."

Caitlin was trying, desperately trying.

Thank goodness twinkling, violet sparks are shimmering in the air just up ahead.

An unearthly, heavenly aroma began to fill Caitlin's lungs, perfuming her very essence. They had arrived at the enchanted springs. All words suddenly left her, robbed by the beauty of the wellsprings.

Scarecrow had been right. The waters *were* a dazzling violet color. And the aroma of the airborne mist was a heady blend of lilac blossoms and sweet, blooming hyacinth bulbs—the fragrance was almost as alluring as the succulent scent of blood. Caitlin sucked in the perfumed air. Her breathing deepened, and her heart rate began to slow.

The edge of a waterfall glinted silvery purple where its waters poured into the brilliant pools.

"I'm jumping in," Caitlin said. "You should too. It'll heal your head wound."

"No way I'm going bare naked in that water! There are boys at the bottom of this mountain, and Peter Pan is somewhere up there—probably spying on you."

There was no time to ponder such thoughts. Caitlin quickly undressed, sliding out of her jeans and panties, yanking off her top, and removing her bra. Then she removed her eye patch.

Natalie shook her head in disbelief. "You got guts, big sister."

"Stay put," Caitlin said, "till I come out." Caitlin waded into the indigo springs. The water was as warm as toast yet soulfully refreshing, and lacquer clear like she imagined the waters of Eden must have been.

She dipped beneath the sparkling surface.

A shimmering, violet-blue aura surrounded her body. As she dipped each of the seven prescribed times, twinkling orbs of light circled about her. Strings of royal-purple light orbited the full length of her body in figure-eight patterns as she closed her eyelids and tilted her head toward the starry sky visible above the Velarium summit.

She raised her arms and opened her eye. The ghastly cracks on her forearms began to fizzle in a ticklish way as they regenerated while she watched. Her stomach wound buzzed pleasantly as the pain vanished. She wouldn't have been surprised if the blood in her veins had turned violet as well.

She splashed more water on her face, inhaling the lilac-hyacinth fragrance. It made her soul swell with grace, humility, and fortitude.

The notions of eating flesh and blood began to seem revolting again as she steadily recovered her human traits.

She had become so enthralled by her surroundings, so caught up in this womb of seventh heaven, it took her a moment too long to realize that a horrific development was unfolding on the banks of the pool.

Natalie was engaged in conversation with a dark-hooded creature who was robed in serrated layers of blasphemous-looking, red-edged, black curtains.

And that's when Caitlin swallowed her heart.

Because the unthinkable had just happened.

Natalie was face-to-face with the Lord of the Curtain.

CHAPTER FORTY-EIGHT

CAITLIN SWAM FURIOUSLY TOWARD THE SHALLOWS. HER FRANTIC shriek rang out across the summit. "Natalie, get away!"

The Enchanter was whispering in Natalie's ear.

Caitlin leaped out of the pool and put her clothes back on as fast as humanly possible.

Just as she was about to dash to Natalie, the Lord of the Curtain raised a shrouded arm.

Woooooooooomph!

A curtain as black as the Devil's eyes sprang open around the pair, encircling Natalie and the Enchanter in a barricade of unspeakable darkness. Caitlin tasted supreme evil.

She whipped her head this way and that, searching frantically for a glimpse of her sister.

"Caitlin!"

A voice called to her from the sky.

She looked to the stars.

Peter Pan was rocketing across the twinkling sky above the summit.

He dropped from the firmament in a reverse two-and-a-half-turn somersault with a twist, landing as gracefully as a cat next to Caitlin.

"Follow me!"

He took her by the hand and sprinted around the dipping pools. "Where were you when I was in the water?" she asked.

Peter Pan didn't answer, but she swore she detected a slight smirk.

That rascal!

They rounded a large boulder and Peter slammed on the brakes. The stop was so sudden, Caitlin plowed into him.

He pulled out his dagger. He slid the tip of his blade into the thin crack of a just-distinguishable, rectangular frame etched into the boulder. With his blade and the fingers of his other hand, he lifted up what looked to be a trap door. Underneath . . . *the shut-off valve!*

The cast-iron spigot looked like the steering wheel you'd find on a bus, only thicker.

Peter Pan quickly stepped back. "I can't touch it."

"Why not?"

"It'll burn me like lava. Only a human hand can turn it."

"Check me," she said as she raised her eyelid.

Peter leaned in close and inspected her eyeball. "Blood-free—bright and beautiful as a summer's sky."

Then he stole a kiss from her lips.

"Peter Pan!"

Caitlin warily placed her hands upon the handwheel.

Please work!

The cast iron was cold. When it registered an authentic human touch, it began to glimmer like moonglow.

Thank you!

Her gaze turned to steel as she eyed Peter. "He's got Natalie—over there, behind the black curtain."

Pan winked and sailed back into the sky. He circled in a holding pattern above the summit, waiting for Caitlin to open the valve. Golden moonlight shimmered on his form like melted butter. His blond locks waved in the wind as if lit by the glow from the lunar orb.

Caitlin tightened her grip like a vise over the handwheel's spokes. She mustered all the strength in her shoulders, arms . . . and then she began to turn it counterclockwise, bit by bit.

A muffled sound of flowing water began to hum in the starry night, drop by drop. The Dipping Pools of Velarium were opening little by little. . . .

Caitlin could hear the rush of unleashed waters cascading down the inner caverns of the mountain. The network of channels designed to unite the male waters from the sky with the female waters welled beneath the ground in massive pools were ready to receive the torrent. At least, that's what Bobby Gramps, Gruncle Derek, Peter Pan, and Scarecrow were all counting on.

But what if those channels are blocked somewhere along the line?

Red-band thoughts!

Resist!

Caitlin shoved the negative thoughts aside.

The next few moments moved as slow as traffic congestion as she continued cranking the valve counterclockwise.

She cranked that handwheel until her palms blistered.

Her finger bones began cramping, her joints swell-
ing . . . and finally, the handwheel could turn no more.

She looked at the wellsprings.

The water levels seemed to be dropping.

Please, please!

She looked over at the neighboring peak. The volcano's
flames were sputtering out.

But what if—

She glanced up at Peter Pan and gave him the thumbs-up.

He jetted toward the barricading black curtain.

He plunged his dagger into the blackened fabric and then
flew around the entire cloak, slicing it open end to end. He
snatched it up like a thief in the night. He quickly sliced it up
into scraps and flung the rubbish into a shredded heap.

Caitlin's eye lit up like a bright star of hope.

The Enchanter *was* weakening.

He was down on one buckled knee, but still clinging to
Natalie.

Caitlin raced toward her sister.

The Enchanter's countenance was obscured by the dense
shadow of his cowl and robe. The dark garments were like a

sucking black hole, swallowing Caitlin's courage and hijacking her will as she approached. Nonetheless, she closed in fast . . .

Caitlin yanked Natalie's arm, releasing her from the clutches of the Enchanter.

"You won't win this!" Caitlin screamed.

The Enchanter paid her no attention. A nondescript voice seemed to radiate out of him, and it was clearly directed at Natalie. But there was no mouth to see, no facial features to discern; the words somehow materialized *inside* Caitlin's mind.

"Eos will be yours, Natalie. It will operate by your chosen laws of nature. Your universe to delight in for eternity. Eos will embody only the violet band of the spectrum—if you join me. The Red Spectrum will be banished. The end of fear. We can create a new realm radiating only a beautiful violet-blue."

Caitlin lost her breath. Not because of what she had just heard. But rather because of what she was seeing . . .

The Enchanter's aura had turned as white as new-fallen snowflakes.

Huh?

Which meant the words he had just uttered were truthful. Genuine. Sincere.

How's that possible?

Natalie squeezed Caitlin. "Get him out of my head!"

"Don't worry," Caitlin replied as she pulled Natalie along

and they began to run away from the Enchanter. "The waters are emptying. He's growing more desperate."

Caitlin glanced back. The Lord of the Curtain was weakening further, down on both knees.

Caitlin glanced at the heavens. Peter Pan still hovered in the vaulted sky. He pointed toward the second star on the right, glinting in the eastern sky just above the summit.

"Run toward the second star!" he shouted. "You need to get Natalie out of here—now!"

The girls sprinted in the direction he indicated. They ended up at the eastern edge of the summit. Caitlin peered over the edge.

Some fifty feet below lay the portrait mountain's twin.

The volcano!

Specifically, the mouth of the volcano.

"Don't worry," Peter Pan shouted down from the sky. "It's like riding the world's largest waterslide."

And then he landed on the summit, right next to Caitlin.

"Lock your eye dead center on the volcano's mouth," he instructed. "Then just jump."

Caitlin did a double take. "Are you insane?"

"The volcano won't erupt, because the wellsprings are dry. Hopefully they will remain dry for a few more minutes."

Yeah—hopefully.

He took hold of Caitlin's and Natalie's hands. "Just remember, ladies—at each intersection in the tunnels, keep veering *right* to make it back to Guildford."

Guildford? Not Glendale?

"I hope the ride is kinda fun," Natalie said.

The resounding *boom* in Caitlin's head was like an atomic migraine explosion. It knocked her off her feet.

"NAATAALLIEEEEE!"

The booming, baleful voice of the Enchanter!

Incredibly, Natalie didn't seem to hear a thing. She was standing by the edge of the summit and preparing to leap off. But then she looked up, as if something had caught the attention of her mind's eye.

"Jump to it," Pan said to Caitlin. "The Enchanter's inside her."

Storm clouds gathered from out of nowhere above the Dipping Pools.

How powerful is this monster?

Violet rain began to fall.

The wellsprings were being fed again. Which meant that the volcano could become active any second.

"Please get me out of here!" Natalie cried out, frightened by what she was seeing in her mind.

Despite her pounding head, Caitlin stumbled back up to her feet. The summit spun and her head throbbed like a gong rung by a mallet.

She managed to turn around; her eye found the Lord of the Curtain. He was back on his feet, arms raised toward the sky. He continued to project his voice inside her head.

"Imagine a world where only violet shines. The calm, contentment, control . . ."

The Enchanter's radiance continued shining a blinding white.

How could this be true?

"I'm not consummate evil. I'm not the monster they portray."

His aura shimmered as white as a snowcapped mountain peak.

Caitlin turned away. She cautiously peered over the summit to locate her target again. The volcano's mouth was moving in jagged patterns as a result of her dizzy spell. She wobbled. She stepped back from the edge to avoid tumbling off.

Peter grabbed her hands. "Get a grip, lass. Breathe slowly."

He massaged her temples. The dizziness began to lift.

"Snap to it!" he shouted.

"But how can all his words be true?" Caitlin cried.

"The Enchanter is cunning."

She shook her head. "But truth is truth!"

"And I speak it, too, my lovely. Now shove off, and get out of here before it's too late."

Just as Caitlin was regaining her balance, a foul breath of wind whipped across the summit. She wobbled again. She stiffened her legs and stretched out her arms to steady herself.

"Okay . . . I think I'm ready."

"Think?" Natalie said worriedly.

"Say goodbye to Gruncle Derek, Bobby Gramps, and everyone," Caitlin instructed Peter. "Hopefully I'll see them sometime, on the other side."

"You'll see them for eternity if we don't jump *now*," Natalie urged.

Peter hugged Caitlin and Natalie. "Hurry! Or these winds will blow you off course, and you'll miss the mouth." His aura shone white.

Nice. So we might just fall to our deaths.

And then, with one great thrust, Peter Pan launched himself off the summit.

Caitlin and Natalie exchanged wary looks.

A hard rain began to fall. Caitlin and Natalie were drenched in seconds.

They peered over the edge.

Sparks sputtered from the volcano.

"On the count of three," Caitlin said. She locked her eye dead center on the volcano's mouth.

Her soaked auburn hair was plastered to her head from the downpour.

The sisters counted in unison.

"One . . ."

Caitlin sensed movement behind her.

"Two . . ."

Someone was creeping up from the rear.

"Three!"

She jumped.

Natalie's cry echoed in the rain-swept Velarium night. "I'm sorry, Caity-Cakes! I still love you!"

Caitlin managed a last look up as she dropped into the black mouth of the volcano.

Her brainiac kid sister Natalie hadn't jumped!

Caitlin's telescopic eye zoomed in.

Raindrops were spilling down Natalie's cheeks.

And then the black-veiled hands of the Enchanter set a gem-encrusted tiara upon her head.

CHAPTER FORTY-NINE

CAITLIN FLETCHER HAD NEVER FALLEN OUT OF THE SKY BEFORE. Not even in her dreams. But now she really was, and she landed on the ground in a forward tumble, which turned into a front roll, and concluded with her lying flat on her back. Her one eye made out a thin slice of curved light that was the October crescent moon.

She was dune dry.

What just happened?

Strange. It didn't feel like she'd physically fallen out of the sky. It felt more like she had just crash-landed in a dream.

And suddenly, she remembered the dream.

She'd been riding the world's largest roller coaster— swerving, speeding, curving, and looping at unfathomable speeds. It had whipped through a pitch-dark indoor coaster hangar that was as big as the Milky Way galaxy, literally. A million other roller coasters were also operating in the same space, entwined and crisscrossing one another in an intricate network, hurtling all kinds of life-forms to different locations in myriad worlds dwelling in countless other dimensions. Some life-forms were corporeal, others ethereal, translucent beings with large diamond eyes.

Some of them exchanged meaningful looks with her as their eyes met. Lifetimes of memories were shared through some kind of unspoken universal language that translated across time and space.

There had been explosions of light and gas that blazed like newborn stars, and hot cosmic gases of purple and blue that swirled nearby, as well as distant supernovas igniting light-years away. There had been smells of hot sulfur mingling with the pristine scents of fresh rain and heavenly gardens.

She remembered the roar of a million whirling wheels gliding along rails, and the continual *whoosh* of million-passenger cars rocketing along the ripping, rolling cosmic coaster. And Caitlin had instinctively kept leaning right, as if her body could control the direction of the track.

It wasn't a dream, though. Any more than Jack and the fairy-tale dimension had been a dream. She had been hurtling through the volcano and its vast network of interdimensional wormholes!

Then she remembered that there was one particular coaster car, far off in the distance, looping and curving and then rushing by her to a distant world. Caitlin's heart had almost stopped when she saw it, because she thought she recognized the people in the passing coaster—her mom and dad?

But then her own coaster had suddenly slammed on the brakes to the screeching sound of scraping metal, and the car jerked to a full stop, flinging her from her seat.

She remembered nothing else.

Now here she was, lying on the grass in deafening silence.

It smelled so familiar.

Like the English countryside during a crisp October fall.

Like the charming town of Guildford.

She turned her head to one side. The cool, crisp grass pressed against her cheek. She read the name on the headstone silently to herself.

Charles Dodgson.

Aka Lewis Carroll.

I'm back!

Then the memory of what had transpired hit like a hammer, inflicting a blunt wound on her soul.

Natalie!

Before she could unpack her next thought, half a dozen hands flashed in front of her face. She took hold of one. More hands reached out from nowhere, latching on to her wrists and forearms, and pulling her to her feet.

She straightened up, locked her knees, and stood firm.

She glanced around.

One. Two. Three. No, wait . . . there's four . . .

Her eye strained, desperate to convince her mind of what it was counting.

Five. Six. Seven . . .

Her jaw dropped as if in slow motion as the shock gradually registered.

She gasped.

Hands cupped her mouth and nose.

Her legs buckled beneath her again.

CHAPTER FIFTY

JACK SPRIGGINS, BARTON SULLIVAN, CINDERELLA, RAPUNZEL, Snow White, Sleeping Beauty, Piper, Paige, and other kids from her school were all gathered in the graveyard at Mount Cemetery. Even Erwin Spencer was there. And the Kingshire social studies teacher and Halloween Masquerade Ball bouncer, Mrs. Sliwinski, as well. They were all staring at her, agog.

The shock of the moment and the emotional trauma of her recent ordeal paled in comparison to the feelings that unexpectedly gripped her like a manacle.

Embarrassment. Shame. Over her looks. Her missing eye. She was wearing a patch. Fearful of being labeled an ugly duckling. And worse, her guilt about being concerned with such vain issues when so much more was at stake.

She bowed her head. Bit her lip. Exhaled. Anything to avoid looking anyone in the face.

What are they all doing here? How did they know?

Was it her post? Blog? Her message to Barton?

She forced to herself to resist the flood of self-conscious doubts that were beating her up on the inside. She had too much to tell them. She began hyperventilating.

"You don't understand," she said frantically, forcing the words out with her breath.

Jack hushed her quiet as he took her in his arms.

Caitlin melted, burying her face in his warm chest. His fresh, foresty scent comforted her. Her other friends gathered around them, and she felt their gentle hands caressing the back of her head, patting her back.

Caitlin sobbed out the words through tears.

"We were at the summit. Mount Velarium. The Enchanter. He's taken Natalie."

Jack tightened his embrace.

Caitlin wept as she wrapped her arms tighter around Jack.

Someone leaned in close to whisper in her ear, "We're here to help you."

Barton.

Caitlin withdrew from Jack and turned to him.

His jasper-green eyes stared intently into Caitlin's eye. "We'll take care of this, Caitlin." He hugged her tight. She smelled his musky cologne.

Cinderella came forward and tapped her on the shoulder. "Listen up, kiddo. That depraved pile of drapes has no clue what's coming."

Caitlin turned to Cindy. It warmed her heart to see

Cinderella again, but how awful and tragic that it had to be under these circumstances.

Sleeping Beauty yawned. "I dreamed you lost your eye. I saw what was happening. So I warned everyone."

"How do we get Natalie back from the Enchanter?"

Beauty raised a single eyebrow. "Did it rain on the summit?"

"At first, no. But then the Enchanter made it rain. To fill the Dipping Pools and regain his power."

Beauty shook her head adamantly. "No, Caitlin. He cannot alter the world. He can form clouds, but he cannot *make* it rain."

"Then who made it rain?"

"Natalie."

Huh?

"When she didn't resist his beguiling words in her mind, her violet sparks transferred over to him. That was the rain you felt!"

Caitlin shook her head, speechless.

"And I had another dream moments ago," Beauty added. "A vision." She was addressing the whole group now. "They're coming here. To this world. Your world. Tonight. Halloween. The werwulves. The Blood-eyed. A full-scale invasion. They've been setting up their portals for some time now."

"Portals where?" Barton asked.

"Patcham—the city where James Halliwell-Phillipps is buried."

"Who is he?"

"He wrote *The Three Little Pigs*. And also Wolvercote Cemetery, where J. R. R. Tolkien is interred. And Great Crosthwaite, where Robert Southey, the author of *Goldilocks* is buried. And—"

"Wait!" Caitlin interrupted. "I don't get it. If this is a battle for Eos, why is the Enchanter sending his ghoul army from hell over *here?*"

Sleeping Beauty's face was enigmatically calm. "Earth *is* Eos."

Oh my gosh!

A tidal wave of questions swam through Caitlin's head.

Jack balled his hands into fists. "We need to spread out. Post people at all the gravesites. We'll need airline tickets. Maps. More soldiers."

Barton spoke up. "I'll round up the nastiest crew of rugby players you ever saw. And I'll cover the costs." Barton winked at Caitlin and flashed a smile. "Sullivan family credit card. Might as well use the money for a worthy cause."

"I've got credit cards, too," Piper volunteered. "My dad will thank me if we save the world."

Sleeping Beauty continued, "The blood-eyed werwulves—the ones who walk upright—I saw them on your streets. They're coming for Caitlin. And the rest of those relentless monsters won't stop until they destroy her—and your world."

Snow White was on the verge of sobbing. "So much devastation."

Caitlin couldn't find the air for her next breath.

Beauty added, "This was the Enchanter's plan all along. But that fiend needed Natalie first."

"How many of these werwulf ghouls are coming here?"

"Thousands."

Caitlin did a double take. "What? We're totally outnumbered!"

"No," Barton said. "You'll post online again. The call to action. We can round up volunteers from your online post."

"Are you serious? Did you not read the comments I got after I posted that? I got ripped open. Slammed. People think I'm psycho."

"No, Caitlin. You actually have a major squadron behind you now."

"What are you talking about?"

Erwin Spencer stepped forward, thumb-scrolling the smartphone in his hand and sporting a smart-aleck grin on his face. "I hacked the doctor in revenge," Erwin said proudly.

"J. L. Kyle?"

"The one and only. Found your original transcripts. I posted them. You touched a lot of people's hearts." Erwin presented her with the comments mounted on his phone's screen.

Thanks, Caitlin! Ur story moved me. I've had panic attacks since I was fourteen. U gave me hope. Courage. U rock.

You wanna fight evil of all evil? I'm down like a clown, Charlie Brown.

And I'm up for it.

I'm game too.

Count me in, Caitlin.

I can dance to that.

Not afraid to die in battle. I die every day during these panic attacks.

Just tell me when and where, when and where, when and where—ooops, a bit of OCD.

I'm all in.

I freaked out two days ago in the mall. Couldn't breathe. Thought I was dying. My mom said it was an anxiety attack. I read your post. I get it now. I really get it. On board w ya.

There were countless more.

"And did you know Doctor Creeptard shot you up with sodium pentothal? It's in the transcripts."

Caitlin hadn't known that.

"Don't worry. We'll take care of him as well."

Watching wiry nerd Erwin Spencer talk tough made her laugh inside instead of crying like she had been about to.

Jack Spriggins punched his fist into his open palm. "It's time. Let's do this!"

Caitlin's face suddenly hardened. She was adamant when she said, "You guys go! I'm staying right here at Mount Cemetery till Natalie gets back."

Barton grabbed her by the shoulders. "Are you crazy?"

Jack grabbed her away from Barton. "Are you a loon?"

Caitlin pulled away from both boys.

"Yes, I'm as crazy as a loon. I know Natalie. She'll make it back. I'm not leaving this place till she returns."

Jack nodded in resignation and turned to Barton. "Leave her for now. She needs some space. And rest. We need to move out."

Sleeping Beauty's face was a mask of concern. "Jack's right. We're almost out of time."

Rapunzel spoke next. "Barton, how long till you recruit more people?"

"Fast. A few texts to a few chaps. Erwin will round up the volunteers."

"Good." She nodded. "Everyone, listen up. We'll meet up at Barton's house to map out our strategy and receive final instructions."

The faces of Piper, Layla, and Paige were pale with concern, but they seemed totally committed to the cause.

Piper kissed Caitlin on the cheek. "Will you be okay here?"

Caitlin nodded. "And thank you for helping. I have no words to—"

Piper covered Caitlin's mouth with her fingertips. "You don't have to say anything. To be honest, I'm a little bit spooked right now. I mean, I read your posts. And Barton and Jack and Sleeping Beauty explained everything to us, but . . . well, seeing Sleeping Beauty and Rapunzel in the flesh . . . this is all so freaky."

Piper shifted her gaze to Caitlin's eye patch. She smiled. "And you look absolutely gorgeous—a genuine badass pirate. Brilliant. No one will dare tussle with you."

Mrs. Sliwinski ambled over and pinched Caitlin's cheeks. Undoubtedly, she was tougher than the whole lot of them.

"Don't you worry, my dear. No zombies are going to crash this party as long as I'm at the door."

"So you believe me?"

She smiled. "Long before I was a social studies teacher, I taught English lit. I know the power of these stories. The reality of the human imagination. And I never missed an episode of *The X-Files*. I know strange things are happening all the time, and we only need to open our eyes to see behind the curtain."

"We go now!" Jack shouted.

Barton led the way out of Mount Cemetery, and the group followed.

Before she could blink her eye, Caitlin was suddenly standing alone. The moment seemed so surreal, she thought the last few minutes might've been a dream.

Without warning, an excessive tiredness overwhelmed her. Her legs also ached from the climb up Mount Velarium; her calf and thigh muscles cried out for relief.

Instead of fighting the sleepiness, she embraced it, for it also distracted her from the hurt in her heart over Natalie.

Besides, she had no choice. Drowsiness was consuming her. Her eyelids were closing. She had to lie down.

Only for a few minutes, she promised herself.

Caitlin laid right down on the lawn, curled up into a comfortable position, and rested her heavy head on her arm. The air was crisp, cool, earthy, and damp. Someone nearby in Guildford was burning a fire. Grassy, leafy scents filled her nostrils—the familiar fragrances of autumn.

She was aching for a cup of hot apple cider.

Before she slipped into slumber, she glanced up at the sky with a tired, tearful eye. She searched and found the second star to the right in the eastern sky. She offered a prayer and a wish before her bedtime in the cemetery.

She prayed that Peter Pan would help Natalie. And she wished her kid sister would somehow find the light. Somehow find her way back home by the break of dawn. And then maybe, just maybe, by that first blush of daylight, her beloved Girl Wonder would be waiting for her when that morning sun rose and Caitlin awoke after some much-needed shut-eye.

EPILOGUE

DAWN BROKE AS A THREAD OF DAYLIGHT BEGAN VERGING ON THE eastern horizon. Not enough to wake her. Then came the girl's whisper. The words entered Caitlin's sleep, and she was delighted to hear them.

"Wake up."

She was aware that she was in the middle of a dream, and hopeful that she would find her prayer had been answered when she finally awoke.

She willed herself out of slumber, forcing her eye open.

I'm still here.

Mount Cemetery.

I must've slept right through the night.

She glanced around, anxiously searching for Natalie. But the graveyard was still dark and as deadly silent as its interred inhabitants.

The girl spoke again. "Are you up? If you are, please help me out of here."

The voice was coming from the grave of Lewis Carroll!

Caitlin leaped to her feet. She clawed her fingers into the dirt and began shoveling away piles of freshly uprooted clods from the top of Carroll's burial site.

A girl's hand poked through the portal.

"Natalie, you did it!" Caitlin shouted with glee. "I knew it!"

Caitlin frantically shoveled away more dirt.

Out popped . . . *Alice?*

Wait—it isn't Alice. But it certainly isn't Natalie.

Caitlin extended a hand and helped the girl climb out of the grave.

She brushed away the soil from her hair and patted clumps of dirt from her body. She was zombified—but still as cute as a button. She wore a gingham frock with blue-and-white checks, and the sunrise lit up her auburn hair and reddish pigtails tied with gold ribbons.

"Dorothy Gale, from Kansas?" Caitlin asked.

She nodded with a smile. "Caitlin Fletcher from Glendale, London, and New York?"

Caitlin returned the smile. "Yes. And I feel like I'm going totally mad!"

"You can't say that Alice didn't warn you."

"She surely did. I know that to be totally true now. What happens next?"

"Let's stroll while we chat," Dorothy suggested.

The fictional farm girl took Caitlin by the hand, and they began to amble through the twilit Mount Cemetery.

"'Once upon a time' is really a great secret," Dorothy said. "And it's also a bit of a problem."

"What do you mean?"

"Time only happens in your world. It's what allows you to tell stories."

"I don't understand."

"Time separates the beginning, middle, and end. Without it, all things would happen at once. And then there would be no story. No suspense. And no fun."

"You talk weirder than Natalie."

"Listen," Dorothy said. "For those of us who live in the other realm, where all the stories reside together, there's no such thing as time. Everything is already written down. Everything is already recorded—because it all exists simultaneously."

Caitlin's eyebrows arched. "You're talking about the Great Book of Records?"

Dorothy smiled.

"And that's how Glinda knew what was going to happen?" Caitlin continued with a sudden twinge in her chest. "She *knew* the avalanche was coming at that precise time, and that's why she took my place in line to cross the bridge?"

"Yes. But it's a teeny bit more complicated than that," Dorothy said. "Because it might not have happened either. But now's not the time to share such details."

Caitlin shook her head. "So why are you even telling me this?"

"I need to show you something."

Caitlin coiled a strand of her pepper-red hair around her pinkie. "Show me what?"

Dorothy pulled out an ornate magnifying glass with a jeweled, baroque frame.

Oh my gosh!

The same magnifying glass that Glinda had used. "Where did you get that?"

"From the Wicked Witch of the West. She received it from Glinda."

"What is it, actually?"

"In your world, you'd call it a search engine."

"What's it for?"

"Well, the Great Book of Records is actually huge. It's hidden away in a large vault that touches the stars. Which makes it far too big to lug around. This charmed magnifying glass allows you to search the entire book for entries."

"And?"

Dorothy swallowed before responding. Caitlin couldn't, because her throat had just closed up.

"I know what happens," Dorothy said.

The sweat beading on Caitlin's brow ran as cold as February. "I'm listening."

"They hunt you down."

"Who?"

"Werwulves."

"And?"

Dorothy didn't answer, which caused a slight nausea to churn in Caitlin's stomach. Her voice trembled as her tone turned angry. "And?"

Dorothy raised the magnifying glass and held it up to Caitlin's eye.

She reluctantly gazed through the glass. A gazillion pages whirled by at the speed of magic.

A sudden flurry of wind swept up the fallen leaves in Mount Cemetery and made the tree branches sway and murmur in ghostly whispers.

Dorothy lowered the magnifying glass. She lifted her gaze above Caitlin's shoulder and stared sadly behind her.

Dread winded Caitlin as she turned around.

Somehow, she suddenly found herself standing by the graves of her parents, Evelyn and Harold Fletcher, and her gramps, Bobby Blackshaw. Except the grassy lawn of Mount Cemetery had turned parched and withered. A blood moon was fixed in a dark and lonely sky.

Caitlin's shocked wail was piercing. Then she went quiet. Wordless. Transfixed.

A tall gray tombstone stood next to the grave of her parents.

Etched in the rock were the words "Caitlin Fletcher."

This was *her* grave. Her fate. The end of her story.

Caitlin crumpled to her knees. Her fingers balled into a hard, tight fist. She pounded the dirt with great force, hopelessness unleashing her full anger.

Her silent scream paired with bitter tears.

"If I just die, then what am I fighting for?"

Dorothy tilted her head to one side as her eyebrow quirked. "You don't know?"

Caitlin lowered her head in shame. Her sorrow was directed at her own situation, herself. That had blinded her.

But now she drew a breath . . . unclenched her fist . . . and rose back to her feet.

She saw what she was meant to with clarity.

She knew what she had to fight for—and for *whom* she had to fight.

Caitlin had to make sure the fate suffered by Harold and Evelyn Fletcher—and soon *her*—did not befall another individual.

Caitlin was now ready to do battle and die—for Natalie.

And for Eos.

But?

"You said everything is already recorded in the Great Book of Records. Which means the end of the story is already known. How can I possibly change anything? What choices do I have?"

Dorothy winked. "Finally, you're asking the right questions."

A bloodcurdling howl shattered the otherwise-tranquil dawn.

"Oh my," a wide-eyed Dorothy said. "The werwulves are already here. They must've crossed over *before* you."

Dorothy's ashen face went even whiter as she leaped into

Carroll's grave. The portal sealed shut after she vanished down the wormhole.

"See ya!" her fading voice echoed.

The howling gave way to a nearby growl, the snarling close as dark to night.

The air smelled like a dog kennel.

A two-legged, blood-eyed, frothy-mouthed werwulf suddenly crept out of the dark of twilight, not more than twenty feet from Caitlin. The creature was frost white, head to claw. Saliva poured from its jaw and drool pooled on the ground beneath it.

Caitlin's eyes shifted to Carroll's grave. It was sealed shut. Useless as an escape route.

A rustling noise sounded behind her. Feet crunching leaves.

"Step away slowly," a male voice said firmly. "I've got a gun on the animal."

Caitlin took a few cautious steps backward and then gingerly turned toward the voice.

Two police officers—one male, one female—had their eyes and guns trained on the wulf.

Thank God!

The female officer raised her gun, tilting it upward. She fired a bullet into the air. It worked. The booming gunshot frightened off the werwulf, and it fled into the darkness with terrible speed.

Caitlin heard other feet—*paws?*—scurrying away in the darkness.

How many werwulves are out there?

"Are you okay, miss?" the male officer asked.

Caitlin wiped the perspiration from her brow. "Yes. Thank you."

"What was that wretched creature?" the male officer asked his colleague. She just shook her head, perplexed.

"Whatever it was,'" he said, "I'm afraid it's still out there, along with a few others."

The female officer approached Caitlin. "You're sure you're all right?"

"Yes, but can we get out of here?"

The female officer pulled out a paper from her pocket. "Are you Caitlin Rose Fletcher?"

"I am."

"Apparently, you've gone missing from your foster home in the States. We have a warrant from a London magistrate to detain you under Section Three of the Mental Health Act. You will be admitted to Foster Home Services under the personal care of Doctor J. L. Kyle, managing director of the agency."

Caitlin's beating heart slammed against the wall of her chest.

Her fingers twitched. Her calves tightened. She rolled up onto the balls of her feet, itching to run.

Should she take her chances with the wolf in sheep's clothing at the orphanage, or the pack of white werwulves lurking in the darkness that surrounded her?

Caitlin had to decide quickly which deadly option seemed the safer bet.